SECRETS

THE WALLACE FAMILY

A. M. Huff

CONTENTS

To Dennis Blakesley and Mary Newman,
for their encouragement, friendship
and for helping me to believe in myself.

ACKNOWLEDGMENTS

With heartfelt appreciation to Marcia Klinge, for her encouraging a shy teenaged boy to write; and to Bruce Fiebach, Patrick Huff, Trudy Kay, Michael Anne Maslow, Eric Meese, and Tamera Somers for all of the encouragement they gave me over the years that kept me writing.

The Wallace Family

Carl James Wallace
m. Ruth Wallace

      1) Morgan (Wallace)
         m. Chuck
           A) Ariel
              m. Mark Jones
                a) Kevin Jones

      2) Tamera (Wallace) Lynch
         m. Daniel Lynch
           B) Danny Lynch (deceased)
           C) Nicholas Lynch

      3) Steven Peter Wallace
         m. Claudia Wallace
           D) Steven Peter Wallace, II

      4) Patricia (Wallace) Ferguson
         m. Roger Allen Ferguson
           E) Steven Colin Ferguson

      5) Bradley Wallace
         m. Amanda Wallace
           F) Benjamin Wallace

David Lynch (Daniel's brother)
Matthew Murphy (Peter's friend)

CHAPTER ONE
THE REUNION

A warm mid-July breeze blew gently through the spreading oak trees of the backyard. Beneath, in the shadows of their many branches, the lighthearted sounds of laughter and splashing water drifted up from the in-ground swimming pool.

"Okay! Okay!" The thin man with graying hair laughed, shielding his face from the barrage of water. "I give up."

"Carl James Wallace!" a familiar stern voice thundered down on the two men. "Get out of that swimming pool and into this house immediately."

The smile faded from Carl's face. He recognized the tone in his wife's voice. He had heard it several times in the past two months since Steven moved back home.

"I'm sorry, son," he apologized. Lately it seemed as though he was doing that a lot. Carl turned around and made his way to the steps, the water in the pool swirling around him.

"That's okay, Dad." Steven nodded. He knew why his mother was acting this way but he still felt bad for his father.

"I guess your mother's upset with me again," Carl said, trying to ease some of the tension that hung in the air while he watched his wife disappear into the house.

"Maybe I should talk to her again?" Steven handed his father a towel. "I'm not a little boy anymore. She doesn't have to worry about me."

Carl looked at his eldest son and for a moment saw the little, brown-haired boy with freckles of Steven's youth. The image was quickly replaced by the tall man with a mustache and graying temples standing before him. Carl smiled. The years had flown by so quickly.

"She's your mother, Steven. It's her job to worry about you and your brother and sisters. It has nothing to do with your age. To her you'll always be her little boy," Carl said, drying himself.

"Well, I thought she understood. I don't want to be babied. I want to—"

"I know," Carl interrupted him, not wanting to hear those words again. "She understands, but her heart doesn't. This isn't easy for your mother. Hell, it isn't easy for me."

Steven looked at his father, for the first time seeing him as a regular man and not a superhero. The strong arms that once lifted him up in the air were not made of steel but of flesh and bone. The dark, fearless eyes that always made him feel safe and secure were red-rimmed from the chlorine in the pool. Or was it from something else?

"But you seem to be handling it fine," Steven said, more to convince himself than his father.

"Yeah, I do, don't I." Carl feigned a smile. Inside his chest, he felt pain and his throat ached as he fought back tears. "Well," he breathed loudly, "let's get out of these wet clothes before the rest of the family arrives."

"Sure thing." Steven put his arm around his father's shoulders. "I love you, Dad."

Carl clenched his teeth and fought harder to keep the tears from his eyes. He turned and hugged his son tightly until the flood of emotion passed.

"Let's go," he said, his voice a mere whisper.

The two walked quietly into the house.

* * *

Steven smiled as he thought about the fun he and his father had been having in the swimming pool only moments ago. He added it to his other cherished memories: camping trips to the lake, catching his first fish, and watching his father save a man from drowning. "You're still my Superman," he whispered to himself.

Slowly he walked back to his bedroom after his shower. His long terry cloth bathrobe felt warm against his skin. As he walked in the open hallway above the foyer, he heard voices coming from behind his parents' bedroom door. He stopped in the doorway of his bedroom and cocked his head to listen. He recognized his mother's voice. She was upset.

Inside the bedroom, Carl sat on the dressing bench at the foot of their queen-size bed, listening to his wife while he finished tying his shoelaces. He understood her concerns, her anger, but it seemed little help as she paced the floor in front of him.

"Ruth," he sighed. "He's not a baby anymore."

"I know that!" she snapped with indignation. "I'm not crazy. Is it a crime for a mother to want to hold onto her children for as long as she can?"

"No." Carl shook his head and sat back. He did not like keeping secrets from his children. For years he and Ruth had taught their children to be open and honest. Now one of them was asking them to keep a secret and it was proving to be the hardest thing they had ever done.

"This isn't about you, or me, for that matter." Carl put as much compassion in his voice as he could muster. "This is about respecting the wishes of our son."

"Well, I can't do it!" Ruth said, nearly screaming at Carl as she stopped pacing in front of him. "He's asking too much from me. I can't. It's just too hard. Tell me, what other mother would agree to such a thing?"

Carl quickly stood up and took his wife in his arms. She wrapped her arms around him and sobbed into his chest.

"It's not fair," she mumbled through her tears.

"I know, Ruth. I know." Carl tried to console her. "But it's his life, Ruth. We have no choice but to accept it." Carl held her trembling body in his arms and wished he could shield her from this pain as she continued crying. "I know it's hard, but we have to try to respect his wishes otherwise we will lose him forever."

"Carl, it's tearing me apart. I don't know if I can," she protested but Carl could tell she was giving up.

"I know, honey. Honestly, I do." A tear escaped his eyes. He quickly wiped it away. He had to be strong for her. He could not let her see him cry even though he wanted to so desperately. Deep down, he knew that everything she had said was true. It was not fair.

Steven pushed himself away from the threshold of his bedroom and walked over to his bed. He sat down and looked around his room, at the familiar pinewood panels on the walls, the bookcase filled with old schoolbooks and childhood memorabilia, and all the things he had left behind when he moved out on his own. Here everything was, just as he left it, waiting for him to return. He looked at the suitcases and boxes stacked next to his old writing desk under the window. True, he had come home, but for how long?

His thoughts returned to his parents' conversation. He knew what he was asking them to do was hard, but it had been just as hard for him to tell them. Telling them meant he had to admit the truth to himself and that was something he had refused to do for two years. He never meant to hurt anyone, especially them, but if the rest of the family knew, it would tear the family apart. That was something he was not willing to do. Family had always been the most important thing to him. He would leave before he let that happen.

He looked at his nightstand and smiled. There, in a wooden frame, was a photograph of his sister Tamera and him taken the summer he turned ten, before she discovered boys. Until then, they had been inseparable. After, their relationship changed, but they were still close. Tears filled his eyes for a moment but he shook them away.

"No," he breathed. "No."

* * *

The front doorbell chimed. Before anyone had a chance to answer, the door opened. A burly man resembling a lumberjack complete with short, wavy brown hair and bushy reddish-brown beard stepped inside.

"Mom? Dad?" he called out in a deep, husky voice.

"Bradley!" Ruth opened her arms, rushing to greet her son. "You made it." She kissed his bearded cheek and pulled away, putting her hand over her nose and mouth. "When're you gonna shave that thing? It's like kissing a Brillo pad."

Bradley chuckled loudly. "Where is everyone?" he asked, looking around the foyer and up at the open hallway on the second floor.

"Well, your father and Steven are out back. As for the rest of the family, they haven't arrived yet." She was distracted by the cute, brown-haired toddler peeking out from behind his mother's skirt as they stepped through the door behind Bradley. "Ah, who's that little angel?" Ruth cooed playfully at him. "Could it be my little Benji?"

Benjamin smiled and buried his face in his mother's skirt, nearly knocking her over.

"Benji!" his mother yelled, regaining her balance without dropping the cake box. "Brad, will you get him?"

Bradley smiled and picked up his son, swinging him into the air. Benjamin giggled and squealed.

"Will you stop that!" she snapped at them.

Ruth looked at her daughter-in-law, surprised by the harshness in her voice. "Here, let me take that for you, Amanda," Ruth said, reaching for the cake box.

"Thank you." Amanda smiled, handing it over. "Do you have any Tylenol? I have a splitting headache."

"Sure, it's in the medicine cabinet in the upstairs bathroom. Help yourself, dear." Ruth watched Amanda hurry up the stairs. "When you're through, we'll meet you in the backyard," she called to her. Turning back to Bradley, she said,

"I think your father could use a hand with that gas barbecuer you gave him last fall. I don't think he's quite gotten the hang of it yet."

"Sure thing." Bradley smiled. "Come on you little monkey, let's go help Gramps." He slung Benjamin over his shoulder like a flour sack which immediately brought on more giggles and squeals as they headed to the backyard.

"Don't let your father hear you call him that," Ruth said with a laugh. She watched them head through the house and suddenly it was like seeing Carl with Bradley all over again. She smiled to herself.

"Mom," Amanda said, descending the stairs. "Can I talk to you alone for a moment?"

Ruth turned around. She noticed the softer tone in her daughter-in-law's voice. "Sure honey, let's go into the parlor."

Amanda walked across the foyer and into the small sitting room. She immediately went over to the fireplace mantle on the opposite wall and stared at the many framed photographs of the family. Her gaze fell on the smiling faces of her and Bradley on their wedding day. She turned away quickly.

Ruth sat down on the edge of the love seat and set the cake box on the coffee table in front of her. She studied Amanda, searching for some clue to what was troubling her. Amanda's long brunette hair was neatly brushed and held back by a butterfly hair pin. Her white blouse hung loosely from her shoulders as though it were still on a hanger. Her skirt was cinched tightly at her thin waist and hung to her knees. She clasped her trembling hands tightly in front of her.

"What is it dear?" Ruth asked, becoming worried.

"Well." Amanda fidgeted. "You know Bradley better than I do. I mean, when he was a teenager and dating. What were they like?"

"They?" Ruth asked, giving Amanda a confused look. "Who?"

"You know, his other girlfriends." She looked at her hands and the diamond wedding ring on her finger. "Were they pretty?"

"From what I can remember, they were just girls, and to be honest, there were only two." She patted the seat cushion next to her. "Come sit down."

Amanda took a step further away. "Bradley and I haven't been getting along so well lately." Her voice was a weak whisper. "He's been distant. I know I haven't been able to lose all the weight I gained with Benji and I can't help but think that maybe that's why. Patty told me that the girls he used to date were fashion models, Barbie dolls."

"Don't listen to Patty," Ruth said, shaking her head. "She's just teasing you. The girls weren't Barbie dolls. They were just *girls*. Bradley loves you. He married you, not them."

"I know," Amanda nodded, "but maybe he'd be happier with one of them instead."

"That's nonsense talk," Ruth said. "Amanda, Bradley is very happy and he loves you. You could be fifty pounds heavier and that wouldn't change a thing. He would still love you."

Amanda's eyes filled with tears and she turned away. "No. No, he wouldn't."

Ruth stood up. Her heart ached for her daughter-in-law. "Amanda, talk to him."

"No. I can't."

"You must. Bradley loves you dearly. You don't need to lose any more weight. He doesn't care about that."

Amanda turned around defiantly. "You'll see. He'll leave me just like my father left my mother when she couldn't lose weight after having the six of us."

"I'm sorry," Ruth sympathized. "I don't know anything about your parents, but I assure you, Bradley isn't like that at all. Trust me, I know him and deep down I know that you know it's true."

"I'm pregnant again!" Amanda blurted and burst into tears. "I am going to get fat and he's going to leave me. I know he will. I can feel it. I lie awake at night and I can't sleep because I'm afraid when I wake up, he'll be gone."

Ruth stifled her excitement at thoughts of another grandchild running around the house. She put a hand over her mouth until her smile faded. "Amanda, I don't know what I can say to make you see that you're wrong. Bradley isn't going to leave you. Talk to him, please."

"Mom, I don't want to have this baby. I can't get fat again." Tears streamed down Amanda's cheeks. "I can't."

Amanda's words hit Ruth's ears like a sharp slap. Her joy gave way to fear and panic. Slowly she walked over to Amanda and cautiously took her shoulders in her hands, fighting the urge to shake her.

"Amanda, dear heart, you have to talk to your husband. You'll see that he will understand and you have no reason to be afraid. Everything's going to be fine. You have to promise me, now. Before you do anything you will talk to Bradley. Promise me."

Amanda looked into her mother-in-law's golden-brown eyes and reluctantly nodded. "I promise." She wiped the tears from her eyes.

"We all love you so very much, Amanda." Ruth hugged her tightly. "You're the best thing that's happened to Bradley. He knows it too." She gave Amanda's forehead a tender kiss and then stood back to look at her. "Now, go upstairs and freshen up," she said with a smile.

"Okay." Amanda nodded, forcing a smile. She stepped around the coffee table and then hurried out of the room. She paused at the foot of the stairs in the foyer and turned back as though she were about to say something then changed her mind and continued up the stairs.

Ruth picked up the cake box and walked into the foyer. She watched the bathroom door close. *This isn't over*, she thought to herself.

* * *

Tamera carefully made her way around the side of the

house into the backyard. She did not want to come to this family reunion because she did not want to face Steven, but at the last minute she gave into her husband Daniel's insistence. Her heart pounded when she saw Carl, Bradley, and Steven huddled around the barbecuer. She took a deep breath.

"Woo-hoo," she called out in a shrill voice. "Hello, everybody, I'm here."

Steven turned around at the sound of her voice. Immediately he smiled and ran around the swimming pool to greet her. As their eyes met, he froze.

"I think I'll go set this stuff down on the table," Daniel said, taking the grocery bag from Tamera's arms and leaning down to kiss her cheek.

"Thank you, Dan," she said, not taking her eyes off her brother standing a few feet in front of her. "Make sure Nick gets back here, too. I don't want him messing around out front."

"Gotcha!" Daniel nodded. "Hey, Steven." He smiled as he brushed past him.

"Hi, Dan." Steven watched his brother-in-law make his way over to the picnic table under the large oak tree. When Steven was sure they would not be overheard, he turned back to Tamera. Her long blonde hair was curled away from her rosy-cheeked, round face. Her blue eyes were filled with tears behind her pink-tinted glasses. Steven took a slow, steady breath.

"Who told you?"

"Mom did. But even if she hadn't, I would still have known. I can tell by the look in your eyes. We've been too close for me not to know," she admitted, wiping the tears from her cheeks.

"Don't cry, please," Steven said, now fighting back his own tears. This was exactly what he wanted to avoid. He did not want to hurt her.

"How dare you ask that of me!" Tamera choked and struggled to keep from raising her voice. "I love you, damn it!" Her tears began to fall too quickly to wipe them all away.

"Please, Tammy," Steven pleaded and stepped closer.

"If you cry, it'll only hurt Mom and Dad more."

"I don't care. I can't help it!" Tamera snapped and stepped away from him. She pulled a handkerchief from the pocket of her floor-length denim skirt and dried her eyes.

"Did you tell anyone else?" he whispered, glancing over his shoulder at Daniel and the others.

"No, I didn't tell anyone," she answered in a tone that sounded as though she was offended by the very question, her tears continuing to fall. "But how? Why? It's not right. It's not fair."

"Life isn't fair. At least that's what you always told me." Steven tried to smile and catch her eyes.

"Oh, that's really nice. Throw that in my face after all these years." A faint trace of a smile slipped across her lips. "How can you make jokes and tease at a time like this? Besides, I only said that to get my own way when we were kids." She finally looked at him.

"Who said we ever grew up?" He smiled at her.

Tamera shook her head and gave in to a smile even though she continued to cry. Taking a deep, quivering breath she relaxed her shoulders a bit. "So, what am I supposed to do now, Steven? For that matter, what're we all supposed to do?"

"There's really nothing you or anyone else can do. Just be happy for me."

"I don't know if I can," she said. Her lower lip began to quiver again.

Steven quickly wrapped his arms around her. "Please, try," he said into her ear. "I don't want you to cry. I love you."

"I love you, too," she said, hugging him back with all her strength.

"Oh, I'm going to throw up!" a woman said from behind them. "Will you two knock it off? What'll the neighbors think?"

They both let go of each other and took a step back. Tamera turned her back on her older sister. "I'll be right back," she said and hurried off into the house.

Steven forced a smile. "Hi, Morgan."

"So what's her problem?" Morgan asked curtly. "I was only teasing."

Steven shrugged. There was no love lost between his two older sisters. They had not liked each other for as long as he could remember. Morgan, always the big sister, badgered Tamera mercilessly about everything from her weight, to her clothes, to her choice of husband. Morgan was always quick to point out everyone else's flaws, a flaw of her own that annoyed him.

"Nothing." He gave Morgan the once over. Of all his siblings, Morgan resembled the family least. Her sandy blonde hair was newly dyed to hide the gray. He did not care for her perm, it was too tight and made her head look even smaller, but that was a critique he thought best to keep to himself. Her blue jeans and gingham blouse made her look more manly than feminine. Even her heeled boots did little to change that. Their father had said Morgan resembled his oldest sister. She was the shortest of his brothers and sisters and quite the tomboy, too.

"So, little brother, don't I get a hug?"

"Of course." Steven smiled and hugged her, ignoring the irritation he felt at her tone and the way she always called him her little brother. After all, he stood a whole head and shoulders taller than her even in her boots, but today he was willing to ignore it. He was just happy she and her family had come.

"So, what's the big idea getting the family together?" Morgan stepped back and looked at him.

Steven knew that Morgan did love him in her own awkward way. He imagined that her growing up five years older made it hard for her to see past the many years of babysitting and taking care of him and the rest of their siblings. If the shoe were on the other foot, he was sure he would resent those lost teenage years and maybe even himself a little.

"Oh, nothing special. I just thought it'd be kinda fun, that's all." He shrugged. "So, where's your other half?" he asked, trying to change the subject. Morgan's jaw tightened at the question even though she tried to hide it.

"Chuck's coming."

"And where are the two love birds?"

"You'll see for yourself. Ariel brought him along too." Morgan nodded behind her. She turned slightly and glanced over her shoulder just as her daughter and the young man in question came around the corner of the house. Without another word to Steven she continued over to the picnic table.

"Hi, Daddy!" Morgan called ahead in a strangely childish tone.

"Uncle Steven." Ariel beamed proudly, escorting a tall, young man with long dyed black hair and brown eyes over to him. "I'd like you to finally meet the guy I've told you so much about. Uncle Steven, this is my fiancé, Mark Jones. Mark, this is my Uncle Steven."

"It's good to finally meet you, Mark." Steven held out his hand.

"The same, sir." Mark shook Steven's hand politely but he seemed a bit distracted, as though he really did not want to be there, much less have to talk to anyone.

"Please, just call me Steven. I may be thirty-eight, but I'm really not old enough to be called sir just yet." Steven smiled at Mark. "So, Ariel says you're in a rock band?" he asked, noticing Mark's black leather jacket and faded denim jeans with torn knees.

Mark's eyes snapped back to the present. He smiled. "Yeah."

"He's the lead guitarist," Ariel interjected.

"Impressive." Steven continued to smile and gave an approving nodded.

"Yeah, we just played a gig over at The Road House last night. This weekend we'll be playing at The Crystal Ballroom in Portland. You should come check it out," Mark informed him.

"I might just have to do that. So, how are the wedding

plans coming?" Steven asked Ariel, but watched Mark for his reaction.

"Oh, don't get her started," he said before Ariel could. "That is unless you've got a week to listen."

Steven laughed lightheartedly. "Not really," he said, immediately noticing the confused looks on their faces. "So, where's your father, Ariel? Your mom said he's coming. Isn't he with you?" Steven looked beyond them, hoping they would let his little comment go. Besides, the last thing he wanted to do was listen to Ariel giggle and coo over Mark. Lately it was hard to hold an adult conversation with her, a condition that seemed to be getting worse as the wedding date drew closer. There was something else about Mark that concerned Steven. Something was definitely going on behind those brown eyes and it puzzled Steven, but he did not have the energy to try to figure it out now.

"Dad?" Ariel said, looking over her shoulder. "Yeah, he's here. He drove up just after us. He must still be out front. Do you want us to go get him?"

"No. He'll be here soon enough." Steven stepped aside and ushered Ariel and Mark past him. "Let's go join the rest of the family, okay?"

Steven followed them around the swimming pool to the backyard.

* * *

"Dad," Bradley said, nudging Carl lightly to get his attention. "Can I talk to you for a second?"

"Sure." Carl looked up from the cooking burgers on the grill. "What's on your mind, son?"

"Not here, Dad," Bradley whispered.

Carl looked at Bradley again. Something was troubling him. "Hey, Dan, you any good at barbecuing?"

"Yeah, I may have done it a time or two," Daniel teased.

"How about watching this for me for a sec?"

"No problem, Dad." Daniel happily stood up from the

table, breaking off his conversation with Morgan.

Carl and Bradley started around the opposite side of the swimming pool toward the house while Tamera rounded the other side to join the family.

"So, what's on your mind, son?" Carl inquired.

"Let's go over there first." Bradley motioned toward the patio chairs.

The two men walked over to the chairs on the patio and sat down. Bradley leaned forward with his elbows on the patio table in front of him. He stared across the pool at the family.

Carl studied his youngest son's dark-brown eyes, trying to figure out what was troubling him. When Bradley was a boy, his face had been an open book and Carl could always tell what was on his mind. But now, at thirty-six, Bradley was no longer a boy and not so easy to read. Carl looked over at the family and then beyond them to where Amanda was pushing Benjamin in the swing.

"So, are you going to tell me what this is all about?" Carl broke the silence.

"I wish I knew, Dad. Something's bothering Amanda and I don't know how to talk to her about it. Everything I say is the wrong thing." Bradley turned his attention to his father. "Have you noticed how thin she is?"

Carl nodded in response.

"Well, she still thinks she's fat. I try to tell her she isn't but then she says I'm lying. I don't know what's going on in her head, but I'm really worried about her."

"Have you thought about taking her to see a doctor or even counseling?" Carl shrugged, not knowing exactly how to answer his son. "I know—"

"Out of the question," Bradley interrupted. "She won't do it. She insists she doesn't have a problem."

Carl turned and looked at Amanda, trying to come up with a solution but his mind was a total blank. He turned back to Bradley again and looked into his eyes. He was waiting for some words of wisdom to come to him, to make it all better for his son, but he was fresh out. He had never dealt with a situation like this before. Or had he? A slow grin spread across his lips as a thought occurred to him.

"You need to find some way to talk to her, today," he said, his grin becoming harder to conceal.

Bradley looked curiously at his father. He saw nothing in their conversation to be smiling about. "Why? What's up?" he asked.

"Oh, I was just thinking about the times your mother would become overly concerned about her weight and nine months later. . ."

Bradley's eyes widened, realizing what his father was hinting at. "You don't think she could be. . ."

"You and she are the only two who can answer that for certain." Carl beamed at the thought of having another grandchild.

"You're right." Bradley nodded. "I'll talk to her, today."

"Good. So how's work going?" Carl changed the subject as the two of them stood up.

"Things are a little slow right now." Bradley shrugged while the two started back around the swimming pool. "The bigwigs say things will be picking up soon. I'll be honest with you, I hope they're right, otherwise I'm afraid layoffs will be coming. I don't know if I'll be able to survive this round."

"Tamera! Dan!" a deep voice thundered from the corner of the house, interrupting everyone's conversations. In unison, everyone turned around to see what was going. Chuck appeared, dragging Nicholas by the arm.

Tamera quickly shot an angry glare at Daniel and jumped to her feet.

"I thought I told you to make sure he was back here," she said and headed around the pool to her son. Again Daniel had not done what she had asked but she did not have the time to figure out who was worse, Nicholas or his father. Right now her attention was required to deal with her overbearing brother-in-law and her son.

"What have you done now?" she snapped at Nicholas. "I thought I told you to get yourself back here when you got out of the car."

"I wasn't doing anything, mom," the brown-eyed teenager with long, shaggy brown hair said, pulling against his uncle's tight grip.

"Come on you little liar, tell the truth for a change," Chuck growled, giving his nephew's arm a jerk.

"Stop it! You're hurting me!" Nicholas winced. "I wasn't doing anything."

"You can take your hands off my son, Chuck. I'll handle this." Tamera glared momentarily at her brother-in-law. She never did like him, ever since he and Morgan began dating twenty-five years ago when she was fifteen. Whenever Morgan was not looking, Chuck, under the guise of teasing, tried to slip his hand under her blouse. She had another reason for hating him, one that she had kept secret for all these years and yet one she had threatened to tell if he did not watch his step.

Chuck could hear the anger in Tamera's tone but he was not about to back down. "You'd better, Tamera, because the next time I'll just call the police." Chuck gave Nicholas' arm one last jerk and then released his grip.

"You keep your hands off my son, Chuck, or I'll be the one calling the police," Tamera threatened, glaring at him.

"Pardon me," he said, stepping closer and putting his mouth near her ear to whisper, "I didn't know he was your son."

Cold panic swept over Tamera, quickly replaced by fear. She cast a quick glance at her son who stood rubbing his arm, unaware of what Chuck had said. She looked back at Chuck as he casually strutted over to the table.

"I hate that jerk!" Nicholas hissed, continuing to rub his arm.

Tamera swung around and faced Nicholas.

"You mind your mouth, young man. Now, for the last time, what were you doing out front?"

"Nothing," Nicholas answered defiantly.

Without warning or hesitation, Tamera slapped his face. Nicholas' head jerked sharply at the impact, and he covered his red cheek with his hand. His cheek stung, but he was more embarrassed seeing everyone looking at him than hurt. Stubbornly he fought back his tears, not willing to give her the satisfaction of knowing she hurt him.

"Don't lie to me. Why is your uncle ready to call the police if you were just *doing nothing*? Do you want to end up in a juvenile home? Because that's exactly where you're going if you slip up one more time, young man."

"Why do you always take everyone else's side? Why do you always believe them? Why don't you ever believe me, your own son, for once? I wish you weren't my mother," Nicholas protested.

The words rang in Tamera's ears and echoed down to her heart. She looked at the boy in front of her. The sunlight caught the small, gold hoop ring in his ear and flashed the light back into her eyes. His black leather jacket and unkempt hair did not escape her notice. She remembered the day she had brought him home from the hospital, so tiny and helpless. She promised herself then that no one would ever hurt her baby. Where had that baby gone? She looked into his eyes and her anger faded. Tears filled her eyes and she said softly, "Don't say that."

"Then believe me for a change," Nicholas snapped back at her.

"Give me a reason to, Nick. Talk to me. Tell me the truth. What were you doing?" she said softly.

Nicholas studied his mother's eyes for a moment.

"Okay," he said cautiously. "I was sitting in Uncle Steven's car." He paused to gauge her reaction, anticipating her flying into another rage as she had so often in the past few months. Nothing. She just stood there and listened. "I found some papers and you wouldn't believe what they say."

"I already know," Tamera said, somberly realizing that

he now knew Steven's secret.

"But Mom, they say Uncle Steven—"

"I already know. Your grandmother told me weeks ago." She took him by his arm and pulled him closer to her. He winced and prepared himself for another slap.

"You have to promise me that you'll keep this between you and me. Do you understand me?" she whispered sternly. "Not a word of it to anyone, not even your father."

"Shouldn't we at least ask Uncle Steven about it?" he asked, trying to get free of her tight hold.

"Absolutely not!"

"But why?"

"Because your uncle doesn't want the family to know, so, out of respect for him, you're to keep this between us. Am I making myself clear?" She looked into his brown eyes, searching for a sign that he understood. "This is very serious, Nick."

"Oh alright, but I don't understand what harm there would be in telling everyone."

Tamera released his arm and he immediately adjusted his jacket. "Your Uncle Steven wants it this way and we have to abide by his wishes. In time the rest of the family will be told, okay?"

"That's cool." Nicholas nodded, his usual detached manner returning.

Tamera looked at her son and shook her head. Suddenly she felt old and wondered when she had turned into her mother. "Cool?" she repeated. "That's not exactly what I would've said. Now, why don't you go see your cousin Ariel and try to stay out of your Uncle Chuck's way and out of trouble."

"Okay," Nicholas answered half-heartedly. Being around Ariel and Mark these days was not on the top of his list of most favorite things to do. Ariel was acting too much like a lovestruck girl to be any fun. *It was only for the afternoon,* he thought to himself. He could suffer through it for that long.

Tamera watched Nicholas walk over to the family but

instead of sitting with Ariel, he stopped under the oak tree and sat down. He pulled his iPhone from his pocket and began texting someone. She glanced over at Daniel. When their eyes met he shrugged, then turned around and joined Carl and Bradley at the barbecuer. Tamera sighed, shaking her head.

"Looks as though you have your hands full," Ruth said, walking up behind her daughter.

"Oh!" Tamera jumped and turned around to face her mother. "That's an understatement, Mom. I don't know what to do with him. Everything I try doesn't seem to work. He either doesn't see what serious trouble he's in or he doesn't care."

"He's just a boy. He'll grow out of it. You all did." Ruth smiled empathetically. "Here, give me a hand with this stuff." She handed Tamera a tray of vegetables and dip.

"Well, none of us ever got into this kind of trouble. So why my son? I don't understand it. You know, some people think it's hereditary, that the bad genes from a parent are passed on so the child turns out bad. If that's the case, it has to come from his father's side."

"I doubt that very much, Tamera." Ruth laughed out loud as they headed over to the table. "Kids haven't changed. They crave structure in order to feel secure, to know they're loved, and to thrive. It's parents who've changed. Nowadays, kids aren't taught to respect authority, let alone their parents, and even those who are can get mixed up with the wrong crowd and, in the excitement of the moment, do stupid things. What Nick did, shoplifting a CD, that's pretty tame stuff compared to other kids out there. Kids are in gangs. They're actually committing murder. They steal cars and do God knows whatever else. It's a good thing Nick was caught now. Maybe it'll keep him from doing much worse. But Tamera, honey, you have to lighten up on him. Don't drive him away from you or he will run to them."

"I'll try," Tamera agreed. She walked the rest of the way to the picnic table in silence, thinking about her mother's advice. Over the years while raising Nicholas she had solicited

Ruth's advice on several occasions. She was happy knowing that she still could.

Ruth smiled to herself as they put the trays down on the table. She could not help but remember the young, teenaged rebel Tamera had been in her youth. Although she never found herself in serious trouble, she had done her share of not following the social norms. Just as Tamera had grown-up, she knew Nicholas would too.

* * *

Slowly Bradley approached the swing set. His palms sweated and his stomach fluttered nervously. He had not decided how he was going to bring up the subject with Amanda, but he knew he had to and that it could not wait.

"Amanda, can we talk for a second?" he asked cautiously.

"Sure." Amanda nodded. "I've been wanting to talk to you, too."

Bradley was surprised by her eagerness. He watched her bring the swing to a gentle stop and help Benjamin down from the wooden seat.

"Go see Auntie Tammy for mommy," she cooed into his ear and pointed across the yard toward the picnic table.

Without a word, Benjamin smiled and scurried off as fast as his little legs would go. Bradley and Amanda watched him until they were sure he would not overhear them. Slowly Bradley turned to face her.

"Amanda," he began again. "What's happened to us? Lately we don't talk anymore, we just argue. It has to stop."

"I know," she agreed. "I've been thinking about that too. If you want a divorce, I understand. You can have it." She sighed and looked at the ground.

"What? Oh god, no!" Bradley gasped, feeling as if she had punched him in the stomach. Tears filled his eyes. This was not going at all the way he thought it would. He took her shoulders in his hands. "Why would you say that? Whatever gave you that idea?"

"Because I'm getting fat. I'm not as thin as I was when you married me." Amanda tried to avoid looking at him. She felt ashamed and embarrassed of her weight.

"Amanda, you are not fat. In fact you weigh less now than before we were married. You have your wedding dress at home in a box. Try it on, you'll see."

"No," Amanda protested. "I just need to lose five more pounds first."

For the first time word *anorexia* flashed in Bradley's mind. It frightened him. *This can't be happening. This only happens to teenagers, not women in their early thirties,* he thought.

"Amanda, I love you. I don't want a divorce and never will."

"You say that now," she said, her voice distant.

"And I'll be saying it for another hundred million years. I love you and I'm worried about you. You're losing too much weight. You have to get help. I don't want to lose you."

Amanda choked and burst into tears. She wrapped her arms around his waist and hugged him.

"What's wrong? Honey, please talk to me," Bradley pleaded, cradling her tightly.

"I-I'm pregnant."

"What?" Bradley's eyes lit up and he could not hold back his smile. "That's wonderful. That's fantastic. We're going to have another baby." Bradley pulled Amanda away from his chest and looked at her. His smile faded seeing her tears. She turned her eyes from him and continued crying. Her whole body trembled. "Aren't you happy?"

"I don't want to get fat again." She shook her head. Bradley froze. "I don't want this baby."

Bradley could not believe his ears. How could she not want their child? He went numb. Words left him. His mind was a blank. He looked at her and released her. She stopped crying and she looked at him.

"Aren't you gonna say something?" she asked.

"What?" Bradley snapped, trying to keep his voice down as anger replaced the shock of her words. "What do you want me to say? That it's okay to get an abortion? Is that what you want? Well, you can forget it. I can't and I won't."

"You just don't understand!" Amanda said, beginning to cry again. "I just don't want to be fat. I don't want to go through what my mother did."

Suddenly Bradley understood what was going on in Amanda's head. "I'm not like your father," he said in a gentler tone. "I'm not going anywhere. I love you. I'm not leaving you, ever. We'll be fine." He took her chin in his hand and raised her head to look into her eyes. "I'm not leaving. I love you," he repeated. "Everything is going to be fine. You'll see."

Amanda nodded but inside she was beginning to feel nauseous. Images of her overweight mother flooded her mind. The taunts of her schoolmates came back to her and echoed in her ears. Feelings of anger and hatred for her mother welled up inside her and then were replaced by a stronger feeling of shame. She really did not want to be obese like her mother.

Now that Bradley knew about the pregnancy, she knew he would never allow her to give it up. Part of her felt secure in that fact and happy about the prospect of holding a baby in her arms again, but the other part of her was frightened at the idea of gaining any weight, no matter how temporary.

"Okay," she said and gave a slight nod. "We're having a baby."

Bradley looked at his wife and smiled openly. "Are you sure you want to go through with this?"

"You sure you won't leave me?" Amanda looked at him.

"Of course," he said without hesitation.

Amanda looked at her flat stomach, fighting her fears, and then back at Bradley. Slowly she stroked his beard. "Then, yes."

Bradley smiled and his anxieties melted. "I love you, Mrs. Bradley Wallace." He kissed her and, for the first time in a long time, she kissed him back. "Let's go tell the others the great news," Bradley said, holding her.

"Not just yet." Amanda pulled back. "Today's for Steven."

Bradley looked at her curiously, wondering what she meant by that. This was just a family gathering. He shrugged off her comment, unable to think about anything but the new baby.

"Okay. We'll tell them later," he conceded.

* * *

Ruth poured another glass of lemonade and set it on the table in front of Ariel, then picked up another empty glass and began filling it. She smiled at the noisy chatter around the table. Ariel and Mark were telling Steven about the concert they recently attended. When she finished filling the last glass, Ruth turned back toward the house. Out of the corner of her eye she noticed Nicholas standing alone under a tree and staring off deep in thought. Slowly she walked over to him.

"Hi, Nick," she greeted, standing beside him. "What're you thinking about?"

"Oh, nothing." He shrugged, running his hand through his hair.

"You seem to be doing a lot of that today." As she looked at her grandson, she remembered the little boy who had been so full of energy that he talked a mile a minute. Anything you asked him, he always gave a lengthy answer, but now, Ruth could tell, something was troubling him; something he was not willing to talk about. *It must be serious,* Ruth thought. She hated the feeling of helplessness it gave her and she hated seeing one of her children or grandchildren troubled.

"Are you sure there isn't something you'd like to talk about? You know I'm a good listener," she prodded.

"Yeah, Grandma," he breathed and glanced at his

mother visiting with the others at the table. "I'm sure."

"Okay, honey," Ruth said and stroked his hair. "If you change your mind, I'll be in the house." She kissed his forehead and continued on her way.

"Thank you, Grandma," Nicholas said and sat with his back against the tree. He wanted to talk to someone. He needed to. The trouble was he promised his mother he would not say a word. What could be so horrible about what he found? Slowly he pulled the paper out of his pocket and looked at it again. He smiled to himself as he read it. Then carefully he folded it up and put it back in his pocket.

As Ruth reached the backdoor, she noticed Morgan sitting alone at the patio table. She was silently staring at something. Ruth walked over to her.

"Care to give me a hand in the kitchen with the salad?" Ruth asked.

"Sure." Morgan nodded without taking her eyes off whatever it was she was staring at in the distance. Slowly she stood up. Without straightening her rumpled blouse and jeans, she walked away from the table.

Ruth smiled and shook her head. Morgan, her eldest daughter, was so different from the others. Ever since she was born she seemed to be so full of anger. Ruth thought about the many photographs of Morgan, always the same: no smile, pursed lips, and an angry stare. After forty-three years it was permanently etched in the tiny crow's feet by her eyes and in the lines around her thin lips.

When she brought Tamera home from the hospital three years later, Morgan wanted nothing to do with her new sister. Afterward, with the addition of each new sibling, Morgan's anger seemed to grow. Ruth tried to spend extra time with her in those years, but Morgan had already shut her out. It was not until Chuck came into her life that Morgan let down the wall between them, at least part of the way.

"So, how're the wedding plans coming along?" Ruth tried to make conversation while she walked back into the house.

"Not well at all to tell you the truth." Morgan shrugged disgustedly. "I can't seem to get Ariel to sit down for five seconds to finalize the guest list, the flowers, the cake, anything. We're already too late to rent a hall for the reception. I don't know what we're going to do. The wedding is only three months away. I just don't understand what's gotten into her." Morgan cast one last look at Ariel just before she closed the back door behind them.

"Sounds like a serious case of love," Ruth said and smiled, "and so familiar, too."

"What did you mean by that?" Morgan snapped and stepped up to the kitchen counter.

"Oh, don't be so defensive." Ruth laughed playfully which angered Morgan more. "I seem to recall another young girl who was so in love she couldn't sit still, that's all." Ruth took the bowl of chopped lettuce and vegetables out of the refrigerator.

"I was never like that," Morgan said indignantly. "Ariel hangs on Mark all of the time. She's forever holding his hand, rubbing his back, giggling and carrying on so. She's twenty-one and getting married. She should grow up!"

"Yes, she should and she will, just as you've settled down, but Morgan, it will take time. Give her a chance." Ruth handed Morgan the salad spoon and fork. "So, what kind of work does Mark do?"

"Don't even get me started. Why Chuck agreed to this marriage is beyond me. The boy says he's a musician and it takes time to build up a reputation. So I guess he plans on letting Ariel support him with her waitressing. What a catch he is," Morgan said sarcastically. "More like a loser," she added as she began tossing the greens.

"So, what do his parents think?" Ruth changed the subject, filling the salad dressing cruet.

"Oh, they're just as irresponsible and useless." Morgan sneered and wiped the counter with the kitchen cloth. "They're too busy with whatever it is they do to be bothered. It's no wonder their son is so lazy."

"Well, let's just hope Ariel knows what she's getting herself into. After all, she's an adult now and can make her own decisions. We just hope for the best," Ruth said, trying to sound positive. She handed the salad dressing to Morgan. "I'll get the plates and be right out."

Morgan started for the back door and then turned around, seemingly deep in thought. "Mom, why was it so important to Steven to get the family together?"

Ruth's breath caught. Her body stiffened. She closed her eyes and was grateful her back was to Morgan. "Oh, nothing special," she answered and shrugged without turning around.

"You know, there's something different about him. Is there something wrong?" Morgan persisted, watching her mother closely.

"No, there's nothing the matter." Ruth tried to keep her voice from breaking. "You just haven't seen him for a while. That's all." Ruth kept her back to Morgan as she stood in front of the stove. "I'll be right out," she said, hoping Morgan would not pursue the conversation and leave.

"You're probably right."

The sound of the back screen door slamming shut brought a sigh of relief to Ruth. Her shoulders slumped as she turned and leaned over the sink, wiping the tears from her eyes.

"I can't do this." She sighed out loud and threw her head back.

"Can't do what, Mom?"

Ruth jumped and spun around. "Patricia, don't do that again!" she snapped at her youngest daughter who was standing in the doorway to the foyer. "You scared the daylights out of me!"

Patricia smiled and gave her mother a hug. Her long auburn hair and dark-brown eyes were the image of her mother in younger years.

"What can't you do?" Patricia repeated, stepping back

and looking at her mother's damp eyes.

"Oh, nothing," Ruth said, trying to think of something fast. "I can't carry all of this by myself," she explained feebly.

Patricia knew her mother was lying. She had been standing in the doorway listening while watching her mother's reactions to Morgan's questions, but she was not going to call her on it. She knew she would find out in time. *This family wasn't one to hold onto secrets,* she thought. That thought comforted her as much as frightened her.

"So, how's the news business these days?" Ruth asked. She was so proud of her daughter's accomplishments. Patricia had worked hard and was finally a reporter for KTVZ, the local television news station.

"Sad to say, it's great." Patricia smiled. "We just uncovered a big story involving fraud and embezzlement right here in Bend. I can't believe big city crime has made its way to our nice little town. I hope that jerk gets the book thrown at him," she answered angrily.

"Well, I hate to say it but Bend is growing. I guess it's to be expected. I'm so very proud of you." Ruth hugged her daughter again. "Let's go out back."

* * *

"Tamera, let's go for a walk," Daniel said, taking hold of her arm and lifting her to her feet.

"Sure, honey." She smiled, stumbling as she stepped over the bench. "What is it?"

"Let's just go over there by the swing so we can be alone first," Daniel said, his tone calm but determined as they walked away from the gathering.

"Hey you two don't go too far," Carl called after them.

"We won't, Dad," Daniel said.

When they reached the swing, Tamera turned around. "Okay, so what's up?" It was obvious by the look on her face and the tone of her voice that she was annoyed at him.

"I want to talk to you about Nick," he said, searching her eyes for any sign of compassion.

"I'm through with talking about him." Tamera folded her arms over her chest, giving him a look that said she was through talking altogether.

"Please, Tamera, you have to ease up on the boy. This was only his first offense. Even the judge recognized that."

"So, now I'm the bad guy?" she snapped and glared at him. "Is that what you think?"

"No, I didn't say that," Daniel said, fighting the urge to snap back at her.

"If I'm being hard on Nicholas, it's because I just don't want there to be a second. He has to learn that if he steals things, he will have to pay the consequences."

"Damn it, Tamera!" Daniel lost his battle and raised his voice just above a loud whisper. "Nick knows he did wrong. He was sentenced by the judge and has forty hours of community service left to do. Let him do his time and forget about it. He's only fourteen years old for crying out loud. He shouldn't be branded for life for one lousy mistake."

Tamera heard what her husband was saying but his words were not registering. In the distance she caught sight of Steven and became distracted by her own thoughts.

"If you don't ease up on him, we're going to lose him. Children tend to live up or down to the expectations of their parents. Treat him like a criminal, and he'll become one. Is that what you want?"

"What?" Tamera looked at Daniel. "Of course not!" she said indignantly. "Daniel, I really can't do this right now, not today," she added in a softer tone.

"Then back off," Daniel said, taking Tamera by the shoulders and forcing her to look at him. "Nick is beginning to think you don't love him anymore. Is it true?"

"No." Tamera looked at Daniel's kind, gentle face framed by his dark-brown hair. "I just, it's just that—" Tamera stammered, not able to find the words.

"What? What is it?" Daniel inquired. For the last couple of months he could tell that something was troubling her. She had been more moody that usual. Whenever he had tried to bring up the conversation, she would change the topic.

"It's nothing," Tamera said, shaking her head. "I'll try."

"That's all I'm asking." Daniel wrapped his arms around his wife and gave her a gentle reassuring hug. Today was no different. She was not ready to talk. Whatever it was that was bothering her would remain hidden; he would not pry. "I love you, Tammy," he said and kissed her forehead.

"I love you, too, Dan." She smiled at him and gave him a soft kiss.

"Let's get back to the family." Daniel turned and locked her arm around his before they headed back to the picnic.

As they neared the table, Tamera spotted Nicholas sitting behind an oak tree, alone. She released Daniel's arm.

"I'll be right back," she told Daniel and left him at the table.

Nicholas did not see his mother approach. He sat with his back against the tree trunk, listening to his iPod. He kept snapping a twig between his fingers and watched the pieces fall to the ground between his legs while the music blared in his ears.

"Nick, honey," Tamera said softly. "I'm sorry I've been so hard on you. I just love you so much. You do understand that don't you?"

Nicholas looked up, pulling the ear buds from his ears. "Wha—?"

"Come here." Tamera held out her hand. Nicholas took her hand and stood up. Without any warning, Tamera wrapped her arms around his thin shoulders and kissed his cheek. As a reflex, he hugged her in return.

"I know I've been hard on you, but I do love you," she repeated, looking into his brown eyes. "Come on, let's get something to eat."

Nicholas smiled uncertainly and looked around before

walking back to the table with her.

* * *

Ruth and Patricia set the plates and hamburger buns down on the picnic table. Ruth smiled proudly, looking around the table at her children and grandchildren. Her eyes stopped and her smile faded when she looked at Steven. He sat quietly next to Bradley, blindly staring off into nothing.

"Okay everyone, line up over here to get your burgers," Carl called.

As everyone rose and grabbed a plate, Ruth leaned over to whisper into Steven's ear. "You look tired, honey. I'll get your plate. You rest, all right?"

"All right," Steven repeated. He blinked and nodded his head. "Mom," Steven called before she could turn away. "Do you have a second?"

"Sure, dear." She smiled.

Steven slowly and unsteadily rose to his feet. Ruth took his hand and walked with him to a quiet tree away from the rest of the family.

Still holding his hand, she looked at her son. His face was pale beneath his brown hair and reddish-brown mustache. A couple of premature gray streaks accented his temples and made him look more like his father. Tiny beads of sweat dotted his forehead. She wiped them away with her fingertips as she remembered the sensitive little boy from so long ago. He had always cared so much for everyone in the family. Always the one everyone could count on for a shoulder to cry on or a listening ear, even for her. Her heart ached seeing him now.

"Are you okay, honey?"

Steven looked at his mother but was having trouble gathering his thoughts. "I don't know," he said softly. "My head hurts a bit. I think maybe I've been in the sun too long."

"Well, if you need to rest, why don't you go upstairs and lie down on your bed for a while?"

"No, it'll pass and I'll be fine." Steven took a deep breath and the pain in his head eased for a moment. "Mom, I know this has been really hard for you, my asking you to keep my secret. I just want you to know that I'm sorry for putting you through this. Truly, I am."

Ruth took a deep breath and looked away. She could feel her throat tighten and knew that tears were not far behind. She forced an unsteady smile as she looked at him. "Steven, I'm trying to understand, but this isn't an easy thing for any parent to accept and have to deal with." The tears arrived and filled her eyes. "But, I love you so very much and I'm trying."

"I know, Mama." Steven's throat tightened as he fought back his own tears. "I'm sorry."

"It's not your fault, honey. You didn't have a choice in this." Ruth pulled him close and hugged him. "Sometimes, we just have to accept what we're handed. It's hard but we'll get through this."

"I love you, Mama." A tear fell from Steven's eyes onto her shoulder as he continued to hold onto her.

Ruth released her son and stepped back to look at him. By the look in his eyes, she knew there was something else on his mind.

"Mom," he began slowly and then stopped. He looked at the ground, avoiding eye contact with her. "Did you ever do something that you wish you didn't? I mean, that you wish you could change?"

Ruth looked at him confused. "Well, I guess just about everyone has made mistakes, it's all part of life."

"No. It wasn't a mistake exactly." Steven shook his head. "Remember when I was away at college?"

"Oh, heavens." Ruth smiled. "That was nearly seventeen years ago. Why?"

Steven continued to look at the ground and struggle with his thoughts. The pain in his head returned with a vengeance. "Oh, never mind." He shrugged. "It doesn't matter now, just foolish thinking." Steven looked around. "I wonder what's keeping Patty."

Ruth jolted. She looked at Steven, becoming concerned and frightened.

"Steven, she's right over there. She carried out the plates, don't you remember?"

Steven's expression was blank. "Oh, okay." He nodded, not really seeing anyone, the pain in his head was too intense. The tiny beads of sweat reappeared on his forehead. His mouth was slightly open as he tried to catch his breath.

Ruth's heart began to race as she looked at her son. She felt so helpless.

"Steven!" she said sharply.

He continued to struggle to breathe.

"Steven," Ruth repeated and put her arm around him tightly. She could feel him tremble and then suddenly he relaxed and shook his head.

"What is it? What's the matter? Are you okay?" she barraged him with questions.

"I'm fine," Steven said, smiling slightly to put her mind at ease. "I just couldn't seem to catch my breath. That's all. I'm okay now but I think I should sit down."

"Okay." Ruth nodded warily and wiped the sweat beads from his forehead again. "I love you so much," she said with a smile and she kissed his cheek. "Come on, dinner is waiting."

"Hey, you two," Carl called out from the head of the picnic table as Ruth and Steven returned to the group. "Where've you been? Your burgers are getting cold."

"Just talking," Ruth said with a smile. "I need to go into the house for a second. I'll be right back."

Carl grabbed her arm as she bent down and kissed his cheek. "Is everything all right?" he whispered.

Ruth looked over at Steven as he sat down at the table. A concerned look came over her and she shrugged.

"I don't know." She gave a nod for him to step back from the table, away from the family. Once away, she leaned closer and whispered into his ear. "There's something troubling him that happened, from what I can gather, when he was away at college."

"But that was a long time ago." Carl looked at Steven but kept his voice down. "What is it?"

"I don't know." Ruth shook her head. "He stopped before telling me. I'm sure he'll tell us when he's ready."

"Is that all?" Carl asked, noticing how pale Steven appeared.

"Something happened while we were talking," she continued.

"What do you mean?"

"He said his head was hurting and then he had a spell where he had trouble breathing."

Carl started to leave, to go to Steven but Ruth stopped him.

"There's one more thing," she said. "He asked when Patty was going to get here."

"But she's already here," Carl said and then the words sunk in. Ruth could see by the sudden change in Carl's expression that he understood.

"That's what I told him."

"Is he okay? Do I need to check on him?" Carl asked.

"No. I think he'll be fine for now. I'll be right back."

"Don't be long," Carl said, giving her a kiss on the cheek before returning to the table.

"Mom," Bradley called, halting her. He glanced at Amanda seated next to him. "You sure it's okay?"

Amanda nodded. Bradley kissed her cheek and smiling proudly. "Before you go, Amanda and I have an announcement to make. I'm lousy at keeping secrets and especially this one." He winked at Amanda. She smiled back. To Ruth it seemed a bit forced, but Bradley was too excited to notice.

Ruth stepped over to Carl's side again and put her arm around his waist. Carl leaned into her.

"Go ahead, Brad," she encouraged, anticipating the announcement.

"Well," Bradley put his arm around Amanda, "Amanda and I are going to add one more Wallace to our family."

"What sort of announcement is that supposed to be?" Morgan scoffed.

"Amanda's pregnant, stupid," he said bluntly. "We're having another baby."

"Just what you need." Morgan sneered at Bradley then turned around and walked away as the table erupted in chatter. Ruth watched Morgan for a moment, surprised by her comment but decided to let it pass for now. Tamera, Patricia, and Ariel huddled around Amanda giving her hugs and congratulations. Amanda was smiling, but her eyes lacked the sparkle of a truly happy person.

Ruth tugged on Carl's arm again. "I think we're in for some rough times with Amanda," she whispered.

"What?" Carl asked, looking confused.

"Look at her plate." Ruth motioned with her head. "We had a little talk earlier today. She's excessively preoccupied with her weight and getting fat."

Carl looked at Amanda's plate, at the untouched carrot stick, the few small pieces of lettuce, and the small stalk of celery. "Oh for crying out loud, as if we don't have enough to deal with already," he sighed. "You don't think she could be anorexic, do you?"

"I don't know that much about it, but what I do know is if she isn't, she's on her way and the baby is the one who'll suffer." Ruth kept her eyes on Amanda.

"It's funny." Carl shook his head. "Bradley talked to me about this very thing earlier too. He said he was concerned about her. I suggested he talk to her, but I guess I'll have to have another talk with him."

"Not today, dear." Ruth gave him a gentle squeeze. "Let them enjoy this moment. We'll have plenty of time later to talk to them. Well, I have to go in the house and check on the dessert, strawberry pie with fresh whipped cream."

"Sounds good." Carl smiled and watched her walk back

to the house.

"So, when's the baby due?" Ariel said over the din of the ongoing chatter.

Bradley looked at Amanda and laughed. "I was so happy, I forgot to ask. When are we due?"

Amanda smiled politely at Ariel. "Oh," she said hesitantly. "I haven't seen a doctor yet but I'm guessing the first of February?"

"We'll let everyone know after we make an appointment with the doc," Bradley assured them, giving Amanda a one-armed hug.

"Oh, that's wonderful," Ariel cooed and put her head on Mark's shoulder. "I can't wait until Mark and I have a baby. I think it'll be so cool to be a mom."

Morgan, who was standing behind Ariel, choked on her lemonade that she had spiked with vodka from her purse. Her face flushed when she noticed all eyes on her.

"Those darned ice cubes get me every time," she said, covering her mouth, afraid that they could smell the alcohol on her breath.

Ariel ignored her mother's attempt at humor, seeing it for what it was, and continued cuddling Mark's arm. She was used to her mother's jabs. She knew all too well how her mother felt about Mark and the wedding but she did not care. *Just a few more months,* she thought, *and I'll be free of her.*

"So, Benji." Steven smiled across the table at his nephew seated next to Amanda. "What do you think about having a new baby brother or sister?"

Benjamin just smiled and kicked his feet as he continued to nibble on his hamburger.

"I'm really happy for you both," Steven said, looking at his younger brother. He wanted to tell Bradley how proud he was of him and that part of him was jealous, but the pain in his head made finding the right words too hard.

"Well, one of these days it'll be your turn," Bradley said, giving him a hopeful nod. "The only problem is we have to find you a wife first." He laughed.

"Yeah." Steven forced a smile. He looked over at Tamera. As their eyes met, his smile faded. Without a word she pushed her plate away and left the table. Steven watched her in silence.

Patricia looked at Tamera and then back at Steven. The reporter in her sensed that something was up. She stood up from the table. "I'll be right back," she said and headed for the house to find Ruth.

The conversation at the table stopped abruptly. Daniel looked over his shoulder in the direction Tamera had disappeared. Chuck took another drink of his lemonade and wished he had Morgan's vodka flask. He glanced at Ariel just as she gave Mark a kiss. He looked away.

"So, you seem pretty quiet, Chuck." Daniel changed the subject. "How's that job down at the mill going?"

"Oh, it's going," Chuck said with a nod, wishing even more for the flask as he took another drink from his glass.

"That bad?" Daniel cringed.

"No. Actually, I've been offered a job as a long haul driver. It means more money, way more, but it means I'd be gone weeks on end. Now that Ariel's moving out. . ." He stopped himself. "I haven't given them an answer yet."

"Oh, that's a hard one to have to make," Daniel teased. He and Chuck were good friends despite the fact that neither Tamera nor Morgan liked each other. "Is the pay really that much more?"

"In a word," Chuck paused then grinned, "yes. A whole lot more."

"Then why don't you just take it!" Morgan snapped, throwing her plate on the table and storming off in a huff.

"Hey, I'm sorry," Daniel apologized, watching Morgan head for the swing set. "I didn't see her there. I hope I didn't make trouble for you."

"Don't worry," Chuck said, brushing green salad off his arm. "I didn't know she was there either and I seriously doubt it would've made a difference." He stood up and took a deep breath. "Guess I should go talk with her."

"Good luck." Daniel nodded and watched Chuck walk over to Morgan.

"I think I'll take Benji inside and clean him up. It's about time for his nap," Amanda announced. "Come on, honey." She took away his napkin and wiped his face before picking him up.

"You can put him in Bradley's old bedroom," Carl called after her. "Well, Nick, you've been awfully quiet. Are you feeling okay?" Carl sat down next to his grandson.

"Yeah." Nick shrugged. "I've just been doing a lot of thinking. That's all."

"About what?" Carl asked.

Nicholas looked around the table at everyone staring at him. He quickly looked down and shook his head. "Nothing. I really don't want to talk right now, Grandpa. I'm sorry." He quickly stood up and headed for the house.

Carl watched Nicholas for a moment and then turned to the rest of the family at the table. "Well, this little party is falling apart fast," he teased. "I hope it wasn't my cooking."

"No, Dad." Bradley looked around the table at the empty chairs. "I think it's something else."

* * *

Morgan leaned against the oak tree just beyond the swing set with her back to the house and family. Chuck walked up to her and stood silently at her side.

"That was just brilliant," Morgan said in a disgusted tone.

Chuck clenched his teeth. He hated the way she always put him on the defensive, making him out to be the bad guy, especially since he had done nothing wrong. "What are you talking about?" He came back at her with the same tone.

"I thought we had an agreement that we wouldn't tell

the family until after Ariel's wedding. I should've known you couldn't be trusted."

"Just what did you mean by that crack?" Chuck snapped. He was not about to back down, not this time.

Morgan turned around to face him. Her eyes were fixed angrily on him. "You know full well what I'm talking about," she hissed in a lower tone so that the family would not hear. "You've been fooling around with that tramp at work."

"What are you talking about?"

"Lisa," Morgan snapped.

As Chuck looked at her, he suddenly relaxed and gave a disbelieving laugh. "Oh, you're a fine piece of work, Morgan." He shook his head and then set his jaw again. "I'm not fooling around with Lisa. I'm not her type. She's a lesbian. Besides, you're a fine one to talk about cheating. Need I remind you of that college boy that you were supposed to be tutoring? Did he get his *problems* worked out?"

Morgan's jaw dropped open as she looked at him. Suddenly she was no longer in control of their argument and that made her angrier. Without warning, she slapped Chuck's face. His head snapped back at the impact but he quickly recovered.

"That's good." He smirked. "I hit a nerve, did I? It still doesn't change the fact that you, my dear wife, were supposed to be tutoring him in literature, not Sex Ed!" Chuck slapped back with his words. "Oh, and as for the family, you don't have to worry. I didn't tell them anything. They still think that we're happily married. So your precious image hasn't been tarnished."

Morgan stood speechless. For the first time, she was totally devoid of a comeback. She turned away and stared blindly into the distance.

"Well, aren't you even going to thank me for that?" Chuck softened his tone.

Morgan remained silent.

Chuck shook his head and ran his hand over his short, dark-brown hair in frustration. Morgan's silence angered him more. "There you go again, making it all about you, poor little Morgan. Well, I've had it! For god's sake, Morgan, you did it in our bed. Do you know how much you hurt me? Do you even care?"

"You still don't get it, do you?" Morgan said calmly, the hostility gone from her voice. "You shut me out of your life years ago. You put your job first. You had no time for me, let alone Ariel. I practically had to raise her on my own. I spent days without anyone to talk to. You weren't there and then Ariel was off doing her own thing. So when this young man showed an interest in me, well, I felt alive again."

"What was I supposed to do? I was working. You're the one who wanted that big house and all that furniture you said you couldn't live without. So I was trying to give it to you," Chuck snapped but his anger started to ebb.

"You fool," Morgan said, turning around to face him again. "The only thing I ever really wanted, ever really needed was you. I just wanted to spend time with you, my husband. That's all." Tears had filled her eyes, not the fake ones she had used on him many times before; this time they were real. "I'm sorry I hurt you. I didn't mean to," she apologized.

Chuck watched the tears roll down her cheeks and his anger melted away completely. He reached out and wiped them away. "All I want is you, too," he said.

"I'm so sorry," Morgan cried, wrapping her arms around him.

He held her tightly in his arms while she sobbed into his chest. He kissed the top of her head. "It'll be okay, babe. We'll be okay," he said, trying to console her. She continued to hold onto him as she cried.

"I know, what we should do," he said, pulling himself free of her grasp so he could look into her eyes. "What do you say if after this wedding business is over, the two of us take a vacation alone? We can go where ever you want. It'll be like a second honeymoon. How does that sound?"

"That sounds wonderful." Morgan looked up into his

brown eyes and smiled. "I do love you, Chuck."

"I love you too, Morgan," he said with a smile then kissed her as though for the first time.

* * *

"Mom," Patricia said softly and she sat down at the kitchen counter.

Ruth turned around without looking at her daughter. She placed the second chilled strawberry pie on the tray with a stack of napkins and forks. "What?" She headed for the refrigerator.

"May I ask you something?"

"Sure."

Patricia made mental notes: no eye contact; appears nervous about something.

"Mom, why are we here?"

"Patty, mankind has been asking that question for eons," Ruth said, placing a can of whipped cream precariously on the tray between the two pies.

"No, Mom, what's going on here? Why is everyone acting so strangely? Bradley and Amanda, Morgan and Chuck, Tamera and Dan, even Steven isn't his usual self."

Ruth turned her back on Patricia and took her time getting the pie server from the drawer. Of all of her children, Patricia had always been the most observant and inquisitive, being a news reporter had been the obvious professional choice. However, at that moment, Ruth wished Patricia had not made it her career.

"I don't know," Ruth said plainly, turning around but still not looking at her daughter. She set the pie server next to the pie and then picked up the tray. "Enough with the questions. Let's just enjoy the day and go out back and have some dessert."

Patricia was more curious than before. She could tell her mother knew more than she was letting on but she could wait. Maybe after everyone had some dessert she would have another opportunity to get to the bottom of whatever was going on with the family.

* * *

Tamera walked back to the picnic table and looked around. "Where's Nicholas?"

"He just went for a walk," Daniel said, taking her hand. "It's okay. He just wants to think. He'll be fine."

"If you say so." Tamera sighed, too tired to keep fighting.

"I do. Now, sit down here with the family for a while." He pulled gently on her arm. She let herself slip into the chair beside him.

"Well, here we are," Ruth announced as she, Patricia, and Amanda walked up to the table. "Who wants dessert?"

Carl jumped out of the way and cleared a space on the table for the tray.

"I'll serve, Mom," Patricia volunteered and counted the heads around the table.

"Be my guest." Ruth smiled and relinquished the knife. She sat down next to Carl, grateful to have a moment's rest. He gently rubbed her back.

"You outdid yourself as usual," he whispered into her ear then kissed her cheek. She leaned into him.

"Benji is sound asleep," Amanda informed Bradley and gave him a quick peck. She sat down next to him on the bench at the table. "I still can't get over how much he's grown. It seems like only yesterday he was just a baby."

"Well, soon you'll have another little bundle to care for and, believe me, you thought you had your hands full with one," Ruth said playfully.

"I welcome the challenge," Amanda said confidently, smiling to herself. For the first time, she meant it and was happy at the thought of being pregnant. "I can't wait until this one is born. Nothing compares to the smell of a baby."

41

"I guess that's one of those *parent things*," Steven teased and pinched his nose.

"Oh, you!" Amanda laughed, throwing a wadded up napkin at him. "I'll save the first dirty diaper for you."

Everyone laughed.

"One of these days, when you have one of your own you'll understand," Bradley informed Steven.

Ruth tightened her hold on Carl's hand beneath the table.

"Yeah." Steven feigned a smile. "Someday. Oh, none for me thank you, Patty," he said, putting up his hand to decline the slice of pie smothered with whipped cream.

"Suit yourself," she shrugged and handed the plate to Daniel.

"I think I should go lay down for a while. My head is really hurting," Steven said, looking at his mother.

"Okay, dear," Ruth said. "Do you want me to help you?"

"No." Steven rubbed his temples. "I'll be okay."

"Are you sure," Ruth asked, not hiding her concern from the rest of the family.

"Yes. I'm okay, really. It's just another one of those stupid headaches that's all. I'll take a couple aspirin and a short nap. I'll be fine," Steven reassured her with a smile.

"Okay, dear." Ruth gave his hand a gentle squeeze as he passed by her. "I love you," she said softly.

"I love you, too." He bent down and kissed her cheek.

"You have a nice rest, son," Carl added, watching Steven head off toward the house.

"I will," he called back without turning around.

Amanda, Bradley, and Patricia watched Steven disappear into the house. All three turned and looked at Ruth and Carl and caught their concerned looks. Bradley looked at Amanda as if asking her what was going on. She shrugged. They looked at Patricia. She shook her head and set down the pie server.

"All right, this has gone on long enough," she said in an authoritative voice. "There's something going on here that you're not telling us." She folded her arms over her chest and looked accusingly at her parents.

Ruth cast a quick look at Tamera. The look did not go unnoticed.

"She knows?" Bradley said, the realization suddenly hitting him. "What's going on here?" he asked, his gentle tone belying his growing irritation.

"Tamera, do you know what this is about?" Daniel asked his wife as he too became concerned.

Tamera looked at Ruth and slammed her hands down on the table. "I don't know what you're all talking about," she snapped and stood up. Before anyone could ask her another question, she ran off to the front yard. Daniel became more confused by his wife's reaction.

"Mom, Dad, please," he said, looking at his in-laws. "We have a right to know what's going on."

"I can't do this anymore." Ruth's shoulders slumped under an unseen weight as she turned to Carl. Tears filled her eyes and began to slip down her cheeks. "I know I promised Steven, but enough is enough."

"What's wrong with Steven?" Patricia looked at her mother in shock.

Ruth avoided her daughter's gaze and continued looking at Carl.

Carl sat forward in his chair and looked around the table at his family's concerned and worried faces. He looked back at Ruth and nodded silently.

* * *

Nicholas nervously approached the closed bedroom door. With a deep breath he knocked lightly and waited for a response. Silence. His heart pounded in his chest and his hands sweated. How was he going to bring it up? What was he going to say? He slowly pulled out the folded paper from his pocket and stared at it. Would Steven be angry? Would his mother? She had told him not to talk to Steven about it. He wanted to turn and leave, but he had to know the reason why it was such a big secret. He folded the paper back up and tucked it away.

"Uncle Steven?" Nicholas called and knocked again.

"It's open. Come in," Steven called faintly from inside.

Slowly Nicholas pushed the door open and stepped inside the bedroom. The shades were drawn to block out the afternoon sunlight, but the room was still filled with a soft honey glow. Steven sat up on one elbow as he lay on his bed.

"What is it, Nick?" he asked.

"Can I talk to you for a minute?" His voice was sheepishly soft.

"Sure. Grab that chair by the desk and pull it around. What's on your mind?" Steven sat up on the bed, leaning against the headboard. He gently massaged the back of his neck, hoping that the aspirin he took would kick in soon.

Nicholas pulled the chair around to face Steven and sat down. He rubbed his hands together and kept looking at the floor. "I've been doing a lot of thinking today."

"I've noticed." Steven nodded. "Is everything okay?"

"Not really." He shrugged. "Ever since this thing with the mall happened, Mom seems to be on my case about everything. I feel really bad about what happened and I don't mean just because I was caught. I know that taking that CD was stupid and I told her that I was sorry. I just don't think she believes me."

"Yeah." Steven nodded again. "I know she's been hard on you, but she does love you very much. She doesn't want to lose you, too." Steven reached out and stroked Nicholas' hair. "Your mother's had it pretty rough in her life. Try to go easy on her and be patient with her, for me?"

"I guess," Nicholas reluctantly agreed. "But why won't she believe me?"

Steven smiled and thought for a moment.

"Maybe you have to do more than just tell her how sorry you are. Maybe you should show her. Take a look at yourself in the mirror." He nodded toward the mirror on the dresser beside them.

Nicholas looked at his reflection. "So?"

"Would you honestly believe the person looking back at you is sorry for shoplifting? Take a look at your hair. The way you're dressed. Does that reflect someone who's truly changed? I know I probably sound old fashioned, but I've been there. Well not exactly there, but I went through a long hair stage myself. The point is you have to let the person you are inside show through on the outside. Otherwise you're sending mixed signals."

At first Nicholas felt defensive about what his uncle was saying, but the more he thought about it the more it made sense.

"Nick, if you want to convince your mother you've changed, show her. You'll be surprised at the outcome." Steven smiled again. This time Nicholas smiled back.

"I will." He nodded.

"Good." Steven's smile faded as the pain in his head increased. "Nick, I really need to lie down for a while."

"Okay." Nicholas stood up and put the chair back. He started for the door and stuck his hand in his pocket. He felt the paper. His heart began to beat faster and he stopped. "Uncle Steven?"

"Is there something else?" Steven asked, propping himself up on one elbow again and squinting as the pain persisted.

"Kind of." Nicholas started back into the room and pulled out the paper. "This afternoon I was sitting in your car and, well, I found this paper." He unfolded the paper to show Steven.

Steven recognized it immediately. "I see," he said flatly. "Have you said anything to anyone?"

"No," Nicholas quickly said. "Well, I started to tell

Mom but she said she already knew and that you wanted to keep it a secret."

Steven realized Tamera did not know this secret and released a shaky, "Thank you."

"Uncle Steven," Nicholas said softly. "Why keep it a secret?"

"I guess," Steven looked at his nephew and shrugged, "it's just that it happened so long ago. I was in college and it was my last year. A group of us flew to Las Vegas to celebrate. We got drunk and did some pretty stupid stuff. This was one of them. See, it can even happen to grown-ups, Nick. All of us make bad choices sometimes."

Nicholas nodded, trying to understand. "Here, you can have this back." He held out the paper to Steven.

"No." Steven put up a halting hand. "You can keep it. Whenever you feel like you're alone, pull it out and look at it. It will remind you that even your Uncle Steven did some pretty crazy things."

Nicholas nodded and half smiled. "Do you ever wonder what would've happened—"

"Sometimes," Steven interrupted him, "but, it's too late for that." The pain was intense. "Go. Please."

Nicholas nodded, folding the paper up and putting it back in his pocket. He turned around just before closing the door. "I love you, Uncle Steven."

Steven lay quietly on his bed. Still.

Nicholas closed the door.

* * *

"So, there you are," Daniel said, walking up to the front door steps.

Tamera just continued staring blindly across the street. Her thoughts kept going back to when she and Steven were children. The time they built the snowman in the front yard and dressed it up in Carl's new hat and scarf. They were grounded for a week and were not allowed to play in the snow again that winter. She smiled unconsciously, remembering the time they were fired from picking blackberries one summer because they kept laughing too much. Steven had always been able to make her laugh no matter what the situation, but not this time. Her smile faded.

"Why didn't you tell me?" Daniel asked, slipping his arm around her.

"It wouldn't have done any good. There's nothing anyone can do about it. It's just one of those things." Tamera shrugged as if giving up.

"Maybe so, but at least I would've understood what's been bothering you. We could've faced this thing together." Daniel turned her around to face him. "I know how close you and Steven are. This news isn't the kind of thing you can keep bottled up inside. I'm a pretty good listener, too, you know."

A lump tightened in her throat and tears filled her blue eyes. She fell into Daniel's arms and cried. "I love him so much, Dan. It hurts so much."

"I know," he said and held her.

The front door opened beside them. Daniel looked up but Tamera turned away. She quickly wiped the tears from her face. Nicholas froze in the doorway when he saw his parents.

"What's wrong?" he asked, looking over his father's shoulder at his mother.

"Nothing," Tamera said, trying to sound confident. She straightened her back and turned around. "Where've you been?" she asked in a gentler tone.

"Well, I," Nicholas stammered and then decided to tell the truth even if he might get another slap. "I was just upstairs talking to Uncle Steven," he said quietly and closed the front door behind him. "I needed to talk to him about the. . ." He looked at his father then back at his mom. "You know," he said, lowering his voice even more.

"I thought I told you not to," Tamera snapped then just as quickly caught herself.

"I know you did." Nicholas looked at the ground for a moment. "But, Mom, I had to. I just don't understand how this could've been kept a secret for so long." Nicholas looked at this father in horror at spilling the beans. "Oh, I'm sorry."

"It's all right, son." Daniel put a reassuring hand on his shoulder. "I know."

"You do?" Nicholas looked at him surprised.

"Yes. Your grandmother just filled us in on what's going on."

"Oh, that's a relief." Nicholas sighed and then thought for a moment. "You know, I think we should throw him a party."

"What?" Tamera snapped in disbelief.

"Yeah, a party," Nicholas repeated, smiling at her.

"I can't believe you said that!" Tamera said angrily. "This is not the time for a party."

He gave her a confused look. "But—"

"Your mother's right, Nick," Daniel interrupted him. "That was a very insensitive thing to say. I think you better not say that in front of your grandparents."

"I don't understand. You guys had one. I've seen the pictures. I don't see why Uncle Steven shouldn't have one."

"Nicholas, that's enough!" Tamera screamed at him. "I don't want to hear another word out of you."

"I give up," Nicholas yelled back that them both. "Nothing I say or do is ever right with either of you!" He turned around, still clutching the paper in his coat pocket, and ran off down the street.

"Nick!" Tamera shouted as he disappeared from her sight.

"Let him go," Daniel said and put his arm around her shoulders.

"What's the matter with him?"

"I don't know."

* * *

A hush hung over the picnic table while Bradley, Amanda, Patricia, Ariel, and Mark took in the news. Ruth looked at her family and held onto Carl's hand. She wondered if she had done the right thing in telling them, but she could not ignore the feeling of relief that grew inside her. It actually gave her a second wind, a burst of strength.

"I don't know what to say." Bradley looked around the table in disbelief. "How could he have kept this a secret from us all this time?"

"You would've thought we would have seen some clue before now," Patricia added.

"So, that's the reason this reunion was so important to him," Amanda realized out loud and leaned against Bradley for support.

"Yes." Ruth nodded in acknowledgement. "But you can't let on that you know. Steven would be very upset if he knew that we told all of you."

"I can't believe you both kept this a secret from us for this long," Patricia said angrily and looked at her parents.

"It was what your brother wanted. Believe me, we wanted to tell you all," Carl said.

"Still you should've told us, warned us."

"Don't you dare judge us!" Carl snapped at her. "I don't care how old you are, we're still your parents and you will not speak to us in that tone. Do you think keeping this a secret from all of you has been easy for us? None of you know what your mother and I have been through these past few months. We've had no one but each other to talk to about this."

Carl looked around the table. Tears filled his eyes. He had tried denying it for so long, avoiding admitting it to himself. Not wanting to think that far ahead, but now he was. He hated that feeling, the pain in his chest.

"So, what's up?" Nicholas said as he walked up to the table and looked at all the sullen faces.

Ariel looked up at him. "Grandma just told us about Uncle Steven."

"Isn't it neat," he said. His smile faded when he looked at the shocked faces round the table.

Without warning Ariel jumped to her feet and slapped him. "No, it isn't neat and it's nothing to joke about," she said and burst into tears. She looked at her mother and then ran off toward the front yard.

Mark hesitated a moment then silently hurried after her.

Ruth glared at her grandson angrily. She could not believe how anyone could say such a thing.

"What?" Nicholas asked, looking at their angry faces. "Did I say something wrong?"

"I need to go check on Benji," Amanda said and stood up. "Mom, do you want me to check on Steven?"

"No," Ruth said, looking at her daughter-in-law. "Let him rest a bit longer. Oh, don't forget to put the child gate up. It's in Steven's closet, so please be quiet."

"Okay." Amanda kissed Bradley on his furry cheek and headed into the house.

"It'd be so easy for Benji to fall down those stairs," Ruth thought out loud. "I don't think I could take much more today."

"That goes double for me," Bradley agreed. "What an emotional roller coaster. First the news about the baby and then this. It almost makes me feel guilty about being happy today."

Nicholas hesitantly sat down at the table. No one was looking at him anymore. It was as if they were intentionally ignoring him. He was confused. Why were they so upset over the news about Steven? Why were they all so sad?

Patricia looked beyond Bradley at Morgan and Chuck in the distance. They were still hugging and kissing each other by the swing like two lovestruck teenagers.

"Do you suppose we should tell Morgan and Chuck?" she asked and motioned with her head in their direction.

"Not now." Carl looked at them and shook his head. "There's plenty of time to tell them later."

"I guess you're right," Patricia agreed and looked back

at Nicholas. "So, you seem to be taking all of this well." Her tone was more accusing than complimentary.

Nicholas looked at his aunt seated on the arm of the Adirondack lawn chair. "Oh, just leave me alone," he mumbled and jumped to his feet. He headed for the house.

Patricia stood up to follow him but Ruth grabbed her arm.

"Let him go," she said, halting Patricia. "He's been in a mood all day. Give him some space."

Suddenly a scream came from inside the house. Everyone at the table jumped.

Bradley sprang to his feet.

"Oh my god, Benji!" he shouted, running for the back door and practically knocking Nicholas to the ground when he pushed passed him.

Ruth looked at Carl as a wave of panic came over her. They both jumped to their feet and headed for the house.

"Please, God, not today," Ruth whispered out loud while she ran into the house.

"Amanda!" Bradley called out, his voice echoing ahead of him. As he entered the foyer, Daniel and Tamera came through the front door followed by Ariel and Mark. Bradley's heart pounded in his chest and his throat tightened as he turned toward the stairs.

"Amanda!" he screamed as he started up the stairs. He froze on the steps when he saw Amanda standing in the open doorway of Steven's bedroom.

"Oh God, no!" Carl yelled and choked, tears nearly blinding him. "Steven!" he screamed in a pained and wounded voice. He cleared the stairs in three leaps and stood in the doorway. Ruth was right beside him when he entered the bedroom.

"Oh God, not my boy, not my son," Carl groaned. "Not now, not today." His heavy sobs echoed throughout the house. Slowly he fell to his knees beside the bed.

Steven lay quiet. Motionless.

Carl took Steven's hand, it was cold. Carl's vision blurred as tears continued falling uncontrolled. His chest heaved with each pained sob.

Ruth reached down and felt Steven's cold wrist for a pulse. Slowly she reached up and stroked his hair. A single, silent tear fell from her eyes as she looked at her son.

"Oh, Steven, my poor baby," she whispered then bent down and kissed his lifeless forehead. "No more pain."

Downstairs, in the foyer, Morgan and Chuck looked around at everyone confused.

"What's going on? Who screamed?"

Amanda looked up from Bradley's arms at her sister-in-law. "Steven's dead," she choked then buried her face in Bradley chest and cried.

"What?" Morgan looked disbelievingly at her. "You liar," she hissed. "That isn't funny."

"It's true, Morgan," Daniel said, hanging up the telephone. "Mom and Dad just told us that Steven found out months ago that he had an inoperable brain tumor. The doctors told him last month he only had a few days left."

"No," Morgan said flatly, turning her face away from him but continuing to look at out of the corner of her eyes. "You're lying." Slowly she moved toward the stairs, not taking her eyes off her brother-in-law. "You're all lying!" she screamed and darted up the stairs.

"Morgan," Chuck called, reaching for her but missing.

Through her tears she could see her parents standing by Steven's bed. "No," she whimpered and collapsed against the threshold, crying.

Carl looked at her. Slowly he walked over to her and helped her to her feet. Putting his arm around her shoulders he whispered reassuringly to her. "It's okay." He guided her back down the stairs.

"Chuck?" Carl said when they reached the main floor.

"I'll take her, Dad." Chuck took Morgan in his arms and helped her into the parlor.

"I've got to call the ah—" Carl fumbled for the word. "Ah—"

"Dad, I've already called the ambulance and they're on their way," Daniel said, putting his arm around his suddenly frail father-in-law.

Carl instantly grabbed hold of him and groaned as he sobbed and cried. "No. No. No," he repeated over and over.

Daniel held him tightly and looked across the room. Patricia stood holding onto Ariel and Mark, their faces wet with tears. He looked up at the stairs just in time to see Tamera step into Steven's bedroom.

Tamera paused when she saw her mother stretch a sheet over Steven's lifeless body. "Mama," she said softly. "May I see him, please?"

Ruth turned around with the sheet still in her hands. She looked at her daughter in silence.

"I need to see him," Tamera said and slowly walked into the room. "I didn't get to tell him goodbye. I-I didn't get to tell him how much I loved him." Tamera crept closer to the bed. "I did love him, Mama. I-I, Mama, no!" Tamera fell into Ruth's arms and cried.

"It's okay, honey." Ruth held her daughter and stared at the wall. "It's okay," she said softly yet firmly. "Steven knew you loved him and he loved you, too."

"He can't be dead, Mama. He can't." Tamera trembled with grief.

"Let him go. He's not in pain anymore." Ruth slowly guided Tamera out of the room and back down the stairs.

* * *

Ruth stood on the front steps watching the black hearse until it disappeared down the street. Slowly she turned around and walked back into the house, closing the door behind her. She turned around and leaned against it. Her gaze wandered up the stairs to the open bedroom door. The sheet that had shrouded

Steven hung over the rail. The house seemed cold, quiet, and empty. It was hard to believe that Steven was gone. Just a few short hours ago he had been alive, laughing and enjoying the family; now, he was dead.

She wrapped her arms over her chest, hugging herself and took a slow deep breath. Her eyes were dry, devoid of tears. She could not cry. The pain was too deep. Every muscle, every bone in her body ached from the pain, but still no tears. Her son was dead but she could not cry.

Slowly she walked over to the parlor. As she stood in the archway, she looked at each of her children. Tamera sat next to Daniel on the love seat, her cheeks still damp from her tears. Bradley quieted Benjamin, gently rocking him back and forth in his arms while he sat in the old wingback chair under the front window. Amanda sat on the arm of the chair, staring at the coffee table, seemingly content to be just near Bradley. Morgan stood wrapped in Chuck's arms, resting her head on his chest silently crying. Ariel sat curled up in the chair in front of Ruth. Her shoulders quivered as she quietly cried. Mark stood behind her, looking lost and out of place, staring at the floor.

Ruth turned without a word and walked into the kitchen. Carl stood at the window in the breakfast nook, staring out at the swimming pool. Ruth looked out at the pool and remembered how just that morning she had scolded Carl for laughing and splashing about with their son. She wished she could go back in time and take it all back, let them have their fun. Why had she been so upset? Slowly she walked over to Carl and slipped her hand into his. He leaned into her, putting his head gently against hers. He sighed a quivering sigh. The two stood and looked out at the backyard.

"It's going to be okay," Ruth softly assured him. "We're going to be okay."

* * *

Nicholas looked inside the bedroom at the top of the

stairs. The room was dark with evening fast approaching. Tears filled his eyes and dampened his cheeks.

"Why?" he cried softly. "Why didn't you tell me, Uncle Steven?"

Slowly he pulled the folded paper out of his pocket. He wiped his nose and tried to dry his tears as he read the large letters at the top of the paper, "Certificate of Marriage." He folded it back up and tucked it away in his pocket and cried.

CHAPTER TWO
THE REHEARSAL

A cool, gentle breeze blew through the branches of the oak tree in the front yard. Autumn leaves gently drifted down to dot the carefully manicured lawn. The flower beds lining the driveway and walk were pruned and ready for the coming winter.

Ruth glanced at the catering truck parked by the curb in front of her house as she opened her car door. The faint sounds of hammering made her look up at the second story bedroom window. She sighed and shook her head. While her mind understood, her heart did not. Turning back to the car, she scooped up the grocery sacks and carefully closed the door with her hip.

Adjusting the bags in her arms to keep from dropping them, she made her way up the front walk to the door. She rang the doorbell with her elbow, then stepped back to look up at the bedroom window. The pounding continued. Again she sighed but this time in disgust, rang the doorbell a second time, then waited. Nothing.

"Carl!" she yelled through clenched teeth. Shifting the sacks in her arms, she dug through her purse for the house key.

"Here, let me help you with that, Mrs. Wallace." A deep voice came up behind her.

Ruth turned around to greet the tan, dark-haired young man in coveralls.

"Thank you, Luke." She smiled, handing him the bags. "How are things going out back?"

"Not bad." He nodded his head.

Ruth took her keys out of her purse and quickly unlocked the front door. "Thank you, so much. I really appreciate this," she said, holding the door open for him.

"Sounds like Mr. Wallace is tearing the place apart up there," Luke said, glancing up at the open hallway above him as he walked into the foyer.

"That it does," Ruth said, frowning and looking at the closed bedroom door at the top of the stairs. "You can put those down on the kitchen counter in there." She pointed in the direction of the open archway to the kitchen. "Thank you again. I'll be out in just a few minutes."

"You're quite welcome, ma'am," he said over his shoulder as he proceeded to the kitchen.

Ruth closed the front door and walked over to the table under the stairs. She set her purse and keys down and looked at the wilted flowers. A sympathy card was still attached. Tears welled up in her eyes but quickly disappeared. It had been three months since Steven's death, but it seemed like only yesterday. She looked at the rest of the table. Something was missing. However, the constant pounding of the hammer upstairs made it difficult for her to think.

"Carl, what have you done?" she said to herself, shaking her head.

Turning away from the table, she headed for the kitchen. Just as she was about to leave the foyer, the front doorbell chimed.

"Now what?" she said, walking over to the door.

"Hi, Grandma," Ariel greeted Ruth as she stepped inside. She gave her grandmother a one-armed hug, shifting her overnight bag to her other hand.

"Hi, Mom," Morgan said, following her daughter inside. "I really appreciate your letting Ariel stay here tonight," she added, looking at her daughter.

Ariel could not stop smiling, her blue eyes sparkling with excitement.

"Don't be silly. You're always welcome here." Ruth smiled warmly and closed the door. "Besides, it only makes sense for you to spend the night since the wedding is here tomorrow afternoon. Why don't you take your things upstairs to the guest bedroom, then come down to the kitchen? Oh, Patty will be spending the night here too, so you'll have to share the room."

"Thank you, Grandma," Ariel said, giving her grandmother a kiss on the cheek before starting up the stairs.

Morgan and Ruth watched her ascend the open staircase. Ariel reached the second floor just as Carl resumed his hammering. Morgan jumped.

"Who's making all that noise?" she demanded.

"That would be your father." Ruth shook her head in disgust. She turned and headed into the kitchen. "He's remodeling Steven's bedroom. He said he just couldn't take the constant reminder any longer."

Morgan looked at Ruth. She could tell that her mother was not in agreement about the change. "I'm sorry." she said, putting her arm around Ruth's shoulders.

"Oh please, I'm fine," Ruth said, shrugging off Morgan's arm. Morgan stepped away. "I hope you're going to give me a hand with the cooking tonight," Ruth continued. "You know, I just can't understand that boy's parents. They've known for months about this wedding. How is it they won't be here?"

"I don't know." Morgan sighed. "Mark said his father was called away on business at the last minute and his mother had to go to help him."

"Well, I know if it were my son getting married, I'd be there," Ruth said matter-of-factly.

"You know, this wedding is fast becoming expensive, with us having to provide the rehearsal dinner too. You'd think with all their money, Mark's parents could let go of a little. After all, it's their son's wedding too." Morgan began to unpack the grocery bag.

"Well, at least we'll make it nice for Ariel's sake," Ruth

said, taking the roast for the night's dinner from the refrigerator. "I hope everyone likes roast beef."

Morgan smiled. She loved her mother's roast beef. It brought back so many nice memories of Sunday dinners around the table when she was growing up. She had not thought about those in years.

"Well, I do," she said happily. "I have a question," Morgan said, her tone changing to a more serious one. Ruth paused and looked at her. "What happened to the family picture that was on the table in the foyer?"

That's it! That's what's missing, Ruth thought to herself.

"I don't know. Your father must've put it away somewhere."

"Oh, not this again," Morgan said in disgust. "You remember when Grandpa Wallace died? Dad went through the house and threw away everything that reminded him of Grandpa. Now he's doing it again."

"Losing a child is never easy," Ruth said firmly, not happy with Morgan's judgmental tone. "We all handle our grief differently. Your father will deal with it in his own way and time. This isn't something you can get over quickly. Three months isn't that long ago."

"That's true," Morgan acknowledged. "I still can't believe he's really gone."

"Tell me about it. It all doesn't make sense." Ruth shook her head. She set the oven temperature and then washed her hands.

"What doesn't make sense?" Morgan asked, turning around to eye her mother. Was there something more she failed to tell her about the day Steven died?

"Oh, I don't know exactly." Ruth shrugged and continued sprinkling seasoning on the roast.

Morgan studied her mother's expression for a moment. She could tell that something was troubling her and it made her more curious. "What is it?" she prodded.

"Did Steven ever tell you about his college days?"

"Mom, Steven and I rarely talked. If anyone would know about that time in his life, Tamera would. Why?"

"Well, he started to tell me something that afternoon but he stopped short of actually coming out with it. I've already asked the other kids and he didn't said a word to any them, so I thought that maybe he might have said something to you. That's all." Ruth lifted the roasting pan from the counter and placed it in the oven. The conversation came to an abrupt halt.

Morgan watched Ruth for a moment, wondering what other secrets the family was keeping from her. She shrugged it off and then changed the subject. "I really appreciate you letting Ariel have her wedding and reception here."

"It's no problem." Ruth picked up the long stemmed flowers from the breakfast table in the nook and began to arrange them in a vase.

"Ariel has so many memories of our family get-togethers here and of swimming out back in the summer. She thinks of this as her second home. I know it means a lot to her," Morgan continued.

"Actually, I have an ulterior motive for wanting it here. Our last family gathering didn't end well."

Silence fell over the kitchen as Ruth continued arranging the flowers and Morgan went about preparing the rest of the night's dinner.

A young man dressed in coveralls opened the back door. "Excuse me, Mrs. Wallace?"

Ruth turned around.

"Yes?" she said, glancing out the window at the canopy in the lower backyard. "How's it going out there?"

"Luke would like you to come out if you have a second or two. He wants to be sure the tables are how you want them before we begin putting the chairs out."

"I'll be right out." Ruth put the last of the flowers in the vase and cocked her head as she looked at them. "That should do it," she said and turned to Morgan. "When you finish with that, would you put this vase on the table in the foyer and throw out the dead flowers from Steven's funeral? I think we can do without those now."

"Sure, Mom." Morgan nodded.

"Well, young man." Ruth smiled at the worker. "Let's go take a look."

The two walked out the back door leaving Morgan alone in the kitchen.

* * *

Morgan set the vase of flowers down on the small table in the foyer. She stretched her back and rolled her shoulders to ease her aching muscles. She picked up the vase of dead flowers and turned around to start back to the kitchen when the doorbell rang.

Just as she reached for the doorknob, the door opened and she started when Bradley walked in.

"Bradley!" Morgan snapped at him. "You almost made me drop this vase. Couldn't you wait for someone to answer the door before you barge in?"

"Sorry, sis," he said, sounding more distracted than sincere as he closed the door. "So, what're you doing with those?" he asked, nodding toward the vase.

"Why do you want to know?"

"You don't have to be so defensive. I was just asking is all."

"I'm not defensive. I'm just busy and Mom wants me to throw these out," Morgan responded in the same snippy tone. She turned around and walked into the kitchen.

"I bet you'll be happy when tomorrow's over," Bradley said as he followed her.

"What's that supposed to mean?"

"Good grief, Morgan, lighten up. I just meant that the wedding will be over and you can relax."

Morgan dropped the dead flowers into the garbage

under the sink. "Here, make yourself useful," she said, holding the bag of garbage out to him.

"No way," Bradley said, taking a step back and holding up his hands. "I no longer take out the garbage around here. You do it."

"Fine," Morgan said and put the bag down on the floor.

"So, is that Dad I hear?" Bradley cocked his head when the hammering began again.

"Yeah, mom says he's been at it all week. I don't know what he's doing up there but whatever it is, I hope he doesn't plan on keeping it up tomorrow."

"I'll go see what he's up to," Bradley said and quickly started for the foyer before Morgan could pressure him into taking out the garbage.

"Good, you do that," she said and went back to preparing the dinner.

As Bradley started up the stairs, the hammering stopped. Cautiously he opened the bedroom door and peered inside. Chalky white dust from the sheets of drywall covered the tarps protecting the carpet in the empty room.

"So, how's it going, Dad?" Bradley asked quietly so he would not startle his father.

"Don't just stand there," Carl said, looking over his shoulder while trying to hold a sheet of drywall in place. "Give me a hand, Steven." Suddenly he froze at his own words. "I'm sorry, Bradley."

"No problem, Dad." Bradley grabbed a hammer from the tool box near the door and a handful of nails, then hurried to help lift the last sheet of drywall into place. "What would you have done if I hadn't come along?" he teased.

"I never thought of that." Carl paused and then began to hammer again. Bradley smiled to himself and joined in at the opposite end.

When they were finished, Bradley put his hammer back in the tool box and looked around the bedroom. The familiar pinewood panels were gone as was the furniture. There was nothing left to remind them that this had once been Steven's bedroom.

"Dad, let's take a break," Bradley suggested, noticing how tired Carl looked.

"All right." Carl nodded, wiping the sweat and dust from his brow with a heavy sigh. "I guess I'm about due for one. So, what do you think?" he asked and looked around the room proudly.

"I guess it's fine." Bradley shrugged. "Dad, I know why you're doing this. It's not going to work."

Carl looked at his son and then away. Anger rose inside himself at Bradley's words. *It will work. It has to work,* he told himself as he bit his tongue.

"I don't know what you're talking about. Your mother has wanted this to be her sewing room for years. I just never got around to it."

"Dad, mom already has a sewing room, Morgan's old bedroom in the basement. This has to do with Steven. You think that by remodeling this room, you can pretend he never existed."

"This has nothing to do with Steven!" Carl snapped, turning around sharply and looking out the window. The empty room echoed Steven's name before falling into deafening silence. Carl's shoulders slumped under the weight and his head fell forward. "You're right, son, it does have to do with Steven," he admitted. "I just can't take remembering him. It hurts too much."

"I know what you mean, Dad." Bradley walked over to his father and put his arm around his shoulders. "I miss him, too. I never really knew how much he meant to me, until now. I don't have a big brother anymore."

"It's more than that, Brad." Carl shook his head. "He didn't tell us everything. There was more."

Bradley looked at his father curiously. "What do you mean?"

"Nothing. That's just it. You think you know our own son and then you find out you really don't. It's as though he were a stranger." Carl shook his head and straightened his back, suddenly realizing he had said too much. "Never mind."

"Dad, you can't leave me hanging here." Bradley looked at his father and dropped his arm back to his side. Carl did not look back; he turned and walked over to the door.

"I'm through in here for a while. I need some fresh air," he said and then disappeared down the stairs.

Bradley looked around the room, confused at what had just happened. He turned and looked out the window at the front yard. "Mom," he said out loud to himself when he saw the catering truck. Without another moment's wait, he turned and hurried out of the room.

* * *

Ariel and Morgan stood by the back door out of the way, watching Ruth direct the caterers on where to move the tables and place the chairs. Morgan smiled as she remembered her wedding day. Ruth had spent weeks orchestrating every detail so the day would be perfect, and it had been. Morgan watched her mother now, and Ruth appeared calm, confident and happy.

"Everything's going as planned," Ruth reported as she walked over to them.

"A lot smoother than my wedding," Morgan teased.

"Yes." Ruth smiled. "This time I'm making sure they don't put any chairs near the swimming pool. So tell Chuck's mother not to worry."

"She'll be happy to hear that." Morgan laughed out loud.

"What's so funny?" Ariel asked, casting a confused look at the two of them.

"Oh, your dad's and my wedding, Grandma Fletcher went to stand up but her chair was too close to the swimming pool. She went over backwards, dress over her head, right into the water. It wasn't funny then, but now. . ."

Morgan continued laughing as she looked across the swimming pool at the workers. Suddenly, her smile vanished and a warm rush of adrenaline swept over her as she recognized one of the workers.

"Mom," Bradley called as he walked over to the small gathering. "Do you have a moment? I really need to talk to you kind of privately." He glanced at Morgan who appeared frozen as she stared at something across the backyard. Bradley nodded his head in Morgan's direction to get Ruth to look.

Suddenly aware of their silence, Morgan pulled her attention away from the worker and looked at the three of them who were all staring at her.

"What?" she said innocently, trying to keep from blushing at being caught with her thoughts.

"Is something wrong, dear?" Ruth asked, glancing over her shoulder at Luke.

"No," Morgan said quickly. "Everything's fine."

"Are you sure?" Ruth questioned. She could tell Morgan was lying.

"Yes," she repeated, annoyed at being questioned. "Come on, Ariel. I want you to try on your dress before everyone else arrives for the rehearsal."

"Thank you, Morgan." Bradley smiled at her.

Morgan gave him a confused glare as she and Ariel left, not sure what he meant by his remark.

"What's on your mind, honey?" Ruth asked, folding her arms in front of her while she continued watching Luke and the other men move the tables to where she had instructed.

"I had a talk with Dad just now and I'm really confused. I thought you might know what's going on," he began.

"What do you mean?" Ruth asked, turning away from the workers and giving Bradley her full attention.

"I was just upstairs helping Dad for a second in Steven's room. Did you know he tore out the paneling?"

"Yes." She nodded. "So?"

"Well, I told him that changing the room wouldn't help

him forget Steven. That's when he implied there was something else Steven didn't tell us. Do you know what he's talking about?" Bradley asked and studied his mother's eyes. Her short auburn hair was flipped back away from her face. She looked away from him and the silence stretched out.

"It's really nothing," she finally said. "Steven implied that something happened when he was away in college. At least that's how I took it. You remember I asked you about it about a month ago? Anyway, so far there seems to be nothing. I'll talk to your father again. Excuse me."

"All right." Bradley nodded, stepping aside to let Ruth pass. She hurried across the backyard to where the workers were setting up the chairs.

* * *

"Hi Morgan," Tamera greeted her sister as she walked into the foyer.

"Hi," Morgan replied, still distracted by seeing the worker. "If you want mom, she's out back," she offered, then headed up the stairs, leaving Tamera to close the front door behind her family.

"What's with her?" Daniel asked and frowned. He watched Morgan disappear into the guest bedroom.

"Who cares?" Tamera shrugged. "Let's go see what's happening out back."

Just as Tamera took a step, a loud bang rattled the walls and echoed in the foyer. Tamera jumped and spun around. "What was that?" she gasped.

"It came from upstairs," Daniel said.

Tamera looked up at the open door of Steven's bedroom. Something was different but she was not sure what. There seemed to be more light coming out of the room than usual.

"Dan, you and Nick go on. I want to see what's going on upstairs." She did not wait for a reply before heading for the stairs.

"Well, son," Daniel sighed and shook his head. "Here we go again. Come on, let's go out back." He put his arm around Nicholas' shoulders and the two proceeded to the backyard.

* * *

Slowly Tamera approached the open doorway and peered inside. She froze at the sight of the room. Across the room Carl put his hammer in his belt loop and continued mudding over the nails. He was aware that Tamera was behind him. Even with all the dust in the air, he could still smell her perfume, a fresh floral scent that was mixed with her hair spray.

"Dad? What've you done?" Tamera was in shock. For as long as she could remember, this had been Steven's bedroom. Even when he had moved out seventeen years ago, the room had remained his. Everything just the way he left it. No one else's bedroom remained intact. Morgan's basement room had been converted into a sewing room. Bradley's room had been turned back into the attic. Even the bedroom she and Patricia had shared had been redecorated.

"What does it look like?" Carl continued to work.

"But this is Steven's room," Tamera protested. "Why?"

"This is my house and I'll do with it as I see fit!" Carl snapped, turning around to face her. "I don't need to explain myself to you or your brother. Is that clear?"

Tamera recoiled at her father's burst of anger. Her eyes immediately welled behind her pink-tinted glasses. She opened her mouth as though to speak but instead turned around and ran from the room in tears.

Carl slowly relaxed his jaw as he looked around the bedroom.

"This is *not* your room," he said out loud, trying to expel the memories from the four walls. Suddenly, his eyes filled with tears. He dropped the spreader into the bucket of mud as he slid down the wall and sat on the floor. "Damn, you, Steven," he breathed. "Why? Why, Steven?" Tears began to streak his white-dusted cheeks. He bowed his head and let them fall.

* * *

"Come on, Ariel, what's taking you so long?" Morgan asked impatiently, staring out the window at the workers in the backyard.

"Mom, are you sure this was measured right?" Ariel asked, squirming as she stepped from behind the antique dressing screen.

"Yes," Morgan answered without looking at her. "All brides feel bloated on their wedding day, so the seamstress made it a little larger. You'll be fine."

Ariel looked across the room at her mother. "You're not even looking." She sighed in exasperation and turned to look at her reflection in the full length mirror that hung on the back of the door. Slowly she ran her hand over her stomach, feeling how tight the lace-appliquéd bodice felt. She turned to look at herself from the side to see if her stomach was noticeable. Her eyes followed the white satin flow of the long skirt and train.

"I can't believe this is actually happening," Ariel breathed, staring at her reflection. "I've dreamt about this day ever since I was a little girl. Somehow, though, I thought it would feel differently. What if I don't really love Mark? Should I still marry him?"

Morgan continued to stare intently at the workers below, not hearing a word Ariel said. Instead, she stood wringing her hands and muttering to herself under her breath.

"Mother!" Ariel snapped. She turned away from her reflection and stood with her fists on her hips. "You haven't heard a word I've said."

Morgan turned around and faced her. Instantly she forgot all about the men working outside, captivated by the sight of her little girl.

"You're so beautiful," she gasped. Tears filled her blue

eyes. She could not help but smile proudly at her daughter. "I'm sorry, what were you saying?"

The moment was gone for Ariel. Her doubts and fears were replaced by curiosity over what was occupying her mother's attention. She walked over to the window and looked out.

"Never mind." Ariel shrugged then turned around. "Is there something wrong?"

"No. Why?"

"Well, you seem to be preoccupied with the caterers." Ariel took another look out the window. "Is something wrong?" At that moment Luke walked out from under the canopy. Ariel glanced over her shoulder at her mother and then back at him. "Isn't that the guy you tutored last spring term?"

"No," Morgan blurted, causing Ariel to turn back around. "I mean," she stammered. "I don't know any of them. I've got to get back to the kitchen. You get changed."

Before Ariel could say another word, Morgan hurried out the door and shut it behind her. Ariel turned back to the window, now more curious than before.

* * *

Tamera closed the back door behind her quietly and walked over to Daniel. He stood with his hands deep in his jeans pockets, watching the workers on the other side of the swimming pool. Tamera wiped the tears from her eyes and stared blankly out at the backyard.

"So, what's dad up to?" Daniel turned to her and smiled. Gently he slipped his hand in hers and gave it a little squeeze.

"He's gone."

"Your dad's gone?" Daniel asked, cocking his head and giving her a confused look.

"No, Steven," she said, wiping her tears from her cheek.

"Didn't we already know that?"

"I know, but now he's *really* gone. Dad tore apart

Steven's room. All of Steven's things are gone." She began to cry. "It's like he never existed."

"It's okay," Daniel soothed, taking her into his arms and holding her. "Losing Steven was hard for all of us. Perhaps this is what he felt he had to do. You know as well as I that Dad loved Steven. Maybe keeping his room was more than he could bear."

"I know, but—"

"Tammy, we all handle our grief differently. You remember."

"Yes. I remember." Tamera looked at the ground. "I just don't understand how he could do it. That was the one place where I felt like I could still be close to Steven."

"Did you ever think it could've been the same for him? Maybe that's why he felt he had to do it, to let go, to get on with his life. Losing a child is, no matter how young or old, the hardest thing to face. We know that all too well."

"But I don't want to forget him." She began to cry again.

"And you won't. Just like we haven't forgotten about Danny." Tears filled Daniel's eyes before he finished saying his name.

Tamera wiped her tears away and remembered that morning so many years ago. She had put her precious little baby boy to bed. He smiled and cooed at her, holding his hands up and kicking his feet. His blue eyes twinkled in the dim light of his nightlight. She stroked his soft blonde hair and gently touched his cheek. She had never seen such a beautiful baby boy and he was hers.

She only left him for a couple of hours. She had been so tired; she could not stay awake another minute. When she woke up she rose from the bed in the nursery and walked over to his crib. She remembered hearing a loud scream that felt as though it was coming from someone else. Daniel rushed next to her beside the crib. He grabbed the lifeless infant from her arms and laid him on the dressing table. Tamera watched while her husband performed CPR on the tiny body.

"It's all my fault," she kept repeating.

"Call an ambulance!" Daniel shouted between breaths.

Tamera stood frozen in place. "I shouldn't have left him. I should've stayed awake."

"For God's sake, Tamera, call 911!" Daniel yelled over his shoulder.

When the police and ambulance arrived, it was already too late. The EMT tried to comfort them, telling them there was nothing they could have done.

"Even if you'd been standing beside him at the exact moment it happened, you couldn't have saved him. It's as if there were a tiny switch inside his brain that shut off. No one and nothing can turn it back on." His words fell on deaf ears. Tamera was slipping away into her grief and refused to be comforted.

"It'll be okay," Daniel said, gently kissing her blonde hair and holding her in his arms while they stood in her parents' backyard. "We'll get through this, too."

* * *

Nicholas stood quietly watching Bradley who was sitting in a lawn chair at the edge of the patio. He could not make up his mind whether or not to talk to his uncle. They had never been really close and Nicholas was not even sure why he was afraid of him. Perhaps it was Bradley's six-foot-two height coupled with his burly build and deep voice. He was not sure, but he had to talk to someone. He felt the folded up paper in his pocket. Taking a deep breath, he cautiously stepped forward.

"Hey, Uncle Brad." His voice was steady even though inside he was shaking.

Bradley turned his head and looked at his nephew.

"Wow, Nick." A smile spread across Bradley's face. "Is that really you? You look great. It's good to see you finally looking like a young man."

Nicholas self-consciously put his hand on his head and smoothed his short hair. It had only been a week since he had his long hair cut off, and he still was not used to people's reactions.

"Thanks." He blushed which made him feel more embarrassed and upset with himself. He hated that. "Uncle Brad, are you busy?"

Bradley looked around and shrugged. "No. Why, do I look like it?" he teased.

"Not really," Nicholas answered, unsure of how his uncle would take his honesty.

Bradley laughed heartily and reached for the lawn chair beside him. Pulling it closer, he said, "Have a seat."

Nicholas slowly sat down, trying to collect his thoughts. He never felt this uncomfortable talking with Steven; that was, until that one day last summer. He leaned forward and rubbed his hands together nervously.

"So, what's on your mind?" Bradley asked, eyeing his nephew and noticing how nervous he seemed. He would be the first to admit that he did not know Nicholas very well. The two had never really spent much time, if any, together. He did not have an excuse since they lived only a mile away from each other. His only reason, and he was not even sure he had given it that much thought before, was that he did not approve of Nicholas' rebellious attitude and did not want him around Benjamin. However, as he thought about it more, he knew that was only a cop out. Benjamin was only two and not that easily influenced. No, the more the thought about it, the more he realized it had more to do with his relationship with Tamera than Nicholas himself. He and Tamera were not very close. The four years that separated them seemed as insurmountable as leaping the Grand Canyon.

"I just wanted to talk to you about Uncle Steven," Nicholas said cautiously. "That is, if you don't mind."

Bradley felt a wave of anxiety sweep over him at the sound of Steven's name. While growing up, he had always looked up to Steven.

Steven had always been popular in school because of his wit and because he was a good listener. People were drawn to him. They opened up to him. Even in the family, Bradley knew that if he ever needed to talk to someone, Steven was always there ready to listen. Steven seemed to be the glue that held the family together. Sure, his mom and dad were there, but it was Steven that kept the peace between the siblings. Now, he was gone. The loss was felt by all and it hurt even three months later.

"Okay." Bradley tried to hide the quiver in his voice with a cough. "What'd you want to talk about?"

"I really loved Uncle Steven but sometimes I get so angry with him," Nicholas said quietly. "I miss him and I know that Mom does too. At night I can hear her crying in her bedroom. I hate seeing her like that and that makes me angry. Is that wrong?"

Bradley smiled to himself because he understood just how Nicholas felt. He had those feelings at times too.

"No, Nick." He shook his head. "Those feelings are normal. They're part of the grieving process. Death is hard for all of us to understand, let alone accept. One minute the person you love is sitting right beside you laughing and talking and the next. . ." Bradley bit his lip and turned his head away from Nicholas as he swallowed his tears.

"Why does it hurt so much?"

"It hurts because you loved," Bradley heard himself say. He looked at his nephew, letting him see the tears in his own eyes. "In time, the pain you're feeling will fade away and you'll be able to remember your Uncle Steven without the tears."

"I don't think I'll ever be able to do that," Nicholas said and sighed. He took the paper from his pocket. "There's something more," he said without looking up.

Bradley looked at the folded piece of paper in Nicholas' hands. His curiosity was piqued. He waited for his nephew to continue.

"The day Uncle Steven died, before he died, he made me promise not to tell anyone about this. I don't know if I should say anything now, but it's too hard keeping it to myself." Nicholas' hands shook as he held the paper. It was bit more tattered around the edges than it had been when he found it.

"Nick, I don't think your Uncle Steven would mind you telling now. Whatever it is, it can't hurt him anymore," Bradley said, still staring at the folded paper.

"Here," Nicholas said and thrust out his hand to Bradley. "He gave me this and told me to keep it as a reminder that even he had made some mistakes when he was young."

Bradley took the paper and carefully unfolded it. His mouth dropped open as he read the seventeen-year-old marriage certificate. This was it. This was Steven's other secret. *How could he have kept this hidden for so long,* Bradley wondered.

* * *

Carl emerged from the dusty upstairs bedroom and wiped the sweat from his brow. As soon as the mud dried, the bedroom would be ready to paint. Then at last, things would be better. The memories that were stored in those four walls would finally be erased. He could walk past that door and not see his son lying dead in his bed. *Everything was going to be all right,* Carl told himself silently and shut the door.

The house was quiet. The hallway and foyer below were deserted. In the distance Carl could hear the faint sounds of voices in the front yard as he descended the staircase. When he reached the foyer, he glanced into the parlor. His eyes went straight to the portrait of Steven on the mantle above the fireplace. A sudden pain jolted him as he realized he had not erased Steven from the house completely. Slowly he walked over and picked up the framed photograph. Gently he stroked the glass over Steven's face with his thumb. A tear came to his eyes. He shook it away.

"Damn you," he whispered under his breath. He turned around with the portrait in his hands and walked back into the foyer. He did not see Morgan standing in the archway to the kitchen watching him curiously. He walked over to the coat closet, opened the door, and laid the portrait on top of the others on the shelf. He closed the door and walked into the family room.

Morgan inched her way into the foyer, keeping an eye out for her father. She tiptoed into the parlor to look at the mantle. Her eyes scanned the many pictures as she tried to figure out which one was missing. She knew in her heart which one it was but she had to see for herself.

A shadow moved across the front window, drawing Morgan's attention. She walked over to the window and drew back the sheer curtain to peer out. Her eyes widened and her heart raced when she caught sight of Luke heading for the catering truck. She abandoned her inspection of the photographs and ran out the front door. Luke turned around and smiled as Morgan rush over to him.

"What do you think you are doing here?" she asked, panic in her voice. "Are you trying to ruin my life?"

Luke's smile faded and he gave her a puzzled look. "I happen to be working here if it's any of your business. What're you doing here?"

"This happens to be my parent's home and my daughter's wedding," Morgan informed him in a hushed whisper.

A smile spread across Luke's face as the realization hit him and he gave a slight laugh.

"What's so funny?" Morgan demanded.

"Oh, I was just thinking about the irony of it all," Luke said, folding his arms over his chest. "You take me to bed. Your husband gets me expelled from college. Four months later, your mother hires me to cater a wedding, and not just any wedding, your daughter's wedding. Who would've guessed our paths would cross again so soon."

"Well, you're fired. Get out of here," Morgan snapped.

"No, no," Luke said, shaking his head. "I'm not working for you. I work for Mrs. Wallace. But if you'd like me to go to her and explain why I have to pack everything up—"

Morgan slapped him across the face, silencing him. He quickly brought his hand to his cheek and smiled at her.

"I owe you one for that," he threatened. "I'm not the naïve little college frosh anymore. You and your husband have messed up my life enough. Now it's time for a little payback."

Morgan began to shake as a feeling of panic overwhelmed her. She knew one word of this to her mother would destroy the fragile relationship she had with her. Slowly she backed away from Luke.

"Just get out of here," she breathed and then hurried back to the house.

"When I'm finished," Luke said, standing his ground. He smiled, rubbing his cheek, and then continued toward his truck.

Morgan froze when she reached the front door and saw that Patricia standing in the doorway had observed the whole confrontation. Patricia flashed Morgan a knowing smile.

"Not one word of this to anyone!" Morgan threatened in her usual bossy tone and started around her to the door.

"So that's why all the drama between you and Chuck lately," Patricia said, nodding to herself.

Morgan spun around in the open doorway. "Chuck and I are fine," she said, looking into her sister's dark-brown eyes. "I don't know what you're talking about."

"Oh, you can pretend all you want but I know differently." Patricia smiled. "You see, I work with Luke's father down at the TV station. He told me all about his son and how he was seduced by his tutor and her husband got him expelled. Only I didn't realize until now that this tutor was my sister."

A feeling of nausea swept over Morgan. She felt like she was losing control, her secret was out. She glared at Patricia and tried to figure out a way to keep her from telling anyone.

"Well, I don't care if you know," Morgan lied. "What do you plan to do, tell Mom and Dad?"

"I might." Patricia gave a little shrug of her shoulders. She smiled at the power she suddenly had over her eldest sister. For as long as she could remember, Morgan had always treated her like a child, bossing her around. It felt good to finally have an equalizer. "But I won't. Not just yet. Telling them today would only hurt another innocent person, Ariel. I'll just wait and when the time's right, if you aren't nicer to me, I'll spill my guts."

Morgan did not say a word as she slammed the door in Patricia's face. Ever since Patricia had been born, Morgan resented her. Stuck at home Friday nights babysitting while her friends were out partying had not been her idea of a fun time. Then the many times she was blamed for Patricia's scrapes and bruises. "Why weren't you watching her?" Ruth's voice echoed in her ears. "You're supposed to watch after your sisters and brothers. After all, you're the oldest." Morgan resented Patricia even more when she saw how close Patricia and Ariel had become. When Ariel chose Patricia to be her maid of honor, Morgan thought she had reached her last straw, but now this. Morgan leaned against the front door to catch her breath before returning to the kitchen.

Patricia waited a moment, watching Luke rummage through his truck and then, with a wrench in hand, return to the backyard. Turning around, she opened the front door and went inside. The house was quieter than she remembered or expected. The smell of roast beef filled the air. *It's strange to be spending the night here again, but it feels good, safe,* she thought silently. She clutched her overnight bag tighter and headed up the stairs.

As she reached the top of the stairs, the sunlight shining through Steven's bedroom window into the hallway caught her eye. She put her bag down and walked over to the doorway. A chill ran up her spine as she looked around the remodeled empty room.

"You're really gone," she whispered. A tear came to her eyes and she leaned against the threshold. Steven was the only one who understood her; the only one whom she could go to for support and a listening ear. He never judged her, never condemned her for how she lived her life. He was the only one whom she could trust with her secret, but now she was all alone. Gently she rubbed her shoulder and turned away.

"Aunt Patty!" Ariel shrieked and ran out of the guest bedroom. "You made it," she beamed happily.

Patricia smiled and forced her memories back into the closet of her mind.

"Of course I did." She laughed and hugged her niece.

* * *

"Look who's here," Ruth announced, carrying Benjamin across the backyard.

Bradley turned around and smiled. "How's my boy?" he said, taking his son. Benjamin wrapped his arms around Bradley's neck and held on.

"Amanda's mother just dropped him off," Ruth informed him.

"Yeah, she took him to see his mother," Bradley said and kissed Benjamin's cheek.

"How is she doing?" Ruth hesitated to ask.

"Physically, she's doing better because the nurses are making sure she's eating. She still refuses to see me. I don't know, I guess she's still mad at me for putting her in there. But what was I supposed to do? She was so sure she was pregnant and even though she claimed she was happy about it when we announced it to everyone, when we got home it was another story. She picked at her food and when she thought I wasn't around, she'd make herself throw up what little she did eat. I couldn't just sit by and watch her slowly kill herself. I had to do something."

"You did the right thing," Ruth reassured him. "As

painful as it is, you may have saved her life."

"She doesn't see it that way. She thinks I betrayed her."

"Give her time."

"I am and I will," Bradley said, patting Benjamin's back. "It's just hard watching someone you love kill themselves slowly. I found her hairbrush and her hair had been falling out. The doctor also told me that Amanda's organs were beginning to shut down. It was getting serious. I had no choice."

"I know," Ruth said and nodded empathically. "You did the right thing, as hard as it is for her and you." She looked at Benjamin and stroked his hair. "I think I know a little boy who would love a cookie." Benjamin perked up and smiled at his grandmother. "There should be some fresh chocolate chip cookies in the cookie jar," she told Bradley.

"Thanks, mom," Bradley said and gave her a kiss on the cheek. "And for the pep talk."

Bradley carried his son into the house. His mind was a jumble of that morning's conversations with his father, nephew, and now mother. He could not understand why his brother had never said anything about being married, and why his father appeared to be angry with Steven. *Does he know,* he wondered. Did his mother? Were they just keeping it all a secret? Why?

"Boy, something sure smells good." Bradley took a slow deep breath and entered the kitchen.

Morgan pushed the roast back into the oven and closed the door. "It's dinner," she said flatly and dropped the hot mitts on the counter beside the stove.

"I can see you're having one of those days too," Bradley commiserated. He sat Benjamin down on a stool at the breakfast bar and walked over to the cookie jar on the sideboard.

"Bradley!" Morgan yelled and rushed over to Benjamin, grabbing him before he fell. She scooped him up into her arms and turned around. "There you go," she cooed and smiled at her nephew as Bradley handed him a cookie.

Bradley smiled, noticing how gentle and motherly his big sister was with his son.

"You can't leave a little one alone like that," she scolded him. "He could've fallen and gotten hurt."

"I'm sorry," he said. "I wasn't thinking. Guess I have just too much on my mind today."

"Like what?" Morgan inquired, still holding Benjamin while he nibbled on his cookie.

"Where's dad?" Bradley asked, looking around the room.

"He's upstairs. Why? What's up?"

Bradley thought for a moment, debating on whether or not he could trust his sister. Just when he was about to tell her, Nicholas walked into the kitchen. He froze in his tracks when he noticed they had stopped talking.

"What?" Nicholas said, staring back at them.

"Would you do me a favor and take Benji out front and watch him for a bit?" Bradley asked, taking Benjamin from Morgan and setting him on the floor.

"Sure." Nicholas took Benjamin's tiny hand. "Say, where did you get that cookie, fella?"

Benjamin pointed to the cookie jar on the sideboard.

Morgan laughed. "I see mom's going to have to find a new place to put that."

"May I?" Nicholas asked, nodding toward the jar.

"Go ahead." Bradley waited until he was sure that Nicholas and Benjamin were gone and would not hear him before he turned back to Morgan.

"Have you noticed Dad and Mom have been acting strangely?"

"As a matter of fact." Morgan raised an eyebrow. "Why? What's up?" She leaned back against the counter and picked up a celery stalk. Without thinking, she bit into it.

"For starters," Bradley lowered his voice to a whisper. "What happened to all the pictures of Steven?"

"Dad put them in the coat closet."

"Good." Bradley sounded relieved. "At least he didn't throw them out like he did with Grandpa's."

"If you want a picture of Grandpa, I have the negatives," Morgan informed him, careful to keep her voice down and crunching the celery as she chewed. "I took them before Dad could find them."

"I'd love a picture of him to show my son," Bradley acknowledged. "There's something else. Have you noticed how angry Dad is? When I asked him he tried to pass it off as Steven said something happened when he was away at college, but Mom said she found it to be nothing. I know what happened but what I can't figure out is why Mom and Dad are keeping it a secret."

"What happened?" Morgan asked, leaning forward and glancing through the window above the sink to be sure no one was around.

* * *

"Aunt Tammy," Ariel said, leaning across the table while she sat on one of the folding chairs. "Aunt Patty said that I should talk to you."

"Oh? About what?" Tamera asked, glancing over her shoulder at the house.

"Well, I have this problem and I don't know what to do. Please don't tell me to talk to my mother, I've tried and she won't listen. You know how she can be. Anyway, it's not like I'm the first one this has happened to." Ariel began to fidget.

"Just spit it out, Ariel. What's the matter?" Tamera asked, growing increasingly impatient, yet concerned and intrigued.

"I think I'm pregnant," Ariel whispered.

The words hit Tamera hard and caught her totally off guard. She tried to hide her shock from Ariel as she fumbled for something to say. "Why do you think that?" she finally asked.

Ariel gave her a look that said, do I really need to explain it to you? "Because I've missed my period for two months," Ariel explained, looking over her shoulder at the men talking in the distance. She lowered her voice even more and leaned closer to her aunt. "I took one of those in-home pregnancy tests a couple of weeks ago."

"And. . ."

"It said I wasn't, but I may have done it wrong or something," she quickly added.

Tamera smiled. "You know those tests can be wrong. You really—"

"I know. That's why I went to the women's clinic in Salem yesterday. I'm still waiting to find out the results."

"I see," Tamera said and looked around the backyard at the tables and chairs. She turned back to Ariel and smiled. "Hey, you're getting married tomorrow, so no problem. After you're married then. . ." Tamera stopped and looked at Ariel who was avoiding eye contact. "Oh, now what?"

"I don't think Mark wants this baby." Ariel looked up at her aunt with tear-filled eyes.

"What?" Tamera raised her voice slightly. This was beginning to sound all too familiar. "He knows about this?"

"No. It's just that he's just getting started with his music career. His group signed a contract yesterday with a record company. They'll be cutting an album and doing tours and a baby would be, well, in the way?" A tear fell from Ariel's eyes. "I've been thinking, maybe I should have an abortion."

The words hit Tamera like a blow to the chest. Her mind flashed back twenty-four years and memories flooded her mind. She looked at the house and then back at Ariel.

"Ariel, there's something I think you should know," she began cautiously. "A long time ago, before your parents were married even, I had an abortion."

"What? Really?" Ariel looked at her aunt with wide eyes of shock and surprise.

"Yes." Tamera nodded and bit her lip as she tried to gather her thoughts. "Your father and mother had been dating for nearly a year. Your father drove me to a clinic in Salem so your grandparents wouldn't find out."

"Was Uncle Dan the father?"

"No," Tamera admitted.

"Who was? Is he still around?" Ariel asked with more enthusiasm than Tamera had expected.

"Yes, he's still around," she answered but ignored her niece's first question. "But the point is, after that happened, I didn't think I'd ever be able to have a child again. When I got married it took a year before I was able to get pregnant, and then he died from Sudden Infant Death Syndrome. I have lived with guilt ever since."

Ariel sat back in her chair, overwhelmed by the news.

"So, Ariel, don't do it. Even if you don't have the same trouble as I did, there'll be the emotional scars, the haunting memories, and the *what if's* that you'll have to live with."

Ariel looked at her aunt not knowing what to say. She was in shock. She looked down at the table again.

"Ariel, talk to Mark. The two of you can work this out," Tamera encouraged.

"But, Aunt Tammy, he's going on the road and if I'm pregnant, I can't travel like that."

"Ariel!" Tamera snapped at her niece. Her anger starting to rise, she tightened her jaw. "You don't have to go with him. You could stay here with his parents or with your grandparents and have this child. Mark can get his music career going and when the child's old enough to travel, then you can go. Believe me, if you abort this baby, you'll regret it for the rest of your life."

Ariel looked at her aunt, surprised by her reaction. She had hoped that Tamera would have been more supportive. "I'll think about it," Ariel said. "I really will." She stood up and started for the house.

Tamera watched her niece for a moment and then shook her head. She was not sure if she had done the right thing by telling Ariel, but maybe knowing her secret would make Ariel to think twice. Slowly she stood up from the table and started back to the house.

* * *

"I don't know what to say," Morgan answered in shock. She turned around and started peeling the potatoes into the kitchen sink.

"Well don't say anything to anyone about this. At least not yet," Bradley said. "I want to talk to Mom about this first."

"Don't worry, I won't," Morgan assured him with a shake of her head.

"So, where are you two going after the wedding?" Bradley snatched an olive.

"Chuck and I are taking a cruise up the coast to Alaska."

Bradley noticed the change in her tone. It was pleasant with no hint of bossiness.

"I've always wanted to go there," she continued. "I've heard it's beautiful during the fall. I can't believe I'm finally getting the chance to see it for myself. If you take another olive, I'll peel your fingers," she warned.

There was that tone! Bradley grinned and pulled his hand back quickly. "How'd you know?"

"I can see your reflection in the window."

Bradley looked outside. The sun was setting and it was starting to get dark.

"So, how long will you be gone?" he asked.

"Three weeks. Chuck and I want to spend a while up there sightseeing before we fly back."

"That's wonderful but, not to burst your bubble, won't it be dark for most of the day?"

"And your point is?" Morgan smiled over her shoulder at her brother.

"Oh, la-la-la-la, too much information." Bradley laughed out loud and covered his ears. "I really hope you two enjoy yourselves," he said sincerely after their laughter died away. This was the first time in as long as he could remember that he really enjoyed talking to Morgan. It made him feel good inside and maybe even a bit closer to being friends with her.

"Well, I guess I'll get out of your way and go see what Benji's up to. See you later," he said, snatching another olive and jumping away before Morgan had a chance to carry out her playful threat.

"Bradley!" A familiar voice called from the parlor as he headed toward the door.

"Patty?" Bradley smiled stopping in his tracks. He quickly rushed over to her and wrapped his arms around her, lifting her off the floor.

Patricia let out a gasp as Bradley's arms pressed against her bruised ribs. Bradley felt her stiffen and quickly released his hold.

"What's wrong?"

Patricia smiled trying to catch her breath. "You just don't know your own strength," she teased.

It was an obvious attempt to dodge answering the question and Bradley was having none of it.

"That's rubbish, Patty," he said, eyeing her suspiciously. "I've hugged you tighter than that before. What's going on? Are you hurt?" Bradley's voice had a distinctive protective tone, one he used every time he felt his younger sister was in trouble.

"It's nothing, really," Patricia tried to assure him. Slowly the pain eased and she straightened up.

Bradley looked at her and knew that she was not telling the truth, but he let the subject drop for now.

"It's really good to see you again." She smiled and sat down on the love seat. "Especially since our last visit wasn't the greatest. It seems so strange, don't you think, without Steven? I can't believe the way Dad has totally changed his bedroom."

Bradley sat down in the chair across from his sister. He looked at his hands while he debated on whether or not to tell her about his conversation with Nicholas. "Yes, it is." He decided to wait until he had a chance to talk to their mother. "So, how's your new roommate working out?"

"Oh, fine." Patricia tensed at the sound of the words. "Fine," she repeated and avoided his eyes.

Bradley looked at his sister and knew there was something more there but it was obvious that she did not want to talk about it.

"So, how's Amanda?" Patricia asked and changed the subject again.

Bradley sat back in the wingback chair. "She's getting better. At least that's what I hear from the doctors and her mother."

"You mean you haven't seen her yourself?"

"She won't see me," Bradley corrected her. "She's still upset with me about putting in the *nut house* as she calls it. But I had no choice."

"Of course you didn't. I should've seen the signs myself. When I covered a health segment on anorexia a year ago, I had to study up on it. I should have realized when she thought she was pregnant that. . . I'm sorry."

"It's not your fault. It's not my fault. She's the one in control. She could stop it if she wanted."

"You don't seriously think it's that easy," Patricia said, giving her brother a disapproving look.

"No, I don't really." Bradley shook his head. "It's just that I'm tired of feeling guilty for her not eating, for putting her in that place, for taking her away from Benjamin. Just for everything."

"I know," Patricia sympathized. "It's hard but it's also for the best."

Before Bradley could say another word, the front doorbell rang.

"I'll get it!" Ariel yelled and rushed down the stairs to the front door. She swung it open and froze, her smile fading. A tall, thin, dark-haired woman and a young man with matching short dark hair and dark-brown eyes stood on the porch. Ariel thought there was something familiar about the boy.

"Hi," Ariel greeted them.

"Hello," the woman said and nodded in return. "Is this the Wallace residence?" Her voice was soft.

"Yes, it is," Ariel said.

"Is Steven home?" the woman asked.

A cold chill ran up Ariel's spine. She glanced over her shoulder at Bradley who had walked up behind her. He stepped forward and opened the front door wider.

"Hi, I'm Bradley, Steven's brother. Won't you come in?" he invited with a smile.

"Is something wrong?" the woman asked and looked curiously at their faces as she stepped into the house. She held tightly to her son's hand.

"No," he said, trying to sound relaxed and natural so he would not frighten her. "I'll get my mother; you can wait in the parlor here if you like."

Bradley motioned for Patricia to escort them and then rushed off to the backyard to get Ruth.

"Please, have a seat," Patricia said, offering the love seat. She could not help but stare at the young man. There was something strikingly familiar about him but she could not place where she knew him from. "I'm Patricia."

"Nice to meet you," the woman said and smiled sweetly. "I'm Claudia and this is my son, Peter. It looks as though we may have come at a bad time. Are you are getting ready for a party?"

"Actually, it's my niece's wedding. She's getting married tomorrow. She's the one who answered the door. She's expecting her fiancé any minute," Patricia explained and looked at Ariel still standing in the foyer. "My mother should be here right away. Excuse me."

Patricia slipped back out to join Ariel standing in the doorway anxiously staring out at the street.

"Don't you think you should come in and close the front door?" Patricia said, more as an order than a question.

"I suppose," Ariel said reluctantly. "I'm just so nervous. Where is he?"

"I'm sure Mark will be here any minute. Stop worrying."

* * *

Ruth stood in front of her bedroom mirror and fluffed her short auburn hair while she considered how she would bring up the subject of Steven to Carl. She hated keeping secrets, first at Steven's request and now at Carl's. She longed for the days when there were no secrets in the family, when they had been open and honest with each other. But, had that ever been true? Were they really as open and honest as she thought or was she just blind to their secrets? With a deep breath she turned around and looked at Carl.

He stood behind her drying his short, graying hair with a towel. The thick hair on his chest glistened with tiny droplets from his shower. His black slacks were zipped up but the top button was still undone. He dropped the damp towel on the dressing bench at the foot of their bed and walked over to the closet to get a shirt.

"Honey, do I have another undershirt in my drawer over there?" he asked her without looking.

"I'll see." Ruth picked up the damp towel and walked over to his dresser. She opened the top drawer and took out a clean, white undershirt. "Here you go," she said and handed it to him. "Carl, there's something I need to talk to you about." Her voice was timid and she began to fold the damp towel to calm her nerves.

"What is it?" He pulled the shirt on over his head.

She walked into the bathroom and hung the towel on the rod to dry. "It's about Steven—"

"No!" Carl interrupted her sharply. "That matter is closed." He began to tuck in his shirttail with such force that Ruth thought he might hurt himself.

"Carl, the matter is not closed," she snapped, her temper beginning to rise. "It's time we talked about this."

"I don't want to discuss it."

"Then you will listen to me." Ruth stood with her fists on her hips, her jaw set, and her eyes fixed on her husband. "Steven was my son, too, and I have a say in this matter."

"Fine. You claim him, but I don't. No son of mine is a—"

"Don't you dare say that!" Ruth interrupted him. "Steven was a kind, sensitive young man. He loved and respected both of us. If that is how he chose to deal with his illness, then we have to respect it. Isn't that what you said?"

"Maybe you can live with it, but I can't. He could've had the operation and he would've still been here with us today. The doctors even said so." Carl turned to the closet and withdrew a white shirt.

"We don't know that for sure. That doctor never even examined Steven. He was talking in generalities."

Carl shook his head, dismissing her comments.

"He also said that kind of operation has its risks. If Steven had taken that chance, and if something did go wrong, he could've suffered brain damage or even died on the table. There were no guarantees. Steven wanted his last days to be happy ones, not ones filled with pain and suffering. That doesn't make him less of a man or a coward."

"Believe what you want." Carl buttoned his shirt.

"That's it. I've had enough." Ruth glared at him, walked over to the bedroom door, and threw it open. "Bradley," she gasped with a start as she almost walked into him.

"Mom, we could hear you two downstairs," Bradley whispered.

"I'm sorry," she apologized.

"There's a lady and her son downstairs. They're asking to see Steven."

Ruth looked over the rail into the foyer below. "Where are they?"

"They're in the parlor."

"Okay," she nodded. "I'll take care of it."

"Mom, there's something I think I should show you first," Bradley said, reaching into his pocket.

"Later, dear," she said, patting his chest to stop him. As she descended the stairs, she peered into the parlor trying to catch a glimpse of the visitors.

She paused at the foot of the stairs when she caught sight of the slender woman and young man seated on the love seat with their backs to her. She calmly walked across the foyer into the parlor.

"Hello, I'm Ruth Wallace," she greeted them with a smile. The woman stood immediately, clutching her purse. The young man turned around and looked at Ruth. When Ruth saw him she gasped and put a hand to her heart.

"Are you okay, ma'am?" he asked and reached for her arm. His brown eyes were full of concern.

She took a step back. "Yes. Yes," she repeated. "I'm all right. It's just that you just remind me of someone, that's all."

"I'm sorry to bother you," the woman said, putting her arm around her son's shoulders. "Your daughter, Patricia told us that you're busy preparing for your granddaughter's wedding."

"Oh, it's all right." Ruth smiled at her but kept an eye on her son. "How may I help you?"

"My name is Claudia," she said with a nod. "And this is my son, Peter."

Ruth looked at Peter again. "Peter," she repeated quietly.

"Yes, ma'am." He nodded to her.

"I was wondering if it would be possible to see Steven?" Claudia asked. "Is he here?"

Ruth looked at Claudia and tried to focus her thoughts. "No, he's not here, dear. Please, sit down."

Claudia took Peter's hand and the two sat back down on the love seat. Peter's grip tightened on her hand and she smiled reassuringly at him.

"Claudia, when was the last time you heard from

Steven?" Ruth asked.

"The last time I saw him was almost seventeen years ago, but we've kept in touch through letters off and on through the years. I guess the last time I got a letter from him was a year ago? Why?" Claudia regretted her question as soon as it left her lips.

Ruth's shoulder slumped and she sighed. "I'm sorry to have to tell you, dear," Ruth fumbled for the words to soften the blow, "three months ago, Steven passed away."

Claudia gasped and covered her mouth with her hands. Tears filled her eyes immediately and rolled down her cheeks. "Oh my god, no."

"Mom?" Peter looked at his mother confused. "Is my dad dead?"

"Dad?" Ruth echoed and looked at Peter again. She knew it was true, he just looked so much like Steven.

"I'm so sorry, baby." Claudia looked at her son and wrapped her arms around him, hugging him.

Peter squirmed and pulled away. "What? How?" he asked.

Ruth took a deep breath and tried to calm her heart. "Steven died from a brain hemorrhage. He had a brain tumor and the doctors feel that contributed to it. He died in his sleep. I'm so sorry, dear."

Claudia continued to hold her son as she tried to recover from her shock. She wiped the tears from her face. "No, I'm the one who should apologize," she tried to smile sympathetically at Ruth.

"You called Steven your father." Ruth looked at Peter. "I'm confused. Steven was never married."

"He didn't tell you?" Claudia said but there was no surprise in her tone. "Steven and I *were* married. We'd been seeing each other off and on during college, but nothing really serious. We were more just close friends really. During our senior year a group of us got together and flew to Vegas. There was a lot of partying and drinking and clowning around. Stupid stuff really. I don't remember whose idea it was, but someone suggested we all go get one of those quickie marriage certificates as a souvenir. So, Steven and I went along and we ended up getting married," she explained, watching Ruth's reaction. Ruth sat calmly listening, her eyes fixed on Peter.

"Most of the others got them dissolved when they sobered up, but Steven didn't want to. He thought we should give it a try. He said that he was raised to believe when a couple married, they were married for life. He said no one in his family had ever divorced.

"So, we moved out of the dorms and into an apartment. It was obvious in just a few months that we were better as just friends, not husband and wife. After graduation, Steven moved out. A month later I found out that I was pregnant. Steven never knew about Peter. I didn't want to burden him with that or make him feel obligated to try to make our marriage work. We stayed friends. We never divorced. I was content being Peter's mother and Steven's long-distance wife. I wasn't looking to get into any other relationship."

As Ruth listened the memory of her last conversation with Steven came flooding back. This was the secret he had tried to tell her that afternoon in the backyard. A feeling of relief replaced her surprise.

"So what brought you out here after all these years?" Ruth asked.

"Peter wanted to meet his father and the man he was named after." Claudia smiled at her son and brushed his hair back with her fingers.

"He's named after Steven?" Ruth asked, sounding both surprised and pleased.

"Yes. Steven Peter Wallace the second. I thought that maybe it was time I told Steven about my secret. Time that he knew he was a father. I guess I waited too long."

Ruth nodded. "It may be too late for Steven, but it's not too late to get to know the rest of your family."

"No!" Carl's voice thundered from the foyer.

Unbeknownst to everyone, he had been standing nearby listening.

"Carl!" Ruth jumped and gasped. She stood up and faced her husband, surprised by the anger in his tone.

"I don't know what you're after, lady, but that's one hell of a con game you've got going. I'm calling the police." Carl turned around, grabbing the phone.

"Carl James Wallace, get back here," Ruth ordered.

"Dad. Stop." Bradley grabbed his arm. "It's true. It's no con. Steven did get married."

Carl glared angrily at his youngest son, telephone receiver still clutched in his fist.

"What're you talking about?" he growled.

"She's telling the truth, Dad." Bradley pulled out the paper from his pocket and unfolded it. "Here, look at this."

Carl hung the receiver up and took the paper from Bradley. His eyes quickly scanned the marriage certificate.

"This proves nothing. She could've had this made up at any cut rate print shop."

"But she didn't," Bradley said firmly. "This came from Steven. He gave it to Nicholas the day he died."

"Rubbish," Carl said and looked at the certificate again, then at Claudia. "That's all this is. Rubbish. She knew Steven died and now she's here to try to claim his belongings. Well, lady, he didn't have anything. Do you hear me?"

Claudia quickly stood up and put her arm protectively around Peter's shoulders. "Come on, son." Together they walked into the foyer and headed toward the front door but then stopped and turned around to face Carl. She took her arm from around her son and stepped forward.

"You are a pathetic old man," she hissed. "It's obvious you never knew your son. Maybe this is why he never told you himself." She turned toward Ruth who was standing in the archway between the parlor and foyer. "I am truly sorry to have upset you."

"No, please, wait," Ruth said, reaching for her. "Please

stay. We need to talk." She turned back to Carl. "You, upstairs, now!" she ordered, pointing at the staircase.

Carl threw the paper on the floor and brushed past Bradley, heading up the stairs. Ruth followed him into their bedroom, slamming the door shut behind them.

"What in the hell has gotten into you?"

"Don't you ever take that tone with me again," he snapped back. "I am not a child."

"Then stop acting like one!" Ruth yelled. "For the last three months you've acted as though your feelings were the only ones that mattered. You stripped this house of everything that was Steven. Did you ever once stop to think about my feelings? Steven was my son too, damn you! I carried him for nine months, not you! I gave birth to him, not you. I'm the one who got up in the night with him, not you. Now he's gone and I'm not supposed to grieve for him? I've had it! I can't take this anymore." Ruth threw her hands up in the air as though giving up. "I'm leaving you," she announced, suddenly calm. She walked over to the closet and pulled out her suitcase. "I've had enough of your self-pity. Steven was more of a man than you give him credit for. He didn't blame other people for his trouble and he dealt with his feelings."

Carl's hostility began to ebb as he silently watched his wife empty her dresser drawers into the suitcase. "Ruth, stop," he said. His anger was gone, and his tone became calm and quiet. Ruth ignored him and kept packing. "Ruth, I said stop it, please." He took her wrist.

"No, you stop it!" she snapped at him and jerked loose of his grasp. "We have a chance to get to know Steven's child. A part of him we never knew existed before and I'm not letting you throw it away. If I have to I'll leave with them. You can wallow in your pity for the rest of your miserable life. I don't care anymore."

"You know that's a lie. Ruth, please, stop." Carl grabbed her shoulders tightly and turned her toward him. "I'm sorry."

"You're too late," Ruth said, turning her head to avoid looking at him.

"No. It's not too late," Carl said calmly. "I was wrong. I've been a fool not to see that. I love you and I'm sorry I hurt you. Please, don't leave."

Ruth looked at her husband, her teeth still clenched in anger. She was not backing down, not just yet.

"This is it, Carl. I'm serious. If you mess this up, I am leaving. I don't know who they are but I want them in my life."

"Okay, okay," Carl conceded. "But please, don't go. I need you."

Ruth's anger slowly began to fade when she looked into Carl's eyes, the same eyes that had melted her heart almost forty-five years ago. She knew that she could never stay angry with him for very long.

"Okay," she said calmly.

Downstairs in the foyer, Patricia, Bradley, Claudia, and Peter stood silently looking up at the closed bedroom door, listening to Carl and Ruth yelling at each other.

"I'm so sorry for all of this," Claudia apologized. "I never meant for this to happen."

"No, no," Bradley said, turning toward her. "We're the ones who owe you an apology. I'm sorry for the way my dad acted. The whole family is grieving, but Steven's death hit him especially hard. He doesn't do well with the whole death and dying thing. Please, come sit down again." Bradley ushered Claudia and Peter back into the parlor. They sat down on the love seat again. Bradley sat across from them in the wingback chair. He looked at the certificate in his hands and then handed it to her. "Here, I think this is yours."

"Thank you." Claudia smiled. She handed it to Peter. "We shouldn't have come."

"No," Bradley stopped her. "You did the right thing in coming here. Give us another chance, please."

"Well, I don't know." The uncertainty was loud and clear in her voice. She looked at Peter. He gave her a slight nod and shrug.

"So, Peter, how old are you?" Bradley asked, looking at him.

"I'm sixteen, sir," he replied.

"Please, don't call me, sir. You can just call me Brad." Bradley smiled at the politeness of his new nephew.

"Uncle Brad," Claudia corrected. She looked at the mantle again. "I was noticing you don't have any pictures of Steven," she said.

"Oh, we do." Bradley stood up and looked at the mantle with a slight frown. "Dad took them down. I guess it's just too painful for him to look at."

"I see." Claudia nodded.

"Contrary to what you said, Dad and Steven were actually close. True, Steven kept this a secret from him, but he kept it from the whole family. When Steven died, Dad just couldn't deal with it. So, he dealt with it by not dealing with it. I guess seeing Peter and you forced him to face his grief and that scares him."

Claudia listened and understood as best she could. "It's quite a shock to all of us."

* * *

Patricia walked into the bedroom, leaving the door slightly ajar. She sat down on her bed and looked at Ariel.

Ariel stood staring out the window at the backyard. She knew her aunt was there. She saw her reflection in the glass. Still, she continued to stare at the darkness outside.

"I suppose you heard what's going on?" Patricia asked.

"I wasn't really listening," Ariel said, turning around and looking worried.

"What's the matter? Didn't you talk to your Aunt Tammy?"

"Yes," she said with a nod. "That's what I was thinking about, what she told me."

"And?" Patricia prodded.

"I'm not going through with the abortion. I want to keep my baby," Ariel said thoughtfully, hugging herself.

"That's wonderful. After tomorrow, you and Mark will be married and then you can announce it to the family. No one has to know." Patricia smiled.

Just then the doorbell rang downstairs. Patricia and Ariel looked at each other and then raced to the door. When they opened it, they almost bumped into Ruth who was also heading down the stairs. The doorbell rang again as they reached the main floor. Ruth ignored it and went straight to the parlor.

Ariel threw open the front door. A smile spread across her lips as she looked into Mark's eyes peeking out from behind a bouquet of red roses. They kissed each other.

"Are you nervous?" he asked her.

"Not anymore," she said and hugged him. "I'm so happy you're here."

"I wouldn't be any place else." He kissed her cheek again and gave her a squeeze.

"Come on inside," Ariel invited. "Where the others?"

"They're on their way."

"Good! Come on, you have to see the back." Ariel escorted him to the family room which was decorated with silk flower garlands and set up with folding chairs.

"Wow! This looks terrific," he said, smiling and nodding his approval.

* * *

"Oh good, you're still here," Ruth said. She sat down on the edge of the coffee table. "I'm sorry for the way Carl acted."

"No, I can apologize for myself," Carl said from behind her and walked into the room. "Claudia, I'm sorry I acted like such a jerk. You were right, I'm a pathetic old man, but if you'll give me another chance maybe I can be different."

"Thank you, Mr. Wallace." Claudia smiled. "I shouldn't have said that. I'm sorry, too."

"Well." Ruth smiled and stood up. "Will you stay for dinner? There are still other members of the family you haven't met. We're all together tonight. It'd be the perfect time."

Claudia looked at Peter.

"Mom, can we, please?" he asked.

"Sure." She hugged him. "We'd be happy to." They stood up.

Ruth reached out and welcomed her with a hug. "It's like having part of Steven back again."

"Sir." Peter looked at Carl. "Uncle Brad said you have pictures of my dad? What did he look like?"

Carl looked at the young man in front of him and tears filled his eyes.

"He looked just like you, son." He tried to smile. "Come, I'll show you." Carl put his arm around Peter's shoulders and led him to the closet where he had stashed all of the pictures.

Tamera walked into the parlor. "Mom," she said, her eyes fixed on Claudia, curious why her mother was hugging this stranger. "Um, I guess we're ready for the rehearsal to begin."

"Tamera," Ruth said, smiling as she looked at her daughter. "I'd like you to meet your sister-in-law. Claudia, this is Tamera, Steven's older sister by a year. Tamera, this is Claudia, Steven's wife."

"Wife?" Tamera's mouth dropped open in surprise and shock.

"Yes," Ruth laughed. "Steven's wife. I'll explain it to you later. There's someone else you should meet, too. Steven has a son, Peter."

"Oh, I have to sit down," Tamera gasped. "This is too much."

Claudia laughed and walked over to Tamera and took her hand. "Steven had written me so much about you. I'm happy to finally meet you."

"Well, forgive me, but he told me nothing about you."
Tamera shook her head uncertainly.

Ruth and Claudia laughed.

CHAPTER THREE
THE ANNIVERSARY

Tiny snowflakes gently drifted down to cover the leafless tree branches. The once green back lawn was now covered in a sparkling blanket of white. Carl slowly turned away from the family room window and returned to tending the crackling fire in the fireplace. He glanced at the clock on the mantle and smiled at his thoughts.

Forty-five years had passed since he stood beside his father, his heart pounding with nervous expectation. His cheeks had hurt from smiling as he looked out at the happy throng of his friends and family. His palms sweated while he waited to catch his first glimpse of his bride. When she appeared, time stood still and everyone else slowly vanished from his sight until it was just the two of them. She looked so beautiful. Her auburn hair had been twisted up and pinned away from her face beneath a shear white veil. Her beautiful brown eyes sparkled with tears. She smiled and his anxiety melted. He remembered it as though it were only yesterday.

Slowly Carl walked up behind Ruth who was standing at the kitchen sink. Her auburn hair was now streaked with gray. Gently he slipped his arms around her waist and gave her a gentle hug. She relaxed and leaned against him.

"Happy anniversary," he whispered into her ear.

"You remembered," she said, turning her head and smiling at him. She gave him a quick kiss but Carl appeared to want more. She squirmed and pulled away. "Carl, I'm almost finished. I don't want to get soap and water all over the kitchen.

Please give me a moment longer?"

Carl nodded and kissed her cheek.

Ruth turned back to her dishes and glanced out the window at the gently falling snow. Her thoughts drifted back to that day. She had been so nervous and yet never more sure of anything as she stood next to her father, steadying herself on his arm.

"You okay, Ruth?" He smiled at her with tears in his faded blue eyes.

"Yes, Daddy." She nodded her head and looked at him. She committed his round face, receding gray hair, and rosy cheeks to memory.

Then the music began to play and the doors of the chapel opened before her. Everyone turned in their seats to see her, but she saw no one but the groom. He looked so sharp standing at the other end of the aisle, every hair in place, his black tuxedo neatly pressed, his shoes shiny. Never did he look as handsome as he did that day. As she slowly walked toward him, he blushed. She lowered her head and smiled at the little boy in him.

The memory felt as though it were new and yet, at the same time, like a lifetime ago. Ruth never imagined they would raise five children together, let alone become grandparents. They had been so young and had their future ahead of them, but now it was all a memory. It had happened so fast.

Her smile faded when she thought about the one person missing from the family, Steven. It had been six months since his death. She never imagined life going on without him, but it did. She closed her eyes and a single tear fell into the dishwater.

In the foyer, Carl nervously paced the tiled floor. He paused just long enough to glance out at the building snow. Impatiently he looked at his watch and the grandfather clock across from the door.

"Where are they?" he murmured and continued to pace.

"So, there you are," Ruth said, walking into the foyer. Carl jumped. She cocked her head and looked at him. "What're you hiding?" she asked playfully as she approached him.

"Ah, nothing," Carl answered less than convincingly. He shrugged and tried to act calm.

"Oh, I get it. We're keeping secrets from each other now, are we?" Ruth said with a smile, continuing to eye him.

"I don't know what you're talking about." Carl began to squirm, a nervous smile spreading across his lips.

Just then they heard a noise at the front door. The doorbell chimed and Ruth looked at Carl with a big smile.

"Ah-ha! Is this the secret?" She started for the front door but he beat her to the doorknob.

Glancing over his shoulder at her, he let go and backed away. "Okay, you go ahead and open it."

"No, you can do it. You beat me fair and square," Ruth said, holding her hands up in surrender.

"No," Carl said and smiled at her. "It's for you." He folded his arms over his chest.

"You're sure about that, are you?" Ruth folded her arms over her chest, mimicking him.

The doorbell rang again followed by a knock. Ruth wanted to continue this little game but relented and opened the door.

"Surprise!" Claudia, Peter, Bradley, and Benjamin shouted. "Happy anniversary!"

Ruth gave Carl a quick glance and shook her head to let him know he succeeded in surprising her. She turned back to her family still standing on the front porch.

"Look at all of you," she said, smiling.

"Can we come in, it's kinda cold out here," Bradley asked and shivered.

"Oh, yes," Ruth said, opening the door wider and stepping aside. "Come in. Come in."

Bradley stepped in first, carrying Benjamin, and kissed his mother on her cheek.

"Bradley!" She gasped and pulled away. "Your beard is like a cold Brillo pad!" she laughed.

"I love you, too," he teased. "Here, this is for you and Dad." He jiggled Benjamin, cueing him to hand the package to his grandma.

"Here, Gamma," Benjamin said, handing her their wrapped gift.

"Sorry about the wrap job. I did it myself," Bradley apologized. "Steven's the gift wrapping expert. . ."

"It's lovely." Ruth smiled, letting the comment pass.

"Mom." Claudia hugged Ruth as she stepped into the warm foyer. "Happy anniversary."

"Here, Grandma, this is for you and Grandpa from us," Peter greeted and handed her another package.

"Thank you both. You really didn't need to," Ruth said accepting the gift and kissing his cheek.

"Don't close that door!" Tamera called and stepped cautiously up the front walk, making sure to step in the footprints made by the others so she would not ruin her shoes. Behind her, Nicholas, Daniel, and Ariel followed, a bit disgusted by her slowness.

"Well, come on in," Ruth invited, shaking her head at her daughter. She greeted Tamera with a cheek to cheek hug. "Oh, you're so cold. You better go on into the family room and get warm."

"Happy anniversary, Mom, Dad," Daniel greeted his in-laws as he stepped into the foyer carrying a cake box. "I'll just put this in the kitchen."

"Here, Grandma," Nicholas said and started to hand her another large present.

"You better give it to your grandfather, dear," she said, smiling at him. "He's got two empty arms and thank you so much."

"Hi, Grandma." Ariel hugged her. "Sorry, I wasn't able to get out. I hope you like it anyway." She showed her an envelope and then handed it to Carl.

"I'm just happy you made it," Ruth said, winking at Ariel and smiling appreciatively.

Ariel closed the front door then took off her coat and hung it next to the others on the rack. She then hurried off to join the others in the warm family room.

"So," Ruth said, turning toward Carl. "This is the big secret?"

"Not all of it, but it's starting." Carl smiled.

"Well, I guess you still have some surprises left in you, old man," she teased. "Come on, let's put these in the other room."

* * *

As Ruth busied herself in the kitchen making a fresh pot of coffee, Claudia took out the cups and saucers. *It was nice to be a part of a family again,* Claudia thought. Her parents were not as understanding as Ruth and Carl. When she showed up pregnant after graduation, they threw her out because she would not tell them who the father was. Since then it had just been the two of them, her and Peter.

"I'm so happy you and Peter decided to move out here," Ruth said and handed Claudia the creamer and sugar bowl.

"So, am I," Claudia said. She glanced at Peter for a moment. "Although, I'm not sure Peter's adjusting to it very well. He's been awfully quiet and withdrawn since about a week before we left."

"Don't worry about him," Ruth reassured her. "When kids are that age, it's hard to leave friends and accept change. They're going through a hard enough time with growing into adulthood."

"I suppose you're right." Claudia shrugged. "But still, I can't help but feel there's something else going on."

"We mothers always worry," Ruth said with a bit of laughter in her voice. "It's part of our job. So, how's the house coming?"

"I think it should close this week. That is, if the weather cooperates." Claudia glanced out the kitchen window at the building snow. "It'll be hard to go anywhere to sign the papers in this."

"True," Ruth agreed.

Claudia turned around and leaned back against the counter. "I can't thank you and Dad enough for all of your help. When I showed up on your doorstep three months ago, I never expected this. Peter and I were just coming out to visit with Steven and then go back home to Indiana. I never dreamt that we would move out here and be buying a house, let alone be welcomed as part of your family."

"I think I speak for everyone when I say we are so very happy you did. About the money, well, that was rightfully yours. Steven took out that insurance policy to help his family. He just didn't know it would be you and Peter," Ruth said, wiping her hands on the towel tucked into her apron.

"That's kind of you to say."

"So, did you find out about getting social security for Peter?" Ruth asked and opened a bakery box containing pastries.

"Yes." Claudia handed Ruth a platter. "I'll be getting a check for him each month until he's eighteen. Then when or if he goes to college, he'll receive it until he's twenty-one. The first check will be retroactive. That'll be a big help."

"That's great news," Ruth said, stacking the pastries on the platter. "If anything good could come from Steven's death, this must be it."

Claudia nodded without saying a word.

* * *

"So how far along are you?" Peter asked Ariel when he noticed her rub her stomach.

Ariel looked up at her cousin, surprised. Since they met, they had barely spoken two words to each other. She smiled.

"About three months," she lied, eyeing her grandfather sitting in his chair watching the fire.

"That's neat," Peter said.

"Let's go in the other room." Ariel stood up from her chair. "We can talk better," she whispered.

Peter followed Ariel to the parlor. He did not know why, but he felt comfortable around Ariel. *Maybe he could confide in her the things he couldn't say to anyone else,* he thought.

"So, how do you like old Bend High?" Ariel asked. She sat down on the love seat and pulled the pillow out from behind her back.

"It's okay," Peter lied. "The school's fine, it's just the people will take some getting used to."

"I bet the girls are all over you, fresh new meat," Ariel chuckled. In a way, Peter had all the physical qualities she found attractive: tall, slender, dark hair and piercing brown eyes. *If we weren't cousins and I wasn't married. . .,* she thought.

"No." Peter shook his head.

Ariel's mouth dropped open in surprise. "You've got to be kidding me. A stud like you? You must've broken a lot of hearts back in Indiana when you left."

Just one, Peter thought, *mine.* He shrugged in reply and then looked away, hoping that Ariel would drop the subject. He had been wrong; he was not prepared to talk about his feelings. "So, how do you like living with your in-laws in that big house of theirs? Mom drove me by it the other day. It's a regular fortress," Peter said to change the subject.

"Actually, they're never home," Ariel said dismissively. "I'm not exactly sure what kind of work Dad Jones does but he and Mom travel a lot. With Mark on tour in Europe, I'm alone most of the time. It's really quite boring actually."

"Don't they have a maid or butler?" Peter asked.

"No. They have a gardener but other than that they do all the cleaning themselves. They won't even let me help."

"Sounds good to me." Peter laughed.

"Actually, I hate it," Ariel admitted. "They won't even

let me have friends over. It's worse than when I lived at home with my parents. Not even they are allowed to come over. If I want to see them, I have to go to their house."

"Now, that's weird," Peter said, shaking his head. "So, what do you do all day?"

"I read, watch TV, and stay in my room a lot."

"If it were me, I'd go out exploring the grounds."

"I tried one day but I ran into the gardener. He threatened to tell Mr. Jones if I didn't promise never to go out wandering again."

"So, did you promise?"

"Hell, yes. That is one creepy dude."

Peter laughed and then Ariel laughed, too. Peter could feel himself relax, his nervousness fading.

"So, what're you two talking about?" Patricia interrupted while she removed her coat.

Ariel let out a squeal and jumped to her feet. "Aunt Patty, you made it!" She threw her arms around Patricia's neck and gave her a hug. Patricia winced in pain. Ariel noticed and immediately let go.

"I'm sorry. I didn't mean to hurt you."

"It's okay. You didn't hurt me that much," Patricia said and rubbed the back of her neck. "So, what did I interrupt?"

"Nothing, we were just talking about stuff," Peter said.

"Let me take your coat," Ariel said, taking the coat away from Patricia and hanging it on the rack in the foyer. "We didn't hear you come in."

"I was trying to be quiet," Patricia said with a real smile. She looked at Peter. "It's nice to see you again."

"Same here." Peter nodded and looked nervous again.

Ariel walked back into the parlor. "Everyone's in the family room."

"Then I'll stay out here a few minutes. That is, if the two of you don't mind."

"No," Peter answered almost too quickly causing Patricia to smile again.

"I have been meaning to ask you something," Ariel said and sat down on the love seat.

Patricia eased herself back into the wingback chair nearest the archway to the foyer.

"You remember what we talked about the day before the wedding in the bedroom?" Ariel said, trying not to give away too much information in front of Peter.

"Yes, about you talking with Aunt Tammy." Patricia nodded. "I remember."

"Well, does everyone know about it?"

"Yes." Patricia nodded her head slowly.

"And Grandma wasn't upset?"

"She was at first. We all were. It wasn't only her child but Grandma and Grandpa's grandchild, my nephew. It was very sad."

"Was she mad with Aunt Tammy?"

"No, why would she be?"

"Because she had the abortion."

"What? When?" Patricia gasped and lunged forward in her chair. Pain shot up her neck and shoulders, causing her to freeze. Gingerly she eased herself back.

Ariel realized she had slipped and said too much. "I'm sorry, I thought you knew. She said it happened when mom and dad were still dating."

"I had no idea," Patricia said in shock.

"Then why'd you want me to talk with Aunt Tammy?" Ariel asked, confused.

"Because she knows what it's like to lose a child. She lost her first child. I didn't know she had an abortion," Patricia whispered. "I guess it just goes to show just because you're raised with someone doesn't mean you actually know them"

Peter sat quietly listening and thinking about the friend he left in Indiana.

"Yes," he said, nodding to himself without looking at either of them.

Patricia cocked her head and looked at him curiously,

noticing the distant tone in his voice.

* * *

Tamera walked into the kitchen and set her teacup down. Daniel followed her under the guise of warming up his already hot coffee.

"Tamera, please, try to relax," he whispered. "You're becoming a nervous wreck." He put his arm around her shoulders and gave her a gentle hug.

"How can I?" she said, shaking her head. "First it was that letter. Then the phone calls started. Daniel, it frightens me."

"Everything will be okay. She hasn't got a leg to stand on, not after all these years."

"I know, but that isn't what scares me. What if he finds out? What will he think of us? I can't lose him, too." Tamera's eyes began to tear.

Daniel turned her toward him and looked her in the eyes. "You won't. We won't," he said trying to reassure himself as much as her. "Everything's going to be fine."

Tamera looked at her husband and thought about what he said. "Okay." She picked up her teacup. "I hope you're right. What did the police say?"

Daniel scratched his head. He had been avoiding this subject since he talked to them three days ago. "They can't do a thing about it unless she begins to threaten physical harm," he admitted.

"I can't believe this is happening." The worry and panic returned to her voice. "I can't handle this anymore." Tamera sank back against the counter and put the teacup down.

"Tamera, stop it!" Daniel said sharply, trying to keep his voice down. "We *will* get through this. Trust me."

Tamera looked at him. She did trust him. He had always been there for her to lean on, but she did not trust the system. She had witnessed too many couples on the news facing similar situations lose everything after trusting that the system would not fail them.

"Okay." Her voice trembled. She picked up her teacup and slowly walked back into the family room.

Ruth glanced at Tamera and smiled from her seat next to Bradley on the sofa. They were watching Carl, Nicholas, and Benjamin setting up the electric train set in the middle of the floor.

"So, how're you doing?" Ruth asked, turning back to Bradley.

Bradley took a deep breath and sighed. "To be honest, not so good. She still won't see me. I've asked her mother to pass Amanda notes for me, but her mother returns them later saying she wouldn't take them."

"We knew it was going to be an uphill battle," Ruth reminded him.

"I know, overcoming the anorexia, but I never expected this. I just don't understand why she's pushing me away."

"Has there been any talk about when she'll be able to come home?"

"Oh, according to her medical doctors her body has recovered. However, her psychiatrist is concerned that once she leaves she'll go back to her old ways. So that's what they're focusing on now. Until then. . ."

"I see," Ruth said, nodding and looking at the boys again.

"It would be nice if she could be home next month for our anniversary on Valentine's Day," Bradley said. "I just think that being around family would help her a lot."

Ruth looked back at Bradley. She put her hand gently on his. "I know you do, but given her present state of mind, not wanting to see you, it could backfire and make things worse."

"I miss her so much," Bradley said, choking back his tears, not wanting to cry in front of everyone.

"I know, dear." Ruth put her arm around his and hugged him.

He leaned over and rest his head on her shoulder. A tear

escaped his eyes.

The telephone rang. Carl looked up at Ruth.

"I'll get it," Tamera announced. Jumping up from her seat, she hurried into the foyer. Daniel followed her and stood by listening.

"Hello?" Tamera greeted the caller.

There was nothing but silence on the other end.

Daniel looked at Tamera. Her hand began to tremble as she held the telephone to her ear. Her blue eyes opened wide behind her round rose-tinted glasses. Daniel stepped closer.

"How did you get this number?" she yelled into the phone. "Why are you doing this?"

"Tamera?" he said softly to let her know he was there.

She looked up at him and her eyes filled with tears. She did not speak but he could tell that something was wrong. She trembled and began to cry.

Daniel quickly grabbed the receiver. "Who is this?" he demanded. "How did you get this number?"

There was silence, then a click.

Daniel hung the receiver back on its hook and took Tamera in his arms. He held her while she sobbed into his chest and tried to regain her composure. He looked over at the empty parlor and slowly directed Tamera to it. They sat down on the love seat hugging each other.

* * *

Peter watched the old steam engine chug around the circle track. Tiny puffs of steam rose from the engine's chimney when Carl made the whistle blow.

"Wow. What a neat train," Peter said as he watched Nicholas and Benjamin playing. "Where did you get it? It looks old."

"It is," Nicholas answered. "It's Grandpa's. He got it when he was a kid."

"It's really great that you kept it so nice and running.

It's really ancient." Peter looked his grandfather's shocked expression. "I mean an antique."

Carl laughed heartily at the horrified look on his grandson's face. He rocked back in his chair. "It's the only store bought toy I can remember ever receiving when I was a little boy. Your great-grandparents didn't have a lot of money for such things in those days. So, I've been extra careful with it."

Peter sat down on the hearth, still watching the train chugging along. "What were they like? Great-Grandma and Great-Grandpa Wallace, I mean."

Carl smiled as he remembered his parents. It had been years since anyone asked him about them. Even though he thought and dreamt about them often, this was different. "Mama, your great-grandmother, was a kind and gentle woman. She was also a hard worker though. She would be up early every morning cooking breakfast for Papa and all of my sisters and brothers. Breakfast wasn't just a bowl of cereal like you kids eat today. No, it was a real meal. Mama would bake fresh biscuits with bacon gravy, eggs and ham, fried potatoes. Sometimes she would even make us pancakes with warm homemade maple syrup."

Peter listened intently, fascinated. The talk of food though was beginning to make him hungry.

"Mama liked people," Carl continued. "She not only looked after us but she never turned away a stranger that needed a cup of soup or a warm place to sleep. It sparked several arguments between my parents as I recall.

"Your great-grandfather was a different story. He wasn't so generous. He was a real stickler for working for your day's bread and butter and didn't believe in charity, giving it or receiving it. He was a very proud man and very stern.

"He was up before dawn tending the farm and if he were up, so were you. If you were late getting to the fields, you'd get a whippin' with his thick leather strap. If you didn't work as hard as he figured you were able, you didn't get your supper. So all of us learned to work hard."

"Wow," Peter sighed and he thought about his own upbringing. As an only child, he never had to share his mother's affection or anything really. It was always the two of them.

"But Papa wasn't all hard and tough, had his soft side. He wasn't one for public affection, but he could still be loving and gentle. When a snake bit my younger sister, he was calm, gentle and knew just what to do. After getting the poison out, he tore up his shirt and bandaged her leg. Then he carried her in his arms all the way back to the house."

Peter looked around the room. Everyone was listening intently to Carl reminiscing. Nicholas and Benjamin had stopped playing with the train. Ruth sat next to Bradley, smiling and watching Carl. He could not believe that his dream of being part of a family had come true. Still, he could not shake the feeling of loneliness growing deep inside.

Claudia and Patricia sat at the breakfast table listening to Carl and watching Peter. Claudia looked at her son's face, at the smile she had not seen in a long time and the sparkle in his eyes.

"I can't believe how much Peter resembles Steven," Patricia commented turning back to Claudia and her coffee.

"I see a lot of his father in him," Claudia said with a nod.

"He's a quiet brooder," Patricia said, glancing at him again. "I don't think I've ever seen him so interested in anything since you moved out here."

"I didn't think anyone noticed but me," Claudia said, surprised by Patricia's comment. She turned and looked at Patricia. "I wish I knew why."

"Maybe it's just the new surroundings. As he gets used to it here, he'll snap out of it."

"That's what Mom said, too." Claudia turned back to Peter. "I hope you're right, because I don't mind saying, I'm a bit worried." She sipped her coffee.

* * *

"Are you okay?" Daniel asked once Tamera had regained her composure. He relaxed as he sat next to her on the love seat in the parlor.

"I think so." Tamera sighed heavily.

"Are you ready to tell me who that was on the telephone?" Daniel prodded.

"It was her. I don't know how, but she got Mom and Dad's number." As she heard herself say the words, her hands began to tremble again and her heart beat anxiously. "What're we going to do?"

"Wait a minute," Daniel said, stopping her. "Who was on the phone again?" He heard what she said. He just could not believe his ears.

"It was her," Tamera repeated, her panic rising. "Nick's biological mother."

Daniel's heart pounded faster as his thoughts started running in all directions. He tried to calm his own fears to keep Tamera from seeing that he, too, was worried.

"What did she say?"

"She just kept saying over and over, 'He's not your son. Give me back my son.' Dan, I'm scared. You talked to the attorney who handled the adoption didn't you? She can't take him away, can she?"

"He said he'd have to get back to me. Normally adoptions are final after a year but there was a clause in ours that we didn't catch. He's looking into it for us." Daniel looked at the floor and a sinking feeling filled his chest.

"Oh, Daniel, what're we going to do? It would kill Nick for him to find out he was adopted." Tamera looked up. "Oh my god!" she gasped. Unconsciously she squeezed Daniel's hand until he jerked it way.

"Ouch!" He grimaced and looked at Tamera. "What?" He turned around looking into the foyer. His mouth dropped open in shock and he sprang to his feet. "Son?"

Nicholas stood in the threshold, a confused expression

on his face. "I'm adopted?" he asked quietly.

"Honey," Tamera said, standing up and reaching out to him. He stepped back.

"Son, come here and we'll—"

"No!" Nicholas shouted. "You're not my parents?" He backed away, holding his hands up as though pushing them back. He continued backing away in a daze until he reached the front door.

"Nicholas!" Tamera shouted but before she could get to the doorway, Nicholas was out the front door and gone. "Oh, god, no!" Tamera screamed, racing after him. "Nick, come back!" As she stepped outside onto the front porch, the cold wind blew the falling snow into her face and around her bare arms and legs, but she did not feel the cold. She squinted to see through the white flurry.

Daniel rushed past her calling after his son, his voice growing fainter and fainter as he disappeared down the street.

"Tamera?" Ruth and Carl appeared in the doorway. "What's going on?"

Tamera slowly turned around, tears streaming down her red cheeks.

"He's gone, Mom," she cried and reached out for her mother.

"What? Who's gone?" Ruth took her in her arms and walked back inside the house.

Carl closed the front door and followed them to the parlor.

"Nick," Tamera said. "He overheard Dan and me talking about his being adopted and he ran away. What am I going to do? I can't lose him." Tamera continued to cry.

"Hush," Ruth said, pulling Tamera away from her. She took Tamera's chin and gently lifted her head up so Tamera would look at her. "Tamera, Dan will bring him back and we'll figure this out together, as a family. Now tell me what started this?"

Slowly Tamera explained about the mysterious letter

and phone calls. Ruth listened quietly.

"Then just a little while ago I answered the phone in the foyer and it was her."

"Here?" Ruth said, cocking her head while she thought.

"They just said on the news that we're in for the worst storm we've had in a long time," Patricia announced as she walked into the foyer, interrupting them. "What's going on?" she asked, noticing the tears in Tamera's eyes and the concerned look on her mother's face.

"I'd best see if I can help Dan find the boy," Carl said and rushed to grab his and Daniel's coats. Returning to the foyer he gave Ruth a quick kiss on the cheek. "Don't worry, honey," he said to Tamera. "We'll find him."

"Carl, be careful," Ruth called to him. The front door closed and he was gone.

"What's all the commotion?" Bradley asked as he and the rest of the family gathered in the foyer.

"Nick overheard Daniel and Tamera talking about his adoption and he got upset. He took off outside. Your father and Daniel have gone looking for him," Ruth said.

"I'd best go help," Bradley said. He grabbed his coat and returned to the parlor. "Patty, watch Benji for me?" He did not wait for her answer but disappeared out the front door.

Moments later, the front door opened again. Tamera jumped to her feet. Ruth stood up too. Morgan walked in, pulling her stocking hat off and shaking the snowflakes from her coat. Chuck followed her, closing the door behind them.

"It's pretty quiet," Morgan said, turning toward her husband and slipping off her coat. "Oh!" she gave a start when she noticed everyone staring at her from the parlor. "There you are. What's going on?"

Ruth explained while Tamera silently walked over to the window and looked out at the falling snow.

"You know." Chuck sneered at Tamera. "This whole thing could've been avoided if you would've told the boy he was adopted in the first place."

"That's enough of that!" Ruth snapped at her son-in-law. "This isn't the time to be pointing fingers and blaming anyone. None of us are innocent in this. We all agreed to respect Daniel and Tamera's decision."

"Speak for yourself," Chuck murmured under his breath.

Ruth cocked her head and looked at him. Suddenly a thought occurred to her. She glanced over her shoulder at Tamera and then looked back at Chuck. Morgan stood next to him with her chin out almost in defiance, a look Ruth hated.

"Tamera, when did you say you received that letter and those phone calls began?"

"About two months ago. The letter came about a week after Ariel's wedding. Then about a week after that the calls started. At first they were coming to the house when Dan was at work. Then a couple times they came to my cell phone. Today, when I answered the phone in the foyer here it was her," Tamera explained.

"I wonder," Ruth said, continuing to look at Chuck and Morgan. "How is it possible that a stranger would know to call my number when it isn't published?"

Chuck shrugged his shoulders. "How am I supposed to know?"

"I think you do," Ruth said, her eyes fixed on his.

Chuck looked at Morgan and smiled. Morgan looked at him curiously.

"What're you talking about?" Chuck asked nervously. "Tamera just said she got a letter, what, the week after Ariel's wedding? We were on a ship heading for Alaska at that time. How could we know anything about this?"

"I'm through playing games with you," Ruth said, her anger growing. "You and I had better have a talk right now."

She walked over to Chuck and, even though she was a head shorter than him, grabbed his arm, spinning him around. Her grip was so tight on his arm that her knuckles were white. Chuck followed her obediently, not having a choice.

The two walked straight into the family room closely followed by the rest of the family. When Ruth reached the middle of the room, she released her grip.

"I think you had better start explaining yourself and fast." She glared angrily at him. "You're messing with my family and I don't like it one bit."

"I don't know what you're talking about." Chuck laughed nervously as he looked at the fire reflecting in Ruth's eyes and at the faces all around him.

Ruth did not move or say a word. Morgan slowly walked over to her husband and faced him. She glanced at Tamera who was crying into Claudia's arms. She looked at her mother, whose glare was fixed firmly on Chuck. She turned back to her husband remembering how he said when they reached their first port that he needed to mail something. At the time she thought it was a postcard to Ariel but now she was not so sure.

"Chuck, if you had anything to do with this, you'd better speak up now," Morgan said softly.

Chuck looked around the room again and then back at Ruth and smirked. "Okay, so I sent a letter and had a friend make a few phone calls, so what. It was a joke." He shrugged.

"A joke!" Tamera repeated through clenched teeth and charged across the room at him. "Well, laugh at this, you son-of-a-bitch." Without warning she slapped him and tackled him to the floor.

Ruth and Claudia grabbed Tamera, pulling her off him and holding her back as she struggled to get free.

"That is enough!" Ruth told Tamera sternly.

Morgan helped her husband to his feet. He rubbed his cheek and then clenched his fists.

"What's the matter with you people," he snapped at them. "Are you all nuts? Can't you take a joke?"

"It's not funny, Chuck," Morgan said to him sternly. "Mom, everyone, Chuck didn't mean—"

"Oh stop it, Morgan," Ruth snapped. Morgan recoiled

and stepped back. "I don't want to hear a bunch of excuses! Chuck, what you did was immature, contemptible, and unforgivable. You hurt an innocent child. You'd better hope no harm comes to him out there."

"I can't stay in the same room with him," Tamera announced, pulling free of her mother and sister-in-law's grasp and walking out of the room.

Claudia looked at Peter. He was quite shaken by all of the fighting but he managed a slight smile as though telling her he was fine. Claudia turned and followed Tamera.

"Mom." Patricia walked over to her.

Ruth turned away from Chuck and Morgan.

"What?" she asked, still seething at her son-in-law.

"Shouldn't they have been back by now? I mean, how long does it take three grown men to find one boy?"

Ruth turned and looked out the family room windows. The snowflakes were larger and coming down so heavily she could barely make out the outline of the trees bordering their backyard.

"I don't know," she said with a bit of concern.

The telephone rang and broke the silence. Ruth looked at Chuck again.

"This had better not be another one of your stunts," she said and went into the parlor to answer it.

Chuck shrugged at her and followed Morgan into the kitchen.

Morgan poured herself a cup of coffee. Her hands trembled as she tried to keep from spilling the steaming brew. Chuck leaned against the kitchen counter behind her.

"Honestly, Chuck," she said, shaking her head and setting the pot back on the stove. She turned around to face him. "I don't understand. Why would you do such a thing? It doesn't make sense."

Chuck just stared at her and shrugged. He never intended it to involve Nicholas, really.

"Tamera's been through enough hell losing Danny and

not being able to have another child. Adopting Nicholas was the only thing that saved her sanity. You doing this just doesn't make sense." Morgan shook her head. "I don't understand."

"I did it for you," he blurted.

"Me?"

"Yes, you. I've watched the way everyone treats you. Your mother has always been cold to you. Steven just tolerated you. Tamera's never liked you. I don't know if it's jealousy or what exactly. She's never treated you with the respect and decency you deserve. Bradley and Patricia have never given you a chance. After everything you've done for them when they were kids, they barely even speak to you now. I did it to pay her and Daniel back for hurting you. I just meant to make them squirm. How was I to know that they'd be so stupid to tell the brat?"

As Morgan listened to her husband explain, she could not help but smile. She looked at him and lovingly wrapped her arms around his waist. "I love you for loving me." She smiled. "You're the best thing that's happened in my life."

Chuck continued pouting boyishly just to keep her feeding his badly bruised ego.

"You've always looked out for me and been there for me. I should never have doubted your intentions for one moment. I'm sorry." Morgan looked into his eyes. "Do you forgive me?"

"I only tried to protect you, because I love you so very much." He smiled and then kissed her tenderly.

* * *

Ruth picked up the receiver. Her heart pounded angrily as she anticipated another one of Chuck's crank calls.

"Hello," she said firmly.

"Hello, Mom?" The voice on the other end sounded distant with loud static on the line.

"Amanda?" Ruth recognized the voice with surprise.

"Happy anniversary. How is everyone out there?"

"Oh, we're all just fine." Ruth looked around at the empty foyer. "It's snowing something fierce right now, but we're all staying warm. How about you? How are you, dear?"

"I'm doing better. They think I should be out of here soon. I can't wait to get back home. I miss my little Benji so much. How is he?"

"He's doing fine." Ruth turned around as Patricia and Benjamin walked into the foyer. She mouthed the words, 'it's Amanda', and pointed to the receiver. Her expression changed to surprise and then sadness while she continued listening.

"I'm sorry, dear, Bradley isn't here just yet. I do expect him back very soon. Shall I have him call?" Ruth asked and picked up a pen. Silently she began writing down a phone number.

"That's okay, he won't call me back. He hasn't returned my calls for weeks."

"Well, I'll make sure he does this time," Ruth promised, a bit confused.

"Then please have him call real soon; they don't let us have calls after dinner." Amanda's voice sounded so different, so childlike. It worried and frightened Ruth at the same time.

"I'll give him the message, dear. I love you. Get well so you can come back to us real soon."

"I will, Mom," Amanda agreed. "Give Dad my love and tell everyone hello for me."

"I will," Ruth replied but the line was already dead. Slowly she hung up the receiver and turned around.

Patricia stood patiently waiting. Benjamin had spotted Peter and run off into the family room. "What did she want?" Patricia asked.

"She wanted to talk to Bradley." Ruth glanced at the front door, silently hoping he would walk through it right then.

"That's great! Isn't it?"

"I sure hope so." Ruth nodded.

* * *

Tamera stood on the front porch straining to see through the falling snow. The cold winter wind swirled around her, stinging her tear-streaked cheeks. She pulled her sweater closed and folded her arms over her chest to shield herself from the biting cold.

"Oh, Nicky." She shivered and cried. "Where are you? Please, come home. I promise everything will be all right."

In the distance she spotted shadows coming closer. Her heart leapt with hope. Her face lit up and she began to run toward them. Her feet plunged deep into the snow that covered the front lawn, coating her legs and filling her shoes but she felt nothing.

"You've found him!" she screamed. "Nick." She ran with open arms to greet him but suddenly, she stopped. As she looked at the three sullen faces of her brother, husband, and father she realized they had not found him.

"No," she whimpered. "You have to find him. You have to find my baby." She fell to her knees and cried.

"Tamera, honey," Daniel consoled her, reaching down and lifting her to her feet, out of the snow. "We couldn't find him but he'll come home when he gets cold enough."

"No." Tamera's voice was near panic. "No, you have to keep looking for him. You have to bring him back to me, Dan." Tamera cried hysterically and pushed Daniel away.

"Tamera Irene Lynch!" Carl said firmly, grabbing her arm and spinning her around. "Listen to me. We've combed the neighborhood. We couldn't find any sign of him. He has to be around here somewhere. He's probably hiding from us, so there's no point in our being out here. Daniel's right, when Nick gets cold enough, he will come back."

Tamera shook her head, not wanting to listen to her father. Fear had gripped her and she it, she was not willing to give up. She began to tremble and shiver in the cold.

"Tammy, you're soaking wet. Let's get you inside,

where it's warm." Daniel put his coat over her shoulders and held her close to him. Carefully they headed back toward the house.

"No," Tamera continued to whimper but let herself be led away.

* * *

The family room was uncomfortably quiet. Claudia sat on the couch and watched Peter and Benjamin across the room. Peter sat holding Benjamin on his lap as they looked out the window watching the falling snow. Occasionally Peter would point out a snowflake and Benjamin would giggle with excitement. Claudia wondered what Peter thought about the things that were happening.

"Welcome to the family," Patricia said sarcastically and sat down next to Claudia on the sofa. "I'm really sorry about all of this."

"No need to apologize." Claudia shrugged. "I guess it's to be expected when you're part of a family. I'm more worried about how all of this is affecting Peter. He's not used to all of this arguing and fighting. Since we've been here, he's been so quiet and withdrawn. That's not normal for him. Back in Indiana, he laughed more and was so happy; here he's a completely different boy."

"He'll be fine." Patricia tried to reassure her again. "Give him time."

"Maybe so," she nodded, "but I don't understand it. Steven told me about your family and growing up here. He made it sound so different. He never mentioned the fighting and always some crisis happening."

"It wasn't always like this," Patricia explained, nodding to herself. She smiled, remembering her older brother and best friend. "Not when Steven was alive." She shook her head. "Steven had a very special effect on the family. When he was around, he acted like a buffer, a counselor. We all went to him with our problems and he'd make us laugh and then somehow whatever it was didn't seem so big. He took our problems on his shoulders and carried them for us. He wouldn't admit it to anyone, but I know he worried about us all." Tears began to fill Patricia's eyes and she turned away. "I sure wish he were here now."

Claudia listened quietly. She wondered if Steven were there, would she have been? She wondered how he would have taken the news about Peter. Would he have been angry with her or would he have forgiven her for keeping this secret? She liked to think that they would still be close friends, that he and Peter would be close as well, father and son. But that could never happen now.

"Mom, look at the snow." Peter turned to his mother. "It's really coming down hard now. The flakes are so big." Peter turned back to the window.

Claudia sat forward on the edge of the couch. "Oh, that poor boy," she moaned softly to herself as she thought about Nicholas being outside in the cold.

The sound of the front door opening brought everyone to their feet. Carl walked into the room and gave Ruth a hug while warming himself by the fire.

"I take it he's still out there," she said quietly to Carl when Tamera and Daniel walked into the room.

"Didn't you find him?" Patricia asked when Bradley walked in alone.

"No." Tamera began to cry and reached out for Ruth.

"It's okay." Ruth held her, stroking Tamera's wet blonde hair. "He'll come back."

"I don't understand it. He couldn't have gone far. It's just too cold and the snow's blowing. We tried to follow what we thought were his tracks but they ended up not being his," Bradley reported. "Tamera, he's just upset now. He'll be back. We just have to wait."

"They just said on the radio that the telephone lines are out in most of the city," Morgan announced as she and Chuck returned to the family room. "The news guy said a tree fell on the lines causing a pole to come down. The weatherman is saying we're in for near blizzard conditions for the next few hours." She looked at their faces and suddenly realized. "Oh, god, you didn't find him did you? I'm so sorry."

"Sorry?" Daniel repeated and looked over at her and Chuck. "For what?"

"Daniel," Chuck said, stepping forward. "If you're going to be angry, be angry with me. I'm the one responsible for all of this, not Morgan."

"You?" Daniel repeated trying to understand. "Not Nicholas' birth mother?"

"Yes." Chuck nodded. "But I never—"

"I don't understand." Daniel shook his head. "Have I done something to you to make you mad? I thought we were friends?"

"I'm sorry. I was just angry at Tamera. I wasn't thinking."

"Wasn't thinking?" Daniel repeated, still trying to make sense of everything. His jaw tightened and he clenched his fists.

"Why you—" Daniel lunged at Chuck. Bradley and Morgan quickly jumped between them, holding them apart.

"Stop it!" Bradley snapped, wrestling with Daniel to keep him from hitting Chuck. "This isn't helping."

"I said I was sorry," Chuck yelled at Daniel.

"Sorry!" Daniel shouted back. "My son is out there and could be freezing to death because of you. You dirty son of a—" Daniel struggled to get closer to Chuck hoping to get at least one good shot in.

"Daniel!" Carl's firm voice thundered throughout the room. "That will be enough! I know you're angry but I will not have you brawling in my house. Besides, hitting Chuck isn't going to bring Nicholas home, is it?"

"No, but it'll sure make me feel better," Daniel said through clenched teeth.

"Well, just cool it!" Carl ordered. "You know deep

down that isn't true anyway."

Daniel quit struggling and relaxed as his temper began to ebb. "You're right." He nodded. "I've got to get out there and find my son."

Cautiously Bradley released his hold on Daniel and stepped back. Daniel looked about the room, then turned around and started for the door.

"Dan," Chuck said. "I'll help you, if you want?"

"You've done enough already," Daniel said without turning around. He continued out the front door. Tamera quickly followed him.

Carl looked around the room without saying a word. Chuck and Morgan retreated to the kitchen. Peter and Benjamin returned to watch the snow falling. Ruth sat down on the couch next to Claudia. Slowly Bradley walked over to Carl.

"So, what about our reservations at The Tower?" Bradley asked, reminding his father.

"Oh!" Carl replied. With everything that was happening he completely forgot about their dinner. He looked at his watch and then out at the snow. "Well, I guess from the looks of things I'd best call and cancel."

"That's what I was thinking. I'll do it."

"Thanks," Carl said and smiled at his son.

"Where's Bradley going?" Ruth asked Carl curiously, watching Bradley leave the room.

"He's going to make a call."

Ruth quickly jumped up and hurried after her son.

"Where's she going?" Carl asked, looking confused.

* * *

"Bradley," Ruth said as she walked into the foyer.

Bradley put the receiver down and turned to face his mother. "Yes?"

Ruth walked over to him so she would not have to talk so loud. "While you were out, Amanda called. She said you aren't answering your cell phone." she said.

"Oh."

"She sounded good. She said she hopes to get out soon. And she asked me to have you call her back." Ruth paused to study Bradley's reaction.

Bradley shrugged indifferently and shook his head.

"Is there something the matter?"

"No. No," he answered, but Ruth could tell it was not the truth. "My cellphone's dead. No service. So's the house phone, by the way."

"Well, I'm sure she'll understand. Don't worry." She gave him a hug, knowing how upset he was. "Let's go back into the family room. It's a bit chilly in here."

The two returned to the family room just as Carl was about to come to check on them. He stopped and turned around with Ruth by his side.

"Well, I guess I might as well let you all know. Due to the weather outside, we've had to cancel our dinner reservations at The Tower."

Ruth's mouth dropped open. She looked at her husband in surprise and disappointment. She had been wanting to go there for years but they had never had the chance. The Tower was the most popular, nicest dinner theater in town. She had loved the theater ever since she saw her first play there back in high school. Having a leisurely dinner and watching a performance was her idea of the ultimate experience, but it was one that would have to wait.

"And, judging by the weather, it looks like you'll all be staying the night," Carl added.

"Why don't you and Bradley go back out and see if you can find Nick," Ruth said, looking at Carl. "The girls and I can start getting dinner and beds ready."

"Sure," Carl agreed. He gave Ruth a kiss on the cheek and then turned around to head back outside. "Come on, Brad," he called as he left the room.

Bradley obediently followed.

"Patty, I think we best be prepared in case the power goes out too. Would you go downstairs and get the candles, just in case, please," Ruth instructed. "As for you two, Claudia and Ariel, would you be dears and get the spare blankets and sheets out of the linen closet upstairs. We'll need enough for the couch in the den, the parlor, and in here."

"Sure, Mom." Claudia smiled and followed Ariel.

"What can we do to help?" Morgan asked as she and Chuck walked back into the family room.

Ruth looked at her daughter and glanced at Chuck, still angry at him. "I could use a hand in the kitchen," she said to Morgan. "And we could use some wood for the fire," she added, not looking at her son-in-law.

"I'm on it, Mom," Chuck volunteered and left to grab his coat. Chuck zipped up his coat and headed outside to gather the firewood from the woodpile on the side of the house. He wondered if, by asking him to help out, Ruth was closer to forgiving him, even if just a little.

Ruth did not acknowledge him. She tied her apron around her waist and busied herself at the sink washing the potatoes while Morgan put on one of the spare aprons from the pantry. She was not as angry with Morgan. After all, it was not her fault her husband did what he did. It was just the way Morgan was so quick to excuse his actions that upset her. If Carl would have done such a thing, would she have defended him?

In the family room, Peter kept Benjamin busy pointing at the falling snow outside. She looked at Morgan and then began to peel the potatoes.

"Let me help you with that," Morgan offered, taking a potato and beginning to peel it.

Ruth took a deep breath. "Honestly, I don't know what's happened to this family," she said.

Morgan did not say a word.

"We used to be so open with each other. There weren't all these secrets. Secrets only bring pain."

"It seems like it all started with Steven." Morgan picked

up another potato.

"No, we can't blame all of this on Steven. Sure, he had a couple secrets, but it's obvious he wasn't the only one." Ruth paused without looking at her. "Tamera wasn't the only one who kept Nicholas' adoption a secret from him, we all did. I can't help but wonder what my other children are hiding. I look at them suspiciously now and I hate that."

Morgan was becoming uneasy with the direction of their conversation.

"So, are you keeping any secrets from me?" Ruth asked as she filled a large pot with water.

Morgan's back stiffened. The potato slipped from her hand and bounced across the counter. "No."

Ruth nodded her head. "That's a relief."

* * *

Patricia opened the basement door and turned on the light over the stairs. Growing up, she was afraid of the basement and dreaded going down there because of the monsters. She was surprised that those fears still lingered twenty-five years later. She took a deep breath and forced herself down the stairs.

The basement was cold and dark. Snow outside had piled up against the windows and blocked what little light there was from outside. Cautiously Patricia made her way past the washer and dryer to the door opposite Morgan's old bedroom.

A damp, musty odor hit her as she opened the storage room. She felt the wall for the light switch. "Please don't let me touch a spider. Please don't let me touch a spider," she repeated to herself. With a sigh of relief, she found the switch and instantly the room lit up.

She had not been in the basement in years, but the storage room still looked the same. Shelves lined the outer concrete wall to her left and a storage closet covered the length of the inside wall to her right. Against the wall directly in front of her were the nightstands, lamps, and bed frame from Steven's room. His desk was covered with a sheet and sat among the many boxes of books and memories that once defined her big brother. A tear came to her eye as she picked up his old baseball glove, remembering how she used to talk to him about her problems while they played catch in the backyard. He had always been willing to listen. She wished she could talk to him now. She put the glove back in the box and turned away to open the closet door.

The box of white tapers sat right in front of her on the middle shelf. She quickly picked them up, shut the door, and turned to leave but froze as something on the lower shelf registered in her mind, sparking memories.

Slowly she opened up the door again. There it was, sitting on a shelf all by itself. She had forgotten all about it. She set the box of candles down and smiled as she picked up the tattered, love-worn teddy bear. She examined its ears, button eyes, and pointed nose. Wrapping her arms around it, she hugged it and closed her eyes. All the feelings of loneliness, pain, and fear of her teenaged self came bubbling back up. She remembered how she used to cry herself to sleep at night. It seemed like such a long time ago and yet like only yesterday. She gave the bear one last hug before returning it to the shelf.

With a deep breath she picked up the candles and closed the closet door.

* * *

Tamera paced the front porch, pausing occasionally to peer out at the darkening street. She no longer felt the cold air that blew against her red cheeks or her numb hands. Still, she paced.

Off in the distance came the sound of footsteps crunching through the snow. She turned around, her heart leaping with hopeful anticipation. She took two steps from the porch and stood in the snow, wanting to catch a glimpse of her son.

Slowly the three figures came closer. Once again Tamera's hopes were crushed as she could see her father, brother, and husband were returning alone. Tears fell uncontrollably from her eyes.

"Tamera." Daniel walked up to her. "We have to stop and get warm for a moment, then we'll go back out. We haven't given up."

Tamera did not say a word. She returned to the porch, leaned against the pillar, and stared out at the street.

"Come inside with us," Daniel pleaded and put his arm around her. "You're freezing."

"No. I have to stay out here." Tamera shook her head. "You go on inside. I'll be all right."

Daniel looked at Carl and shrugged helplessly. Carl motioned for him and Bradley to go inside. They silently obeyed.

"Tamera, honey." Carl walked over to his daughter and rubbed her back. "Please come inside for a few minutes."

"Daddy, I can't." She shook her head again. "I need to be out here watching for my son." Her body jerked at the sound of the word *son*. She smirked to herself. "My son," she said, rolling her eyes. "I was such a fool to ever believe that he was really mine. I should've told him the truth years ago, but when would it have been the right time? When he was two? Five? I guess I didn't want to tell him, because I would've had to admit to myself that I could never have another child of my own. I'm still not ready to do that. Oh, Daddy, what have I done?" She turned and hugged him as she cried on his shoulder.

"You haven't done anything wrong." Carl took her by her shoulders and pulled her back so he could look into her blue eyes. "You did what you thought was best and the family is behind you. You have nothing to be sorry for. I'm so proud of you."

"Did I really, Daddy?" Tamera turned back to the pillar. "Then why is he out there freezing in the cold, lost and confused. His whole world has been destroyed, turned upside

131

down. Face it, I'm a lousy mother. I couldn't even keep my own son from dying and now I may have killed someone else's. If anything happens to Nick, I'll never forgive myself."

"Stop that kind of talk right now," Carl snapped at her, taking her in his arms again and holding her tightly. "You know you don't believe that. What happened to Danny was out of everyone's control. Even if you or the best doctors in the world were standing right there, there was nothing anyone could've done to save him. SIDS just happens. As for Nick, don't sell yourself so short. You've done a wonderful job of raising him. You may not have given birth to him, but he is your son and you are his mother."

Tamera listened and held her father tightly. She stared out at her SUV and suddenly noticed its fogged up windshield.

"Everything is going to be all right." Carl kissed her cold cheek. "Just give him time."

"Okay." Tamera nodded, transfixed by her car.

"Now, come inside, please," Carl coaxed.

Tamera stepped away and leaned against the pillar again. "I will, in a few more minutes. I promise," she said without looking at him.

"Okay." Carl nodded and then disappeared into the warmth of the house.

* * *

Ariel and Claudia returned to the family room, their arms loaded with blankets and sheets. Ariel dropped her armload into a pile on the sofa and looked around at the room.

"So, where's everyone going to sleep?" she asked.

Claudia shrugged, deferring the answer to Ruth.

"Well." Ruth wiped her hands on her apron as she walked over to them. "I was figuring that Peter, Nicholas, and Benjamin could sleep on the floor in here with Bradley. You two and Patricia could sleep in the den. Your parents could have the parlor, and Tamera and Daniel could take the guest room.

Unless someone has a better idea, that is."

Ariel and Claudia looked at each other and nodded. "Sounds good to us," Claudia answered for them.

"Good," Ruth sighed. "Dinner will be ready in about an hour. Why don't you get started making up the rooms for me?"

"Sure." Claudia smiled. "You get started in here," she said to Ariel. "And I'll take the den."

* * *

Tamera turned her sweater collar up against the cold wind. Slowly she made her way down the front walk toward her SUV. The street lamps flickered and then came on, casting a yellow glow across the snow-covered street and sidewalks. There was an eerie silence up and down the street.

The top and side of the SUV exposed to the wind were blanketed in snow. The fogged up windshield and telltale crack in the snow around the back passenger door were all she needed. Her heart pounded as she tried to figure out what to do next. She walked around to the driver's door and opened it. Without looking in the back seat, she sat down behind the steering wheel.

The air inside the car was so cold she could see her breath. She shivered and rubbed her arms, wishing she had her purse with her car keys. She put her hands on the steering wheel and leaned her head against her arms. "Oh, Nick, where are you?" she cried.

Slowly the blanket in the backseat began to stir. Nicholas poked his head out from beneath it. He listened while she cried.

"I can't lose you, too," she said, looking up and wiping the tears from her cheeks. "Please come home. Please come back to me."

Slowly Nicholas sat up. He reached out and touched her shoulder. She jumped and turned toward him in her seat. "Nick!"

"I'm sorry," he said quietly.

"No baby, I'm sorry," she cried, this time her tears were real. "You're okay?" she asked and hugged him over the back of the seat. "You had me so worried. Please, don't ever run away again. I love you so much."

"I love you, too," he said out of habit, still uncertain about what he really felt.

"Come up here and sit next to me," Tamera instructed. "Bring the blanket, it's cold in here."

Nicholas climbed into the front seat. He turned around and grabbed the blanket, then sat with his back against the door. Tamera mirrored his pose and spread the blanket over both of them.

Nervously Nicholas studied the dashboard trying to get up the courage to ask her what he needed to know. Finally he looked at her. "I have to know," he began slowly. "Is it true? Am I adopted?"

Tamera reached out her hand and touched his cheek. He instantly pulled away, not because of rebellion but because her hand was cold. Tamera quickly took it back, not understanding why he pulled away. She wiped the tears from her face and tucked her hand beneath the blanket again.

"Nick, there's something I want to tell you before I answer your question. I never told you this before because I never talk about it. Before your father—" She stopped herself. "Before Dan and I were married, when I was a teenager, I was raped and became pregnant. I was scared. I didn't know what to do. I terminated the pregnancy. I had an abortion."

Nicholas' eyes widened in surprise as he listened.

"After Dan and I were married," she continued, "we had a baby. He was a beautiful little boy. He had the softest blonde hair and big blue eyes. We named him after Dan, but called him Danny. Then one night, when he was only four months old, I couldn't get him to go to sleep. He wasn't fussy. He just wasn't sleepy, but I was so tired. At two in the morning I put him in his bed. He looked up at me with his beautiful eyes and smiled. I just couldn't stay awake, I was so exhausted. I lay down on the bed next to his crib and fell asleep. I was only asleep for a couple hours, maybe not even that long. When I woke up and looked at my baby, I knew something was wrong. His eyes were open and he was just staring up at the ceiling. His rosy cheeks were blue and cold." Tamera choked back her tears and continued. "I screamed and grabbed him, holding him to my chest, patting his little back. Daniel came running into the nursery and took him from me. He tried to revive him, but Danny was gone. My baby was dead." Tears streamed down her cheeks but she did not wipe them way. "Sudden Infant Death Syndrome, the doctors told us. But I knew that God was punishing me for having that abortion. It was my fault.

"Dan and I tried to have another child. I miscarried three times. After months of testing, the doctor told me I would never have another child of my own. I was devastated. I wanted to die.

"It took Dan almost a year to convince me that we should adopt a child. I didn't want to but I could tell that he desperately needed to, so I agreed. We saw a lawyer and he arranged for us to see you. You were so beautiful, tiny and helpless. I instantly knew you were my son." Tamera smiled through her tears and touched his cheek. This time he did not pull away, he just looked down. "So, yes, honey, you were adopted. Dan and I aren't your birth parents, but we couldn't love you more if we were."

Nicholas turned and looked at the snow covered windshield in front of him. The words rang in his ears. He nodded to himself, telling himself it was okay. Then slowly he found his voice. "So, what about my real parents? Do you know who they are?"

"We were never told their names." Tamera bit her lip as she tried to see his face, to read his expression. "What we were told was your birth mother was only fifteen, just a child herself. She said that she couldn't raise a child on her own and wanted you to have a home with a mother and a father. Through the attorney, we offered to send her pictures of you each year but she said no. We don't know anything about your birth father."

Nicholas continued to stare at the windshield. He did not really hear what Tamera was saying. Inside, his thoughts and emotions were at war. Flashes of memories of growing up, family gatherings, and trips all came flooding back. Mixed in with them were the bad times, the hurtful words, the groundings, and the hours spent in his room as punishment. They did not sting as much now. He thought of his bedroom, his own personal space, and wondered if he would have had that with his birth mother.

"Nick," Tamera said, trying hard not to cry again. "Nick," she repeated. He turned his head and looked at her. "If you want me to, I will do everything I can to find your birth parents with you."

Tears filled Nicholas' eyes.

"Would you like that, honey?" Tamera asked, secretly dreading his answer.

"No," he cried and lunged forward, hugging her. "No, I want to go back to the way things were before. I want you to be my mom and Dad to be my dad again."

Tamera hugged him tightly and stroked his hair. "We are, baby. We are." She kissed the top of his head as her tears of relief began to fall.

* * *

Daniel stood at the back door and looked out the window at the darkening night. The snow had begun to ease up, gently falling in slow, feather-like drifts. His thoughts turned to Danny and the morning when Tamera's screams woke him. He sprang from their bed and raced to the nursery. Tamera stood over the crib, holding their little boy close to her chest. He looked at Danny's hands, so tiny, so blue, so lifeless. His heart raced and his throat tightened causing him to gasp for air as he realized what it all meant. Tears flooded his eyes but he choked them away. He grabbed Danny out of her arms and ordered her to call the ambulance. He laid the tiny, limp body down on the dressing table and began administering CPR just as he was trained by the instructor before Danny was born. Only Danny did not respond. *No, this can't be happening,* Daniel had thought to himself. *No. Not Danny. Not my son. He's just a baby.*

Daniel's thoughts turned back to the day when he and Tamera received the news that their son was waiting for them, a beautiful, healthy baby boy. The first time he looked into Nicholas' eyes, all the pain of losing Danny was eased, replaced by the joy of the little bundle in his arms. He could not have been more proud if Nicholas were his own flesh and blood. To him, Nicholas was.

Now, the pain was back. The familiar tightening in his chest, that same helpless feeling, all of it had returned. Not because of losing Danny, but because of fear of losing his son, Nicholas. Tears fell from his eyes; he wiped them away.

He turned from the window and looked at Carl standing in front of the fireplace.

"Ready to get back out?"

Carl turned around. "I guess so. Brad—" He froze when he looked at the archway to the foyer.

"Dad?" a voice said.

Daniel slowly turned and looked in the direction of the foyer.

"Dad," Nicholas repeated, seeing the tears in his father's eyes. He ran across the room with opened arms.

"Nick!" Daniel choked, tears streaming down his cheeks. "Nick," he repeated and he held his son tightly in his arms. "You've come back to us. Don't ever leave us again."

"I'm sorry, Dad. I'm sorry." Nicholas cried with him. They stood holding each other in the middle of the family room, oblivious to everyone around them.

"I love you so much, son," Daniel said. He closed his eyes tightly and said a silent thank you to his unseen helper.

Ruth and Carl walked over to Tamera and gave her a

hug.

"He's really home, Mom," Tamera said, her eyes filled with tears of joy. "And this time, he chose us."

"Dinner's ready," Morgan announced and smiled at the sight of Nicholas back where he belonged.

* * *

The house was quiet as Ruth walked toward the stairs. She paused by the guest bedroom and listened to the sound of Tamera, Daniel, and Nicholas sleeping peacefully at last. She smiled to herself. She was glad that the secret of Nicholas' adoption was out in the open and that it turned out well. Descending the stairs, she looked at the parlor. With the light from the nightlight in the foyer she could just make out the sleeping forms of Morgan and Chuck. She still was uncertain how she felt about Chuck's little *joke*, but her anger was gone. She turned toward the family room but a dim light from the dining room caught her eye. Curiously she made her way toward it.

Bradley sat at the table staring at the framed photograph of his wedding day. A glass of warm milk sat on the table in front of him. Beside it, his cell phone. He shook his head and turned the photograph face down on the table just as Ruth walked into the room.

"Couldn't sleep either?" she said softly and sat down in the chair next to him at the end of the table. She looked at the cell phone, picture frame, glass of milk and then at him.

"No. Not really," he sighed without looking at her.

"Were you able to get ahold of Amanda?" Ruth tried to look into his eyes but he kept his head down.

"No," he said. "I suppose she told you that I haven't been calling her."

"She did mention it. Why, may I ask?"

Bradley looked up at the ceiling and took a deep labored breath as he collected his thoughts. "I just can't," he said. His throat tightened as he fought to keep his feelings in check.

Ruth watched her son and felt his anxiety. She gently stroked his short dark-brown hair. "Please, tell me what's troubling you, maybe I can help?"

"She asked me for a divorce," he said and looked at her with tears in his eyes. "I don't know what to do."

"Oh honey," Ruth responded, surprised. She tried to find the right words to ease her son's pain, but her mind was a blank.

"I figure, if I avoid talking to her, maybe she'll change her mind," Bradley continued. He shook his head.

"When did she tell you this?" Ruth asked.

"Three weeks after she entered the clinic. She calls nearly every day leaving messages for me on my voice mail. She wants to know if I've seen an attorney yet and when she can expect the papers."

"But what about Benjamin?"

"Oh, she wants him. She says no judge will take a child away from its mother. She even has her mother in on it."

"Why didn't you tell us?" Ruth asked, putting her hand on his shoulder.

"I didn't want to burden you with my problems. You had enough to deal with already."

"Nonsense, I am always here for you, Bradley. That's what moms are for. You can always come to me. So have you talked to a lawyer?"

"I had an appointment to see one tomorrow." He glanced at the darkened window. "If a divorce is what will make her happy and get her well, then I'll give her one, but I'll be damned if I'll let her have full custody of our son." Bradley wiped the tears from his cheek.

Ruth picked up the photograph and turned it up so they both could see it. "I remember when this was taken," she said.

"It feels like a lifetime ago." Bradley sighed. "I can't stand looking at it and yet I find myself staring at it all of the time. I just don't know what to do anymore. I still love her with all my heart. Can't she see that?"

Ruth sat quietly holding his hand. She did not have any answers for him and it pained her deep inside.

* * *

The bedroom was dark except for the soft glow that reflected off the snow outside and through the window. Ruth slipped into her bed and lay next to Carl. The warmth from his body and the flannel sheets felt good against her skin. She lay on her back, staring blindly at the ceiling. She felt her wedding ring and smiled to herself. Forty-five years filled with joy, laughter, sorrow, and pain. A lifetime really and yet it passed by so quickly.

Carl slowly turned over, putting his arm around her. She looked at him and he smiled.

"Happy?" he asked.

"Yes." Ruth smiled back to him.

He kissed her softly and they fell asleep in each other's arms.

CHAPTER FOUR
THE SHOWER

Tiny blossoms hung from the branches of the tall oak trees in the backyard. The sounds of birds chirping and the fresh sweet scent of flowers filled the air, announcing the arrival of spring.

Ruth smiled to herself and looked up at the clear blue sky. *A perfect day for a baby shower,* she thought as she carried the tray of punch glasses out to the picnic table. She glanced at her watch then hurried back into the house.

"Carl," she called as she entered the kitchen. "I need a hand in here." She removed the tray of hors d'oeuvres from the oven.

"Here I am," Carl announced, walking into the kitchen. "What can I do?" He smiled as he watched his wife. It was obvious to him that she was having the time of her life. She always did love having people over for a party, something he did not care that much about. It seemed the older he grew, the more he liked the quiet.

Ruth glanced at him. "The girls will be here any minute. Would you please take the punch bowl out to the table for me? Be sure to leave it covered; there are a lot of bees out this afternoon. Oh, and light the tiki torches for me."

"I'm on it," Carl said, carefully picking up the punchbowl without spilling its contents. Moments later the back screen door slammed shut behind him.

Ruth quickly but gently slid the tiny pastry hors d'oeuvres onto a platter then turned her attention to the cake on the counter. With the skill of a professional cake decorator, she added the finishing touches to the icing decorations and then smiled to herself. Everything was coming together nicely. *Ariel will be pleased,* she thought.

She picked up the cake and started for the back door when the front doorbell chimed. Frantically she looked around for a place to set the cake. Finding none, she returned it to the kitchen counter and hurried off to answer the front door.

"Coming," she called right as the doorbell chimed again.

"Hi, Mom," Tamera said when Ruth opened the door. "Are we early?"

"As a matter of fact, yes." Ruth smiled and stepped aside to let Tamera and Nicholas enter. "But that's quite all right, I could use the help. The guests will be arriving soon and I still have a lot of things to do."

"Great." Tamera smiled. "I hope it's all right that I brought Nick. I thought that maybe he could keep Dad busy while the party is going on."

"That's fine, more hands make less work for all," she said and winked at her grandson. Nicholas smiled at her.

"Claudia is bringing Peter, too, so between the two of them, they should be able to handle your father. Come on. The kitchen awaits."

Ruth shut the front door and started back to the kitchen.

"Nick," Tamera said and turned to her son. "Be a good boy and watch the front door. When the guests arrive, have them meet us out back."

"Sure, Mom." Nicholas smiled even though he hated being called a boy. He was hardly a boy anymore. He was fifteen, a young man, almost an adult.

"Tamera?" Ruth called from the kitchen.

"Coming, Mother." Tamera hurried off to the kitchen.

"Would you get the door for me?" Ruth motioned toward the back door with her head as she picked up the cake.

"Oh, Mom, the cake is beautiful," Tamera said and held

the screen door open.

Tamera followed Ruth outside. The long table had been covered with a pale yellow tablecloth. Festive pastel pink and blue balloons hung in midair, tethered by matching ribbons. Streamers twisted from the tree branches above the table to the poles near the swimming pool to form an open canopy. Tamera smiled as she remembered the baby shower Ruth had thrown for her when she brought Nicholas home from the hospital. Time had truly flown by.

The back door opened and Bradley stepped out carrying a wrapped gift. Ruth looked up at her son and a smile spread across her lips.

"Bradley, what a surprise." She went to him and gave him a hug and a kiss.

"I just thought I should stop by and drop this off for Ariel." He shrugged.

"That's so sweet of you." Ruth took the gift. "How're things with Amanda?"

"She relapsed after receiving the divorce papers but seems to be doing better now. I thought it was what she wanted since she kept asking for it. I just don't understand her anymore."

"Did they say when she'll be able to come home?" Ruth took his arm as they walked over to the gift table.

"Nothing definite, maybe in another month or two."

"Well, it'll take time, honey." Ruth squeezed his arm. "In the meantime, how're you and Benjamin holding up?"

"He really misses his mom," Bradley said, purposely avoiding answering the whole question. "But I think he understands as best a three year old can."

"Kids are stronger than we give them credit for," Ruth assured him.

"I guess," Bradley said, not as convinced as his mother. "If it's okay with you, do you think I could just hang out in the house for a while?"

"Sure, that would be fine, dear." Ruth looked at her son

with concern. He seemed quiet and somewhat depressed. "There's some fresh coffee on the stove. Help yourself."

"Thanks, Mom." Bradley kissed her cheek and disappeared into the house.

Tamera slowly walked over to her, still staring at the back door. "He sure doesn't seem like himself these days. Is everything okay?"

"I don't know," Ruth said with a sigh. She shook her head, trying to shake the thoughts from her mind and refocus on the party that was due to begin at any moment. "Well, looks like we're almost ready," she said and looked around the backyard, unconsciously waving away a bee with the back of her hand.

* * *

Nicholas opened the front door and stepped aside to let the small group of chattering girls enter.

"Everyone's in the backyard," he said, pointing the way.

"Hold the door," Claudia called as Nicholas started to close the front door. Immediately he opened it wider and smiled as she entered.

"Hi, Aunt Claudia," he said and then noticed Peter. His smile faded.

"Hi, Nick," Peter greeted him with a smile.

Nicholas ignored him, turning toward Claudia. "Everyone's to go out back," he informed her and closed the front door.

* * *

"Claudia!" Ruth called from the kitchen seeing her heading for the back door. She rushed over and gave her daughter-in-law a hug. "I'm so happy you made it. I know you're busy with your new job. How do you like it?"

"I love it." Claudia smiled proudly. "I just wish Peter

was as happy here."

"He's still not liking it?" Ruth asked while she walked back to the kitchen to get the pitcher of lemonade to top off the punchbowl.

"I don't know. He's not his normal self. He's quiet and withdrawn."

"What about school?"

"It was so nice of Nick to offer to show him around, but from what I gather they had a falling out."

"Over what, pray tell?" Ruth asked. She started to pick up a tray of hors d'oeuvres but Claudia took it from her.

"Let me help you with that," she said. As they headed for the back door, Claudia glanced at the foyer, to where Peter and Nick stood by the front door. "I wish I knew."

Claudia followed Ruth out the back door and over to the refreshment table. A bee buzzed by her head and she ducked, nearly dropping the tray.

"Oh, my," she gasped, looking at the handful of bees that were buzzing over the table. "Mom, look at the bees."

Ruth turned around from emptying the pitcher into the punchbowl.

"Oh no, this isn't good." She glanced at the lit torches, which were positioned too far away to be helpful. "Here, grab that torch over there while I get the other one. We can put them at either end of the table. That should keep them away."

Claudia and Ruth pulled up the torches and stuck them into the ground at either end of the refreshment table. The bees quickly flew off. Ruth smiled. "Take that, you pesky bees!" she laughed.

* * *

Patricia walked into the dining room.

"Hi, Brad. What're you doing hiding out in here all alone?"

Bradley did not answer. He just he stared blindly at cup

of coffee in front of him, deep in thought.

"Is everything all right?" Patricia asked, sitting down next to him.

"I suppose you heard already," he said quietly, still not looking at her.

"Heard what?" she asked.

"Amanda and I are getting divorced."

Patricia looked at her folded hands on the table. "Yes, I did hear about that. I'm sorry."

"I'm the one who's sorry." Bradley smirked and then sipped his coffee. "I should never have put her in that place."

"No." Patricia reached out and put her hand on his. "You did the right thing."

Bradley looked at her, tears in his eyes. "Did I?" he asked. "She hates me now. She thinks I betrayed her."

"Brad," Patricia said softly yet with firmness in her voice. "You can't blame yourself. If you didn't step in and do that, then she could've died."

"I know," he admitted. "But now she's trying to take Benjamin from me to punish me. She even has her mother helping her spy on me."

"Is that where Benji is now?"

"Yes." Bradley looked back at his coffee.

"Oh, Brad, I'm so sorry."

"I used to think that I still loved her. That by giving her time she would come to her senses and we could be a family again." He frowned and shook his head. "Not any more. I don't want her to back. She and her mother take a flying leap for all I care."

"What about Benji?"

"There's no chance in hell a judge will give him to her," he said confidently and with a tone of defiance.

"Don't be so sure about that," Patricia cautioned him. "It's not about what is morally right, it's about what is legal. There is a difference."

The words hit Bradley like a brick. He sat back in his

chair in stunned silence as he let the possibility of losing Benjamin sink in. He looked at the wall in front of him and then back at her.

"There is no way I will lose my son," he said matter-of-factly.

"Remember what mom always says, 'Prepare for the worst but hope for the best.'"

Bradley nodded in silence.

* * *

The backyard was abuzz with the chatter and laughter of the crowd of women. In the center of it all was Ariel. She sat next to the table of gifts, rubbing her round stomach through her bright green-and-yellow floral maternity dress. Her long, blonde hair was pulled back in a ponytail by a matching sheer green scarf. She basked in the attention.

"So, when's Mark coming home?" Claudia asked and took a sip of her lemonade.

Ariel looked at her aunt and her eyes sparkled. "Tomorrow, and I can't wait. It's been really lonely in that big, empty house."

"Where're his parents?" Ruth asked.

"They're off on another business trip," she answered.

"Tamera," Morgan whispered as she stood beside Tamera, watching Ariel unwrap her gifts.

"What?" Tamera said coldly, looking at her.

"Can I talk to you for a moment, alone, please?" Morgan asked sheepishly.

"Fine." Tamera glared at her sister. Only three months had passed since Chuck's so-called joke, yet it was still fresh in her mind.

The two walked away from the gathering to a quiet corner of the yard. Their departure did not go unnoticed. Claudia nudged Ruth and motioned with her head in their direction. Ruth looked at them and frowned. She knew about the tension still between them and hoped they would not make a scene.

"What do you want, Morgan?" Tamera's tone was curt.

"I just want to apologize again. I know what Chuck did was wrong. He shouldn't have done it," Morgan said quietly.

"He shouldn't have done a lot of things!" Tamera snapped at her. "He may be your husband, but I don't have to like him and I don't have to like you either." Tamera turned around and headed back toward the tables.

"Tamera," Morgan called after her. "You're not being fair."

Tamera froze and turned around slowly. "Fair?" she repeated and walked back toward her sister. "Fair," she said louder. "You and that good-for-nothing husband of yours nearly destroyed my family and you say I'm not being fair?"

"Well, what about your interfering with Ariel the day before her wedding?"

"Just be thankful I did or we wouldn't be here today." Tamera tried to keep her temper under control.

"What are you talking about?" Morgan looked at her confused and suddenly without anger.

Tamera looked smugly at her sister.

"Ariel found out that she was pregnant before the wedding and wanted to get an abortion. So I convinced her not to. I did you a favor, Grandma," Tamera said flatly, then turned and walked away without another word.

Morgan stood in dumbfounded silence.

* * *

"Hey, Nick." Peter followed his cousin into the family room.

Nicholas ignored him, grabbing the TV remote and turning the television on.

"Nick, where's Grandpa?" Peter asked and stepped in front of him, blocking his view.

"He's out in the garage tinkering with the lawn mower.

Get out of the way," Nicholas ordered and turned up the volume.

"Do you want to go out front and shoot hoops?"

"No."

Peter sighed. He had hoped, even though they were two years apart, since his mother had bought a house close to theirs and they attended the same school that they could be friends. Suddenly Nicholas had begun to avoid him, and Peter did not understand why.

"Do you want to play catch?"

Nicholas muted the television and then turned to face his cousin. "Don't you get it? I don't want to play anything with you. Leave me alone." He turned back to the television and unmuted it.

Peter looked at Nicholas for a moment and tried not to let his hurt feelings show. Without another word he turned around and walked out of the room.

"Faggot," Nicholas said under his breath and glared at the doorway.

* * *

A roar of laughter rose from the backyard as Ariel opened her gifts, holding each one up for their approval. Wrapping paper littered the ground around her feet, and the bows were piled up next to her opened gifts.

"Who is that one from?" Ruth asked while she wrote the gifts down in the baby book.

"It's from Aunt Patty," Ariel said and then smiled. "Thank you, very much," she said, looking at her aunt.

Tamera smiled and turned away from the group. She headed over to the punch bowl to get another cup of lemonade. She was lost in her thoughts and not paying attention to the buzzing around her ears. Unconsciously she swatted at the sound.

Suddenly there was a sharp pain behind her ear. She screamed and spun around, falling into the table and knocking over one of the torches. The torch splattered hot oil across the lawn, igniting the grass.

"Oh my god," Ruth gasped and grabbed the table cloth off the empty table nearby. She ran to the burning grass and began swatting the flames. "Morgan, get a bucket of water, now!" she called over her shoulder.

Morgan quickly grabbed the punchbowl, half filled with lemonade. She upended it over the fire, extinguishing it.

Ruth looked up at Morgan standing back from the burned end of the table cloth, empty punchbowl in hand. Their eyes met and Ruth laughed.

"Sorry, Mom. I just grabbed the first thing I could."

"Whatever works," Ruth said, turning around and looking at the shocked faces of her guests "It's okay. It's over. Everything's—"

"Mom, Tamera!" Claudia screamed, running over to her sister-in-law lying on the ground a few feet away from the table.

"Morgan, get your father out here, now!" Ruth ordered as she knelt down beside her daughter and checked her neck for a pulse. "Ohmygod," she gasped, feeling the swollen knot behind Tamera's ear. "And get Tamera's purse, on the double!" she screamed as Morgan reached the backdoor. "Tamera! Tamera!" Ruth repeated and shook her daughter to try to bring her to.

"Ariel, take everyone into the house and tell your mother to hurry up," Ruth ordered.

Everyone grabbed the gifts and food and rushed into the house. Morgan returned with Tamera's heavy purse and handed it to her mother. Ruth grabbed it and emptied it onto the ground beside her.

She frantically dug through the contents. Makeup, hair brushes, mints, tissues, books, coupons, more makeup, wallet. "It's got to be in here," she said and continued searching. "Where's your father? There it is!" she said, grabbing the black beesting kit. She quickly opened it and took out the syringe. At first she had been nervous about giving her little girl a shot every time she was stung, but after years of doing it as Tamera grew up, she had become quite used to it. Slowly she pushed the contents of the syringe into Tamera's arm. She withdrew the needle and sat back, holding Tamera's head in her lap.

Carl ran up to them just as Tamera opened her eyes. He glanced at the burnt lawn and empty punchbowl. "What happened?"

"Tamera was stung by another bee," Ruth answered. "Behind her ear. Her breathing is becoming normal again, but I think you should take her to the emergency room and have her looked at, just to be sure. She may have hit her head when she collapsed."

"Sure thing." Carl turned to Morgan. "Get Bradley out here to help me."

Morgan hurried off to the house, reaching the back door at the same time as Nicholas emerged.

"Mom!" he shouted, seeing Ruth and Carl helping Tamera to her feet.

"She's okay, Nick," Ruth assured him. "She was just stung by a bee. She'll be fine."

Nicholas looked at his mother. Tiny beads of sweat dotted her forehead and her eyes were glassy. His heart pounded in his chest. He had seen her before when she had been stung, but this time she looked different, not completely there inside.

"Mom?"

"I'm okay, baby." Tamera nodded to him, still groggy. Her mouth was dry and her tongue felt thick.

Bradley ran over to them and took Tamera's arm from Ruth.

"Help your father get her into the car. He's taking her to the emergency room," Ruth instructed Bradley.

"I'm going, too," Nicholas insisted.

"No, you're not, young man," Ruth said firmly, grabbing his arm. "She'll be fine. Besides, there isn't anything you can do there that you can't do here."

Morgan held the back door open and the five made their way into the house. "I called the emergency room and they'll be waiting for her," Morgan informed them.

Moments later, Morgan, Ruth, and Claudia stood on the front steps watching as Carl and Bradley helped Tamera into the car. Nicholas stood on the front walk obviously upset that he could not go along.

"Boy, I don't remember Tamera being this allergic to beestings. Has it gotten worse?" Morgan said.

"Apparently so," Ruth agreed as the car pulled out of the driveway and started down the street.

"Is she going to be okay?" Claudia asked.

"I think she will." Ruth nodded. "We've been through this several times over the years. It's almost a yearly occurrence."

"I don't know how you stay so calm," Claudia said, looking at Ruth. "This whole thing is very unsettling."

"We do what we have to for our kids." Ruth watched Nicholas walk out onto the front lawn. Peter stood under the basketball hoop, watching Nicholas intently.

"Well, I better get back to the guests," Morgan excused herself and disappeared into the house.

"Thank you, dear," Ruth said, turning back Nicholas. "I'll be in in a moment."

Peter walked over to Nicholas with the basketball tucked under his arm. He saw the car turn the corner.

"Hey, I'm sorry about your mom. She's gonna be fine," he said and put his hand on Nicholas' shoulder.

"Get your hands off me, you queer!" Nicholas snapped and pushed Peter away.

"Hey. What did you call me?" Peter's anger blazed. He dropped the basketball and shoved Nicholas back.

"You heard me, faggot." Nicholas doubled up his fist and punched Peter in the jaw.

Peter lunged at Nicholas, grabbing him by his shirt, and the two tumbled to the ground.

"Boys, stop it!" Ruth screamed, running across the lawn. Claudia and Patricia followed close behind her. Ruth grabbed Nicholas' collar and yanked him off of Peter. "Stop it! I said."

Nicholas ignored her, continuing to struggle in her grasp.

Claudia helped Peter to his feet. All of the sudden Nicholas slipped from Ruth's grasp and took one last swing at Peter, connecting with his mouth. Peter tripped and fell backward onto the ground, blood seeping from his lips.

Ruth's temper flared. She grabbed Nicholas by his arm and spun him around. A sharp slap across his face brought him to attention. "I said that is enough!" Ruth said through clenched teeth as she glared at him. "Now, what started this?"

"You gonna tell them?" Nicholas hissed and looked at Peter while Claudia helped him to his feet.

"No!" Peter glared back at Nicholas, wiping his mouth with the back of his hand.

"Go ahead and tell them what everyone calls you at school," Nicholas egged Peter on.

Peter looked around at the faces of his mother, aunt, and grandmother. Panic came over him. Without a word he turned around and ran off down the street.

"Peter!" Claudia called and started to go after him.

"No, Claudia, wait," Ruth said, halting her. Claudia turned around facing Ruth. Ruth motioned with her head for her to come back.

"Suppose you tell us what this is all about?" Ruth asked, glaring at her grandson, still furious over his fighting.

"Well," Nicholas hesitated for a moment, looking at his aunts and grandmother, "Dustin, he's a guy in my class, he told me his brother caught Peter checking him out in the shower after PE. So now everyone's calling him a fag."

Claudia gasped, her eyes widened and she covered her gaping mouth with her hand. Ruth looked at her sympathetically and then turned back to Nicholas.

"And what did you do?"

"Grandma, I'm no fag. I'm staying away from him. That's gross!"

"I'm really disappointed in you," Ruth said, shaking her head. "I thought you'd have a bit more loyalty to your family than that." Ruth turned her back on Nicholas and faced Claudia and Patricia.

"I better go after him," Claudia said.

"No, Claudia," Patricia stopped her. "Let me. Maybe he'll talk to a stranger."

Claudia looked at Patricia and reluctantly nodded. She watched helplessly as Patricia hurried to catch up to Peter.

"As for you, young man," Ruth said, turning back to Nicholas. "Get in the house and get cleaned up. You best never let me hear you using those words again. Is that understood?"

"Yes, Grandma," Nicholas answered but did not move.

"Now!" Ruth ordered.

Nicholas jumped and quickly obeyed.

"Claudia," Ruth said, turning to her daughter-in-law again. "Don't worry, boys go through this name calling thing. It's part of growing up. Peter will be fine."

Claudia nodded but deep down she wondered if there was something more going on. She had heard these same types of rumors before, from the last school Peter attended in Indiana. She thought it would be different for him here, but now she was not so sure.

Ruth and Claudia slowly walked back into the house.

The family room was filled with the noisy chatter of the guests. The gifts were stacked on the coffee table in the center of the room and the party continued. Ruth busied herself in the kitchen, pouring fresh bowls of chips and restocking the trays of cookies. She did not notice Claudia slip away.

"I just wanted to thank you, Mrs. Wallace, for letting us move the party inside," one of Ariel's friends said as she leaned over the counter.

"You're quite welcome, dear." Ruth smiled, handing

her a tray of cookies. "With the bees outside, we didn't have a choice. Pass those around and I'll fix us some more punch."

* * *

"Peter!" Patricia called as she ran after him. "Wait up."

Peter kept running, heading for the park just around the corner. It was only three blocks from the house and the only place he could think of to go. Never had he felt so alone as he did at that moment. Tears streamed down his cheeks, stinging the cut on the corner of his mouth. He did not care. He just had to get away.

Finally he stopped and leaned his back against a tree. He could not run any longer. He slid slowly down the trunk until he sat on the ground. He buried his face in his crossed arms and cried.

Patricia stopped running after him when she entered the park and saw him sitting on the ground. Slowly she walked over to him, trying to catch her breath. She stopped and stood beside him for a moment before she spoke. "Mind if I sit down?"

Peter kept his head down and wiped away his tears. Patricia took his silence as an invitation and sat down beside him. She stared across the park at a man walking his dog and two children playing on the swings with their mother.

"Boy, I haven't run like that in years," she said, finally catching her breath. "Do you want to talk about it?"

"No."

Patricia nodded to herself and continued to stare at the trees across the park.

"You wouldn't understand," Peter continued much to Patricia's surprise.

"Probably not, but you never know."

"You don't know what it's like to grow up without a father," Peter said, sitting back and resting his head against the tree. He stared straight ahead, avoiding eye contact with his aunt. "There was this guy, Matthew, at school back in Indiana.

He was a couple years ahead of me and really nice. Other kids bullied me because I didn't have a father. But Matthew wasn't like them. He protected me. We became friends and after school we would talk. Sometimes we would go on a walk or just hang out in the gym. He liked basketball. Mom liked him, too. She thought it was nice that I had *big brother* to talk to.

"Well, after school one day some guys cornered me. They called me a bunch of names and beat me up. I got away and I hid in the gym under the bleachers. Matthew heard about it somehow and he found me. He took me over to the locker room to help me get cleaned up. I sat down on the bench and he helped me get my shirt off and cleaned me up. I don't know how or why it happened, but he kissed me, a real kiss." Peter looked down again.

Patricia nodded. "Did you tell your mother?"

"No. I couldn't," Peter said quickly, fear and panic in his voice.

"Why? Did he threaten you?"

"See, you don't understand," Peter said, shaking his head. He turned and looked at his aunt. "I kissed him back. I wanted to. Mom would never understand and she'd be angry. She probably wouldn't let me see him again. I couldn't do that to him. I love him."

Patricia was silent. She did understand more than he realized, but she just listened.

"I guess I've always known that I was attracted to guys," Peter continued. "Since I was in the fifth grade, really. There was this guy in my class; all the girls had a crush on him and so did I. When we played during PE one team would be Shirts and the other Skins. I used to like looking at him without his shirt on. He had a great body for a fifth grader. So, you see, Aunt Patty, I'm gay, but I can't tell my mother. I don't want to disappoint her."

"Why do you think it would disappoint her?" Patricia shifted and turned to face Peter. "Has she ever said anything to you like that?"

"No," Peter shrugged, "but wouldn't any parent be disappointed if their son turned out queer?"

Patricia looked away. She realized at that moment what he said was true. Any parent would be upset if their son or their daughter, for that matter, turned out to be gay.

"You know, Peter," she said reassuringly. "One thing I've learned over the years is that you have to be true to yourself. You can't live your life to be who everyone else expects you to be. You have to be who you are, gay or straight, otherwise you'll be miserable and your life will be empty."

Peter quietly let her words sink in. Patricia ducked her head to get a look at Peter's eyes.

"It doesn't matter to me that you're gay," she said quietly, gently stroking his hair. "And thank you for telling me. It took a lot of guts."

Peter looked up at his aunt and smiled. "Thanks."

"I still think you should tell your mother," she urged. "I know she's very worried about you."

Peter suddenly felt nervous. "No, I can't." His eyes widened as he realized what he had just done. "Please, don't tell her. I'd rather die than be a disappointment to her."

"I won't say a word." Patricia smiled and gave his hand a gentle squeeze. She looked at Peter's bruised cheek and swollen lip. "Looks like we better get back to the house and get some ice on that. What do ya' say?"

"It does hurt a little."

Patricia stood up and dusted the dirt from the seat of her blue denim jeans and then held out a hand to Peter. He grasped it tightly and pulled himself to his feet.

"Wow." He smiled. "You're pretty strong for a girl," he teased.

"Well, don't mess with me," she teased right back.

* * *

Ariel laughed out loud as she picked up another

package.

"Let me guess," she said, closing her eyes and squeezing the sides of the gift. "I bet I know what this is." She looked at the girls gathered around her. With a sharp tug, she ripped off the colorful wrapping paper and looked at the contents. "More diapers!" she screamed and laughed, showing them to everyone before setting them beside the other two packages. The whole room roared with laughter.

The clock on the wall chimed four and as though on cue three of her friends rose at once. They made their apologies and then their goodbyes. Ruth escorted them to the front door. The girls stopped briefly to thank her again for her hospitality before leaving.

Ruth turned around, heading back to the party, when someone knocked on the front door. She smiled to herself.

"Okay, what did you forget?" she said, swinging the front door open. "Oh," she said with a start upon seeing a woman she did not recognize standing there. "I'm sorry. I thought you were someone else. May I help you?"

"Is Patty here?"

"No," Ruth said, puzzled by the woman's demanding tone. She looked the woman over, noting her short-almost manly-haircut, plaid shirt, faded jeans, and hiking boots.

"Liar!" the woman snapped, pushing her way into the foyer. "Patricia get your skinny butt out here now!" she yelled into the house.

Ruth took a deep breath and tightened her jaw, grabbing the intruder's arm. "Now, see here, young lady—"

"Patricia!" The woman jerked away from Ruth's grasp and ignored her. "I know you're here, don't make me find you," she yelled up at the second floor and started for the stairs. She stopped when Claudia and Morgan came running into the foyer. Ariel and the remaining guests huddled in the arch to the family room watching curiously.

"Mom?" Morgan gave her mother a puzzled look.

Ruth shrugged and then grabbed the woman's arm and

spun her around. "Look, I don't know who you are, but you have no right to come into my house and—"

Just then the front door opened and Peter and Patricia walked into the house. Patricia froze as her eyes met with the intruder's. Fear and panic gripped her and she took a step back.

"There you are, you bitch," the woman cursed and lunged at Patricia. Her hands closed around Patricia's throat and the force of her jump sent them crashing backward into the front door. Patricia's head hit with a loud thud.

"No one leaves me!" The woman tightened her grip the more Patricia struggled unsuccessfully to break free.

Ruth's temper flared. In one swift movement she grabbed the woman by her hair and jerked her head backward. The intruder let go of Patricia as she was sent crashing to the floor.

"Get out of my house!" Ruth demanded.

Morgan quickly ran to Patricia and helped her into the parlor. Patricia coughed as she tried to catch her breath, unable to speak. Peter backed into a corner and watched in wide-eyed shock.

Fire blazed in the woman's eyes. She sprang to her feet and grabbed Ruth, throwing her down. "I'm not leaving without Patricia!" she screamed and lunged at Patricia again.

Morgan protectively stepped in front of her sister and pushed the woman back. Her heart pounded faster as adrenalin coursed through her veins. She was surprised by her instinctive reaction to protect her sister and yet it gave her a sense satisfaction too.

The woman glared at Morgan. She clenched her teeth. "Okay, you wanna play too, bitch?"

"Hold it right there!" Claudia shouted pointing a pistol at the woman.

The hostility in the woman's eyes was replaced by fear. She stepped back as Claudia cocked the hammer.

"I don't know who you are, but you weren't invited and you're not welcome here," Claudia said in a cold, firm voice.

"Mom?" Peter looked at his mother in surprise.

"Claudia, no." Patricia found her voice and rushed back into the foyer. "It's okay. Please, don't."

Claudia kept her aim on the woman, not looking away.

Ruth stood up, shocked at the sight of a gun. Never before had such a thing been brought into her house. She had even forbidden her sons to play with toy guns when they were young. Yet, at that moment, she was glad it was there. Ruth looked at the woman and then at Patricia.

"Patty, what is going on here?" she demanded.

Patricia looked at the woman, then slowly at each of the faces around her and then finally at her mother.

"Please, Claudia, put the gun down," Patricia almost begged. "Mom, this is Jo, my ex-roommate," she said and glared at Jo.

"Your lover, don't you mean?" Jo blurted out.

Ruth looked at the woman, this time confused. She was not sure of what she just heard. What did she mean by that remark? What was she implying? She looked at Patricia.

"Shoot her, Claudia," Morgan snapped. "Obviously she's out of her mind or on drugs."

"Try neither, bitch!" Jo cursed at Morgan. "Go ahead, tell them," Jo said to Patricia.

Patricia stood in stunned silence, her mouth open as though she were about to speak only the words would not come out.

"Aunt Patty?" Peter looked at his aunt.

Patricia's eyes filled with tears as she looked at Peter and then at her mother. She took a deep breath.

"It's complicated," she said to her mother and then turned back to Jo. "We're through and I want you out."

Ruth shook her head in disbelief. "I've had enough of this. Get out of my house, now, or I'll call the police." She pointed directly at the front door.

Jo backed away, toward the open front door, her eyes still fixed on the gun in Claudia's hand even though it was no longer aimed at her. She slipped away without another word.

Patricia looked at her mother with tears in her eyes.

"Mom, I'm sorry," she cried. "I—"

"Patricia, not now," Ruth said, her mind reeling from all that just happened.

"Mom, please, let me explain," Patricia pleaded.

"I've heard enough, already. I can't do this right now." Ruth turned around and left the room. Claudia hesitated for a moment, then set the gun on the table next to the phone and hurried after her mother-in-law.

Patricia looked around the foyer at all the stunned faces and then ran out the front door.

"Aunt Patty," Peter called and followed her outside.

Patricia stopped on the front walk and turned around to face her nephew, tears dampening her cheeks. She tried to smile, to reassure him, but it was no use.

"You see, Peter," she said. "I do understand, but I guess I was wrong." She turned around and headed for her car.

"No, you weren't wrong!" Peter called to her as she backed out of the driveway and sped off. He wiped the tears from his eyes.

* * *

Ruth walked across the backyard, her head still reeling from the images of the intruder, the gun, Patty. Moments before, on the front lawn, everything had been clear, but now she did not know what she thought, let alone how she felt about what she heard. She slowly began to pick up the torn wrapping paper and ribbons.

Claudia walked around the swimming pool, watching Ruth stuff the trash into a plastic garbage bag. She wrung her hands nervously as she mustered up the courage to speak.

"Mom," she said, cautiously. "I'm sorry. I should've told you about the gun."

"Yes, you should have," Ruth answered flatly without

looking at her.

"I've carried it for years, ever since I was mugged two years after Steven moved back here. I just forgot that it was in my purse," Claudia explained. "I'm sorry."

Ruth looked at Claudia. Her mind had frozen on the word mugged. Her anger melted away to be replaced with empathy.

"I'm the one who should be sorry. I didn't know."

"I never told anyone before," Claudia said, smiling slightly at the relief she felt in telling someone. "I guess we all have our little secrets that we keep to ourselves. It's safer that way, sometimes, I guess."

Ruth nodded and returned to picking up the napkins and paper plates that littered the lawn. She tried not to think about Patricia but she could not stop.

"Mom," Claudia said softly. "You need to talk to Patty. You can't let her leave here, not like this."

Ruth looked up at Claudia, confused by her own conflicting emotions. She knew Claudia was right, but she just could not. She felt like such a hypocrite. When they were talking about Peter being called names at school, it was different, but Patricia was her daughter, her child. It went against every part of her being, every part of her moral upbringing. It was not natural. No. She did not have to discuss it. The memory of her words to Nicholas suddenly flashed in her mind. She stopped and looked up at the sky, trying to push the memories away.

"I wouldn't know what to say."

"Then just listen. Give Patty a chance to explain," Claudia pleaded. "You don't want to lose her, too."

Ruth froze. Slowly she turned away, her heart aching, tears filling her eyes. "I don't know if I can." She searched for answers in the tree branches and in the flower beds that lined the fence. "I don't know how to deal with this."

"You're not alone, Mom." Claudia walked over to her mother-in-law and put her arm around her. "We're all here. Together we can handle this. We just need to give Patty a chance."

Ruth nodded. She turned and hugged Claudia.

* * *

"Well, they're all gone," Ariel said, closing the front door and leaning against it. She watched her mother place the telephone receiver back on its cradle. "Who was that on the phone?"

"It was your grandfather," Morgan said. "He and your uncle are on their way back with your aunt Tammy. She's fine. Where's Nick?"

Ariel thought for a moment. "I think I saw him last in the dining room."

"Thanks," Morgan said and headed for the dining room.

Despite all of the excitement, Ariel thought, *that was the best party ever.* Excited over the many gifts she had received, she walked back to the family room. She could not wait to show Mark all of the cute baby clothes and toys.

Ariel noticed Peter immediately as she entered the family room. He stood by the window with his arms folded over this chest, staring out at his mother and grandmother in the backyard. Images of the expression on their faces when Patricia revealed her secret were permanently etched in his mind. He never wanted them to look at him that way. *No,* he thought, making up his mind, *I can never tell them.* He turned around and gave a start when he saw Ariel standing in the doorway staring at him.

"Hi, Peter." She smiled at him.

"Hi," he replied, avoiding eye contact as he quickly left the room. He was not in the mood to talk to anyone. He headed into the foyer and seconds later the front door closed with a bang.

Ariel did not appear to notice. She busied herself picking up the baby's gifts and packing them into an empty box.

* * *

Peter walked over to a quiet corner in the front yard and sat down under a tall oak tree. Tears filled his eyes as he thought about Matthew. *If only I had put up more of a fight to stay in Indiana,* he thought, *but then I would've had to tell mom my secret. No. She wouldn't have understood. How could she? I don't even understand it.*

Tears began to roll down his cheeks. His heart ached. He missed spending afternoons with Matthew. With Matthew's strong arms wrapped around him, he had felt safe, secure, and at peace. He closed his eyes and took a deep breath, remembering the scent of Matthew's cologne mixed with sweat. He touched his lips, feeling the softness yet firmness of Matthew's kisses.

"I miss you so much," Peter cried quietly. *You're the only one who understands me,* he thought. *I can't go on without you, without my best friend, I just can't.*

He looked at the pistol in his hands. He fumbled with the tumbler while he thought about Patricia's words, "You have to be true to yourself. You have to be who you are, otherwise you'll be miserable and your life will be empty."

"My life is already empty," he said, tears streaming down his cheeks. Slowly he brought the barrel up to his lips. The metal felt cold against his tongue. He smelled the oil from the barrel as he took a deep breath.

* * *

Claudia opened the back door and stepped into the family room, Ruth behind her. They set the punch bowl and empty platters down on the counter in the kitchen without a word.

"Ariel," Ruth turned to her granddaughter. "Where's your mother?"

"She's in the dining room talking to Nicholas, I think.

Grandpa and Aunt Tammy are on their way home right now," Ariel replied and continued to fold the baby clothes she received.

Ruth looked at Claudia and the two of them hurried off to the dining room.

"Morgan, may I see you in the parlor, please?" Ruth interrupted as she paused in the dining room archway. "Now."

Morgan obediently stood up from the table and followed Claudia into the parlor. They both sat down and waited for Ruth to speak.

Ruth walked over to the fireplace and thoughtfully touched Patricia's photograph. She did love her daughter, that fact was never in question. She just did not know what to do. What to say. What to think. Slowly she turned around and faced the two women.

"I know I've never been one to keep secrets from any of you, and especially your father," she began. "However, I do not want anyone to tell him about what went on here this afternoon. I need to talk to Patty first. So, please, don't say a word."

Morgan readily nodded her consent.

"Shall I try to call Patty for you?" Claudia offered.

"No." Ruth looked back at the photograph. "I need to do it myself."

Claudia nodded silently and smiled. She was glad that Ruth was not going to leave things the way they were. She liked Patricia, liked being her friend and her sister-in-law, no matter what.

She looked at the coffee table and noticed her open purse. Suddenly she remembered her pistol. She had not put it back. *Where did I leave it?* she thought. Her heart began beating faster as panic set in. She looked toward the foyer and tried to remember.

Ruth noticed the purse in her daughter-in-law's hands and looked toward the foyer. "Oh my god, Claudia." Her tone was almost a chastisement as she realized what was bothering

Claudia. "Where is it?"

Claudia looked at Ruth, panicking. She stood up. "I don't know." She walked into the foyer, thinking through the earlier events, trying to place when she had last seen it.

"What's wrong?" Morgan asked, standing up.

"The gun," Ruth said. "Claudia, when do you remember having it last?"

"I was standing right here," she said and stood in the foyer, facing the front door. Her thumb and forefinger extended and aimed at the front door. She lowered her hand. "That woman left, then Patty," she continued thinking out loud. "You left and I followed." As she turned toward the family room arch, she unconsciously extended her gun hand toward the table, she froze. "That's it!" she yelled. "I set the gun down next to the phone."

"I used that phone when dad called. It wasn't there," Morgan said.

"Peter, Nicholas, Ariel," Ruth yelled, her voice amplified by the open foyer.

Immediately Ariel and Nicholas came running. They could tell that something was wrong by the looks on the three women's faces.

"Were either of you in here this afternoon—"

"Have either of you seen my pistol?" Claudia interrupted. "I set it down right here." She put her hand next to the telephone.

Ariel and Nicholas both shook her heads.

"No," Nicholas said. "Why?"

A shot rang out in the front yard. Everyone jumped and stepped back. Ruth ran to the front door, followed closely by Claudia. Together they stepped onto the front porch and froze.

"Peter!" Claudia screamed spotting her son leaning against the oak tree facing away from them. "Oh, god, no." She ran over to him and knelt down.

Peter did not move.

Claudia grabbed him up in her arms only to let go when

he pulled away.

"Peter!" she snapped, grabbing his arm and pulling him to his feet. "What's the matter with you?"

Peter looked at her; he could see the anger in her eyes.

"Nothing,"

"Where is it?"

"Where's what?"

"Don't play games with me. That gun isn't a toy," Claudia said and tightened her grip on his arm.

"I don't have it." He squirmed his way free of her grasp. "What's going on?"

"Then what was that shot we just heard?"

"That wasn't a gun shot. That was a car backfiring," Peter said and pointed down the street. He laughed silently at the lie he had come up with.

Claudia looked at her son's eyes and then over her shoulder at the empty street. As her fear and anger subsided, she felt foolish. She started to apologize to him but shook her head and walked back to Ruth. Peter watched her and then slowly sat back down and leaned against the tree.

"Oh that boy," Claudia said to Ruth as she walked over to her.

"Don't be too hard on him, or yourself," Ruth consoled her. "Perhaps one of the guests took the gun. We better notify the police."

"Let's take another look around first," Claudia said.

Peter sat with his ear turned toward the house, listening. When he heard the front door close behind them, he glanced over his shoulder just to make sure they were gone. He smiled proud of himself that they both had believed him. Slowly he stood up and walked across the street. Cautiously he stooped down and picked up the pistol from the bushes where it had landed when he'd thrown it. He stashed it into the front of his jeans and covered it with his shirt.

* * *

"Aunt Claudia, we've looked everywhere and still can't find it," Ariel reported as she walked into the parlor. She sat down in the chair by the doorway and rubbed her round stomach.

Ruth wrung her hands. "I guess we have to conclude that one of the guests must have taken it."

"I suppose you're right; although I can't imagine who it would have been," Claudia conceded. She rubbed her slender neck, massaging her tense muscles.

"Should we call the police and report it?" Morgan asked, more concerned about her reputation with her women friends than about the missing gun.

"I know I should," Claudia said, looking at the floor to avoid their gaze. "But I can't. I don't have a permit to carry it."

"But it's registered in your name isn't it?" Ruth asked. Claudia nodded.

"Then what if something should happen to the person who took it? Or worse yet, they commit a crime with it," Ruth continued. "You could be opening yourself up to a lot of unnecessary trouble."

Ruth was right but Claudia was still concerned about her lack of a concealed weapons permit.

"No one has to know the gun was in your purse," Morgan said. "None of us saw you get it out. It could have been in a drawer somewhere. Besides, you're within your legal right to protect yourself and family inside your home."

Claudia nodded. What Morgan said did sound good. "Okay," she agreed and started for the telephone.

The front door opened and Carl helped Tamera into the foyer. Ruth grabbed Claudia's arm, halting her.

"Sorry, I messed up the party," Tamera apologized in a tired voice. A large white-gauze bandage was taped to her neck over the beesting.

"Nonsense," Ruth reassured her, putting her arm around her shoulders and giving her a hug. "You didn't ruin a thing. If you don't believe me, just ask Ariel."

"No, Aunt Tamera, you didn't," Ariel said. "Although you did give us quite a scare. I'm glad you're okay." Ariel gave her aunt a hug and kissed her cheek.

"Mom!" Nicholas shouted running back into the foyer. "You're okay!" He threw his arms around her and hugged her tightly.

"Of course, I'm okay," she gasped. "I'm fine, honey." She kissed the top of his head.

"So, what did the doctor say?" Ruth turned to Carl and asked.

"The same old thing, keep that beesting kit close and be careful." Carl took a deep breath and sighed.

"Well that's sure comforting." Ruth smirked. "Doesn't he realize it's spring and bees are everywhere?" she asked rhetorically and shook her head. "Okay."

"Well, Mom, I think it's time I took Ariel home. I need to be getting home, myself. I still have to make dinner," Morgan said as she looked at her watch.

"Okay, dear." Ruth gave them each a hug and a kiss. "Thank you for your help this afternoon. I really appreciate it."

"Nick, could you help me out with my things?" Ariel asked her cousin.

Nicholas looked at his mother, still holding fast to her arm.

"I'm fine, go help her," Tamera said.

Reluctantly Nicholas let go of his mother and went with Ariel into the family room to retrieve her gifts.

"I think it's time for us to get going, too," Tamera announced. "It's been quite a day and I'm a little tired."

"I don't think you should be driving just yet," Ruth said. "Carl, would you please take her home for me? With everything that has happened today, I don't need any more worries. You and Dan can pick up your car tomorrow," she added to Tamera.

"Sure, honey." Carl took out his car keys and kissed

Ruth's cheek.

"Thank you."

Ruth and Claudia watched everyone gather their belongings and head for the front door.

"I'll stay and give you a hand with the dishes," Claudia told Ruth.

"That would be great." Ruth smiled, knowing that Claudia was really talking about taking care of their other problem.

Just then Peter walked in the front door. He looked around as, one by one, his aunts and cousins filed out the door in front of him.

"So, is everyone leaving?" he asked and looked at his mother.

"Yes." Claudia nodded. "But we're going stay for a bit."

"Mom, can I spend the night here, if it's okay with Grandma, please?" Peter looked at his grandmother and then back at his mother.

Ruth looked at her grandson and smiled as she stroked his hair. She could not help but see Steven when he was Peter's age. He had Steven's eyes and smile, even the same hopeful look. He was definitely his father's son.

"It's okay with me," Ruth said with a little laugh.

"If you're sure he won't be a bother," Claudia said, more as a warning to Peter than a question to Ruth.

"Gee, thanks, Mom." Peter kissed his mother's cheek and then gave Ruth a hug. "I really appreciate it, Grandma."

"You can sleep in the guest bedroom. Why don't you go wash up and I'll fix us a snack before dinner."

"Okay." Peter smiled and started up the stairs. "Bye, mom."

"You be good," Claudia told him and watched him disappear into the bedroom and close the door behind him. "Well, I guess I'll be on my way," Claudia said and picked up her purse. She took out her car keys. "I'll stop by the police station on my way home and fill out the report."

"I think it is a wise decision," Ruth said. She gave Claudia a hug and kissed her cheek, then watched from the front step while Claudia drove away.

Ruth walked back into the house and closed the front door behind her. She glanced up at the closed bedroom door. The house was finally quiet. She took a deep, restful breath, and walked over to the telephone. She dialed quickly from memory and then listened. The phone rang once. Twice. Three times. A click and Patty's voice messaging came on. Ruth sighed as she waited for the beep. She hesitated for a moment, trying to find the right words to say.

"Patty, this is Mom. Please come back home. We need to talk. I need to talk to you. Please, come. I love you. I'm sorry." She hung the receiver back on its hook and then walked into the kitchen.

* * *

Peter cautiously opened the bedroom door and raised his head to look over to the rail. The foyer was empty. Quietly he shut the bedroom door and leaned his back against it. He folded his arms and rubbed his shoulder. Thoughts of his conversation with Patricia returned.

Slowly he lifted the front of his shirt and took the pistol from his waistband. He walked around the bed and knelt down beside it, facing the door. As he stared at the pistol he replayed in his mind the message he just overheard his grandmother leave. Now he was more confused than before. He looked at the pistol and then shoved it deep between the mattress and box spring.

* * *

Ruth held the garbage can lid while Peter lifted the sacks of trash into the can. They closed the garbage can and

Ruth put her arm around his shoulders.

"Let's sit out here for a moment," she said and walked over to the bench.

Peter felt a little nervous anxiety, not knowing what she wanted. Still he went along with her. They sat down on the bench and stared up at the setting sun.

"Thanks for letting me stay," Peter said in an attempt to keep the conversation on a safe, neutral topic.

"Anytime you want to stay over, you can." Ruth slipped her arm around his and hugged him. "I want you to feel comfortable here."

Peter smiled at the words, but the truth was, he was not comfortable anywhere except in Matthew's arms, and that was something he could never tell her.

"Peter," Ruth continued. He noticed that her tone had changed and his heart began to pound nervously. "I heard what Nick said this afternoon."

"Yeah, it's nothing," Peter said, trying to sound disinterested, like it did not really bother him, hoping she would drop the subject.

"Do the kids at school really tease you?" she asked.

Peter rubbed his hands on his knees. This was not a conversation he wanted to have. His mouth went dry as his anxiety grew. He felt sure Ruth could hear his heart pounding in his chest.

"Yeah," he nodded, "but they tease a lot of the new guys."

Ruth furrowed her brow. "I hope it isn't true," she said. "I want you to know, if you ever want or need to talk about it, I'm here."

Peter nodded his head. Ruth smiled and kissed his forehead. She stood up and walked silently back into the house. He stayed seated and listened for the sound of the screen door closing. Hearing it, he put his head back and looked up at the star dotted sky. "Why didn't I just stay behind with you?"

* * *

The fire in the fireplace crackled, filling the family room with a warm glow. It was not really cold out; it was more for creating a relaxing ambiance. Ruth sat in her chair watching the flames. The house was quiet. Peter had gone to bed hours ago. Carl had been up and down twice to ask when she was coming to bed. She told him she could not sleep and she would be up later. She just wanted to think about Patricia.

How could she have been so foolish? Sure there was a lot to take in: the intruder, the gun, Patricia's confession. *She is still your daughter,* her conscience reprimanded her.

Feelings of guilt overwhelmed her and tears filled her eyes. Could Claudia have been right? Had she lost Patricia, too? Why would Patricia not return her calls? Ruth looked away from the fire and wiped her tears from her eyes.

The front door opened. Patricia quietly stepped into the foyer and closed the door behind herself. She tucked her house key back into the pocket of her jacket. The flickering glow of the fire in the family room told her where to go. Slowly she walked over to the doorway.

In the light of the fire, she could see her mother sitting in her chair. She hesitated to speak. Maybe this was not such a good idea after all. The look on her mother's face, in her eyes, was indelibly etched into her memory. The feelings she had, the loneliness and fear, engulfed her again. She turned away.

Ruth looked up and caught a glimpse of Patricia walking back into the foyer. Her heart leapt and she jumped to her feet.

"Patty?"

Patricia stopped and turned around. She looked at her mother. "You phoned?"

"Yes. I did," Ruth said. "Please, can we talk?"

"I guess." Patricia shrugged her shoulders.

"Would you like some hot tea?"

"Sure." Patricia followed her into the kitchen.

Ruth quickly poured hot water into two cups and dropped a tea bag into each. She motioned toward the dinette table where the cream and sugar bowls were already set.

The two women sat down.

Patricia played with the tea bag, dunking it several times but not really paying attention to it. She looked up at her mother.

"Patricia, I'm sorry about this afternoon," Ruth began. "It was all so overwhelming."

"I know, Mom, I'm sorry too. I never meant for that to happen."

"You wanted to tell me something, but I brushed you off. I'm listening now."

Patricia removed the tea bag and set it on the saucer. She took a sip of her tea and then set the cup down. She had rehearsed this moment over and again since she heard her mother's voice message but now her mind was a blank.

"Where do I begin?" she said, taking a deep breath. "When I was away at college, I met Jo. We were just friends. We'd hang out and talk. I knew she was a lesbian but it didn't bother me. After graduation, we went our separate ways and lost touch.

"Last summer I was covering a story about gay marriage and I ran into her. We talked and she mentioned she needed a place to stay, so I invited her to stay with me. I never dreamed it would turn out as it did."

"So, were you two lovers then?" Ruth asked.

"No, not exactly."

Ruth gave her a curious look that did not go unnoticed.

"I'm getting there," Patricia promised and continued. "Jo and I lived our own lives. She had her friends and I had mine. That was until I met Roger. He's a cameraman at work. He was assigned to work with me on another story. Well, Jo noticed that I was spending more and more time with him and she became jealous. When I told her I thought our being roommates wasn't working out and suggested it was time for her to move out, she threatened to tell everyone I was a lesbian and ruin my career."

"So, you never actually had sex with this woman?"

Patricia looked away, embarrassed and slightly ashamed. She looked back at her mother. "I was curious but it only happened a couple times, right after she moved in. It wasn't like she made it sound. We weren't lovers."

"But she thought you were," Ruth said, starting to understand both sides. "So, what about this Roger person, what does he have to do with this now?"

"Roger and I started seeing each other secretly, at least secretly on my part. I didn't tell Jo. I'd just tell her I had to work late. But then she started following me. One night, the night before Ariel's wedding rehearsal, I came home late and she met me at the front door. She demanded to know where I was, why I was late. I told her I had to work late. That was the first time she hit me. I threatened to go to the police, but she only laughed. She told me if I did she would say it was Roger who hit me. It would be her word against mine. The police would believe her because they would say I was just protecting him. So, I kept quiet and hoped it would pass.

"Last February, Roger took a job in Seattle. We stayed in touch. He told me about an anchor position opening at his station and I applied for it. This morning the station called the house to tell me I got the job, only Jo took the call. That's why she came here."

Ruth listened quietly. She did not know what to think or what to say. Seattle was only six hours away, but at that moment it felt like the other side of the world. Her baby would not be close by anymore.

"Mom, I'm really not gay," Patricia said, trying to reassure Ruth. "I was just going through a phase of finding myself. I know that I want to be married and have a family and the white picket fence. And I want to take a chance and see if Roger is the one for me."

Ruth sighed. How could she have been so blind to all

that was going on in her daughter's life?

"I'm sorry," she finally said, putting her hand on Patricia's. "I had no idea. I wish I could've been more of a help to you instead of acting as I did."

"It's okay." Patricia smiled. "It's over now. I spent the afternoon at the police station filing a report with them. When we went back to the apartment, Jo and all of her stuff were gone. I don't think she'll be back."

"But what about your career?" Ruth looked surprised. "Aren't you afraid she may still try to ruin it for you with her lies?"

"There are more important things in life than work, Mom." Patricia smiled. "Family."

"That's right." Ruth smiled back and squeezed her daughter's hand. "And family sticks together, in good times and bad."

CHAPTER FIVE
THE GATHERING

The warm mid-July sun shone brightly across the rolling hillside. Except for the occasional caw from a crow in the tall trees, a peaceful quiet filled the air. Below, stone images of angels stood guard over the bright, colorful flowers that dotted the hillside. Urns and marble slabs stood proudly in rows as remembrances of lives gone by.

In the distance, the gentle hum of an automobile engine drew closer. The dark-navy blue Bonneville slowed to a gentle stop at the crest of the hill. The engine shut off and the quiet once again returned. Ruth slowly got out of the passenger's side. In her hands she held a bouquet of summer flowers. She stood quietly staring out at the lovely view that only the visitors could see.

It seemed as though it were only yesterday when she and Carl stood on this very spot and chose this view for Steven. He would have liked it. She smiled at the thought.

Carl walked up beside Ruth and slipped his hand into hers. He smiled a nervous smile at her and wondered if she could read his thoughts. Could she tell how frightened and uncomfortable he was, not of the cemetery, but of himself? It had been a year since he had last come here. He could not bring himself to do it, to face the pain or the memories, not even the joyful ones. His heart pounded and his throat tightened. He looked at Ruth. She smiled and in her eyes he could see that she understood.

"Are you ready?" she asked, giving his hand a gentle

squeeze after seeing the tears in his dark-brown eyes. "I'd like us to have a few moments alone before the rest of the family arrives."

Carl swallowed hard, trying to force down the lump in his throat. He drew a deep, quivering breath. His hands were sweating. He nodded and they took a step onto the grassy hillside.

They walked passed stone after stone in silence. Carl glanced at the names and dates but not really reading them. Ruth stopped beside a gray marble stone and released Carl's hand. Slowly she walked around and faced it. She bent down and put her hand on the cold rock. She moved her hand over the inscription, gently tracing the letters as she had done every time she came there. She whispered, reading aloud from the headstone, "Steven Peter Wallace. Remember me with joy and laughter."

Carl's heart pounded in his chest. He dug his hands deeper into his pockets, turned his head away, and remembered. The small boy that caught his first fish, the excited look in his eyes as he reeled it in, and his proud grin when he showed his mother. The sparkle in his son's eyes and the smile that lit up his face as he looked in surprise at his first bicycle. That morning a year ago how he and Steven splashed about in the swimming pool, having fun. A smile found Carl's lips even as the tears fell from his eyes. It hurt to remember, remember that Steven was gone.

Ruth slowly laid the flowers on the ground at the base of the headstone. She looked up at the dates on the stone; images of the day she brought Steven home from the hospital filled her mind. He had been so tiny, so helpless. Her first son. She took a deep breath and slowly stood up. She slipped her arm around Carl's.

"It's hard to believe a year's already gone by." She sighed.

"Yeah," Carl agreed and nodded, afraid to say more.

"I remember thinking I couldn't imagine life without

him, how could I ever go on, and yet, here we are," Ruth continued, taking a deep breath and looking at her husband. "You poor dear," she said, turning to him and taking him in her arms, seeing his tears.

Carl held onto her tightly, his sobs breaking the peace of the morning.

"It's okay, honey," Ruth whispered into his ear, trying to reassure him.

The sound of an approaching car caused them both to look up. Carl took out his handkerchief and wiped his tears away. They started slowly back up the hillside. Carl smiled, watching the SUV stop behind their car on the edge of the narrow road.

"We made it," Tamera announced. She closed the passenger door and then froze when she looked at the headstone in the middle of the hillside below. She bit her lip and fidgeted while her parents approached.

"I don't know if I can do this, Mom," she whispered while giving Ruth a hug.

"If your father can do it, so can you."

"I'm gonna try." Tamera smiled nervously. She turned and hugged her father.

Daniel and Nicholas walked around the car and stood a few feet away. Nicholas had a single white rose, nervously twirling the stem in his fingers. He had picked the rose from the bush he had planted in their backyard in memory of his uncle. The first bloom of the year. White roses were Steven's favorite, or at least that's what his mother had told him. He looked down the hillside at the gray headstone and then up at the sky. Slowly he took a deep, unsteady breath.

"So, how're you doing, Dad?" Daniel shook Carl's hand and smiled.

"I'm actually doing better than I thought I would," Carl said with a smile. "I'd be lying if I said it didn't hurt, but it's getting better."

"Time, the healer of all wounds," Daniel said.

"Yeah," Carl agreed and nodded. "It's just that some wounds are deeper than others and will take a lot more time."

Another car pulled to a stop followed by a fourth and a fifth. The rest of the family had arrived. Ruth greeted Morgan with a kiss on the cheek.

"I'm so glad you made it." Ruth grasped Chuck's hand and smiled. "It's very nice of you."

"I wouldn't miss it. Although Steven and I weren't close, we were still brothers." Chuck smiled. He glanced over at Daniel and his smile faded. It had been nearly six months since their big blow up and they had not spoken to each other since. Chuck looked away.

"Tamera." Morgan walked over to her and held out her hands.

Tamera hesitated for a moment and then smiled. She hugged Morgan. Again Morgan whispered an apology into her ear.

"I know," Tamera whispered back. "It's okay, really."

Morgan looked at Nicholas as she and Tamera let go of their embrace. She noticed the white rose in his hands. Nicholas smiled politely at her. She turned around and rejoined Chuck.

Ariel and Mark slowly walked over to Ruth and the family. Mark carried a tiny blue bundle in his arms. Smiling proudly, he pulled back the blanket to show Ruth his sleeping son.

"He's so beautiful," Ruth cooed at her great-grandchild.

"He is, isn't he?" Mark beamed. "Wake up, Kevin," he said, gently bouncing him in his arms and lightly stroking Kevin's soft cheek.

Kevin grimaced but continued to sleep.

"Honey, let him sleep," Ruth said, giving them a welcoming hug.

"Hi, Grandma," Ariel said.

"Thank you for coming," Ruth greeted Ariel with a quick hug.

"Hi Mom, Dad," Bradley called while he and Benjamin

walked over to the gathering.

Ruth smiled at her son. She could tell by the way he stood that the divorce was taking its toll on him. She put her arms around his shoulders.

"Hello, son," she said into his ear and kissed his cheek. "I'm glad you finally shaved," she teased. "How're you both getting along?"

"As well as can be expected, I guess. Now it's a game of tug-of-war. She's still insisting on full custody of B—" he stopped himself and motioned with his head toward Benjamin. Ruth nodded. "But I'm not willing to give that. She's proven that she can't take care of herself, how is she going to take care of him?"

"You have a point," Ruth agreed and nodded. "Just don't lose sight of what is best for. . ."

"That's all I ever think about these days, Mom." He looked down at his son and smiled.

Ruth looked at her grandson and bent down. "My, that's a pretty white rose. Is that for me?" she asked playfully.

"No." Benjamin turned away to hide the flower from Ruth. "Is for Unkol Steeben."

Ruth smiled at how he was beginning to talk in sentences. So grown-up, and it warmed her heart that he was being told about Steven. She touched his cheek then stood up.

"So, do you think that Patty will make it?" Bradley asked while they walked over to join the others under the shade of a nearby tree.

"I don't know," Ruth sighed. "I've tried calling her cell phone and Roger's, but no answer. I don't know. It's hard to say."

"Since she moved to Seattle, it's a wonder if anyone ever hears from her," Bradley said, shaking his head. "What does anyone know of this guy she's seeing anyway?"

"Only that he was a cameraman when he worked down here. Patty seemed smitten by him but she didn't say much else." Ruth looked back, hearing another car approaching.

"Excuse me," she said and patted Bradley on the shoulder, gently nudging him to continue toward the others.

Claudia stepped from between the parked cars. In her black dress and pillbox black hat, she reminded Ruth of Jackie O. The three white roses she held contrasted sharply with her black-gloved hands.

Slowly Claudia walked over to Ruth. Her heart pounded nervously. Ever since she and Peter moved to town, she had avoided coming to the cemetery. *Somehow,* she thought, *seeing his grave would make it all too real.*

Peter closed the car door and stood looking out at the hillside filled with headstones. He put his hands into the pockets of his black dress slacks. He had refused to wear his suit. It'll be too hot, he complained, but actually he was never comfortable wearing the thing. He felt the envelope in his pocket and gave a heavy, quivering sigh. He looked over at Nicholas and then looked away as soon as their eyes met. Nicholas did the same.

"I'm so happy you made it," Ruth said and gave her daughter-in-law a hug. "Are you going to be okay?"

"I don't know," Claudia admitted. "We almost didn't come. All this time I've been kidding myself. Pretending Steven's just away on a trip or something. Coming here means that I have to face the truth, that he's gone and never coming back."

"Reality can be hard to take sometimes," Ruth said, nodding understandingly. "It's tough, I know, but eventually we all have to face it." She glanced over at Peter. He stood alone by the car staring down the hill at the headstones. "How's Peter doing?" she asked without looking at Claudia.

"I don't know." Claudia turned and looked over her shoulder at her son. "He's changed so much since we moved out here. After school ended for the summer, he's gotten to be so quiet. He keeps to himself a lot more. Something's bothering him and I don't know what it is or how to approach him about it," she said and sighed. "He received a letter the other day from a friend of his back in Indiana. It was the first time in a long time I've seen him smile, but that didn't last long. I wish I knew what was troubling him."

Peter began to walk down the hillside, his feet dragging. He looked at each of the headstones, reading the names, searching for the one that bore his father's name. Ruth and Claudia watched silently as he neared the grave.

Peter stopped sharply at Steven's grave. He crouched down and touched the engraving as if somehow by touching it, he was touching his father. The stone was cold. He stood up and looked at the ground beneath his feet. A tear came to his eyes for a man he never met. He looked up at the headstone.

"I know you can't hear me," he said softly. "You died before we could ever meet, but I wish we had. Maybe we would've even been friends. Then I would have someone I could talk to." He looked down at the ground again and a tear fell from his eyes and ran down his cheek. "I know that Mom loves me, but I can't tell her the things I'm feeling. I'm so confused. I don't know where to turn." He looked at the stone, then bowed his head and began to cry.

Ruth glanced over her shoulder at the line of cars, hoping that at any moment she would see Patricia. She desperately wanted the entire family together for this gathering to remember Steven. Disappointed, she turned back to her family and the group began to walk down the hillside to join Peter.

As the group gathered around the upright headstone, Claudia put her arm around Peter. The two took their place in the semicircle that formed around the grave. Mark stood between Morgan and Ariel, patting Kevin's back and rocking him gently in his arms. Tamera stood beside Nicholas, holding his hand. Every now and again, Nicholas shot a glare at Peter, a look that was meant to be noticed. Bradley knelt down next to Benjamin and they both looked at the headstone. He whispered into his son's ear and slowly Benjamin stepped forward. He dropped his rose on ground at the base of the headstone then quickly rushed back to his father's arms. One by one the rest of the family stepped forward and laid their flowers down.

After laying her rose down, Ariel knelt down and Mark handed Kevin to her. With one hand she touched the cold headstone and a tear came to her eyes.

"Uncle Steven," she whispered softly. "I wish you were here to meet your great-nephew, Kevin. You would've loved him like you did all of us." She kissed her fingers and pressed them against the stone. "I love you, Uncle Steven," she said and stood up. Mark helped her back into line.

"I miss you, big brother," Bradley whispered while he stood holding Benjamin in his arms. "I could sure use someone to talk to."

Ruth looked up at the top of the hill. Suddenly, a movement caught her eye. She took a step closer and strained to see. It was gone.

"Are you okay?" Carl asked while the family made its way back up the hillside to their waiting cars.

"Yes. I just thought I saw someone watching us. I guess it was just my eyes playing tricks on me."

As they reached their cars, the sound of a car approaching caused everyone to look up. A taxi stopped and Patricia stepped out, followed by a tall, slender, brown-haired man. Patricia straightened her black skirt, and then took the man's arm. She smiled as she walked over to the family.

"Hi, Mom, Dad," she greeted them with a kiss and quick hug. "I'm sorry we're late. Our flight was delayed and then the taxi driver. . . Don't get me started," she apologized and glared at the taxi driver as he drove away. "But we made it."

"I'm happy you did," Ruth said and gave her another hug. Her family was together again. When she stepped back, she looked at the man beside her daughter and held out her hand. "You must be Roger."

"I'm sorry," Patricia gasped. "Where are my manners? Mom, Dad, this is Roger Ferguson. Roger, this is my mother Ruth and my father Carl," she introduced.

"Pleased to meet you," Roger said in a deep voice. He

shook their hands.

"Well, the family has already placed their flowers and shared a quiet moment. If you want to go ahead, we can wait?" Carl invited.

Patricia looked at Roger then nodded and tugged on his hand. Roger gave in and the two slowly walked down the hillside together. Patricia glanced over at Peter and smiled a silent hello to him.

Peter did not smile back. He was confused seeing her with a man. She said she understood, but had she really? He turned away and a feeling of loneliness filled him. He walked back to his mother's car and sat down.

Tamera casually walked over to Ruth and stood next to her. The two watched Patricia place her flower on the grave.

"I see she's late as usual," Tamera said, irritated.

"At least she's here," Ruth said. "That's all that matters." Ruth looked at Tamera and then headed back to her car to wait for Patricia and Roger.

* * *

Ruth busied herself in the kitchen preparing lunch for the family. The scent of freshly brewed coffee and warm bread filled the house. She took the hot bread pans from the oven and set them on the cooling racks on the counter.

* * *

Outside, the second the SUV came to a stop at the curb in front of the house, Tamera opened the passenger door and stepped out. Daniel quickly took the keys out of the ignition and jumped from behind the wheel.

"Tamera!" he called to her as she started up the walk. "May I have a word with you?"

Reluctantly she nodded and waited for her husband to catch up.

"Go on inside," she instructed Nicholas. He hesitated for a moment then went on ahead.

"What's going on? You haven't said a single word since we left the cemetery," Daniel asked, guiding her across the lawn to the shade of the oak tree.

"I'm just thinking is all," she said, not intentionally being vague.

"About what?"

"I don't know," she answered. "I'm just having a difficult time with Patty's new beau. There's just something about him that bothers me and I can't quite put my finger on it."

Daniel shook his head. "Leave it alone, Tammy. Just let Patty be happy for once. Mom told us what she went through with Jo. Just be happy for her, okay?"

Tamera looked at Daniel's eyes while she thought. "Oh, all right," she conceded.

* * *

Morgan tied an apron around her waist and closed the oven door.

"That smells wonderful, Mom," she said, taking a deep breath. "I just love your cheese bread."

Ruth smiled proudly. She loved baking, especially when it was appreciated. "Thank you. Would you grab the lunch meat platter out of the refrigerator, please?"

Without hesitation Morgan did as she was asked. She set the tray on the counter and removed the cellophane wrap, still trying to organize her thoughts.

"Mom," she began cautiously. "Have you talked to Bradley since he started this divorce thing?"

Ruth continued to slice an already cooled loaf of bread. "A little. He's not much for conversation these days. Why?"

"I was just wondering how he's doing," Morgan said. "He doesn't seem himself these days."

Ruth paused for a moment and thought. It had been a

while since she and Bradley sat down for a good mother-son talk. The last time they spoke, he was worried because his attorney had the feeling the judge was siding with Amanda. She sighed and shook her head.

"I'll see if I can get him to talk to me this afternoon," she said and continued slicing the bread.

Morgan opened her mouth to say what was really bothering her, that she suspected Bradley was drinking again, but decided it would be best to wait. She returned to the refrigerator and retrieved the relish tray.

* * *

Tamera opened the front door and stepped into the foyer. She froze, causing Daniel bump into her.

Across the room Patricia stood wrapped in Roger's arms. She smiled at him, looking into his blue eyes and feeling his short, dark-brown hair, mustache, and goatee with her fingertips. He was everything she had dreamt of. Strong, handsome, hardworking, but most of all, in love with her. She kissed him.

"Oh, that's so disgusting!" Tamera quipped as she walked past them. "Get a room!" She disappeared into the family room.

Patricia looked at Daniel with questioning eyes.

"Don't mind her," he said, closing the door behind them. "She's in a mood."

"I guess." Patricia laughed and pulled herself free of Roger's arms. "I didn't get the chance to introduce you two at the cemetery. This is Roger Ferguson, my. . ." she paused and looked at him. He smiled and nodded. "My boyfriend." She smiled back at him. "Roger, this is Dan. He's my sister's husband."

"I got that." Roger laughed and held out his hand to Daniel. "Pleased to meet you." They shook hands.

"Likewise," Daniel said. "Please forgive Tamera. I

don't know what's wrong with her today. Could be just *today*."

"No problem," Roger answered. "I understand. Patty's told me how special Steven was and what he meant to the family. I know it's rough."

"Thanks," Daniel said. "Good to meet you. I'll see you later." He smiled at them and then continued on his way.

Roger waited until they were alone before he looked at Patricia, pulling her back into his arms. "What's wrong? Why didn't you tell him?"

Patricia kissed him and then pulled herself free of his arms. She really did want to let the family in on their secret, yet she was not sure that the anniversary of Steven's death was the right time. She looked back at him.

"I think we should wait a bit and see how the day goes." She frowned. "Besides, you have to ask my dad first, remember?"

"Sure," Roger said and smiled. He took her hand and the two of them joined the others in the family room.

Claudia was not really listening to Tamera going on about Roger while they sat on the sofa in the family room. She was watching Peter through the window. He was standing by the edge of the swimming pool in the backyard.

When Patricia and Roger walked into the room, Tamera instantly shut up. Claudia took the opportunity to excuse herself and went outside.

Slowly she walked over to her son and put her arm around his shoulders. "Are you okay?" she asked.

Peter looked at her and shrugged. Claudia frowned.

"Still thinking about your father?" she asked, trying to get him to talk.

"Yeah," Peter said and continued to look at the shimmering water by his feet. He could not tell her what he was really thinking about. She would not understand.

He felt the letter in the pocket of his slacks as he dug his hand deeper. He'd been carrying it around with him since the day he received it. When he first saw it in the pile of mail on the kitchen table at home, he was ecstatic. He recognized Matthew's handwriting. He took the letter to his bedroom, sat down on the floor and leaned against his bed. He read it four times, before finally looking up. He closed his eyes and took a deep breath, savoring the warm feeling inside his chest.

His joy had been short lived, however, because two days later another letter arrived. This time from a neighbor to his mother. The neighbor had recognized the boy in the picture as the one who used to hang around with Peter. The letter explained that she had clipped the article from the local newspaper and mailed it, thinking Peter might want it. When Claudia showed it to him, Peter could not believe his eyes. The article had a photograph of Matthew with his arm around a girl, both with big grins on their faces. Beneath the photo was an announcement of their engagement. Peter forced a smile and tried to act unaffected by the news. He had told his mother he was happy for Matthew and then gone to his bedroom. Shutting the door, he turned around and leaned against it. Sliding down to the floor, he buried his face in his arms and cried.

"I wish you had met him," Claudia continued, unaware of Peter's real thoughts. "Your father was such a thoughtful, fun guy to be around. I think if you had those memories to draw on, it would be a comfort for you now."

Loud laughter coming from the family room caused Claudia and Peter to look over their shoulders.

"I wonder what that's about?" Claudia said, hinting that they both should go into the house.

"Go on in," Peter suggested. "I really don't feel like partying right yet."

"You know," Claudia said, frowning sympathetically and looking into his eyes. "Sometimes it helps to be around other people when you are feeling down."

"I know," he agreed, "But right now I just want a few more minutes to myself."

"Okay," she relented. "Just don't stay out here all day." She kissed his forehead and then went back inside to the family, leaving Peter and his thoughts by the pool.

"Better grab a plate and get some food before it's all gone," Carl called to her.

Claudia smiled at the sight of the family all crowded around the kitchen counter. Ruth held out a plate as she walked over to get in line.

"Don't worry," she told Claudia. "There's plenty."

Ruth took another sip of her coffee and stepped back to let Claudia squeeze her way up to the counter. Ruth noticed that Roger was standing back, politely waiting his turn.

"Don't be shy, Roger." Ruth laughed. "You've got to elbow your way in if you want something."

Morgan emerged from the crowd, her plate piled high with a sandwich, potato salad, coleslaw, and baked beans. She walked over to her mother and picked up a mug. Ruth filled it with coffee.

"A bit hungry today?" she teased.

"No, I'm going to go find Bradley. Would you make sure someone gets Benji something to eat?" she asked.

Ruth nodded to her daughter, pleased that she had taken an interest in the family. Things were changing. Her children were finally growing up. She smiled.

* * *

Morgan paused when she saw Bradley sitting alone at the dining room table. She walked over to him and set the plate down in front of him.

"I thought you might be hungry," she said quietly.

Bradley looked at the sandwich plate. He smiled and lifted the top slice of bread. "You remembered," he said.

"Of course I did." She laughed. "I was the one who made your sandwiches every day when we were kids. Dry, no mayo and lots of lettuce and tomatoes."

"Thanks, sis," he said with a nod. "But I can't eat."

Morgan sat down at the table across from him. She

looked around and sighed.

"Boy, this brings back memories, doesn't it?" she said and looked at her brother again. "We always sat across from each other when we were kids, and look at us now."

Bradley did not look up. Instead, he looked at the melting ice in his glass and sipped on the water.

"I brought you some coffee. I thought you could use it," she said, motioning toward the steaming cup. Bradley did not look at it.

Morgan looked around the room for a moment to collect her thoughts. She was nervous about bringing up the subject, not knowing how he would react. She looked at her hands and then back at Bradley. "I've noticed that you've been awfully depressed since you started this divorce," she began.

"You think?" he retorted sarcastically.

"Bradley," Morgan snapped. "I mean it. How are you doing?"

"How do you think?" he said in the same sarcastic tone. "I'm losing my wife, maybe even my son. How do you think I feel?" He looked around the room as though searching for something, then he turned back to her, his expression softening. "Have you ever done something totally stupid and wish you could go back, change it?"

The image of Luke's young face flashed in her mind. She nodded quietly in response.

"I think I made a big mistake," Bradley continued.

"What do you mean?"

"I should never have put her in that center. Then she wouldn't have felt I betrayed her, and she wouldn't have insisted on this divorce or be trying to take my son away from me."

Morgan fought the urge to say something when he paused to take a sip from his empty glass; she wanted him to keep talking. Silently she slid the coffee cup closer to him. He did not take it, did not even look at it.

"I still think about her constantly," he continued.

"Everywhere I turn in that house, she's there. I've taken down pictures, rearranged the furniture, even repainted some of the rooms, but she's still there. Why didn't I put up more of a fight about the divorce?"

Morgan reached out and touched her brother's hand. "I'm sorry," she said. "I know it doesn't help much, but I do care and am worried about you. Have you been able to talk with her?"

"Only through the lawyers," he said. "I don't want to do this anymore. I still love her."

"Have you told her?"

"Don't be ridiculous. I can't tell her that now. My lawyer said it would be a sign of weakness and then her lawyer would have a field day with me." Bradley scoffed.

"Then maybe it's time you moved on. I mean, sell the house and get a place for you and Benji to start over," Morgan suggested cautiously.

"I can't. She wants the house too." He finally looked at the coffee cup. "Do you have anything stronger than that?"

Morgan looked at the coffee and then back at him.

"Bradley, you don't need to start drinking again. You've done so well for so long, don't go back."

Bradley smiled smugly. "Too late," he said, holding up his empty glass and then giving a little laugh.

Morgan slumped in her chair, disappointed, concerned, and worried for her brother.

"Well, I can't help you there," she said. "Correction, I won't help you with that. You and I both know what happened the last time you started drinking. Think about it." She stood up and left him alone again with his thoughts.

* * *

The front doorbell chimed. Tamera jumped up from the table in the breakfast nook. "I'll get it."

The doorbell rang a second time as Tamera crossed the

foyer. "Coming!" she called. "Some people," she muttered under her breath.

She opened the front door wide to find a young man with blonde hair and blue eyes standing on the porch. From the look of his letterman's jacket she guessed he was into sports in school.

"May I help you?"

"Is there a Peter Wallace here?"

Tamera glanced over her shoulder just as Peter walked into the foyer. *He has the same disinterested expression that he had at the cemetery,* Tamera thought.

"Hey, Peter," she called to him. "It's for you."

Peter looked up at his aunt and then noticed the man in the doorway. He gasped and smiled, rushing to the door and nearly knocking Tamera out of the way. He threw his arms around the man and hugged him, giving him a quick peck on the check.

"What're you— How—" Peter kept cutting himself off as his mind whirled with questions.

"I take it you two know each other?" Tamera asked, eyeing Peter and the visitor curiously.

Peter turned around, his arm still around the man's shoulders.

"Yes, Aunt Tammy," Peter said, still grinning happily. "This is my friend, Matthew," he half-introduced them. Grabbing Matthew's arm he tugged. "Come on in," he invited.

Matthew pulled back, fixed on Tamera's suspicious expression.

"Actually I can we go somewhere and talk, privately?" he said.

Suddenly Peter remembered the picture from the newspaper and the engagement. The excitement drained from his face as quickly as it had come.

"Sure," Peter said and stepped away from him. He looked at Tamera.

"Go ahead, I'll tell your mother," she said, ushering

them out the door.

"Thanks, we'll be at the park."

Tamera nodded silently, watching them until they were out of sight. She closed the front door slowly and replayed the scene in her mind, remembering how Peter's face lit up when he saw Matthew, their hug, the sudden change in Peter when Matthew would not come inside, the kiss. Even though it was on the cheek, it still seemed an odd thing for a boy of his age to do to another boy. Without reaching a conclusion, she turned around and returned to the family room.

* * *

Ruth poured Claudia and Patricia another cup of coffee then set the pot down on the warming plate in the center of the breakfast nook table. She slipped into the chair across from Claudia.

"Ah, it feels good to sit down at last," she sighed, smiling at her daughters.

"So, what do you think of him?" Patricia asked, nodding her head and looking across the room at Roger. He stood talking with Chuck and Carl by the fireplace. Every now and again, he would glance over at her and wink.

Ruth turned her head and took a quick look at Roger, then shrugged and sipped her coffee. "He seems nice, but I really haven't had a chance to talk to him," she said in her best disinterested tone.

Claudia did not say a word. She glanced over in Roger's general direction but her thoughts were on Peter.

"I think he's the one," Patricia whispered and continued to grin.

"Oh?" Ruth sipped her coffee and continued her little game. "That's nice, dear. The one for what?"

Patricia cocked her head and swatted at her mother. "Mom, you know," she said and laughed. "The one I want to marry."

"Oh," Ruth said, nodding with raised eyebrows. "Has he asked you yet?"

Patricia's smile faded. She had not been expecting that question. "Ah," she hesitated. "Well, we've talked about it," she said, avoiding a direct answer.

"Well, you let us know when he has and we'll have our little mother-daughter talk," Ruth teased and patted Patricia's hand.

"Mother," Patricia sighed. "I'm trying to be serious here."

"I know," Ruth said sincerely. "I just can't help teasing you. You know, this is the first boy you've brought home to meet the family in a long time."

Patricia recoiled at her mother's observation although she tried not to show it. What did she mean by that? Was she trying to bring up Jo? Patricia suddenly became uneasy. She looked across the table at Claudia, desperate to change the subject. "Well, you sure are quiet this afternoon."

Claudia looked at Patricia and then Ruth. "I'm sorry. I'm just concerned about Peter. That's all."

"How's he doing? I haven't really had a chance to talk to him since I moved away. Did he finally come out of the closet?" Patricia asked carelessly.

Claudia looked at Patricia with wide, shocked eyes. "What?"

Immediately Patricia realized what she had done. "Oh, there I go again," she chastised herself. "Forget I said that."

Claudia put her coffee cup back on the saucer and reached over and grabbed hold of Patricia's hand, squeezing it tightly. "No, you need to tell me what's going on," she said through clenched teeth.

Patricia looked to Ruth for help. It was not going to come. She looked back at Claudia and continued to try to pull free. "Okay! Okay," she gave in.

Claudia released her hold and put her hands around the warm coffee cup.

"You remember three months ago, at the shower, when he and Nick were fighting? Well, I went after Peter and we had a talk. He told me that he's gay. He's known it for years but is afraid to tell us, you, for fear of being rejected," Patricia said quietly.

Claudia listened but did not know what to say. She looked around the room but her mind was blank.

"He met a boy at school and fell in love. He didn't want to move out here but he wanted you to be happy. He knew how important it was to you," Patricia finished.

Claudia looked at her. "I had no idea," she finally said. "That explains why he's been so depressed. Oh how could I have been so blind?" She looked down at the table.

Ruth's mind flashed back to her conversation with Patricia the night of the shower. Even though it went against every sense of morality, she had been willing to overlook it for the sake of her daughter. She remembered the feeling of relief when she found out it was not true. But now this, this was different. Peter was not her child. He was Steven's; the only part of Steven still with them. She could not bear the thought of losing him all over again.

"It's okay," she heard herself say to Claudia. "You can't know everything. Children do keep their secrets from us."

"The one fear he has," Patricia said to both of them. "He's afraid that if you knew, you would be ashamed of him and stop loving him."

"Oh, that would never happen," Claudia said, shaking her head. Her eyes filled with tears as she realized how isolated and lonely he must be feeling. "He's still my son and I want him to be happy, no matter what. If he's gay, then he's gay. I'll always love him."

"Then let him know," Patricia urged gently. "He needs to know that."

Claudia stared at Patricia for a moment. "Did he say who his friend was?"

"I think he said a boy named Matthew?"

"Hey, Claudia," Tamera said returning to the table. "Peter wanted me to tell you that he went to the park with a guy named Matthew."

Claudia's heart jumped, and she looked at Tamera in shock. "He's here?" she said.

"No," Tamera said, confused. "They went to the park."

Ruth glared disapprovingly at Tamera.

* * *

The park was nearly empty. Matthew and Peter walked shoulder to shoulder. The warm summer breeze gently stroked their faces and ruffled their hair. They walked over to a picnic table in a secluded part of the park, away from view. Matthew sat down on the table, putting his feet on the attached wooden bench, and faced Peter. He remembered all the special moments they shared and thought about the things he came to say.

Peter avoided eye contact with Matthew, choosing to look at the ground instead. Ever since they moved away nearly nine months ago, he had dreamt of Matthew showing up on his doorstep and whisking him away in his arms. Matthew was here and everything was going to be all right again, but that was only a dream. The image of Matthew with that girl kept popping up in his head.

"How did you find me?" Peter asked.

"It wasn't easy," Matthew said. "When you weren't at your house, I tried looking in the phone book. I must have called every Wallace listed before one of them told me where your grandparents lived."

"So, how long are you going to stay?"

"I don't know." Matthew shrugged. "My sister lives not too far from here and I'm staying with her. She wants me to move out here, but I don't know."

"I hope you do," Peter said and then realized his slip. "But you're getting married. Our old neighbor sent us the newspaper clipping."

Matthew looked down. He struggled with what he had come to say.

"Pete," he said softly, his voice deep and manly. He hesitated. "Thank you for the graduation gift. You didn't need to get me anything, you know."

"I know, but I wanted to," Peter said and shrugged.

Slowly Matthew stood up and ran his hands through his hair. It was obvious to Peter that he was frustrated about something. Matthew turned his back to him.

"You're not making this easy," he said and turned back around. "Peter, I came all the way here because we need to talk."

"Okay."

"Pete, when you and your mom left, I did a lot of thinking. What we had between us was wrong—"

"What?" Peter gasped. "Wha-what do you mean, wrong? For the first time in my life, I felt normal. I felt that someone in this world cared about me. It wasn't wrong. What's wrong is you marrying that girl. That's wrong."

"Peter, stop," Matthew said and reached for Peter's hands.

"Me stop?" Peter stepped back and pulled his hands away. "What about you? I can't believe you came clear out here, just to tell me this." Tears began to fill his eyes and blur his vision.

Matthew sighed and looked at his hands. "No. I didn't. There's something else."

Peter shook his head in disbelief. He looked up at the sky as if to say, *Why me, God?* His heart was breaking. He turned back to Matthew. "No. I don't want to want to hear anymore. I can't. Get away from me." He choked and began to cry. "Leave me alone." Peter took a step away from Matthew.

"Pete, I'm sorry," Matthew said feeling a lump rising in his throat and tears welling up in his eyes. "I still love you."

"Don't!" Peter snapped, holding one hand to his lips and the other held up to keep Matthew away. "Don't say that to me again," he said firmly though his voice trembled.

"But, it's true," Matthew pleaded.

"No! You love her. That's what the paper said," Peter snapped and looked around frantically, not really knowing what he was looking for. "Why did you have come here? Why don't you just shoot me?"

Peter turned around and began to run. Matthew stood looking around confused. How could this have gone so wrong? *Why wouldn't he let me explain*, Matthew thought. He looked up and saw Peter leaving the park at a blind run.

"Pete, please, wait!" He began to run after him, knowing Peter was not about to stop.

Tears blinded Peter so that he could not see where he was running. He tripped on something and hit the ground hard. He lay on the ground, out of breath and sobbing, as much from the pain in his knee as in his heart.

Matthew stopped and gently turned Peter over. He wrapped his arms around Peter and held him tightly to his chest while Peter continued to cry and struggle to free himself.

"I'm sorry. I'm sorry," Matthew repeated.

Peter stopped struggling and hugged Matthew back until he could not cry anymore.

"Let's get you back to your grandparents," Matthew said and lifted Peter to his feet. "Do you think you can walk? Just lean on me."

Peter gave in without a word, letting Matthew help him back to the house. He looked at his jeans. The right leg at the knee was torn, dirty, and red from his blood. When they reached at the front door, Matthew turned Peter around to face him.

"Are you okay?" he asked.

Peter looked at him. "Why does it matter, how I feel. You said so yourself, it's wrong. So, I'm wrong. You were all that kept me going. It's over now. She won."

"Pete, you have it all wrong. I told my parents—"

"I can't do this. You know my aunt once told me that I should be myself that if I try to live a lie then life's not worth living. So, just go."

Peter turned around and walked into the house, closing the door behind him. The sounds of laughter and noisy chatter emerged from the family room. He looked up at the guest bedroom door and started up the stairs.

* * *

"So, what do you do now?" Carl asked Roger as they stood by the fireplace in the family room.

"I'm still a cameraman for KOMO-TV News as well as doing some freelance work. Whenever anyone needs a spare cameraman they call me. I film footage for commercials, movie location shots, whatever," Roger explained. He looked over at Patricia and winked.

"Sounds interesting." Chuck raised an eyebrow and smiled. "Is there much money in that?"

"It brings in enough. I'm not rich by any means. It would take me a long time before I could ever think of owning a place like this even. The main thing for me is that I enjoy what I do. Not many people can say that about their nine-to-fives."

"True," Carl agreed with a nod and a sip of his coffee.

"Do guys in your line of work move around a lot?" Tamera asked.

"I guess so. I started out in Sacramento then moved to San Diego. Before coming to Bend I worked in Salt Lake City and Denver. Now I'm in Seattle. So, I'd have to agree. You have to go where the news is."

"That why you stayed single?" Chuck probed.

Roger gave a hearty laugh. "I guess so, but who said I was single?" Roger sipped his coffee while Chuck choked on his.

Carl laughed. "Roger, you got him that time." He turned to the family. "That's enough of the interrogating. Let's not scare away Patty's guy."

"Thank you, daddy." Patricia walked over and put her arm around Roger's back.

The conversation drifted into sports and other mundane banter. Patricia noticed Roger's coffee cup was empty and went to get a refill.

Walking into the kitchen, she noticed Tamera was making a fresh pot. She glanced back at Roger. He was involved in a conversation with Carl.

"So, what do you think of Roger?" Patricia asked as she leaned against the counter. She could tell that Tamera did not approve of him.

"Don't ask," Tamera said, trying to avoid a confrontation.

"No." Patricia nudged her playfully. "I really want to know."

"All right," Tamera said coldly. "You could do better."

"What?" Patricia laughed out of shock. She had not been expecting such a blunt answer. When Tamera did not laugh too, Patricia started to get angry. "Fine. Why do you say that?"

"How well do you really know him?" Tamera said and looked at Roger. "I get this feeling he's hiding something. I don't know what it is, but I'm sure of it. I've seen his type before. You'd be better off dumping him before things get serious."

Patricia sucked in her cheeks and glared at her sister while she mulled over what Tamera said. Inside she struggled to keep from lashing back at her. "Exactly what type is that?" she asked, remembering the guys that Tamera dated before Daniel.

"Oh, they're clever," Tamera said with a sneer. "They give a good first impression. Very smooth. Say just the right things. All hugs and kisses. Then the ax falls and their true colors show. I haven't figured out yet what he's hiding, but I will."

"So, what's Dan hiding?"

"Hey, you asked me, remember?" Tamera said, taking offense to Patricia's insinuation.

"Oh my, I hit a nerve." She laughed. "Think what you

want, but all I have to say is, you're barking up the wrong tree. Roger's not like you, he has no secrets."

A shiver ran up Tamera's spine. She looked at her sister and wondered what she meant by her comment. "Patty, we all have our secrets, even you," Tamera retorted.

"Believe what you want," Patricia snapped. She grabbed the coffee pot, filled Roger's cup, and then stormed out of the kitchen.

Tamera turned back to the sink more determined than before to find out what Roger was hiding. She could not explain it but something was not right. He was hiding something.

* * *

Claudia walked into the parlor and looked around. She sighed, nervously wringing her hands, and walked back into the foyer. She looked up and noticed Ariel coming down the stairs with Kevin in her arms.

"Have you seen Peter?" she asked, walking over to the staircase.

"No, Aunt Claudia," Ariel said and shook her head. "Why? Is something wrong?" She noticed how nervous her aunt seemed.

"No." Claudia smiled. "I just wanted to talk to him, that's all." She turned around and started back to the family room.

Ariel watched her curiously. Carefully she stepped off the stairs so not to wake Kevin. The front doorbell chimed. Kevin jumped in her arms and began crying.

"Oh, damn it, people!" she cursed, patting Kevin's back and rocking him. She turned around and opened the door. Standing on the front steps were two uniformed police officers. They removed their hats when they saw her.

"Good afternoon, ma'am, my name is Officer Martin Bead," the middle-aged, gruff-looking officer greeted her.

"How can I help you?" she asked politely but

cautiously.

"Is there a Mark Jones here?" he asked.

"Why do you ask?" she said without thinking. Her thoughts were racing in every direction, trying to guess what the police would want with her husband.

The younger officer smiled at her, realizing her shock. "It's okay, ma'am. We just need to talk to him," he assured her.

"Certainly." Ariel's voice cracked nervously. "Please, come in." She stepped aside, holding the door open with her back as the two policemen entered. "I'll get him. You can wait in the parlor." She motioned toward the empty room, then used her foot to kick the front door closed.

"Thank you," they said, walking into the parlor.

Martin began to look over the photographs on the mantle. He paused when he saw the one of Mark and Ariel's wedding. Picking it up, he turned around to his partner.

"Hey, Tom, take a look at this," he said and handed over the framed photograph.

"What do you know, Martin," Tom nodded and handed it back. "Mrs. Jones."

Moments later Mark walked into the parlor followed by Ariel, Ruth, and Carl.

Martin set the photograph back on the mantle and turned around to face them.

"This is my wife, as you have seen by the picture," Mark said, to let them know he saw them with the photo. "And these are her grandparents, Mr. and Mrs. Wallace. They own this house," he added as an explanation to why they were there.

"I'm Officer Martin Bead and this is my partner, Officer Tom Poe." Martin nodded to them and then turned back to Mark. "We'd like to ask you a few questions if we may. When was the last time you saw your parents?"

Mark looked confused. "About a week ago. They're away on business."

"What sort of business?" Martin pressed further.

"Maybe you should be asking them?" Mark said,

increasingly uneasy with their questions.

"I think it would be best if you and Mrs. Jones sat down," he instructed.

Mark turned and motioned for Ariel to sit down on the love seat with him. She did so without a word.

"What's this all about?" Mark insisted.

Tom looked at his hat in his hands and then at Ruth and Carl. Martin straightened his back and took a deep breath and looked at Mark.

"I regret to inform you there has been a plane crash," he said gently.

Mark sat back on the love seat and looked at them, confused. Ariel gasped and grabbed hold of Mark's hand while she covered her mouth with her other. Mark did not say a word.

"Your parents' private jet went down just after takeoff in Columbia. There were no survivors. I'm sorry."

The words hit Mark like a blow to the gut. He gasped for air and leaned forward on his knees. Ariel tried to put her arm around him but he pulled away. There were no tears, just shock. Slowly he sat back as he caught his breath and looked at Ariel.

"I need to go home," he said in a daze.

"I'm afraid that won't be possible, son," Officer Bead said. "The FBI has been investigating a group of cocaine smugglers. As part of the War on Drugs, your parents' house and property have been seized under the assumption that it was all purchased with money from drug trafficking."

"But Grandma," Ariel said, looking at her for help. "Kevin's clothes and crib?" She turned to the policemen and her anger blazed. "My baby's clothes and his things were not bought with drug money. My family and friends gave those to us and you have no right taking them."

"Ma'am." Tom stepped forward. "When the FBI is through with their investigation any property wrongfully seized will be returned."

"When will that be? When he's fifty?" she snapped at

the officer. She looked at her husband. He did not say a word, just stared blindly at the coffee table.

"Officers," Ruth said stepping forward. "Is it possible to continue this at a later time? This is quite a shock." She looked at Mark and Ariel with sympathy.

"Certainly, ma'am," Martin said, nodding understandingly. "But we need to take Mr. Jones with us, flight risk and all."

"What? No!" Ariel protested. "Mark?" she said, turning toward him.

Mark looked at her and then at the policemen, still unable to speak. Memories of the many trips his parents had taken over the years suddenly made sense.

"We'll vouch for him," Carl said. "He can stay the night with us and we'll bring him down to the station in the morning."

"Just give me a few minutes," Mark said in an unsteady voice. "I'll answer your questions. I don't mind."

Ariel drew back and looked at her husband. Her anger toward them was replaced by confusion.

"Mark?"

"It's okay," he assured her.

"Are you sure, son?" Carl asked.

"Yes, Grandpa, I am."

"Okay," Martin said and nodded to his partner.

"Well, in that case, may I get you some coffee?" Ruth offered.

"Sure, that would be nice," Tom said.

"I'll just be a minute." Ruth smiled and left the room, grateful for the chance to leave and process what she had just heard.

As she entered the kitchen, she motioned to Morgan and Chuck. The two of them walked over to her. She quietly relayed the news to them and they immediately left to be with their daughter and son-in-law.

* * *

A. M. Huff

Peter sat on the floor behind the bed in the guest bedroom. Images of his many walks with Matthew flashed in his mind; laughing, talking, feeling safe. Then suddenly Matthew's voice echoed in his ears, turning everything ugly. Wrong! Wrong! Wrong! Tears continued to stream down his cheeks. Slowly he turned around and reached deep between the mattresses. His hand found what it was searching for. He pulled it out and turned around, his back against the bed. He stared at the pistol, turning it in his hands as though inspecting it.

In the foyer below, the front doorbell chimed. Carl excused himself and went to answer it. Claudia rushed into the foyer just as Carl opened the front door.

"Hello," Matthew said, smiling nervously at Carl. "Is Pete here?"

Carl turned and looked at Claudia. Claudia rushed to the door.

"Matthew," she said and gave him a hug. "So good to see you."

"Hi, Mrs. Wallace," Matthew greeted her. "I'm looking for Peter."

"Wasn't he with you?"

"No. Yes. I mean, he was. We went for a walk and to have a talk. He got upset and started running back here. He tripped and hurt his knee, so I helped him back. He told me to leave but I just walked around the block."

"I'll leave you two," Carl excused himself and returned to the parlor.

"Why would he be upset?" Claudia asked.

Matthew's heart beat faster as he became nervous. He thought about whether or not to tell her and then decided to just say it. "Can we talk privately?" Matthew invited her outside.

"Sure." Claudia stepped out and closed the door behind her.

The two walked silently over to the bench by the side garden and sat down. Matthew looked up at the sky and rubbed his hands on his legs.

"Matthew," Claudia said softly, anticipating what he was about to say. "I already know about you and Peter."

Matthew's head turned sharply and looked at her in surprise. "You, you do?"

"Yes." She smiled.

"But how?" he asked, still shocked and confused. "I was sure we were careful. How long have you known?"

"I just found out. I admit it's quite a shock."

"Pete told you?" Matthew asked but did not really expect an answer. "I suppose you also know that I'm supposed to be getting married?"

"Yes, I saw the newspaper article," she said and looked at him. "You don't seem very happy about it."

"No, I'm not," he admitted. "That's why I came out here. I don't want to get married. I've just made such a mess of things," Matthew said, feeling exasperated.

"Perhaps it would feel better if you talked to someone?"

"Oh no." He shook his head. "I'm through with shrinks."

Claudia nodded. "Maybe just talking with a friend would be better."

Matthew turned and looked at her. "I wish my parents were as understanding as you, but they're not. My father and mother have great plans for me. I was supposed to work for the family business, get married, and have the specified number of children. They've got it all mapped out." He stretched out his arms in front of them as though showing Claudia his future.

"At first I tried telling them that I had other ideas about what I wanted to do with my life, but they wouldn't listen. They said the decision was already made.

"So, I told them that I was gay. Big mistake. It took two weeks for my black eye to go away. Then I spent every Friday night for the rest of my senior year in therapy.

"The whole marriage thing and the newspaper article, that was their idea. She's the daughter of my dad's business partner."

"Does she know how you feel?" Claudia asked.

"Yes, I told her from the start. She wasn't really behind this marriage idea either. Seems her parents were forcing her to get married because she's pregnant and they didn't like the guy she was seeing.

"So, I sort of ran away. My sister lives in Redmond and offered me a place to stay, so I jumped at it. I tried to explain it all to Pete, but I even messed that up. He got the wrong idea and is really upset. I think I hurt him and honestly that was the last thing I ever wanted to do."

Claudia smiled at Matthew. "I'm sorry you had to go through all of that. From a parents' viewpoint, when your child's born you have all these hopes and dreams about how they'll turn out. You want only the best for them. You want them to be healthy and happy. You dream of grandchildren one day. Learning that your child is gay, it's more than just a shock. It's not the life I would've chosen for Peter. But like my sister-in-law told me, that's my problem, not his. And while I'm disappointed that I'll never be a grandmother, I'm happy being his mother. Gay or straight doesn't matter to me, I just want him to be happy and I know how happy he was with you."

Suddenly the crack of a gunshot rang out from inside the house. Claudia and Matthew jumped to their feet and ran into the house.

Inside, the two officers ordered everyone down on the floor. They crept into the in the foyer, guns drawn, looking up at the second floor. When the front door burst open, the two officers spun around, guns aimed directly at the shocked and surprised pair. Claudia and Matthew froze in the doorway, hands in the air, hearts pounding.

"Don't shoot!" Matthew yelled.

The officers started to relax and lower their guns.

"Peter!" Claudia screamed and lunged for the stairs.

Officer Bead grabbed her around the waist and held her back.

"Let go of me!" she screamed and twisted in his arms.

"Calm down! Calm down!" he repeated, tightening his hold on her. "Let us check it out first. Tom, go on," he called over his shoulder.

Tom cautiously crept up the stairs, his back against the wall, gun trained on the bedroom door directly above the foyer.

Matthew fell back against the threshold of the front door. A sinking feeling drained him of all his strength as he thought about what Peter said. He pressed his hands on his scalp and slumped down to the floor.

"Please, God, no," he said softly as tears filled his eyes.

Claudia began to cry hysterically as she watched Tom move slowly across the open hall above toward the bedroom door. His pistol at the ready, he turned the doorknob with his free hand then kicked open the door.

"Martin, get an ambulance. Now!" he yelled at his partner, then disappeared into the room.

"Peter, no!" Claudia screamed and collapsed on the floor. Ruth rushed to her and held her in her arms. She glanced at Carl as he dialed.

Martin ran up the stairs and into the bedroom.

"The ambulance is on its way," Carl called out to the officers. He walked over to Ruth and helped her and Claudia to their feet.

"Do you have any clean rags or bandages?" Tom shouted from the bedroom.

"Yes," Ruth answered quickly. She looked at Claudia. "Stay here."

Carl put his arm around Claudia while Ruth hurried up the stairs to the linen closet and pulled out a brand new, white sheet. "Will this do?" she asked walking into the bedroom.

"Yes," Martin said, grabbing the sheet from her. In one swift movement, he tore it in half.

Ruth stood in the doorway, frozen. For a split second she saw Steven lying in his bed, staring blindly at the ceiling, cold and lifeless. She gasped and covered her mouth.

"I could use some help over here," Tom said as he pressed his hands over the wound on the side of Peter's head.

"Mrs. Wallace!" Martin's voice jolted her out of her thoughts. "Help him!" he ordered as he continued ripping the sheet into strips.

Ruth rushed to Tom's side and began handing him the pieces of torn sheet. Her heart skipped a beat as she looked at Peter lying on his back across the bed. Blood splattered his face and soaked the bedspread around his head and left shoulder. She covered her mouth with her hand and fought back the tears that flooded her eyes.

"Is he. . ." she asked, fearing the answer.

"No. The bullet appears to have grazed the side of his head," Tom said and placed a folded piece of the sheet over the wound and applied pressure to try to stop the bleeding. "The bullet lodged in the wall near the ceiling. Here, hold this tightly but not too tight, we don't know if his skull was fractured."

Ruth moved quickly to do as she was instructed.

"Oh, Peter," she breathed and looked at his pale face.

Tom ran to the other side of the bed and knelt next to Peter's head. He took a long strip of the sheet and began wrapping it around Peter's head to hold the pad in place and maintain the pressure.

"Where did he get that gun?" Tom asked in a businesslike tone while he worked.

"It's his mother's," Ruth said. "He must've taken it from the table months ago and hidden it."

"Is there any reason why he would want to kill himself?"

Ruth looked up at him surprised by his comment. She looked back at Peter. "What makes you think he tried to kill himself?"

Tom tore the end of the strip in half and tied it around Peter's head. "I've seen this a dozen times but usually they aren't so lucky."

Ruth stepped back as both of the officers gently lifted

and turned Peter onto the bed. As Tom began taking Peter's pulse, Ruth looked at her blood-reddened palms. Slowly she walked to the bedroom door.

The sound of clanking and voices downstairs brought her to the rail. The EMTs were bringing a backboard up the stairs. The gurney was left in the foyer, waiting to carry Peter to the ambulance and then the hospital.

Ruth stepped out of the way to let them by and then went down the stairs. Claudia and Matthew gasped at the sight of her hands. Patricia quickly handed Ruth a damp towel she retrieved from the kitchen.

"Is he?" Claudia asked, tears streaming down her face.

"He's still alive." Ruth hugged her.

No one noticed Matthew slip past them and up the stairs. He walked into the bedroom just as the paramedics lifted Peter onto the backboard. The sight of Peter unconscious and the blood was more than he could take. He choked and tears began streaming down his cheeks.

"Please," he said pushing his way to Peter's side. "I have to tell him something."

The paramedic on the other side of the bed looked at Matthew and reached across Peter, touching Matthew's arm to get his attention. "We have to get him to the hospital," she said in a gentle voice.

"But I just want him to know that I love him," he told her. "He has to know that I need him."

The woman released Matthew's arm, not sure what was going on and not really caring. "You'll have to step out of the way," she said, the gentleness in her voice gone. "Okay, on three. One, two. . ."

Martin grabbed Matthew by the arm, pulling him out of the bedroom and out of the way. He restrained him as the EMTs emerged from the room and headed down the stairs. Matthew followed, still being held back by the policeman. When the paramedics reached the foyer, they placed Peter on the gurney and wheeled it out the front door to the waiting ambulance.

Martin then released his firm hold on Matthew.

"This is all my fault," Matthew cried.

"No, Matthew." Claudia took his arm and hugged him. "This isn't your fault."

"We best get to the hospital," Ruth said, putting her hand on Claudia's back.

Carl grabbed the car keys from the table next to the telephone. "I'll drive," he said. He glanced at the policemen who gave him an approving nod.

Ruth, Carl, Matthew, and Claudia rushed out the front door. The police turned and looked at Mark and Ariel. Tom gave them a sympathetic smile.

"You promise not to leave town?" Martin said to Mark.

"I'm not going anywhere," Mark assured them.

"Then we'll talk tomorrow. Be down at the station at ten."

Mark nodded and watched them walk out the front door.

"Oh my god," Patricia said, resting her face against Roger's chest. "Poor Peter."

Tamera looked at Patricia. "What do you expect from a couple of queers," she said and shook her head.

Patricia turned around and glared at her sister, shocked by her callousness. "You don't know what you're talking about, so why don't you keep your mouth shut!" she snapped, furious.

Tamera's mouth dropped open in shock at her sister's tone. "I saw them kissing," she said disgustedly. "They're queers."

Without thinking Patricia slapped Tamera across the face. Tamera responded by clenching her fists and glaring back at her sister.

"Don't you ever say that about them again!" Patricia yelled through clenched teeth. "You're not so perfect yourself. Do Mom and Dad know about your little secret?"

Tamera's mouth dropped open as she stood staring at her sister in shock, growing angrier as she realized what Patricia knew. Not willing to back down, Tamera pointed her finger at

Patricia's face.

"I'll let this one go, but don't ever slap me again, or it'll be the last thing you do." She turned around, grabbed her purse, and stormed out the front door. "Nick, Daniel. We're leaving!" she yelled over her shoulder.

Daniel and Nicholas quickly followed without a word.

Roger wrapped his arms around her protectively Patricia. "What was that all about?" he asked looking at the open front door.

"She's just been a bitch today," Patricia said with lingering hostility. She pulled free of Roger's embrace and walked back into the kitchen.

Roger looked at the others and shrugged before following her.

Morgan gently handed a sleeping Kevin to Ariel.

"Here, honey. I should see if I can clean up the bedroom before they get back. We can talk later, okay?" She gently touched both Mark's and Ariel's cheeks and smiled sympathetically.

Ariel nodded, her head still spinning. She was overwhelmed and could not focus her thoughts. She turned around and walked back into the parlor.

Mark closed the front door, still numb and in shock over the news that his parents were dead. He could not even begin to process the news about the drugs. He looked at Ariel and wondered what she was thinking. Slowly he walked into the parlor.

Ariel sat on the love seat and gently rocked Kevin. She did not look up at her husband. She just kept looking at her peaceful, sleeping baby.

* * *

Bradley stepped into the doorway of the bedroom, silently watching Morgan strip the blood-dampened comforter and sheets from the bed. Aside from the soiled linens and the hole in the wall, the bedroom did not look any different than before. He watched Morgan tie the sheets into bundle.

"Could you use a hand?" he asked quietly.

Morgan looked up and nodded. "Sure, Brad." She smiled.

Together they finished bundling up the rest of linens and then turned back to the bed. The blood had not reached the mattress. *At least that's good,* Morgan thought. She threw the blood dampened pillow next to the bundle of linens.

"Would you get a clean set of sheets and the spare pillow out of the closet?" she asked and pointed down the hall.

"Sure," Bradley said and retrieved the items she requested. "What a day," Bradley commented, dropping the linens on the bed.

"Tell me about it," Morgan said, unfolding one of the sheets. "First mom tells me that Mark's parents are killed in a plane crash and now this. I don't know about this family sometimes."

"I know what you mean. I haven't been much help either, with my moping around and all. Damn, I wish that Steven were still here. I could always talk to him and he always knew what to say. In a way, like you did earlier."

Morgan looked up at him as she tucked the sheet in on her side of the bed. She could not remember what she had said earlier. She smiled uncertainly.

"You're right. Drinking isn't the answer and it sure isn't going to help me keep Benji," Bradley continued. "Maybe it is time for another change too. I think I'll talk to a realtor."

"Good," Morgan said and smiled at him. "If you need any help, I'm here. Now, grab that pillow case for me."

Bradley smiled and handed her the pillow case.

* * *

Mark sat down next to Ariel and looked around the room, at the mantle with its many pictures of the family, the wingback chairs, and the crystal floor lamp. He had never really noticed how nicely the room was decorated before. How warm and safe it felt.

He looked at Ariel and Kevin and thought about his own childhood. His parents' home never felt this warm, comforting, and safe. It always seemed so cold with its marble tiles and stark white walls. Even in his bedroom, the one room that was totally his, he had never felt like it belonged to him.

Gently he put his arm around Ariel. He realized the reason why he had no tears for his parents was because they were strangers to him. As far back as he could remember, they were always gone on business trips or to parties, so they said. As a child, he never questioned it, not even when the police had searched the house in the middle of the night.

"They're just checking for monsters, so you can sleep safely," his nanny would tell him.

Now everything was so clear. How could he have been so blind? He took a deep breath and kissed Ariel's cheek. She leaned into him.

"Everything's going to be okay," he whispered.

Ariel looked at him. "Is it?" she asked disbelievingly. "What's going on, Mark? What did those policemen mean when they said Mom and Dad were trafficking drugs?"

"I guess it's true, but, Ariel, I had no idea and I was never involved in it. Now when I think about it, the things that happened when I was growing up finally make sense."

"It's true?" Ariel repeated, shocked. Her thoughts becoming muddled. "What're we going to do? What about Kevin? Mark, where are we going to live?"

"Let me worry about that. Everything will be all right. Tomorrow, I'll tell the police what I know and then we'll go from there."

"Oh, Mark, I'm scared." Ariel laid her head on his shoulder.

Mark took a deep breath. He was frightened too, but he could not let her know.

CHAPTER SIX
THE WEDDING

A warm September breeze blew through the trees in the front yard as Daniel parked the SUV next to the curb. Tamera pursed her lips as she looked out at her parents' house. Two white mesh paper bells hung on the front door. The white and pink crape paper streamers, draped along the walk on lawn stakes, gently waved in the air. Tamera turned her head away from the house.

"Tamera, just let it go," Daniel said sternly, taking her hand in his.

"I can't," Tamera seethed and jerked her hand away from him. "I can't just forget what I found out about that bum my sister's about to marry."

"Nothing was proven. He was never under any suspicion. The paper said it was a break-in accident, for god's sake. It could've happened to anyone," Daniel pleaded.

"That's exactly why I can't let it go. What if Patty were next?"

"Mom, look who's here," Nicholas interrupted.

Tamera looked out her window just as Claudia opened the front door for Matthew and Peter. Matthew held Peter's arm, helping him step up and through the doorway.

"Oh great," Tamera said, throwing her hand in the air. "What's a wedding without a couple of fairies?"

"Tamera!" Daniel snapped at her. "What in the hell has gotten into you? I will tell you this right now, if you so much as say one word out of line today, we're finished. I'm leaving.

You've been nothing but a bitch since you heard about this wedding and it has got to stop."

Tamera continued to look out her window, unfazed by his threat.

"Tamera, do you hear me?"

"Yes. I heard you!" she turned and snapped at him.

"I'm not kidding this time," Daniel said and opened his car door. "I'll be inside." He slammed the car door and walked into the house alone.

"Dad isn't going to leave us," Nicholas said, patting her shoulder.

"I know," Tamera sighed. "He just doesn't understand. That's all."

"Are we going inside?" Nicholas asked, looking out the window while more guests arrived.

"Yes." Tamera heaved another sigh as she opened her car door.

* * *

The family room was filled with excited chatter. Guests signed the guest book and then made their way into the backyard. Ruth looked up from directing the flow of guests to the back door and smiled when she saw Claudia, Matthew, and Peter walk into the room. She hurried over to them.

"Oh, I am so happy you all made it." She gave Claudia a hug and a kiss on the cheek.

"You look wonderful, Mom."

Ruth looked down at her ivory dress studded with silver rhinestones. She had not been sure about wearing the dress. Tradition dictated that only the bride should wear white, but the salesgirl insisted that times had changed and anyone, especially the mother of the bride, could wear whatever color she chose. Ruth did not quite believe her, but she bought the dress anyway. Now, with Claudia's compliment, she felt more at ease about her decision.

"Thank you." She smiled. "Well, we'd better get you up those stairs and changed if you're going to be the matron-of-honor."

Ruth turned and looked at Peter and Matthew. "My, don't the two of you look nice." She smiled at them and gave them both a welcoming hug and peck on the cheek.

"Thank you, Grandma," Peter said, returning her smile. "Matthew picked out my suit," he said, looking at his lightweight, gray-blue suit. The color matched Matthew's suit with just enough difference in style that they were not identical.

"Well, you sure do have good taste in clothes, Matthew," Ruth said and nodded at him. "I'm glad you made it too and I know your aunt Patty will be happy to see you both." She smiled again at Peter, placing a gentle hand against his cheek. The scar from the bullet was very noticeable just above his temple. "How are you feeling, dear?"

"I'm doing okay." Peter nodded and smiled at her despite his being lightheaded and weak. "Mom and Matthew are helping me a lot." He looked up at Matthew lovingly.

"That's wonderful." Ruth looked at Matthew. "I truly mean that. Thank you for helping Peter."

"I'd do anything for him, Mrs. Wallace. He means the world to me," Matthew said.

"I know." Ruth nodded, noticing the sparkle in Matthew's blue eyes whenever he looked at her grandson. However, despite her trying to be open-minded, she still felt a little repulsed by the thought of the two boys being together. "Why don't you boys go out back and find yourselves a seat. I need to get your mother upstairs on the double!"

"Okay, Grandma." Peter nodded, careful not to move his head too quickly. He held tightly to Matthew's arm as they made their way through the back door.

Claudia watched the boys until she was sure they were safely seated.

"Still worried about him aren't you?" Ruth put her arm around Claudia's shoulders, guiding her toward the stairs while they talked.

Claudia sighed and looked at her mother-in-law. "I can't help it. I hoped he would be well by now but I guess I have to be more patient. I'm still worried though."

"I imagine it's hard, even though the police report said it was an accident, knowing that your child came that close to actually killing himself has to make for some sleepless nights."

"It's not just that. Peter's still having these really terrible headaches and has been so dizzy lately. As you noticed, he's still having trouble walking."

"What have the doctors said?" Ruth asked, opening the door to Bradley's old bedroom. On the bed, carefully laid out, was Claudia's dress.

"They keep telling me it's normal for this type of injury and it takes time for the body to heal itself. I don't know." Claudia shook her head as she unzipped her skirt and stepped out of it. "I just can't help but worry. I came so close to losing him, too. Did you know the police wanted to take Peter away from me? One of the paramedics heard what Matthew said up here that day and figured Peter needed more help than he was getting at home. A woman from Social Services even paid me a visit."

"I heard rumors to that effect," Ruth said as she zipped up the back of Claudia's dress. "Don't let that bother you. Peter is and will be just fine. The police don't know everything."

"Thank you, Mom."

"For what?" Ruth smiled.

"For staying by us. I know this isn't easy for you. I remember our conversation about six months ago out back." Claudia patted Ruth's hand as it rested on her shoulder.

"It's true. I don't understand or profess to agree with his lifestyle, but I do love him very much and have to respect him for who he is." Ruth gave Claudia a gentle hug.

Claudia turned around and looked at her reflection in the mirror. She ran her hands over her stomach and adjusted the bodice. "Why do they have to make these things so hideous?"

she asked.

"It's so the bride always looks best," Ruth said with a laugh.

* * *

Matthew sat silently next to Peter, still holding onto his arm while the rows of chairs filled up around them. He could not help but notice when one of the ushers escorted a couple to the empty chairs next to them, the man whispered something to the usher, who then turned around and showed them to different seats. Matthew looked at Peter, hoping that he had not seen what happened, but by the look in Peter's eyes, he had.

"Maybe I shouldn't have come." Peter sighed, near tears.

"Nonsense," Matthew said, putting his arm around Peter and hugging him. "Remember, we're here for Patty and to hell with everyone else."

"But this is my family," Peter protested. "I could take it from strangers, but it's different when it's family."

Matthew nodded understandingly and hugged Peter even tighter.

Daniel stood in line at the back door and watched as one by one the ushers escorted the guests to their seats, avoiding the empty chairs next to Peter and Matthew. He was angered by the obvious shunning the boys were receiving from people who should be supportive. Even Morgan and Chuck were escorted to seats three rows away from them. *Intentional or not, they could've chosen to sit with the boys,* Daniel thought. He watched as an usher approached him.

"Are you with the bride's family or the groom's?" the usher in a black tuxedo asked.

"The bride's," Daniel replied. "There are actually three of us. My wife and son will be out here in a few minutes."

"Fine, sir. Right this way."

Daniel followed the usher up the center aisle between

the rows of folding chairs. The usher directed him to a row in front of Morgan and Chuck. The row was already crowded, with only three chairs left unoccupied in the middle. Daniel stopped next to Matthew and put his hand on Matthew's shoulder. Speaking directly to the usher, Daniel said in a voice loud enough to be heard by many of the guests. "I think my family and I will sit here with my nephews."

The usher's mouth dropped and he blushed with embarrassment. He quickly joined Daniel and pretended to show him to the seats.

Matthew looked up at Daniel and smiled. It was the first time anyone had included him as part of the family. *It feels good,* Matthew thought.

Daniel winked and smiled. Matthew helped Peter to his feet and they moved further down the row to make room for their uncle and his family. Daniel took his seat next to Matthew.

Tamera stood at the back door, looking around the backyard. Rows of chairs were set up between the house and swimming pool. The pool, shimmering in the sunlight, was dotted with floating bouquets of red roses and daisies surrounded by greenery. A sturdy wooden bridge, constructed perfectly by Carl, spanned the swimming pool, dividing it in half. Garlands of greenery and roses were draped along its handrails. Just beyond the bridge, one of the large trees had been cut down to make room for the new gazebo that stood at the end of the aisle. Everything looked wonderful. She could not help but feel a little jealous. *My wedding wasn't this grand,* she thought.

She glanced to the buffet tables set up beneath the kitchen window on the patio to her left. A four tier wedding cake dominated the center of the longest table, flanked by tapered candles. Slowly Tamera walked over to the table. She picked up the champagne glass with the word *Groom* etched onto it. She was tempted to drop it, shattering it on the concrete, but then thought better of it. She set it back down and turned around just as Roger stepped through the back doorway.

He looked at Tamera and smiled. Then he did the unexpected, he walked over to her.

"So nice to see you again," he said, trying to be polite. "How have you been?"

Tamera met his smile with an intense glare. "I know all about your little secret," she whispered.

Roger pulled his head back, giving her a confused look. "Oh, you do, do you?" he said. "And just what is it?"

"I know about your first wife," Tamera hissed.

"So does Patty," Roger answered, unconcerned.

"Does she know you killed her?"

"What?" Roger nearly shouted. He took her by the arm to move her to a more private place but she twisted out of his grasp. He lowered his head and glared at her. "Are you crazy? I did *not* kill Christine."

"Is that so?" Tamera smiled to herself seeing his reaction. "Is that why KWGN news in Denver fired you? They seemed to think otherwise. Yeah, I know all about that too," Tamera said smugly, noticing the surprised expression on his face. "If you think for one minute I'm going to just sit back and let you marry and then murder my sister, you've got another think coming!"

Roger clenched his jaw tightly, struggling to keep from making a scene. "I did *not* kill my wife, Tamera, and you can go to hell," he said and turned around before Tamera could reply. He calmly made his way around the chairs toward the gazebo.

Tamera watched him greet the guests along his way. Her anger was still raging inside her when she saw him stop and shake Peter's hand. She caught sight of Daniel seated next to Matthew and her mouth dropped open.

"That son-of-a-" She stopped when she spotted Nicholas walking her way.

"Mom, do you see where dad's sitting?" he asked, looking over his shoulder at his father.

"I'll take care of this!" she snapped. "Nicholas, come on."

Ignoring the ushers, she marched down the aisle, stopping at the end of the row where Daniel, Matthew and Peter were sitting. Daniel looked up at her and he motioned to the two empty seats beside him. Tamera's face reddened to the color of the dark-pink roses that dotted her mid-calf length dress.

"Daniel, there is no way I'm sitting next those two faggots," she cursed through clenched teeth, loud enough that everyone turned around and looked at her.

Daniel smiled and stood up. He walked over to her and leaned down to her ear. "You will sit where I tell you to sit. Now get your fat ass over there, sit down, and keep your mouth shut." He glanced at Nicholas who appeared about to protest. "And that goes for you too, Nicholas. March."

"Do I have to, Mom?" Nicholas protested.

Daniel grabbed his son's arm tightly. "When I tell you to do something, young man, I expect you to do it. Do you understand me?" Nicholas looked at his father in quiet shock. "Now sit down and shut up."

When Daniel started back to his seat he noticed Matthew helping Peter to his feet. "Where are you two going?" he asked.

"It's okay, Uncle Dan, we're leaving." Peter was trying not to cry in front of his aunt. "It's obvious that no one wants us here."

"Peter, no. Don't go," Daniel pleaded.

"We appreciate everything you've tried to do for us, Uncle Dan," Peter said, trying to smile as a tear fell from his eyes. "But I think it would be better for Aunt Patty if we left."

Just as Matthew helped Peter into the side aisle, Ruth quickly walked up.

"What's going on here?" she asked in a hushed voice.

"Matthew and Peter are leaving because of your daughter's mouth, Mom," Daniel answered.

"What?" Ruth said, looking at Peter. Her protective instinct kicked in when she saw his tears. Immediately she took his face in her hands. "Matthew, please help Peter back to his seat. You two aren't going anywhere." She turned to Tamera. "You, get in the house, now! I want a word with you," she said sternly. She turned around without letting Tamera respond and headed back into the house.

Suddenly Tamera felt like a child. Memories of being disciplined by her mother came flooding back to her. She could not stop the feeling of panic that began to engulf her. Her anger was gone, replaced by fear. She looked at Daniel as though asking for help. He turned his face away from her, still incensed by how cruel and intolerant she was behaving. Tamera pushed Nicholas into the chair next to his father before heading back to the house.

Nicholas quickly moved back into the seat on the end of the row, away from Daniel. He looked straight ahead, ignoring everyone, folded his arms over this chest, and pouted. Daniel turned toward Matthew and Peter. He reached over and took Peter's hand, giving it a reassuring squeeze. "Don't let people like your Aunt Tamera win," he said and smiled. "Don't give them more power. They're not worth it."

"Thank you," Peter said gratefully.

Daniel smiled back with a nod and wink. He sat back in his chair. Peter reminded Daniel of someone he had not thought about in years. He too had been gentle, kindhearted, and gay. *If only things had been different back then maybe he wouldn't be just a memory,* Daniel thought.

Daniel looked at the gazebo. His thoughts returned to the present. Roger stood beside the justice of the peace, laughing and talking in hushed tones. *Tamera hasn't ruined the day,* Daniel thought.

* * *

Tamera closed the back door quietly behind her. The family room was empty except for Ruth standing in front of the fireplace. Cautiously, Tamera walked over to her. Ruth sighed heavily and Tamera knew she was angry.

"Just what is the matter with you? You've done nothing but berate Peter and make him feel unwanted ever since you found out that he's gay."

Tamera felt her muscles tighten in defiance. She was no longer a frightened little child who cowered in front her mother, fearing her anger.

"I think what they're doing is disgusting and I don't want my son subjected to their perverted behavior," Tamera said boldly.

"What?" Ruth raised her voice and an eyebrow as she looked at her daughter.

"I don't want them to try to recruit my son into being queer like them. There, is that blunt enough for you?"

Ruth slapped Tamera across the face. "Don't you ever use that tone with me again, Missy! I'm still your mother and I will not put up with it."

Tamera covered her reddened cheek and tried not to cry.

"As for the boys," Ruth continued. "Don't be so stupid and ignorant. No one can make anyone gay. You either are or you aren't. Furthermore, Peter is part of this family, like it or not."

"Well, I don't have to like him because you say so!" Tamera snapped back at her mother.

Ruth felt her temper growing. Part of her wanted to take Tamera and shake some sense into her, but another part understood her revulsion. Homosexuality went against everything she ever believed in. It was not natural. However, she understood too that it was not Peter's or anyone's fault. He was the way he was, just as Tamera was, but that did not give her the right to treat Peter and Matthew so rudely.

"It is true. I can't force you to like anyone, but I can tell you this. This is my house and in my house all of my children are to be made to feel welcome and that includes Peter and his friend, Matthew. If you don't like it, you know where the door is. Is that blunt enough for you, missy?"

Tamera drew in a deep breath. She looked at her

mother. She could tell that Ruth was furious and that at any moment she could lose her temper, but at the same time she was too stubborn to give in. "Yes," she retorted.

"The choice is yours. Either stay and keep your mouth shut and pretend to be human, or get the hell out of my house and don't ever come back!" Ruth snapped back and then left the room.

Tamera stood by herself in the empty room, weighing her options. She looked out the window at the gathering in the backyard and thought about why she came. It was settled. She would stay. She had more important business to tend to.

* * *

Ruth opened the door of her bedroom and walked inside. She smiled proudly as she looked at her baby girl standing in front of the mirror in her wedding dress. Patricia looked so beautiful. Her auburn hair was twisted and pulled up in the back, making her neck seem long and statuesque.

Patricia turned her head and looked over her shoulder as her mother walked up behind her. She took a deep but shaky breath.

"Nervous?"

"A little," Patricia admitted.

"It's okay, I was on my wedding day," Ruth assured her. She picked up the strand of pearls from the vanity.

Patricia turned back to face the mirror. Ruth reached around hung the pearls around her daughter's neck. She fastened the clasp and put her hands on Patricia's shoulders. "There, something old," she told her. "Your grandmother put these on me on my wedding day and now, I give them to you."

"They're so beautiful. Thank you, Mom." Patricia turned around and hugged her mother.

"You are beautiful," Ruth whispered into Patricia's ear.

When Patricia turned back to face the mirror, Ruth noticed the sudden change in Patricia's expression. She put her hands on Patricia's shoulders.

"What's the matter, dear?"

"I don't know, Mom," Patricia said, looking at their reflections in the mirror. "I just have a strange feeling that something's going to go wrong."

"Everything's going to be fine. Honestly, you worry too much, dear."

"I guess," Patricia agreed. She turned back around to face Ruth. "When you married Daddy, how did you feel?"

"Oh, I felt excited, nervous, and scared all at the same time. But I also I knew I couldn't live without him and that's what got me down that aisle," Ruth said, remembering her wedding day.

"Mama, I don't think I love Roger," Patricia blurted.

"What?" Ruth gasped, surprised by Patricia's sudden revelation.

"I mean, I do love him," Patricia said, trying to sort out her feelings while she spoke. "I'm just not sure I'm in love with him. I'm so confused."

"Patricia, you think too much," Ruth said, taking her daughter's hands. "Not everything needs to be analyzed to death. You've got cold feet, that's all. Getting married is a huge step. 'Until death do you part,' remember? It's only natural to be a little nervous. But you'll be fine. Roger's a good man. He loves you, without a doubt. Everything will be fine."

"I hope you're right," Patricia said and smiled uncertainly.

"I am and you'll see that too."

A knock at the door interrupted their conversation. Ruth turned around. "Yes?"

The bedroom door opened and Carl stepped into the room. Ruth smiled at her husband. He looked so handsome in his black tuxedo and white shirt.

"Well, it looks like everyone has shown up down there and we're about ready to start," he announced.

"In that case, I best be getting down there." Ruth leaned

forward and gave Patricia a soft kiss on the cheek. "I love you, dear. I'm so proud of you."

"I love you too, Mama," Patricia said, fighting back tears. "Thank you for everything."

Ruth left the room and hurried down the stairs. As she reached the foyer she glanced at the parlor and froze. A smiled spread across her lips and she rushed into the room.

"Amanda." She hugged her former daughter-in-law. "I'm so happy to see you. How are you?"

Amanda hugged Ruth tightly not wanting to let go. "I'm fine," she said as Ruth pulled away.

"Honest?"

"Yes, Mom, honest," Amanda said, nodding. "I see you still have Brad's and my wedding picture on the mantle." She glanced over her shoulder at the family pictures.

"Yes," Ruth sighed. "I guess I'm still hopeful that you and Bradley will get back together."

Amanda gave an uncertain smile and looked at the floor, then back up at Ruth. "I received an invitation to Patty's wedding," she said, changing the subject. "So, here I am."

"Well, I'm sure she'll be happy you came," Ruth said and hugged Amanda again. This time Ruth noticed that Amanda had gained a few pounds over the last year. She was no longer just skin and bones.

"So, have you seen Brad?" Amanda asked and straightened her dress.

"Yes, he and Benji are out back."

"Is he with someone?"

"You mean did he bring a date? No. To be perfectly honest with you, he hasn't been seeing anyone."

The sound of the bedroom door opening upstairs caught Ruth unprepared. She glanced over her shoulder and then back at Amanda

"Come on," she said, taking Amanda's hand. "We've got to find you a seat."

The two hurried out the back door. The ushers were

already standing in their places by the bridge, waiting to take the bridesmaids across. Ruth held up her hand, stopping them from leaving their post and helping her to her seat. She walked down the center aisle quickly, stopping next to Bradley.

"Here," she said, directing Amanda to the empty chair next to Benjamin, not giving her a chance to object. She rushed off and took her seat in the front row.

Bradley jumped to his feet and stepped into the aisle, giving Amanda room to get to her seat. For a second, their eyes met and he smiled. Amanda looked down but smiled and bit her lip.

"Mama!" Benjamin squealed, reaching for her as she sat down beside him.

Bradley took his seat again. The music began to play. He could not take his eyes off her. He could not believe she was there. She looked at him while she held Benjamin on her lap.

"Hi," he mouthed a greeting to her and continued to grin.

"Hi," Amanda mouthed back, smiling coyly. "You look great."

"Thanks," he mimed and looked at his gray suit, the same one he had worn to their wedding over four years earlier. He was surprised that it still fit, but he had lost weight himself since the divorce.

"Are you here with someone?" Bradley asked, looking around.

"No," Amanda responded, shaking her head.

Bradley smiled bigger.

Everyone turned toward the aisle.

In the family room, Claudia handed Patricia her bouquet of roses and baby's breath. She smiled at her sister-in-law but could not help feeling a bit envious. She wished she and Steven would have had a wedding like this.

"Well, this is it, Patty," she said. "Be happy. You deserve it."

"Thank you, Claudia," Patricia said, smiling through

her veil.

Claudia, dressed in a pastel pink, ankle-length bridesmaid dress with matching pumps, slowly walked down the aisle following the other bridesmaid.

As soon as Claudia was across the bridge, Carl turned to his daughter. "You ready?" he whispered.

"I think so." Her voice quivered and she tightened her grip on his arm.

Outside the last refrains of the music from Love Story faded away. There was a brief moment of silence and then the familiar chords of the Wedding March began. Carl and Patricia stepped through the doorway into the backyard. Everyone stood up, turning toward the aisle as they slowly made their way to the bridge.

Ruth watched her daughter, smiling proudly through her tears of joy. Morgan held tightly to Chuck's arm, tears streaming down her cheeks. *That fraud,* Ruth thought and smiled, *you do love your sister after all.* Ruth looked at Roger. He looked so handsome in his tux standing by the bridge waiting to take his bride across.

Patricia glanced at the guests as she passed each row. She smiled and winked at Peter and Matthew. *They made it,* she thought.

However, her smile vanished when she saw Tamera's disapproving stare. She turned her head away and fought the feeling that something was going to happen to spoil her day. She looked back at Roger and the feeling vanished.

Roger glanced over at Tamera. When their eyes met, he glared at her, almost threatening her to keep her mouth shut. Tamera defiantly glared back.

Daniel noticed the exchange between them and put his hand on Tamera's and gave it a firm squeeze. Tamera looked at him and winced.

"Don't you dare say a word," he whispered firmly to her, then turned his attention back to the wedding.

Carl kissed Patricia on her cheek and whispered, "I love

you," into her ear. He took her hand and placed it in Roger's. With a smile he left them to sit next to Ruth. Roger then guided Patricia cross the bridge and into the gazebo where they stood before the justice of the peace.

The music faded away and the Justice opened with a few words of greeting to the congregated family and friends and then turned to Patricia and Roger. Patricia kept looking into Roger's brown eyes. She could not stop smiling. All she could think about was becoming Mrs. Roger Allen Ferguson.

"Is there anyone here present that knows of some reason why these two should not be united, let them speak now or forever hold their peace," the Justice asked, looking beyond the couple at the faces of the guests.

Roger held his breath, knowing that Tamera was behind him staring at his back. The silence seemed to drag on for an eternity. His heart pounded. His hands began to sweat. Tiny beads of sweat formed on his brow and he wiped them away. He looked at the Justice and tried to signal him to continue.

"Well, then," the Justice said, breaking the silence. "Let's continue."

Roger heaved a heavy sigh of relief and smiled at Patricia.

"I'm sorry. I can't let this happen," Tamera called out from behind them.

Patricia suddenly snapped back to the present. She was confused. Had she really heard what she thought? She turned around and looked at the faces of her family and friends. There standing in the middle of them was Tamera. Daniel had ahold of her arm and was pulling at her to sit back down.

"No. Let go," Tamera said and pulled away from him.

"Tamera, you're making a fool of yourself," Daniel said sternly. "Have you no feelings for your sister?"

"Yes, I do," Tamera said, stepping into the aisle. "I do have an objection," she stated firmly to the gathering.

Patricia looked at Ruth in shock and disbelief. How could this be happening? Ruth saw the hurt in Patricia's eyes and she felt her pain and embarrassment. As she turned her head to look at Tamera her anger grew. She and Carl both sprang to their feet and rushed her.

"What do you think you're doing?" Carl snapped.

"This time you've gone too far, Tamera," Ruth added.

"Family, friends, please," the Justice said stretching his hands out over them. "Please return to your seats and remain calm. I've been marrying people for years and so far there hasn't ever been a wedding actually called off. Please, stay in your seats." Turning his attention to Tamera, he said, "Mrs. Lynch, please meet me in the house and tell me what this is all about. Patricia, Roger, please come with me."

"I hope you're satisfied," Daniel sneered as Tamera pushed passed him.

She did not respond. She just walked smugly toward the back door.

Patricia nearly threw her bouquet at Claudia as she gathered the train of her gown and threw it over her arm. Her hands were shaking and her eyes were filled with tears and rage as she marched up the aisle almost at a run. Carl stepped in front of her, seeing her anger.

"Honey," he said calmly.

"I'll kill her!"

"Patricia!" Ruth snapped.

Roger and the justice of the peace caught up with her. "It's nothing to worry about, babe," he assured her and took her arm.

"We're Patty's parents," Carl told the Justice. "We're coming too."

The five of them walked back into the house, leaving the guests behind. Claudia walked over to the DJ and asked him to play something calming. Within seconds, music covered over the whispers and murmuring.

Amanda looked over her shoulder at the back door. "Poor Patty," she whispered to Bradley. "How could Tamera be so cruel?"

"I don't know," Bradley said, shaking his head and looking at the gazebo and the bridal party huddling together. "Ever since the day she met Roger she's had it in for him. No one knows why."

"That's awful." Amanda sighed, turning back around in her chair and facing the gazebo. "I can't believe all the changes back here, the bridge, the gazebo. Did Dad and Mom do all of this?"

"Yes." Bradley nodded to himself. "Mom wants to open up a wedding consulting business and use the house and grounds for weddings. She wants to keep herself busy and really enjoys doing weddings."

"Well, she sure has the knack for it," Amanda said, smiling. "I remember our wedding reception here. It wasn't like this but it was really something. Mom really out did herself with the flowers, food, and decorations. Everything was so beautiful."

"Yes, it was," Bradley agreed and smiled. He snuck a quick look at Amanda. *Beautiful as always,* he thought. He was so happy she came and wondered if she suspected that he was the one who sent her the invitation. He had tried to disguise his handwriting, but he still thought it was obvious. But if she did know, she was not letting on.

"Ah," Bradley hesitated and looked over at Amanda. His heart fluttered and his hands begin to sweat. He had to look away for a moment to gather himself.

"Yes?" Amanda said, leaning toward him.

Bradley looked at her again. He smiled at the sight of Benjamin sitting on her lap. "You wouldn't want to go out for coffee or something after the reception, would you?"

"I'd love to." Amanda smiled and reached over and took his hand. "I would absolutely love to," she repeated.

Bradley looked down and exhaled in relief. When he looked up at her again, he was grinning like a schoolboy. *It worked,* he told himself.

"I wonder what that is all about," Chuck said, turning

sideways in his chair and looking back in the direction of the house.

Morgan did not turn around. She put her chin in the air and took deep breath through her nostrils.

"Don't know and don't care," she answered flatly. "I'm staying out of this one."

"No. I mean about Bradley and Amanda," Chuck said. He turned back around.

"What?" Morgan gasped, looking at him and then glancing over her shoulder. "Who invited her?" she asked, not expecting anyone to answer. "Oh, this is too much. I can't take this family." She shook her head and settled back in her seat. "They're all a bunch of lunatics."

Ariel, standing next to Claudia in a bridesmaid dress, looked at Mark and shrugged her shoulders. Mark motioned for her to come to him, but she shook her head.

"What's Aunt Tamera trying to do, ruin Aunt Patty's wedding?" she whispered to Claudia.

"I have no idea." Claudia shook her head. "I feel so sorry for Patty. How embarrassing, in front of all of these people. Why didn't Tamera say something sooner?"

"Like yeah!" Ariel said, slipping back into her best airhead speech.

Claudia gave her a curious look and fought the urge to laugh.

"Well, this is taking way too long," Daniel muttered and stood up. "I'm going in there. You stay put," he instructed Nicholas firmly, pointing his finger at him for emphasis.

"But, Dad," Nicholas pleaded.

"Nick, I'm not in the mood. Do as you're told for once and shut up!" Daniel snapped. He brushed past Peter and Matthew, not wanting to use the center aisle.

Nicholas looked at Peter. When their eyes met Peter smiled. Nicholas glared at him and turned his head away. He folded his arms over his chest and stared straight ahead, pouting again.

Peter smiled to himself at how ridiculous his fifteen-year-old cousin looked. He sat back and looked at Matthew. "Thank you for coming with me," he said and patted Matthew's hand.

"Hey." Matthew looked at Peter and smiled. "Where you go, I go. I want us to be together forever."

"Me too." Peter's smile faded and his tone became hushed. "So, what did your parents say when you called off your wedding?"

"They flipped, I'm sure. Even after I told them I was gay, they continued with their plans. They just don't get it and they never listen to me. So, I had Monica call mom and tell her that I wouldn't be coming home, that the wedding is off and that I'm going to live my life the way I choose. I'm through being made to feel guilty. Mom will listen to Monica."

"But what about your dad?"

"He's probably disowned me by now." Matthew shrugged his shoulders to show his indifference. He looked at Peter. "But I don't want you to worry about that. Just focus on getting better."

"Okay." Peter smiled. "I love you, Matthew."

"I love you, too, Pete." Matthew winked at him.

* * *

When Daniel entered the family room the shouting stopped. Roger stood with his arm around Patricia's waist, restraining her. Even from his angle, he could tell Patricia was in tears but fuming. Tamera stood behind the Justice who had his hands held up over his head as though calling a time out.

"I can't believe you're doing this to me," Patricia cried and glared at her sister through her tear-filled eyes. "Why can't you let me be happy for once? Why do you always have to ruin things for me?"

"It's for your own good," Tamera said coldly without empathy.

"For my own good?" Patricia nearly screamed at her. "I'm an adult. I can decide for myself what's for my own good. I don't need you sticking your fat nose in my business."

Ruth stood beside Patricia, whispering for her to calm down, but deep down inside, she was angry at Tamera too. This was by far the worst stunt she had ever pulled on Patricia, topping switching her shampoo with green hair dye when Patricia would not loan her money from her allowance. Patricia's hair was easy to fix compared to this.

"Tamera, this had better not be another stunt," Carl said sternly. He stood next to the Justice, staying between Tamera and Patricia.

"Yes, Tamera, this better be good," Daniel said, folding his arms over his chest and looking every bit as angry at her as the rest of the family.

"Okay, everyone please, calm down," the Justice said. "Mrs. Lynch, please come around here where I can see you."

Hesitantly, Tamera moved over next to Carl, glancing at Patricia fearfully.

"First I want to hear the reason why you stopped the wedding," the Justice said, looking directly at Tamera.

Tamera drew a deep breath and folded her arms over her chest. She looked at Roger in her usual cocky manner. "Shall I tell them or should you?"

Roger glared at Tamera. Even though he had only met her once before, he knew he did not like her. Over the years he put up with a lot of people like her, unwilling to listen to the truth and eager to believe the lies, always out to ruin his life.

"Why don't you tell everyone, since you obviously think you know it all," he said through clenched teeth.

"Mrs. Lynch, enough of these games. What is it?" the Justice asked.

"Okay." Tamera looked at Patricia. "I'm sorry I interrupted your wedding but I had to. You see, Roger was married before."

Patricia shook her head in disgust. "So, I already knew

that. What difference does that make?"

"Did he tell you what happened to her?" Tamera continued. "That after her father died she inherited all of his millions. That she caught him cheating and planned to divorce him. But he didn't want to lose all that money, so he strangled her and tried to cover it up by making it look like a robber broke into their house? Now he's running from the law."

"Bravo. Bravo," Roger repeated, clapping his hands. "You watch too much TV."

"Roger?" Patricia said, looking at him confused, her body trembling.

"Don't listen to her," Roger said, putting his arm around her and pulling her closer.

"Is it true?" Patricia asked him.

"Of course it isn't true." Roger cast a glare in Tamera's direction.

"Please explain," the Justice urged.

Roger looked at Carl, Ruth and the Justice and nodded his head.

"Okay. It's true that I was married before. Christine's father was a wealthy man, a widower. When he passed away he did leave his estate to Christine. But it wasn't worth millions as some of the more disreputable newspapers and tabloids purported.

"As for our marriage, we married very young, right out of college. The first years were rocky. We argued a lot. Christine did her share of fooling around, and so did I, I admit. It was a like a game to us. However, when her father died, it was a turning point for our marriage. She suddenly felt mortal and seemed to grow up overnight. I didn't. She wanted more out of life, stability, a family, the white picket fence. For a time we went to a marriage counselor. Things were starting to get better between us. We talked more instead of yelling. We got to know each other better and found that we really did love each other.

"I was in Vale covering a story for KWGN-TV News. You can check the police reports. I have witnesses also who can verify it. Christine wasn't feeling well and insisted that I go without her. When I came home at three in the morning I found the house surrounded by the police. That's when I found out someone had broken into the house and killed my wife. They made off with a few hundred dollars and jewelry from the bedroom safe.

"As standard in cases such as these, the police did interrogate me, but I was never a suspect nor was I ever accused or arrested," Roger said directly to Tamera.

"Well, aren't you leaving out something?" Tamera interjected. "The part where she had filed for a divorce that very morning?"

"No!" Roger snapped back at her. "When that story came out in the papers, I contacted her lawyers immediately. They informed me that one of their clerks ran across some old papers from when Christine and I were having trouble. Thinking she made a mistake, she filed them with the courts. The next day, her attorney discovered the erroneous filing and acted to rescind it. Neither Christine nor I had any knowledge of it. After my call, the attorney contacted the newspapers and had a retraction printed and, as things go, no one ever saw it buried on page twenty-six. It wasn't front page news!"

Tamera smirked disbelievingly. "What about the money?"

"I think we've heard enough," the Justice interrupted. "Mrs. Lynch, I advise you to be quiet."

"I can do better than that, Your Worship, sir. I'll take her home," Daniel said.

"No!" Tamera gasped. "I'm sorry; I was only trying to protect my sister. I'll keep quiet."

"I don't believe you," Daniel said.

Tamera was speechless. She looked at Ruth who immediately turned away. Carl stared at her with pursed lips, obviously angry with her.

Patricia stepped forward and glared at Tamera through her tears. "I will never forgive you for this. Never!" she yelled at her. She turned back to Roger and he took her in his arms.

"Well, as tragic as this all is," the Justice said, nodding sympathetically to Roger and Patricia. "There's no reason why we can't proceed with this wedding. What do you say?"

Roger looked at Patricia, deferring to her.

Patricia looked at everyone standing around her and then at Roger. She was so confused by everything that had happened. So many emotions flooded her that she was numb.

"I don't know," she said in a shaky voice, she touched Roger's face. "I don't know," she repeated and ran from the room in tears.

"Patty!" Ruth called after her. She turned and glared at Tamera before she hurried after her daughter.

Carl looked at Roger. He could not imagine the pain that he must be feeling. "Go to her, son," he urged.

Roger looked at the Justice. "Please, can you give us a moment longer?"

"You're my only appointment today, Mr. Ferguson. I'll give you all the time you need," he said, smiling sympathetically at Roger.

"Thank you. I really appreciate that." Roger nodded and then hurried after Patricia.

"Well, are you happy now, little miss know-it-all?" Daniel said to Tamera as he stood in front of her. "You just couldn't keep your mouth shut and your nose out of everyone else's business could you."

Tamera looked over at her husband and her anger grew. "Oh, shut up," she hissed and pushed passed him, heading for the back door.

Daniel grabbed her arm and pulled her back. "Hold it right there. You're not going outside. If you get to stay, you can watch from in here." He glanced at Carl and the justice of the peace. They both nodded.

"I'm truly sorry about all of this. But, what can I do, she's headstrong and stubborn," Daniel apologized.

"Don't I know it," Carl said, nodding his head in

agreement and frustration.

* * *

Peter leaned forward in his chair and looked at Nicholas sitting at the end of the row. "What's going on in there?" he asked, trying to make conversation.

"Oh, shut up and mind your own business!" Nicholas snapped.

Peter sat back and smirked. "Guess he doesn't know either."

The back door opened and Daniel walked out. All heads turned at once to watch him. He walked up to Nicholas and said, "Come on."

Nicholas stood up. "What's going on? Are we leaving?" he asked and stepped into the aisle.

Several other guests stood up ready to leave. Daniel quickly raised his hands. "No, no," he said, stopping them. "They'll be out in a moment. Everything's fine." The confused guests returned to their seats.

Morgan stood up and rushed over to Daniel.

"What's going on in there?" she asked.

"Tamera really blew it this time. She made a bunch of accusations about Roger's past and it sort of blew up in her face. I tried to stop her before but she wouldn't listen," he replied, shaking his head.

"So, what about the wedding?"

"I don't know," Daniel replied. "Patty and Roger are talking now. I better get back inside before Tamera does any more damage."

Ariel nudged Claudia as they stood in their place by the gazebo. "I wonder what's going on. Uncle Dan just came and got Nick."

"I don't know," Claudia said. "But he did say for us to stay, so that must mean something good."

The back door opened Carl and the justice of the peace

stepped out. No one was smiling. Claudia got a sinking feeling in her chest.

"This doesn't look good," she said to Ariel.

The two walked up the aisle together until Carl took his seat. The justice of the peace walked over to the gazebo and stood, his hands folded over his black book, waiting for some signal that the wedding was still a go.

After a few minutes of silent thinking, Carl stood up in front of the assembly. He looked at the familiar faces of his family and those of the other guests.

* * *

Roger knocked lightly on the bedroom door. He regretted not telling Patricia everything about his life with Christine, but it was still too painful a topic and not one he liked talking about. He silently cursed Tamera under his breath, yet at the same time he was relieved that everything was all out in the open. If only Patricia could understand. If only she would go through with the wedding. A wave of panic rolled over him while he stood outside the door. *What if she won't marry me? What will I do then? How will I go on?*

"Come in," Ruth called in answer to his knocking.

Roger opened the bedroom door. Ruth sat alone on the bench at the foot of her queen bed and looked up at him. Patricia stood, leaning against the wall and staring out the window and thinking about the gathering in the backyard. She was not crying, that much he could tell.

"I'll leave you two alone," Ruth said standing up.

"Mom, tell them I'll be down in a minute," Patricia said without turning around.

"Okay, dear." Ruth nodded and kissed Roger on the cheek before she disappeared out the door.

Roger felt his cheek and thought about the kiss. He wondered if it was a good sign or bad omen. He shrugged his shoulders as though shaking off the thoughts and turned his attention back to Patricia.

"Are we okay?" he asked nervously.

"Why didn't you tell me about Christine's murder?" she asked, still not turning around.

Roger looked at the floor and then turned back at Patricia. "I guess I didn't want to think about it. I've tried hard to get on with my life and put it all behind me. I didn't want her to come between us."

"And the money? What happened to that?"

"Well, after Christine's death, I inherited it," Roger said, a bit uneasy about her question. "It's in a separate account that I haven't touched since. I just didn't feel right using it. It was her family's money."

"So, exactly how much was it, since it wasn't millions?"

"Actually, at the time it was slightly over a million dollars."

"Wow," Patricia responded almost sarcastically and without any real feeling. "Then you're working as a cameraman is just for what? To show everyone you're a good deed doer?" She turned and looked at him coldly.

"No," he said and shook his head. "I do it because I enjoy it and I'm good at it. I want to show people the truth behind the news they hear and expose the two-bit reporters out to make a name for themselves by twisting facts for ratings. And I take pride in earning my own pay."

Patricia turned back to the window. "What do we do now?" she asked softly.

Roger took a step closer to her. "Well, let me ask you a question, do you still love me?"

Patricia looked at him with tears in her eyes. "With all my heart."

Roger knelt down on one knee. "Then Miss Wallace, will you marry me?" he asked, holding one hand over his heart and the other out to her.

"Well." She looked at her dress. "Seeing how I already

have this dress on. . . Yes. I will marry you Mr. Ferguson." Patricia smiled and took his hand.

Roger stood and leaned into her to kiss her but she quickly turned her head.

"Not so fast, Sparky. I don't have a ring on this finger yet," she said playfully, holding up her bare hand.

Roger laughed and kissed the back of her hand. "Well, let's go do something about that."

* * *

Morgan was standing next to Carl by the gazebo when Ruth walked up. They both looked at her in hopeful anticipation. Carl noticed that Ruth was not smiling and suddenly felt uneasy. He greeted her with a quick kiss.

"So, what's the verdict?"

Ruth drew a deep breath and looked back at the house. "I wish I knew. The news really knocked Patty for a loop. It's hard to say what she'll do."

"Well, thank you, Tamera," Morgan said sarcastically.

"It's not all Tamera's fault. Although she picked a really lousy time to speak up," Ruth said in Tamera's defense, even though, deep down she was still angry with her.

Suddenly the music stopped and everyone turned around to see why. There by the back door, stood Patricia holding onto Roger's arm. She smiled reassuringly to her parents and Wedding March began to play. Slowly the two walked down the aisle while Ruth, Carl, and the others retook their seats and the bridal party took their places.

"I guess we have our answer," Ruth said and gave Carl's hand a gentle squeeze.

* * *

The guests applauded wildly as Roger kissed his new wife and then cut into their cake. Patricia laughed playfully as the cameras clicked all around. Roger held a piece of cake in one hand while fending off Patricia's with his other. His reassurances that he would be gentle did not seem convincing with frosting still smeared on his cheek. Finally, he lovingly fed her the first bite of the cake. With icing still on her lips, he grabbed her about the waist and drew her to himself and kissed her.

"That is so neat," Peter said to Matthew, leaning against him to steady himself. "Wouldn't it be great if one day we could do that?"

"Yeah," Matthew said, looking into Peter's brown eyes.

"Oh, don't make me sick," Tamera barked from behind them.

"Aunt Tamera!" Peter jumped, nearly losing his balance as he turned around to face her. His head spun from moving too quickly.

"You two are disgusting."

"You know, for someone who just made a fool of herself trying to stop this wedding, you sure don't know when to quit, do you," Matthew said, standing between her and Peter. "I'll tell you what is disgusting, for someone to have such a narrow mind and be so hateful toward people they know nothing about. You're nothing but an ugly, overweight bigot."

"I'd rather be a bigot than a faggot like you," Tamera said and spit on the ground by Matthew's feet. "Weddings are for straight people, a man and a woman, not two sissy boys. Why don't you two just leave?"

"We'll leave when we're good and ready," Matthew snapped back.

"And another thing, don't you ever come near my son, or I'll press charges."

"Why? For what?" Peter asked, confused.

"Think about it," Tamera hissed and walked away.

Peter stumbled and fell back into a folding chair.

"Are you okay?" Matthew gasped and knelt down beside him.

"Yeah," Peter said, keeping his head still. "Just a little dizzy is all. I guess I let her get to me. I don't understand what happened to her. She wasn't always like this. When I first met her she was really nice. I know it's hard to imagine it now."

"Are you sure you're okay?" Matthew noticed the dark circles under his Peter's eyes. "You look a little pale."

"I guess I am a little tired. Maybe we should go inside and sit in there."

"Good idea," Matthew said, relieved to be getting away from the crowd.

As Peter held onto Matthew, they made their way to the back door. Claudia quickly excused herself from chatting with Bradley and Amanda and went to check on her son.

"So, how are you, dear?" she asked and kissed his forehead, as much out of affection as feeling his temperature with her lips.

"I'm okay."

"Are you really?" Claudia asked, gently lifting his chin to look into his brown eyes.

"No," Peter admitted. "I guess I let myself get worked up over things Aunt Tammy said. What's her problem, anyway? Have I done something to her and don't know it?"

Claudia looked over her shoulder at Tamera going through the line at the buffet table. "No. You haven't done a thing."

"Then why is she so hateful? She even said that if either Matthew or I get near Nick, she'll press charges. Is she implying that we would molest him or something?"

"Just ignore her as best you can," Claudia said, looking at him with worry in her eyes. "She's the type that has to keep things stirred up. Don't let her get to you."

"I'll try, but it's hard not to when she gets in your face like that, Mom," Peter explained then grimaced in pain. His head hurt.

Claudia wrapped her arms around him and kissed the top of his head. "Peter, honey, please don't upset yourself. It's not good for you."

"That's what I've been trying to tell him," Matthew agreed, his blue eyes reflecting his fear and deep concern. "I'm going to take him inside to find a quiet place for him to sit down and rest."

"I won't keep you then," Claudia said, releasing Peter to Matthew's capable hands. She watched them enter the house before turning around to find Tamera. She spotted her leaving the buffet table with a plate of food in her hands and walked over to her.

"What do you want?" Tamera asked, seeing Claudia approaching.

"I'd like a word with you, dear sister-in-law," Claudia said, feeling her blood pressure rise.

"I've nothing to say to you," Tamera said, ignoring her and looking for an empty table.

Claudia grabbed Tamera's arm before she could walk away. "Then you can just listen because, I have plenty to say to you." Claudia took Tamera's plate and set it down on the nearest table and walked her over the bridge and past the gazebo to the back lawn.

"Look at that, Dan," Carl said, nudging Daniel and motioning with his head. Daniel looked just as Tamera and Claudia walked over to the swing. "I wonder what that's all about. Neither one looks too happy"

"I don't think I want to know," Daniel said. "Think I should go see?"

"Probably." Carl sipped his coffee, watching the two in the distance.

* * *

Tamera turned around once she reached the swing set, her arms folded over her chest and anger in her eyes. "So, what do you want?"

"Just what is your problem?" Claudia snapped back.

"Problem? I don't have a problem. However, it looks as though you do. You really should try to relax," Tamera said in her best passive-aggressive tone.

"Don't pull that with me, Tamera," Claudia said firmly. "Ever since the day you found out that my son's gay you've done nothing but harass him and be outright mean to him."

"So, your point is?"

"Back off! Unless you want to deal with me."

Tamera looked at Claudia and could see the anger in her eyes, but she had already been humiliated once today and she was not going to let it happen again.

"Oh, nothing is going to happen to your precious little girl," Tamera mocked.

All at once Tamera's head jerked sharply as Claudia slapped her, hard. Her cheek stung and her eyes watered at the pain. She looked back at Claudia and covered her reddened cheek with her hand. "Why you, bitch!"

"Don't you ever talk like that about my son!" Claudia ordered. "And stay away from him! His doctors said if his blood pressure gets too high, he could have a stroke or a cerebral hemorrhage and I could lose my son. I think you, of all people, know how that feels."

The image of Danny flashed in Tamera's mind. She nodded silently, afraid if she said anything her voice would crack and be taken as a sign of weakness. She looked past Claudia for the first time and noticed Daniel standing nearby watching them. From the look on his face, she knew he heard everything and was angry.

* * *

Amanda smiled and hugged Patricia as they stood by the swimming pool. The gentle breeze cooled the late afternoon air around them.

"I'm so happy for you. You look absolutely beautiful," Amanda said.

"Thank you," Patricia said, smiling. "You look wonderful yourself. Did you come with Bradley? I saw you two sitting with each other."

Amanda shook her head, a bit confused. "No. I came alone."

"You did?" Patricia said and then realized the surprised tone in her voice. "I mean, of course. I'm sorry. Forgive me; it's been a crazy day."

"Don't worry about it," Amanda exclaimed. "I remember Bradley's and my wedding day, I was a bundle of nerves but it was nothing compared to today. I don't know what got into Tamera."

"She crossed the line this time," Patricia said. "I don't know if I'll ever be able to forgive her for this."

Amanda sensed Patricia's hostility. Suddenly she felt uneasy and began to fidget with her empty glass.

"Well, I guess I'll go get myself something to drink. I'm just so happy that you have finally found yourself a man. I'll see you later."

Patricia watched Amanda walk away. As her smile faded she could not help but wonder what Amanda meant by her comment.

* * *

Daniel watched Claudia walk by him, heading back to the party. Memories flooded his mind from years ago of similar fights and arguments, tears and pain. Slowly he walked over to Tamera and took out his wallet.

Tamera watched her husband in silence. Daniel removed an old worn photograph from his wallet and stared at it. Tamera's curiosity grew while she stood watching him in silence. He did not say a word. He just kept looking at the picture.

"What's that?" she demanded.

Daniel wiped his mouth and gave a slight sniff as he

struggled to keep his tears to himself. He handed her the picture.

Tamera looked at the photograph and smiled at the familiar face of Daniel at sixteen. She had seen that picture before. In fact, a larger one sat on their mantle at home in their living room, she remembered, handing the picture back to Daniel.

"So, you carry a photo of yourself in your wallet?"

"It's not me," Daniel said.

"What?" Tamera said, looking a bit confused. "Of course that's you."

"No, it's not," Daniel corrected her. His expression was serious, his tone dry. "I never told you this, but this is my twin brother, David."

"What?" Tamera repeated, nearly laughing in disbelief. "You're joking."

"I'm serious," Daniel said through clenched his teeth, angered by her insensitivity. He looked at the photograph again. "I have an identical twin brother."

Tamera was dumbfounded. She could not believe what she was hearing. After all these years, how could she not have known about this? She looked at Daniel.

"Why didn't you tell me this a long time ago?"

"Because it was something my family never talked about," Daniel began. "This photograph was taken of the two of us when we were both sixteen. Mom tore David out of the picture and threw it away. I dug it out of the trash and hid it."

"Why?" Tamera was confused.

"Because David is, to quote you, a faggot, a sissy boy, a queer."

Tamera recoiled from the look in Daniel's eyes. There was no love, just cold disgust and repulsion.

"About two months after this photo was taken, David told me that he was gay. He'd known for years that he was attracted to men, but he continued to play the straight game. At first he actually went out with girls, although none of them ever stayed with him for very long. Then he met a guy and we began the charade. We'd leave the house, saying we were going out on a date with our girls but we'd really pick up his boyfriend two blocks away. They'd drop me off with my date at the theater and come back later to pick us up. I didn't mind, because we covered for each other all the time.

"But then one night it all fell apart. The other boy's parents confronted our dad and mom when we were out. They had found a picture of David and a love note from him in their son's backpack. When we got home there was a huge fight. My parents were more concerned about what the neighbors' might say than they were about how David felt. He was forbidden to see the boy again and my parents had him admitted to a psychiatric hospital to straighten him out. The day he went into the hospital, my parents forbid us to ever say his name again. They threw out all of his belongings and tore up all his photographs. That's when I realized that they had no intention of getting him out. To this day they only claim to have two children, my sister and me.

"Anyway, three months later, the hospital called and said that David ran away. We haven't seen or heard from him again." Daniel gave a heavy sigh and put the picture back into his wallet.

"Oh, Dan," Tamera said sympathetically, reaching out to take his hand. "I'm so sorry."

Daniel pulled away and glared at her. "No you're not."

Tamera stepped back, shocked at his rejection. "How can you say that?"

"What do you mean, 'how can I say that?' You know damn well how I can say that," Daniel snapped at her. "Look at the way you're treating Peter and Matthew. You're just as ignorant, bigoted, and judgmental as my parents, and the worst part of it is, you're raising our son to be just like you." Daniel shook his head. "I've had enough. I'll pack my things and be out tonight. I'm going to find my brother."

"No, Dan," Tamera pleaded and reached for him.

"Don't touch me. I can't even stand the sight of you

right now." Daniel turned around and walked away.

Tamera stood stunned, her mind echoing Daniel's words over and over. She gave a slight laugh. *Daniel's not leaving,* she thought. They'd weathered much worse than this and survived. He could not be serious.

She watched him disappear around the side of the house, heading toward the front yard. Slowly the realization of his words began to stir doubts in her mind.

"Dan?" she said quietly, beginning to follow him. "Dan?" she called louder and began to pick up her pace. Her hands shook with fear at the idea that he may have been serious this time.

"No, no, no, no," she muttered as she rounded the side of the house to the front yard. The sound of a car engine starting sent a wave of panic washing over her. Her eyes filled with tears as she realized he was serious. Her heart pounded. She ran down the driveway.

"Dan!" she screamed. "No stop! Please, stop!" she cried.

Their SUV pulled away from the curb and disappeared down the street.

"Dan, no!" Tamera screamed. "I'm sorry, I'm sorry. Come back," she fell to her knees in the grass of the parking strip and covered her face with her hands.

* * *

Patricia stepped out the back door dressed in her purple cotton shirt dress. She kissed Roger as they stood together, looking out at their friends and family. As if giving a silent signal, Patricia looked at her bouquet and bounced it in her hand. It felt a lot heavier than she thought it would and she wondered if she would have enough strength to toss it over her head. All of the single women stepped forward and huddled together.

"Aren't you going to see if you can catch the bouquet?"

Amanda asked Claudia playfully.

"Only if you try," she teased.

"Well, we are single eligible women," Amanda said, cocking her head.

"True." Claudia nodded in agreement. "Okay. Let's give it a shot."

Claudia and Amanda walked over to the group of young, single girls and stood in the back. Claudia did not really want to and felt slightly embarrassed by being there, after all, she had been married before. She looked at her former sister-in-law beside her. *It was nice to see Amanda laughing and having fun,* she thought.

Patricia smiled seeing Claudia and Amanda join the group.

"Is everyone ready?" she asked, looking directly at the two of them.

"Yes!" they all shouted in response.

For a brief second Claudia's eyes met Patricia's and suddenly she realized what Patricia had in mind. She quickly looked away, her stomach full of nervous butterflies and her pulse racing.

Patricia turned around and prepared herself to throw her flowers over her head with all her might. It had been years since she had thrown a football on her high school powder-puff team and this bouquet weighed a lot more than that old pigskin.

"Okay, on the count of three," she called out. "One. Two. Three!" She swung the flowers with all her might into the air and then turned around quickly to see where they went.

The bouquet flew high over the heads of the younger girls as she had hoped. Patricia watched the expression on Amanda's and Claudia's faces change as they realized the bouquet was headed their way. Both women, hands reaching into the air, backed up to try to catch the flowers, unaware that they were getting closer and closer to the swimming pool. Patricia screamed to warn them but it was too late. Both women grabbed for the bouquet and immediately toppled into the pool.

Patricia ran through the crowd of women as Amanda surfaced with the bouquet, laughing.

"I got it," she said proudly holding the dripping flowers over her head.

All at once the entire assembly applauded and laughed with the two of them. Bradley bent down and offered Amanda his hand. He helped her out of the pool, careful not to get soaked in the process. Meanwhile, Ruth hurried over with two large towels for the girls.

As he wrapped a towel around Amanda, Bradley looked into her eyes. "So, I guess this means you're the next in line to get married."

"First you have to be seeing someone," Amanda said, looking at him. "Bradley, I have a question."

Bradley smiled nervously; he hated it when she said that. It always meant he had been caught at something.

"Okay," he said reluctantly.

"Mom tells me you moved out of the house, but haven't sold it. Why?"

"Well, I-I don't know. I guess I'm just not ready to close that chapter of my life yet."

"You sent me that invitation, didn't you?" Amanda said bluntly.

Bradley looked at her in shock. "Who told you?" he blurted and then realized he just had. "Yes. I confess. I sent you the invitation. I was hoping you'd come if you thought that Patty sent it to you."

Amanda smiled and put her hand against the side of his face. "I would've come even if you asked," she said. Slowly she took her hand away and looked down, biting her lip. "Bradley, I'm so sorry. I've been such a fool. I should never have blamed you for putting me in that place. I realize now that it was for my own good. Divorcing you was the biggest mistake of all. I still love you and am still in love with you. I'm so sorry I hurt you."

Bradley looked at her, feeling the familiar butterflies from long ago returning to his stomach. "There's nothing to forgive," he said, shaking his head. Tears of joy filled his eyes. He could not believe what he hoped to hear had finally been said. "Amanda, I love you so much," he said back to her.

Without thinking, Bradley wrapped his arms around Amanda and pulled her soaked body to his. He did not feel the wetness seeping into his suit and even if he had, he would not have cared. He kissed Amanda and lifted her off the ground. Suddenly he stopped, put her down and stepped back still holding her hand. As all the guests continued their noisy chatter all around them, he knelt down on one knee.

"Amanda, will you marry me, again?" he asked her.

A full smile spread across Amanda's lips and a lump formed in her throat. "Yes, Bradley. I'll marry you."

Bradley stood up and took her in his arms again to her laughter. They kissed to seal the deal.

Peter nudged his mom as she tried to dry herself off. They both smiled when they looked across the pool at Bradley and Amanda.

"I guess the right one caught the bouquet," Claudia said, putting her arm around her son and hugged him. Peter shrunk back from the dampness of her dress.

* * *

Ruth closed the front door as the last of the guests drove away. She sighed quietly. Everything considered, the wedding had turned out fairly well. *At least it was memorable for Patricia and Roger, something to tell their children,* she thought.

Carl walked up behind Ruth and wrapped his arms around her. He kissed the back of her neck and turned her around.

"Well, Mrs. Wallace, now that the last of our children is married, what do you say we go upstairs and relax in a nice hot bath together?"

Ruth looked into Carl's eyes and smiled at him. "Why, Mr. Wallace, whatever do you have in mind?"

"Come along, my dear, and I'll show you," he said playfully. He took Ruth's hand and started to lead her up the stairs.

"But what about the mess down here?" Ruth protested, pulling back.

"It can wait until tomorrow." Carl playfully tugged on her hand.

"Whatever you say, dear," she said and followed him up the stairs.

CHAPTER SEVEN
THE ANNOUNCEMENT

The cold December wind howled through the barren branches of the trees in the front yard. The ground was frozen solid and the few leftover leaves from autumn rattled against the blades of grass as they were blown across the lawn. The pine wreath rocked on its hanger against the front door.

Morgan turned up the collar of her brown wool coat as she and Chuck walked up the front steps. Her breath billowed in front of her face while she stood in front of the door. She was not pleased about being summoned out of her warm home into the elements without any explanation.

"This had better be good news," she said, her teeth beginning to chatter.

"I'm sure it is," Chuck said confidently, smiling at her as he knocked on the door.

"Oh, no one could hear that," she snapped at him. "Here let me." She rang the doorbell.

From inside the house she could hear Kevin crying and knew that Ariel and Mark were already there. The sound of footsteps coming nearer seemed to make Morgan colder. She shivered. "It's about time. Someone could freeze to death out here."

"Morgan, it's not that cold. So, stop complaining," Chuck said and laughed to himself.

The front door opened and a rush of warm air greeted them. Morgan instantly bolted into the foyer, nearly knocking over her mother. Ruth looked at Chuck, who shrugged. She turned and looked at Morgan.

"Well, hello, Morgan," she said, closing the front door. "Hang up your coats and come on into the family room. Everyone's here and waiting."

Chuck watched his mother-in-law disappear into the family room. He turned to Morgan and handed her his coat to hang up. She let it drop on the floor.

"I'm not your slave. You know where the coat rack is." She headed for the family room.

Chuck shook his head. He could tell it was going to be one of those days again. He picked up his coat and hung it on the brass coat rack beside the front door.

"Great." Morgan strained, peering into the family room. "We're always the last to hear about everything."

Chuck took her arm and whispered in her ear. "If we'd left when I wanted to we wouldn't have been the last to arrive. Now, come on."

The two walked into the family room and looked around. It was true everyone had already arrived, Patricia and Roger, Claudia along with Peter and Matthew, Ariel and Mark with baby Kevin, Bradley and Amanda with Benjamin, and Tamera with Nicholas. Almost everyone, Chuck thought to himself.

"Come on in," Carl welcomed them from his chair next to the fireplace. "Get yourselves warm."

Morgan noticed that everyone appeared to be in a good mood. That fact seemed to calm most of her fears, but she could not help but remember the last time she had been summoned to the house over a year and a half ago and the news had not been so good. Not wanting to delay the suspense any longer, she walked over to an empty chair opposite Carl by the fireplace and sat down.

"So, now that I'm here, what's going on?" she asked impatiently, looking at her father.

"This is your brother's show."

Bradley looked around the room at the faces of his

family. Slowly he stood up and took a deep breath. He straightened his navy blue Dockers and smoothed the front of his long-sleeved argyle sweater. Letting his breath out with a heavy sigh, he grinned from ear to ear.

"I want to thank you all for coming," he began. "You all know how rough it's been for Benji, Amanda, and me this past year."

Patricia looked at Roger and grinned. Memories of seeing Amanda and Bradley at their wedding three months ago were still fresh in her mind. Roger shrugged at his wife. He did not have a clue as to what was going. He looked back at Bradley.

"Some of you may not have been aware of it, but I fell off the wagon for a time during the divorce. But, thanks to Morgan and her tough love speech, I stopped drinking and went back to AA."

Morgan smiled proudly, looking around the room to make sure that everyone noticed her. *It's about time I received some credit from the family,* she thought.

"One thing she said to me really hit home," Bradley continued and nodded to his sister. "She said I needed to get on with my life. But it wasn't so easy. Benji and I moved out of the house and into an apartment, but I still couldn't move forward.

"There's a prayer we say every meeting at AA. To accept the things we cannot change and change the things we can. So," Bradley continued and looked over at Amanda.

"Come on," Morgan interrupted, rolling her eyes. "What is it? Don't tell me, you two are dating again?"

Bradley frowned. "No. We aren't dating again."

"Oh, good," Morgan said, giving a relieved sigh louder than she realized. Seeing everyone's shocked expressions, she quickly added, "Oh, no offense, Amanda."

"None taken, Morgan," Amanda said and flashed a forced smile. She had never been very comfortable around Morgan. Perhaps it was because she always seemed a little bossy. Still, she did not totally dislike Morgan.

"May I continue without any more interruptions?"

Bradley asked, looking directly at his oldest sister. She nodded. He scratched his short, dark-brown hair. "Great. Now, I've lost my train of thought," he admitted and rolled his eyes, not hiding his disgust. "Well, bottom line, last week Amanda and I took a little trip to Reno and got married. There, that's it." He looked down at Amanda and smiled. She smiled back at him. The room erupted in applause.

"Congratulations," Claudia said, putting her arm around Amanda as they sat on the couch. "I'm so happy for you."

"Thank you."

"Way to go, Brad. Not taking any chances, eh?" Roger grinned and then shot a glare in Tamera's direction.

Ruth noticed Roger's exchange and looked at her daughter. Tamera sat quietly at the breakfast table in the nook, away from the rest of the family. She looked tired. Her blue eyes were red as though she had not slept in days. She had not even tried to cover the dark circles under them with makeup. Her blonde hair looked hurriedly brushed, not its usual neat coiffure.

Ruth walked over to her. "Is this seat taken?" she asked and sat down in the chair next to Tamera without waiting for her to reply.

"You look as though you're a million miles away." Ruth tried to catch Tamera's eyes.

"I wish I were," Tamera answered truthfully.

"What's wrong, honey? Do you want to talk about it?" Ruth asked, trying not to pry.

"No. Everything's fine. Nothing's wrong. Life's wonderful," Tamera said, not even trying to hide the sarcasm in her voice.

"Tamera," Ruth said, lowering her voice. "I'm your mother. I know when you're lying. There is something wrong. What is it dear?"

Tamera looked at her. "I don't want to talk about it right now," she said flatly. Her blue eyes began to tear. She quickly stood up and left the room.

Ruth shook her head and sighed at her daughter. The happy chatter of family gathered around Bradley and Amanda, brought back the smile to her lips. She stood up to address the family. "Now it's my turn to share a secret." Ruth beamed.

The entire gathering became silent. Everyone turned to look at Ruth with shocked faces. Ruth laughed out loud.

"It's not that kind of secret," she assured them. "Amanda and Bradley, everyone else too, come into the dining room."

Amanda glanced at Bradley curiously as they walked through the kitchen and into the dining room. Her eyes lit up and a smile spread across her lips when she looked at the table. There, in the center of the lace-covered table, was a small, two-tier wedding cake, complete with bride and groom. Carl and Ruth quickly lit the candlesticks on either side of the cake.

"Surprise!" they shouted together presenting their gift.

Bradley gave his parents a confused look. "How did you know about our secret? We were so careful?"

Carl laughed at the thought of having a secret of his own. "It wasn't easy. Believe me."

"Amanda, Bradley," Ruth interrupted. "Why don't you two go ahead and start cutting the cake? Claudia, would you help me get the coffee and punch?"

"Sure, Mom." Claudia started for the kitchen.

"Wait." Bradley halted his mother. "Aren't we supposed to cut the first piece together while someone takes our picture?"

Ruth smiled at her sentimental son. "Yes, that's right."

Amid camera flashes and applause, Bradley and Amanda cut the first slice of cake and fed each other a first bite. Ruth looked around the room at her children and grandchildren. Her smile faded when she looked at Tamera.

Again, Tamera stood off by herself, leaning against the archway into the foyer. She appeared distracted, picking at something on her long, blue denim dress. *She was definitely not herself,* Ruth thought. However, she knew in her own time,

Tamera would tell her what was troubling her. Ruth turned around and went back into the kitchen to get the coffee cups and punch glasses.

"So, Mark." Chuck walked over to his son-in-law. "What's the word with your appeal to the courts?"

"Not as good as I'd hoped. The District Attorney is claiming since my parents' bodies were found along with illegal drugs, then under some law they had every right to confiscate all of my parents' property and funds. My attorney is arguing that since my parents were never arrested or charged with any crime that law doesn't apply. He's also pointing out that it still doesn't give them grounds to seize my personal funds and property. The house was in my name, not theirs."

As Chuck listened, he nodded his head. He then turned toward Mark, looking him directly in the eyes. "Were they trafficking drugs, son?"

Mark understood his father-in-law's question. It was not about whether or not his parents were innocent. It was about whether or not he could win his case and get his hands on the money. Mark looked Chuck directly in the eyes and, without flinching or hesitation, said, "I don't know."

Chuck nodded and put his hand on Mark's shoulder. You've been through enough losing both your parents at once. You don't deserve this added stress and grief. I'm really hoping you win and stick it to 'em," he said and winked at his daughter before walking over to Carl.

Ariel looked at her father and then at Mark. "Why did you tell him that?"

Mark smirked at his father-in-law across the room. "Ariel, if your father knew we won our case, then he would be hitting me up to back him in his new trucking scheme. We have our own plans for that money. Remember the music store? If I tell him the truth, then we'll never see it happen. Do you understand?"

"I do," Ariel agreed with her husband as she rocked Kevin in her arms. "But, honey, he's going to find out sooner or later."

"True," Mark agreed and kissed Ariel's cheek. "But if it's all the same, I'd rather it be later. For now, let's keep it our little secret, okay?"

"You. . ." Ariel smiled at him and shook her head.

* * *

Tamera stood silently watching Peter and Matthew across the room. Thoughts of Daniel's face, the anger in his eyes when he told her he was leaving her filled her mind. His words echoed in her ears. She began thinking about how she had been treating her nephew and his friend. It was true; they had never done anything to warrant her hostility. It was not about that, she told herself. It was about protecting her son. But deep down, she knew that was not true. She continued to question herself and stare at them.

Peter leaned closer to Matthew as they stood against the wall. Matthew smiled at him then whispered something into Peter's ear. Peter blushed.

Suddenly, an image flashed in Tamera's mind and she had her answer. She turned around and walked into the parlor.

* * *

Roger sat next to Patricia at the table and cuddled her. His short beard tickled her when he kissed her neck. She pulled away laughing.

"So, do you think we should tell them?" he whispered loud enough for only her to hear.

Patricia looked around the room at the family, making sure that everyone who mattered to her was there. "Why not?" Before Roger could say another word, Patricia put her hand on his arm. "Give me a minute," she said.

"Why? What is it?" he asked.

"I want to check something first," she said and stood

up.

Roger watched Patricia walk across the room toward Nicholas. "Oh no," he said and shook his head. "Here we go again."

"Hi, Nick," Patricia greeted. She leaned against the wall next to him.

"Hi," Nicholas grunted, obviously disinterested in everything that was going on.

"How're you doing?" she asked, trying to sound less like a reporter and more like an aunt.

"Okay, I guess." His answer was as enthusiastic as his greeting.

"That bad, eh?" Patricia frowned at him then smiled. He did not notice. "So, how's your dad?"

Nicholas' throat tightened and his heart ached. He struggled to fight back his tears, remembering what his mother told him. A fifteen-year-old boy did not cry, especially in front of grown-ups. He looked at his aunt.

* * *

Tamera stared at the photographs on the mantle. Her eyes stopped when she saw Morgan's and Chuck's wedding photo. She recognized herself immediately. How she let her mother talk her into being one of Morgan's bridesmaids, she could not remember. The only thing she knew was that she could not tell her mother or Morgan the truth why as to why she had not wanted to or about why she disliked Chuck so much.

As she stood staring at the photograph, her bitterness seemed to fade. She was no longer filled with anger seeing Chuck's face. To her surprise, she felt nothing.

"Still millions of miles away?" A soft voice came up from behind her.

Tamera jumped and spun around, her heart racing. She watched her mother walk into the room.

"I'm sorry. I didn't mean to startle you."

"You didn't," Tamera lied. "Well, maybe a little. It's okay."

Ruth walked over to the love seat and sat down. She looked at her daughter and patted the cushion next to her. "Come, sit down," she ordered, more than asked.

Tamera obediently did as she was told.

Ruth took a deep breath and let out a heavy sigh. She patted Tamera's knee. "Honey, I know something's bothering you," Ruth said softly. "Why don't you talk to me about it?"

"I don't know how." Tamera began to cry.

Ruth put her arm around her daughter. She could not help remembering the frail little girl from years ago. As a child, Tamera always wore her heart on her sleeve. Whenever she liked someone, she fell fast and hard, and always ended up being hurt. Ruth remembered many nights sitting in that very room, her arm around Tamera's shoulders, comforting her while she cried. Now seemed no different.

"It's okay. You can tell me anything. You know I love you and that will never change."

Tamera wiped her eyes and sat up. "It happened so long ago, but it still hurts like it was yesterday. I tried to forget about it, to say it happened to someone else, but I can't. I've never talked about it to anyone."

Ruth was becoming confused. She was expecting Tamera to tell her about why Daniel suddenly left her, but this sounded like something else. "It's okay, dear. You can tell me."

Tamera looked into her mother's soft, brown eyes. "Will you still love me, no matter what?"

"Of course." Ruth gently wiped away a tear from her daughter's cheek.

"You promise?" Tamera insisted.

Ruth suddenly felt worried about what Tamera was about to tell her. She looked intently into her daughter's eyes. "I promise," she assured her.

Tamera nodded to herself and took a deep breath.

"When I was fifteen, I was. . ." Tamera's voice trailed

off as the words seemed to stick in her throat. It was proving harder to say than she thought.

Ruth sensed Tamera's anxiety. She struggled with her own curiosity and growing concern while patiently waiting for her daughter to continue.

Tamera looked at her hands in her lap. "I guess there's no easy way to say it. I was raped," she said and her tears began to flow again.

Ruth silently gasped, shocked by what her daughter just admitted. She was saddened to think that her daughter had dealt with this on her own and hurt that she had not come to her sooner with this news.

"Oh, baby, I'm so sorry," she empathized, holding Tamera in her arms and not knowing what else to say, yet knowing anything would not be enough.

"There's more," Tamera said hesitantly, pulling away to look at her mother.

"More?" Ruth questioned.

"I-I became pregnant," she admitted and looked back at her hands and lowered her head in shame. "I had an abortion."

Ruth's eyes widened in shock. She could not believe one of her own children would have done such a horrible thing, yet, at the same time, she understood.

"How—" Ruth tried to speak.

"Chuck took me to a clinic in Salem."

"Chuck? Why would he. . ." Ruth realized the answer to her question and suddenly the years of hostility between the two of them made sense. Gently she stroked Tamera's hair. "I'm so sorry. I had no idea."

"Please, Mama, don't say anything to them. Morgan doesn't know and she loves him." Tamera looked at her. "Over the last couple months I've been doing a lot of soul searching. For years I've lived with all this anger. I lashed out at people because if it. I took it out on Nicholas, then Peter and Patty and it cost me my husband. I should be angry at Chuck, but I'm not." Tamera finally looked at her mother. "I know everyone thinks

I'm a mean, heartless bitch."

"Oh, I don't think so," Ruth tried to reassure her.

"It's true, Mom," Tamera protested. "Patty hates me. Roger won't speak to me."

"They're hardly everyone," Ruth said. "I know for a fact that Peter doesn't hate you. Bradley and Amanda don't. Your father and I don't. As for Patty and Roger, give them time. I'm sure they'll come around."

"I might as well tell you, Daniel's not away on business. He left me the day of Patty's wedding. He was upset with me because of the things I said to Peter and Matthew. He showed me a picture and told me about his twin brother he hasn't seen in years because his parents kicked him out for being gay. He said he couldn't stand to be around me anymore because I was a cold-hearted bigot. I don't know where he is and I haven't heard from him since."

Again Ruth was stunned. This was more than she had expected and more news than she could take in. She did not know what to think. "Honey, Daniel's an intelligent man. I'm sure wherever he is, he's fine. Maybe he just needs some time for himself," Ruth said, grasping at straws to try to reassure her daughter and failing miserably.

"He went looking for his brother. I just want him to come home, Mama," she started to cry again.

"He will," Ruth said, trying to sound positive. "And when he does, you two should talk and you should tell him what you told me. He'll understand."

Tamera tried to smile but deep down she had her doubts about how understanding Daniel would be. "I'll try," she said.

* * *

Bradley cornered his father in the kitchen. The steam from Carl's cup of freshly brewed coffee momentarily distracted him.

"Come on, Dad," Bradley whispered. "How did you

find out about Amanda and me? We didn't tell anyone we were going."

Carl smiled at his son. He loved teasing Bradley and remembered years ago when he and Ruth brought him home from the hospital. He would lie on the couch with Bradley on his chest. He would wait until Bradley fell asleep and then playfully touch his soft cheek. Bradley would grimace without waking up, and Carl would laugh. As Bradley grew up, the teasing continued between them both, one always trying to outdo the other.

"Think, boy." Carl poked Bradley in the stomach playfully. "You did tell someone."

Bradley cocked his head and looked at his father. He searched his memory trying to figure out whom he told. "No, Dad. I didn't tell a soul. I'm sure of it," he said, shaking his head confidently.

Carl grinned and then looked very serious. "Where did you leave Benjamin?"

"With the sitter, but I only said we were going away for the weekend and would be back."

"What about Amanda?" Carl asked, grinning and loving his little game.

Bradley thought for a moment. At first he was ready to dismiss the whole idea that Amanda said something, but then a thought occurred to him. "She could have," Bradley admitted and then with a smug expression asked, "So, how do you know Benji's sitter?"

Carl looked at his son and recognized that look in his eyes. "Oh, don't you even think that," he laughed. "Your mother ran into them at the grocery store. She told your mother and that's how we found out."

"Aha!" Bradley laughed. Finally the secret was out. He had his answers and he was satisfied.

* * *

A. M. Huff

Claudia sat quietly beside Patricia at the breakfast table thumbing through the pages of Patricia and Roger's wedding album. She was pleased to see that the pictures turned out quite nicely. The photographer did an exceptional job, even capturing a shot of her and Amanda as they tumbled into the swimming pool while reaching for the bouquet.

"That is a wonderful album," Claudia complimented, closing the book. "Thank you for sharing it with me."

"No problem," Patricia said proudly. "After all, you were the matron-of-honor; you should be the first to see them."

"Well, again, I thank you." Claudia nodded.

"So, how's Peter doing?"

Claudia looked over her shoulder in the direction of the dining room. She thought about what to say. "He's stubborn as ever. He insisted on stopping the home schooling and returning to school last October. He wants to graduate with his class this spring."

"Do you think he can do it?" Patricia asked.

"If his determination was all it required, I'd have to say yes, but he's still having some bad headaches and dizzy spells. Thank goodness he only has school for half days, so they haven't interfered too much with his classes."

"Do the doctors know what's causing his headaches and dizziness?"

"They want to run some tests but Peter is refusing to do them until after he graduates. I have to say, I'm worried."

"Speaking about after he graduates, does he have any plans?" Patricia inquired.

"I've tried not to think about it," Claudia admitted quietly. "He wants to get an apartment with Matthew right away. I don't blame him. I understand. It's just hard letting him go. He's so young and after all he's been through, I just don't know if it's a good idea."

"I know this is going to be rough on you, but it's bound to happen sooner or later. Just like it was for our parents when we moved out, it will be for us when our children go out on their own."

"I know," Claudia agreed. Then suddenly she looked at Patricia in surprise.

Patricia grinned and put a finger to her lips.

Claudia looked around the room and then ducked her head and smiled at her sister-in-law.

* * *

Carl sat down at the dining room table across from Peter and Matthew. Peter reminded him so much of Steven: the same sparkle in his brown eyes; the same cowlick over his right eyebrow. A tear came to his eyes as he remembered the story he told Steven about how he came to have that silly cowlick. When he showed Steven the cows on his father's farm in the country, Steven was so afraid the cows would lick him again, he would not go near them. Carl wondered if Steven ever grew out of his fear.

Carl looked at Matthew. He never understood how a man could be attracted to another man, he did not. He did not want to really, but at the same time it did not bother him as much as he thought it would. Matthew's love of sports, fishing, and hunting helped break the stereotype in Carl's mind of what he thought a gay guy was like. With so much in common, Carl was willing to overlook the gay thing.

"So, how are things at work?" Carl asked Matthew.

"Things are going pretty well," Matthew said and nodded. "I can't thank you enough for getting me that security job. Working nights gives me a chance to take some classes at the community college during the day."

"Well, I'm just glad I could help. It's nice to know they still remember me down there. Usually after you retire, you're forgotten by the time the door closes behind you," he said and chuckled. "So, what courses are you taking?"

"Right now just some basic requirement courses. I haven't decided on a major," Matthew admitted. "I'm not sure what I want to do yet."

"Well, you have time. Just be sure whatever you choose it's something you enjoy doing. That way you'll be able to stick with it. I know I enjoyed my job so hanging in there 'til retirement wasn't all that bad. Sure, it had its moments and the last few months about drove me crazy, but it was worth it." Carl looked at Peter. "So, how're you doing, son?"

"I'm doing okay," Peter answered confidently. He had not really talked to his grandfather since the incident but he could tell that it bothered Carl. Carl seemed to keep his conversations brief and on neutral topics, never too deep. "Can't wait to graduate," he added.

"It'll come quick enough." Carl looked at his coffee cup. "Well, I guess I need a refill." He stood up. As he walked by Peter, Carl placed his hand on his shoulder. "I love you, son."

"I love you too, Grandpa," Peter said and reached up to touch Carl's hand, but Carl took it away too quickly.

Peter turned and looked at Matthew. Matthew glanced around the empty room and then took Peter's hand giving it a gentle squeeze. He leaned closer to Peter and gently kissed him on the cheek. Peter closed his eyes at the touch of Matthew's soft lips.

"Ahem." Tamera pretended to clear her throat as she stood in the threshold between the foyer and the dining room.

Matthew and Peter both jumped and looked at her. Matthew sat back in his chair and glared at her with angry eyes. Peter blushed. He looked at his aunt, realizing they had been caught in an act of showing public affection.

"I'm sorry, I didn't mean to disturb you," Tamera said in a quiet voice.

Peter gave Matthew a puzzled look and then turned back at his aunt. "That's okay, Aunt Tammy."

Tamera sheepishly entered the room and stood holding the back of the chair at the head of the table. Her hands shook slightly as she tried to find her words. She looked at the table cloth and the remaining wedding cake. Chocolate, she thought and smiled to herself. She took a deep breath and turned back to the boys.

"May I talk to you both for a moment?" she asked and actually waited for a reply.

"Sure." Matthew gestured toward the chair she was standing in front of. "Have a seat."

Tamera sat down immediately and nervously put her hands in her lap.

"Peter, Matthew," she began. "I know I've gone out of my way to be mean to you both and said some pretty nasty things."

"I'll say you have. You've been a regular bitch toward us," Matthew scoffed bitterly.

Peter quickly put his hand on Matthew's to silence him. He realized the tone in his aunt's voice was different, softer, apologetic, and sincere. He wanted to hear what she was about to say.

"I deserve that," Tamera said, nodding and biting her lip. "I tried to tell myself I was justified because I was protecting my son, but that was a lie. It's just I was running from some painful memories that I've tried to forget. I lashed out at Nick, at Patty, at you both. I realize now it was misdirected anger and I'm sorry. I hope you both can forgive me and we can be friends again."

Peter looked at Matthew who sat expressionless, stunned by Tamera's seemingly sudden change in personality. A smile spread across Peter's lips and he turned back to his aunt.

"Sure, Aunt Tammy," he said. "Apology accepted and everything's forgotten."

"Thank you," Tamera said and stood up. "I'll leave you two alone now."

Peter watched his aunt leave the room and then looked back at Matthew who sat staring blankly at the wall, seemingly deep in thought.

"What are you thinking about?" Peter asked.

"I wonder what memories she was talking about."

Matthew looked at him. "What's her secret? Do you think she's a lesbian?"

"Aunt Tamera?" Peter said and laughed. "You're joking, right?"

"Then what?"

The smile faded from Peter's lips when he began to think about what his aunt said. "I don't know. Maybe Ariel will, though."

* * *

Claudia leaned against the doorpost of the back door and stared at the cold, wintry scene in the backyard. The tall oak trees stretched their naked branches toward the sun as if begging for its warmth to return. A foggy mist rose from the uncovered swimming pool. The lawn chairs and picnic tables were put away for the season. The yard looked so bare and lifeless. Claudia shivered at the sight.

The words of the doctor echoed in her head. Words that she wished she could erase. She had asked for a second opinion, but even that came back with the same painful news.

Ruth noticed Claudia standing alone and walked over to her. Of all of her children's spouses, she felt most like an equal with Claudia, not like mother and daughter-in-law, but more like peers. Perhaps it was because she'd never known Claudia as Steven's wife.

"Penny for your thoughts," Ruth said softly, standing beside Claudia and staring out the window with her.

Claudia looked at Ruth and pretended to smile. "I'm not even sure if they're worth that much," she sighed.

"Something troubling you, dear?" Ruth asked, slowly turning to face Claudia.

"You could say that."

"Peter, I take it?"

Claudia nodded. "Yes. How did you know?"

"I'm a mother, too. I recognize the look," Ruth said

empathetically. "Do you want to talk about it?"

Claudia looked around the room. The family had all regrouped in the family room and were busy chatting with one another. An occasional burst of laughter broke the constant drone but then vanished just as quickly. "Sure." Claudia nodded. "Let's grab something to drink and go in the other room."

The two walked into the kitchen. Ruth took two coffee cups from the cupboard and set them on the counter. Claudia filled them with freshly brewed coffee.

"I've noticed that Peter seems to be getting around better," Ruth said as they headed for the parlor.

"His balance is better but he still has headaches and dizzy spells that concern me."

The two women walked into the parlor and sat down; Ruth on the love seat and Claudia across from her in the chair closest to the fireplace.

"So, what do the doctor's think? Will this be permanent?" Ruth asked.

Claudia drew a deep breath and held it for a few seconds, trying to maintain her composure. A lump grew in her throat and she thought about the doctor's words again. "Ah," she fumbled to find the words the doctor used, "the doctors suspect there may be splinters, possibly bone fragments, that have lodged in Peter's brain near his ear. They think these could be the reason he gets dizzy and also has been having those headaches. They also said that given his father's history, there may be another reason but without more tests they can't know for sure."

"Oh, poor Peter." Ruth set her coffee cup down on the coffee table in front of her. "So, when are they going to run the tests?"

Claudia looked down and then set her coffee cup on the table too. "That's just it." She shrugged. "The doctors want to run the tests as soon as possible, but Peter is refusing until after graduation."

"But that's still at least five months away," Ruth protested.

"I know. That's what worries me. If it is a tumor, like Steven's, the longer we wait the. . ." Claudia looked away and willed her tears not to fall. "His doctor said they could successfully remove the fragments and splinters but if it is a tumor then they need to know so they can call in a specialist."

Ruth put a hand over her heart as thoughts of the worst filled her mind. She shook her head trying to erase them. "So, what are you going to do?"

Claudia looked up at Ruth. Her eyes were filled with fear and tears. "I'm leaving it up to Peter. We had a long talk with the doctors and he knows all the risks, but he wants to finish school first."

"What about you?" Ruth looked at Claudia. "What do you think?"

That was all Claudia needed to hear. The tears began to fall down her cheeks. "I am so scared," she confessed. "I've never been this frightened in all my life, or felt this helpless. I have to admit, I haven't tried very hard to sway him into having the tests sooner."

"Oh, Claudia." Ruth sighed and shook her head. She could understand the anguish that Claudia was feeling. Just two years earlier, she was faced with the same situation when Steven moved back home.

"His doctors have scheduled the tests the week after the graduation ceremony," Claudia said, wiping her tears away. Claudia looked at Ruth. "I would appreciate it if you and Dad would be there with me."

"You don't have to ask," Ruth reassured Claudia. "We all will be there, and when he's well enough, we'll celebrate not only his graduation, but also his recovery."

"Thank you, Mom," Claudia said, managing a brief smile.

* * *

Patricia walked over to Roger and put her arm around him while he talked with Carl in the family room. Roger winked at her and smiled. She kissed his cheek and then looked at her father.

Carl stopped mid-sentence and looked at his daughter. He could tell by the look in her brown eyes that she had something up her sleeve.

"Okay, Patty," he said, raising his head. "Out with it. What're you up to?"

"Me?" Patricia said, feigning innocence. "Nothing," she teased and looked at Roger.

"Can we tell them now?" Roger asked.

Patricia looked up just as Ruth and Claudia returned. The family was all present.

"Sure," she said to her husband.

"What's this?" Carl asked.

Roger put his coffee cup down and wrapped his arm around Patricia's back. "Everyone," he raised his voice over the din. "May I have your attention for just a moment? Patty and I have an announcement to make."

Ruth looked at Carl and grinned in anticipation. Ever since the wedding, she secretly hoped that Patricia and Roger would move back from Seattle. She wondered if this was it.

Tamera looked at Patricia. She still had not talked to her to apologize or explain why she had disrupted her wedding. Every time she mustered up the courage, Patricia was already talking with someone else.

"You may have noticed that Patricia is putting on a little weight," Roger teased.

Patricia grimaced and elbowed him in the ribs. "I am not getting fat."

"That's right," Roger agreed and laughed. "We're having a baby!"

There was a collective gasp of surprise and then the room burst into applause and happy chatter. Everyone jumped up to congratulate the proud couple.

"Oh, honey, that's wonderful," Ruth said, giving her youngest daughter a hug. "When are you doing this?"

"I'm due in June," Patricia answered proudly.

"Congratulations," Carl said, shaking Roger's hand. "You're in for quite a thrill. You'll be amazed at yourself and the memories of your own childhood as you teach your little one. It's truly a blessing."

"Thanks, Dad." Roger nodded proudly.

Tamera made her way across the room toward her sister. Patricia turned away from hugging Morgan and their eyes met. Slowly Patricia smiled and reached out her arms to hug her sister.

Tears fell from Tamera's eyes. She wrapped her arms around her sister, hugging her. "I'm so happy for you and I am so sorry for what I did."

"Let's not talk about it. It's in the past," Patricia said, giving Tamera a gentle squeeze and then releasing her. She looked into Tamera's blue eyes and was surprised to realize that she was no longer angry. "Besides, we're sisters."

Tamera cried and hugged Patricia again. "I do love you, Patty," she choked.

Patricia glanced across the room at Ruth. Ruth winked at her and nodded her approval. The sound of the front doorbell chiming caught everyone's attention. Ruth looked at Carl curiously.

"I wonder who that could be?" she said.

Before anyone could respond, Nicholas jumped up. All the talk about babies and the hugging and crying was making him uncomfortable.

"I'll get it!" he shouted and ran to the front door.

He opened the front door and froze as he stared at the man on the doorstep. His heart leapt.

"Dad!" he shouted, throwing his arms around his father's neck. "I've missed you. Where've you been?"

Tamera jumped when she heard her son cry out. She

quickly ran into the foyer just as Nicholas pulled the visitor into the house. Tamera stopped and looked at her husband.

"Dan!" she screamed. She wrapped her arms around his neck, hugging him. "I'm so sorry. I'm so sorry," she repeated and cried. She closed her eyes and pressed her cheek against the side of his face. She felt a sharp prick but didn't care. She took a deep breath, smelling his cologne. The scent was different. Suddenly she realized he was not hugging her back. Slowly she released him and stepped back. A single diamond stud earring sparkled from the light of the chandelier. "Daniel?"

The front door opened wider and Daniel stepped inside. All at once he and the man in front of Tamera started laughing.

Nicholas stepped back and shook his head, confused.

"Wha-What's going on?" he stammered.

Daniel dropped his coat on the floor and opened his arms to Tamera. Immediately she rushed over to him and was surrounded in his embrace. He kissed her with all the passion he had on their wedding day and held her tightly in his arms.

Tamera was still in shock and so happy to have her husband back. However, she kept staring at the identical stranger behind Daniel.

Daniel looked around the foyer at the shocked faces of his family as he held Tamera in his arms. Slowly he peeled her arms from his waist and moved her to his side. She continued to hold onto him. He smiled and held out his arm to the man beside him.

"Everyone," he greeted. "I'd like to introduce you to my twin brother, David."

Nicholas shook his head in disbelief, wondering if he were dreaming. His mouth was agape in shock and his eyes darted back and forth from his uncle to his father.

"David," Daniel said, nodding toward Tamera. "I'd like you to introduce my wife, Tamera."

"We've already met," he said with a smile.

Tamera's mouth fell open, even David's voice and smile were identical to Daniel's.

"And, this is our son, Nick," Daniel continued his introductions, motioning for Nicholas to step forward.

"Hi, Nick," David greeted. He shook the boy's hand.

"Uh, hi," Nicholas said, still confused.

Daniel went around the room and introduced the family to his brother. He could tell by all of their shocked expressions that he had some explaining to do.

"I know you all have questions and I'll be happy to answer them, but first I'd like a moment alone with Tamera. Nick, will you take your uncle into the family room? We'll be back in just a few minutes."

"Okay," Nicholas said, still wary of his new uncle.

"Come on, David," Carl said, offering him a welcoming hand. Together with Nicholas and Ruth, he ushered their new guest into the family room.

Daniel turned to Tamera and nodded for them to go into the parlor. She walked over to the love seat and then turned around. From the look in his eyes, Tamera sensed the situation between them was still uncertain. She sat down without a word.

He looked at his wife and remembered his parting words nearly three months ago. With his anger gone, he regretted them. He walked over to the love seat and sat down facing Tamera.

"Dan," Tamera said, unable to take the tension between them any longer. "Ever since you left, I've been doing a lot of thinking about what you said. I've already apologized to Peter, Matthew, and Patricia. And I want you to know that I'm sorry."

Daniel looked at her and raised an eyebrow. "And?" he said, urging her to continue.

Tamera slumped and looked at her hands in her lap for a moment and then back at her husband. "You were right. I was being unfair and totally unreasonable and I'm sorry. I realize now why I was acting that way and I've changed. I mean it sincerely. I am sorry, truly sorry, Dan. . ." Tamera's words trailed off.

Daniel took a deep breath and looked away from her for

a moment. He still had his doubts as to whether or not she had actually changed, but he was willing to accept her at her word for now. The real truth was he missed her and while he was away he never stopped thinking about her.

"I accept your apology," he nodded. "And, I want you to know that I'm sorry for what I said. I was hurting and angry but what I said was harsh and just as cruel."

Tamera wrapped her arms around Daniel's neck, hugging him and kissing his cheeks.

"Okay, okay," Daniel said, laughing and pulled her away.

"I love you so much and I've missed you."

"I missed you too," he said, standing up and helping her to her feet.

"So, how did you find David?" she asked as they headed for the family room.

"It wasn't easy," Daniel admitted. "I contacted a company, Seekers of the Lost. They took the little information I had and came up with a list of people with the same name. One by one I narrowed it down to a man in San Francisco but by the time I got there, he'd moved. So, I talked to his former landlord and found out his forwarding address. We met up in Philadelphia. Come on, I'll explain it all when I tell the others."

Tamera wrapped her arm around Daniel's waist and pulled his arm around her. "I love you, Dan," she breathed.

"Me, too," Daniel replied.

CHAPTER EIGHT
THE GRADUATION

The May sun shone brightly in the clear blue sky above the Bend Senior High School campus. The groundskeeper had done a wonderful job mowing the lush, green lawn between the parking lot and gymnasium. The flower beds were in full bloom and meticulously pruned. The eighty-year-old man in faded blue coveralls went about his work on his hands and knees, pulling the tiny weeds from the far edges of the flower bed seemingly unaware of the many people that passed by him.

Peter stepped up to the curb and looked around. He had no feelings toward the school he had attended for nearly two years. The school was filled with people who had harassed his friends and him unrelentingly. Even the faculty seemingly turned a blind eye toward the teasing and physical bullying. He drew a deep breath and let it out, as though cleansing himself of those memories. He was just happy to finally be through with all of it.

Claudia stepped up to Peter's side and proudly put her arm around him. What a strange twist of events. Who would have thought that twelve years ago, her son would be graduating from the same school as his father. She smiled, remembering Steven, and wished that he could have been there to see his son.

Matthew handed Peter his mortarboard. His blue eyes sparkled with pride as he watched Peter put on his blue cap with gold tassel. He took Peter's hand in his and gave it a reassuring squeeze. "Congratulations Peter. You made it."

"Oh, not quite," Peter teased him. "I still have to get my

hands on that diploma. Then it's goodbye and good riddance to this place."

Claudia was not surprised by her son's comment. She knew the trials he endured here and she did not blame him for his lack of school loyalty.

"Well, I guess I should be going. I'm supposed to meet with the rest of my so-called classmates in the cafeteria," Peter said, looking at them both as he leaned on his cane. "You two better go on in and get seats."

"We will," Claudia assured him, kissing his cheek. "Just as soon as your grandparents arrive."

"Do you want me to help you?" Matthew offered.

Peter turned to his companion and put his hand gently on Matthew's cheek. "No, Matt," he said softly. "I'll be okay."

Matthew closed his eyes and leaned against Peter's touch. "Okay," he relented.

Claudia took Matthew's arm. They watched Peter walk off toward the school building.

"He's doing so much better, isn't he," Matthew exclaimed, noticing that Peter was barely using his cane.

"Yes." Claudia nodded in agreement. "Who'd ever guess just how bad he has it."

Ruth and Carl walked up behind Matthew and Claudia. They had seen Peter walking away as they pulled into the parking lot. Ruth's heart ached and her mind momentarily flashed back twenty-two years ago, to a memory of her watching Steven run off with his friends, all talking excitedly. How happy he had looked. He had worked hard in school, becoming the student body treasurer and editor of their yearbook. She had been so proud of him. Ruth sighed as the memories faded and were replaced by the present.

Carl looked at the old school building and thought back to his graduation day so long ago. The school building of his youth had been smaller than the current gymnasium. It had long since been torn down and replaced by the newer one that stood before him. This was the third generation of Wallace's to graduate from Bend Senior High. His chest swelled with pride.

"Well, are we all set?" Ruth asked, putting her arm around Matthew's.

Matthew gave a start, then smiled and relaxed.

"Hi, Grandma," he said, looking at Ruth.

Ruth smiled at the sound of Matthew calling her Grandma. He had never done that before. She was surprised at how, deep down, she really liked it.

"Hi, honey," she said. "Well, let's get inside."

"What about the rest of the family?" Carl asked, looking back toward the parking lot.

"We can save them seats," Ruth said, winking at Matthew and holding fast to his arm. "Coming, Carl?"

Carl walked over to Claudia and offered her his arm. She slipped her and around his arm and the four of them walked into the gymnasium.

The excited rumbling of the gathering crowd inside was almost deafening. Rows of folding chairs were placed on the main floor to create a center aisle. Claudia quickly claimed a row about midway up. As Ruth sat down she looked around the huge open room. Long banners hung down from the ceiling, forming a wall at the far end of the gym. Large poster-size photographs of the various members of the class, taken throughout their four years, were adhered to the brightly colored cloth banners along with words Ruth did not take time to read. Instead she excitedly scanned the pictures for her grandson's face. She turned away from the last one disappointed. Suddenly the banners were ugly to her, just examples of the vanity of an elite group of graduating students.

"Do you think we have enough seats?" Ruth asked, looking at their row the chairs.

Carl looked over the chairs again and counted. "I think so," he answered confidently. He turned to Matthew. "Hey, son, why don't you go outside and see if the others are here yet."

"Yes, Grandpa." Matthew hurried off to find the rest of the family.

Ruth smiled to herself. She looked at Claudia seated beside her in the chair nearest the aisle and noticed that she was looking at a piece of paper. The letterhead was from the hospital.

Ruth smiled reassuringly and looked at Claudia. Amid Claudia's long brown hair, neatly pulled up in a Gibson bun hairstyle, a few gray hairs were beginning to show. Beneath Claudia's brown eyes were dark shadows caused by worry and lack of sleep. Even in her loose fitting, brightly colored silk dress it was obvious that Claudia had lost too much weight.

"So, how is he, really?" Ruth asked, nodding at the letter in Claudia's hand.

"Oh, he's doing fine." Claudia nervously folded up the letter and gave a slight shrug. "Better than I am." She hesitated for a moment then looked at Ruth.

"I didn't want to say anything because I didn't want to upset you or Dad, but you should know. About two months ago, Peter had a bad spell. Matthew and I had to rush him to the hospital. I had them run their tests, an MRI and a CT scan. They confirmed the bone fragments but they also showed a tumor."

Ruth gasped and put a hand over her mouth. Memories of Steven lying cold and lifeless in his bed rushed over her, taking her breath away.

"I'm sorry," Claudia apologized, taking Ruth's hand. "I didn't want to tell you because. . ."

"It's alright." Ruth found her voice, though it was a bit shaky. "So, today's surgery is to do what?"

"They called in a specialist, Doctor Hough. He's going to do the operation to remove the bone fragments and the tumor." Claudia looked at the ceiling fighting to keep from crying.

"He's going to be just fine," Ruth said, gently patting the back of Claudia's hand.

"I keep telling myself that," she said and bit her lip, tears in her eyes. "They told me there are always risks involved when operating on. . ." She reached over and hugged Ruth. "I'm so glad you're here."

"I will always be here for you," Ruth whispered into Claudia's ear.

* * *

Outside, Matthew spotted Tamera walking across the parking lot toward him. His opinion of her was still guarded even though she had apologized to Peter and him last winter. Deep down, there was something about her that made him feel uneasy. He shrugged it off for the moment and focused on the ceremony that was about to begin.

Tamera stopped and turned around in the middle of the parking lot and yelled for Nicholas to hurry up. Nicholas had been lagging behind. He had not wanted to come to his cousin's graduation. Not because he was gay, he had half-lied to his parents, but because he found the whole idea boring and resented having to wear a suit and tie. Especially the tie. "After all, I'm not the one graduating," he tried to argue with his mother before she put her foot down.

Despite his complaining, he looked very handsome in his gray pinstriped suit. His brown hair, just recently trimmed, was neatly combed. Not a bad looking young man, his uncle David commented upon seeing Nicholas all dressed up. The comment had creeped Nicholas out, knowing that his uncle too was gay.

"Now, remember, just sit still and be quiet," Tamera instructed Nicholas and took his arm.

"Like I'm the one who's gonna make a big scene. I'm sure," Nicholas scoffed. Tamera tugged on his arm. She knew what he meant and she did not find it funny.

"Hi, Aunt Tammy. Hi, Nick," Matthew said as the two approached him on the sidewalk. "The rest of the family's inside about halfway up the center isle on the right."

"Thanks, Matthew," Tamera said. "By the way, how's Peter this morning? Is he worried about the operation later this afternoon?"

The words hit Matthew hard, nearly taking his breath away. All morning he had tried to forget about what was going to happen that afternoon, and he had nearly succeeded, but suddenly all his fears and anxieties returned in full force.

"He's doing fine," Matthew managed to say. "He's just taking it one step at a time. Right now, he's graduating. He's not thinking about anything else."

"That's good. Let him enjoy his successes."

"Yes," Matthew agreed and nodded. "Go on inside. I have to wait here for the rest of the family," Matthew explained, trying to change the subject while ushering them along.

He watched in silence as Tamera and Nicholas disappeared into the gymnasium. Damn her, he thought to himself as his fears returned. His mind flooded with thoughts about all the "what if's" and things that could go wrong with the operation. Peter had been so calm when the doctor discussed the possible negative outcomes of the surgery with them. He had not even flinched when the doctor said there was the risk of permanent brain damage that could result in his inability to walk without a cane, being bedridden for the rest of his life, or even death. Peter had been so strong in front of his mother, but he knew Peter was just as frightened as he was.

"Hello, Matthew," Daniel said, jarring Matthew from his thoughts.

Matthew jumped and turned around to face Daniel and his twin brother, David. He quickly looked at each ones left ear to see who wore an earring, the only way to tell them apart.

"Hello, Uncle Dan," he said but he was looking at the tall, handsome man with dark-brown hair and brown eyes standing beside him. *If I was not already committed to Peter,* Matthew secretly thought, *I could really get to like that man.*

"You look very nice, Matthew," David said, aware that Matthew was staring at him. Even though he was old enough to be Matthew's father, he had always been attracted to blonde, blue-eyed, athletically built men like Matthew. Still, he respected commitment and Matthew was definitely committed to Peter. He held out his hand to Matthew.

As he firmly shook David's hand, a shiver ran up Matthew's spine. He blushed and was sure both David and Daniel noticed, which only made it worse.

"Thank you," Matthew said, looking away for a moment to regain his composure.

"Well, I guess we should be getting inside, don't you think?" Daniel said, letting Matthew off the hook.

"Yes," David agreed. "Coming?" he asked Matthew.

"Not yet, I need to wait for the others. Halfway up the center aisle on the right," he informed them and then watched the two men head for the gymnasium.

As Matthew turned around, he saw Morgan and Chuck hurrying across the parking lot toward him.

"Was that Daniel?" she asked Matthew without saying hello.

"Yes it was."

"Well, good morning everyone," Bradley said as he, Amanda, and Benjamin walked up. "What's going on?"

"Nothing, we're just waiting for you," Matthew answered. "Now that everyone's here, shall we go inside?"

* * *

Inside the gymnasium, the seats were filling up rapidly. Even the bleachers on either side of them were beginning to fill up. Ruth glanced at her watch; the ceremony was only minutes away from starting. She proudly looked down the row at the faces of her family. Everyone was there, even Patricia and Roger, who made the six hour drive down from Seattle. Ruth looked at the end of the row and noticed that Amanda was holding a gift wrapped in blue and gold paper on her lap. She was pleased by her daughter-in-law's thoughtfulness and yet wondered if she knew they were all going to the hospital directly after the ceremony.

Patricia squirmed uncomfortably in her seat between

Roger and her father. She tried shifting her weight and turning slightly to get a more comfortable position but nothing seemed to help.

"Are you alright?" Roger asked, noticing his wife's discomfort.

"Yes, only two more weeks to go," she said, rubbing her very pregnant stomach. "I am so ready for this to be over." *This whole being pregnant thing,* she thought, *is highly over rated.*

Roger smiled at his wife and put his arm around her. She leaned back and nestled against him.

Suddenly a trumpet blew and the gymnasium went silent. As the band joined in, everyone turned and looked toward the entrance. The procession entered slowly, first the principal and then his assistant, both dressed in their black college graduation robes and caps. Following behind them was the guest speaker, a man that Ruth did not recognize, and then the school faculty. All kept up the slow-paced procession and took their seats in the first row chairs.

There was a pause, and then the band began to play the familiar tune of Pomp and Circumstance. All eyes were fixed on the entrance as the senior class entered single file.

Claudia watched the students pass in front of her. Proud tears filled her eyes. She smiled as Peter finally came into view.

He walked slowly, leaning a bit more on his cane than he had earlier. He flashed a brief smile to his mother as he walked past her, hoping she would not notice how dizzy and light-headed he was. He looked at Matthew and blinked. Matthew smiled and did the same; their secret signal to each other.

Peter slowly made his way up the steps onto the raised platform with help from the short girl behind him. *The first kind gesture from a class of strangers,* Peter thought. He was grateful to some unknown organizer for having the students at the top of the alphabet sit on the top row of the riser because it meant he had no more stairs to worry about. He walked across the stage to his chair and stood facing the audience until the last few classmates found their seats. The music ended, and the audience applauded the graduates.

Claudia was not really listening to the discourses of the various faculty and student speakers. Her thoughts were fixated on the operation that awaited her son in just a few short hours. No matter how hard she tried to stay focused on the ceremony, it was no use. She looked at Peter and smiled.

Applause echoed loudly throughout the gymnasium as the last speaker took his seat and the principal returned to the podium. He proudly announced the names of the students who received various scholarship awards. Peter watched but was oblivious to the whole affair. His head felt as if it were spinning. It was worse than ever before. Still he struggled to stay focused. It is just all the excitement, he kept telling himself.

The applause continued unceasingly as one by one each student stepped forward and received their diploma. Claudia took Matthew's hand and held it tightly as Peter stepped forward and accepted his diploma. Again, he looked out at the audience and spotting Matthew, blinked. Matthew smiled proudly and blinked back.

After the last graduate returned to their seat and the applause faded away, the vice principal stepped forward announcing that the PTA had arranged for a reception to be held in the cafeteria immediately after the ceremony. Once again the band, with renewed enthusiasm, played Pomp and Circumstance as the graduates filed out of the gym. Spontaneously, everyone stood and applauded the passing graduates.

Ruth looked at Claudia who was crying proudly and gave her a hug.

"So, is everyone meeting at the hospital?" Bradley asked Morgan who sat next to him.

"As far as I know," she stated matter-of-factly.

"How're you doing?" Roger looked at his wife.

Patricia sat rubbing her round stomach. She had

continued to be restless during the ceremony and felt sorry for those around her for distracting them, but it could not be helped.

"I'm okay," she replied uncertainly. "I think."

Roger gave her a curious look. "Pains?"

"No. Just uncomfortable, that's all."

Roger nodded, relieved that she was not in labor. Even though they had taken all the birthing classes together, he was still nervous about being in the room during the birth. Bradley tried to encourage him earlier, saying it was the most beautiful experience he had ever had, but the look on Amanda's face said otherwise. Carl told him when all of his children were born, husbands were not allowed in the room. Roger secretly liked that idea best.

* * *

The waiting room at Saint Charles Medical Center was warm and peaceful. The wall sconces were dimmed, casting a soft glow on the powder-blue walls. The black-and-tan-paisley upholstered chairs were inviting. Green, living plants and a bouquet of fresh, spring flowers added to the feeling of calm.

Chuck rest his arm around Morgan's shoulders as they sat on the small couch. Occasionally he glanced at Tamera and Daniel seated directly across the room from him. Tamera kept her head down, although she knew he was watching her. Daniel knew it too and tried to stifle his rising anger.

Bradley and Amanda sat next to Mark and Ariel watching Benjamin and Kevin play on the floor. Bradley sat forward and reminded his four year old son to be easy with Kevin. It was hard to believe that Kevin was already a year old. *Where had the year gone,* he thought. He looked at Amanda seated next to him and gave her a kiss and a one armed hug.

"I love you," he whispered into her ear.

Amanda smiled back at him without a word.

"My, aren't we all a bunch of Gloomy Guses," Patricia said, walking into the room. "I guess I'll just have to liven up the party a tad!" She did a comical shuffle in the doorway.

"Oh, Patty," Morgan sighed. "We aren't here to party."

"Well, we aren't here for a funeral either," Patricia retorted. "So, lighten up guys."

Patricia and Roger walked over and sat next to Tamera and Daniel.

"So, where's Nick?" Patricia asked, looking around the room.

"He's down at the cafeteria with David," Tamera replied coolly. She did not want to be there, much less talk to anyone. She just wanted it all to be over so she could go home.

"Oh." Patricia nodded and gave Roger a shrug as though telling him she gave up.

"Aunt Patty," Ariel said. "Have you and Uncle Roger decided on a name for the baby?"

Patricia smiled at her niece, happy that at least someone was willing to try to breathe some life into the gathering. She looked at Roger for a moment. He gave her one of his smirks.

"Well, we're still discussing it," Patricia admitted, ignoring her husband's forced cough. "We've narrowed it down to Jessica Marie if it's a girl. I want to name it Roger Steven if it's a boy."

"But I want to name him Colin Steven," Roger interrupted, glancing at Patricia.

"Wow," Ariel said. "They're both really good names, but I have to go with Uncle Roger's choice."

"Traitor." Patricia playfully glared at her niece.

Ariel laughed. "I like yours, too," she tried to cover up. "But Colin Steven Ferguson has such a nice ring to it."

"I guess it comes down to who gets their hands on the birth certificate first," Patricia teased and laughed.

"I guess so," he replied.

* * *

Peter lay quietly on the gurney in the prep room. His

hand trembled as he held onto Matthew's. He looked into Matthew's blue eyes and tried to see the calmness he could always count on. It was not there this time, only concern and fear. He tried to smile. Matthew did the same.

"No matter what happens," Peter said quietly yet firmly. "I want you to know that I love you with all my heart and soul and will always love you."

Matthew fought hard to hold back his tears. A lump rose in his throat and his vocal cords tightened. He nodded, fearing to speak and break his concentration.

"You've been everything to me." Peter continued to look lovingly at Matthew. "I've never been as happy in all my life as I have this past year with you."

"Stop it," Matthew said, finding his voice. "Nothing is going to happen to you. You'll be fine. You'll see. We'll have many years together. Don't talk like that."

A single tear fell from Matthew's eye and he wiped it away quickly. "You're going to be okay," Matthew repeated, more for himself than for Peter.

"That's right, honey." Claudia stepped up to the side of the gurney. She looked at her son and barely recognized him with his head shaved. All of his beautiful thick brown hair was gone. Tubes ran from the IV bags down into the back of Peter's hand. Her heart ached for her baby.

"You'll be out in no time and everyone will be here waiting for you," she assured him.

"Excuse me." A voice from behind them interrupted. "It's time to get him down to surgery."

Claudia gave a start and turned around. She looked at the nurse standing in the doorway. She was not ready to let Peter go, not just yet. She looked back at Peter, forgetting to hide her worry. Peter saw her expression and a fearful tear flowed down the side of his face.

"I love you, Mama," he said and reached for her.

Claudia bent down and hugged her son, holding him as tightly as she could. Tears continued to escape her tightly shut eyes.

"I love you, Peter," she whispered into his ear. She gave him one last squeeze and a kiss, then let go and left the room in a hurry.

"Come back to me, dear man of mine," Matthew whispered into Peter's ear as he hugged him.

"I will. I promise," Peter replied and kissed Matthew's soft lips. "I promise," he repeated and held Matthew's face in his hands. "I love you."

"I love you, too," Matthew breathed. "Forever."

Peter looked at his grandparents for the first time and smiled at them. "Take care of my mom, for me."

"We will, son." Carl winked. "Now, don't you worry about anything. Just think about getting better."

"You'll be fine, Peter." Ruth patted his hand and then stooped down and kissed his forehead. "You will be fine. See you in a couple hours after you're through in there."

"Okay, Grandma," Peter said. "I love you both," he called as they left the room.

Ruth walked into the hallway just outside the prep room. She was greeted by the sound of Claudia crying and the sight of her holding onto Matthew. Carl's eyes were red with tears. He shook his head and headed down the hall toward the waiting room. Ruth knew that look. He hated hospitals, much more seeing one of his own in them. She turned back to Claudia and walked over to her.

"Claudia," she said quietly yet firmly. "Stop it. Peter is going to be just fine. This is not good. You have to be strong."

Claudia looked at her mother-in-law and struggled to suppress her tears and worries. Her throat tightened as she swallowed back her tears. "Okay," she breathed. "I'll try, Mom."

"That's my girl," Ruth said with a smile. She put her arm around Claudia. "Now, let's go get something to drink and then join the others." Ruth led Claudia down the hallway toward the cafeteria. "Coming Matthew?"

"No, I think I'll stay here. If that's okay?"

"That's fine." Ruth nodded.

Matthew quietly watched them disappear. He fell back against the wall and slid down to the floor. He folded his arms over his knees and rested his forehead on them. He could not cry. He could not think. When he closed his eyes, all he could see was Peter lying on the gurney looking up at him. Slowly he looked up at the door across the hallway.

"Come back to me, dear man, please," he begged softly.

* * *

Ruth sat quietly next to Carl and watched Claudia pace in the hallway through the glass wall of the waiting room. She sighed out loud and shook her head. She understood Claudia's uneasiness and inability to sit and wait. It was even difficult for her. She looked away.

Patricia sat next to Roger. As Ruth watched her, she noticed Patricia grimace occasionally and continue to rub her stomach.

"Patty, are you okay?" Ruth asked.

Patricia looked over at her mother. "I'm not sure," she replied honestly.

Suddenly a sharp pain in her groin took Patricia's breath away. She lunged forward and gave a guttural moan.

"Mom!" she gasped and looked over at Ruth.

Ruth recognized the look and immediately jumped to her feet. Morgan, Tamera, Amanda, and Ariel also recognized what was happening and tried to mask their smiles with looks of concern.

"What is it?" Roger leaned forward and tried to get Patricia's attention. "What's the matter?"

"Get a wheelchair and nurse in here right away," Ruth ordered Roger.

"Why? What's wrong?" Roger looked at his mother-in-law confused.

"You are about to become a father," Ruth informed him. All the color drained from his face. "Oh no." Ruth barely got the words out when Roger collapsed in a dead faint on the floor at Patricia's feet.

"Bradley, get the nurse in here!" Ruth ordered as she helped Patricia to her feet and into the hallway.

Carl immediately revived Roger and helped him back into his chair. He tried hard not to laugh at his bewildered son-in-law. "Are you okay?"

"What happened?" Roger asked, his head still in a daze.

"You passed out, my man," Chuck said, slapping him on the back and laughing.

"Chuck, be nice!" Carl said, frowning at his son-in-law.

"Sorry, Dad." Chuck hid his smirk and returned to his chair across the room.

"I've got to go with Patty," Roger said with a bit more confidence.

"No. You should stay here. Ruth is with her. They'll be fine," Carl assured him.

Roger did not argue. He sat back in his chair and tried to calm himself. Every now and again feelings of guilt for not being by Patricia's side crept up but he immediately dismissed them, remembering Carl's words.

"Well, isn't this great!" Morgan said in her usual sarcastic tone. "This family never ceases to amaze me. Nothing is ever simple is it?"

"What's that supposed to mean?" Tamera looked at her sister.

"For starters, Pete's in the operating room as we speak and now Patricia is on her way to the maternity ward. We can never have things simple, just one thing at a time. Nope. They all have to happen at once."

"Oh, mother," Ariel sighed. "Aunt Patty didn't do this on purpose."

"No one said she did!" Morgan snapped at her daughter. "I'm just making an observation, that's all."

"Well, I don't care to hear it," Ariel mimicked her mother's tone.

David excused himself and slipped into the hall. He felt like an outsider intruding on a private family moment. As he looked up the hall he saw Matthew sitting on the floor.

"I'll be right back," he mouthed to his brother and pointed up the hall. Daniel nodded but David had already left.

David walked toward Matthew. He could not stop thinking about how much Matthew reminded him of someone he once knew and loved. Someone he was supposed to grow old with but who had left him two years ago. Seeing Matthew stirred feelings in him that he had not felt in a long time.

"Come on," David said with authority, holding out his hand and looking at Matthew.

Matthew slowly looked up at David. His blue eyes were still dry but filled with worry. Cautiously he reached up and took David's hand.

"Let's go get a cup of coffee," David said, not giving Matthew a chance to decline.

The two headed for the cafeteria in silence.

* * *

Daniel leaned back in his seat, grateful that the commotion with Patricia was over and the room was quiet once again. He looked at Chuck across the room and thought about what Tamera had told him. He remembered her words and her tears as she told him the truth about why she had the abortion. Even though he promised her he would not say anything, he was finding it difficult to sit in the same room as Chuck and keep silent.

Tamera noticed Daniel was staring at Chuck and knew what he was thinking. She put her hand on his. He looked at her hand and then at her blue eyes.

"Please," she said quietly. "Let me put this behind me."

Daniel nodded, giving in to her wishes and stifling the

feelings inside his chest.

* * *

The cafeteria was quiet. The lunch rush was over. Only two nurses remained, sitting together in a booth along the far wall. They sat quietly sipping their coffees and reading their books.

Suddenly there was a loud bang as the kitchen door swung open, hitting the wall. A busboy pushing his metal cart entered the room and froze when he saw Matthew and David standing at the counter.

"Sorry," the busboy apologized, ducking his head and then going about cleaning the tables.

"Oh, pay him no mind," the short round woman at the cash register said, taking David's money for the two coffees.

Matthew walked over to a clean table by the windows, on the opposite wall from the women and sat down. David joined him after putting away his change.

"Thank you for the coffee," Matthew said, staring at the dark brew in his cup. He was not really thirsty.

"You're welcome," David said. He sat across from Matthew and studied the young man's face. He could tell that Matthew was worried. He wondered if his face showed as much when he sat in a similar chair two years ago.

As he looked at Matthew he saw the image of the blonde haired, blue-eyed man he had loved. He smiled unconsciously at the memories. John was so full of life, always laughing and optimistic, even to the end. He never once complained about the many days and weeks he had to spend in the hospital during his therapy, or the painful shots and procedures that he had endured to prolong his life, to give them one more day to be together. Then finally the day came and he was gone.

David looked at the emerald and diamond ring on his hand. John had given it to him on their ten year anniversary. He had been so sentimental, always the romantic. A tear fell from

David's eyes. He quickly brushed it away and hoped that Matthew did not see it. After all, he was there to cheer Matthew up, not worry him more.

"Peter will be just fine," David said reassuringly. He reached across the table and patted Matthew's hand.

Matthew looked up and nodded without smiling. "I know he will. I just worry about him."

Matthew reached into his pocket and took out a jewelry box. Matthew opened it and stared at its contents.

"When he wakes up, I'm going to give this to him," he said out loud, more to himself than to David. "I'm going to ask him to be my life partner. I love him so much."

David smiled and looked at the gold wedding band set with a row of five small diamonds. "That's wonderful. I hope you two will be as happy as John and I were."

Matthew looked at David. He had never mentioned a man in his life before. He only even know that David was gay because of what Tamera had said.

"John?" Matthew asked, not trying to pry.

"Yes, John was my life partner. We met, of all places, at the bus stop one rainy winter evening in San Francisco. There was just something us that clicked. That very night we had our first date. We were together for thirteen years."

"What happened?" Matthew heard himself ask before he realized it. "I'm sorry," he quickly apologized. "It's none of my business."

David smiled again. It had been a long time since anyone had asked. It almost felt good to be able to speak of him again. "It's okay. John passed away a couple years ago. He died from cancer. People thought he had AIDS but he didn't. He wasn't even HIV positive."

"I'm sorry. I mean, not that he didn't have AIDS, I mean, that he died," Matthew stammered and then felt embarrassed.

"It's okay," David said. "I understood what you meant. I carry John with me wherever I go, in here," he said, patting his chest over his heart.

"I understand," Matthew said, smiling and nodding. "Thank you for telling me about John and you. It's encouraging."

"Don't mention it." David winked. "You and Peter are going to be just fine. Are you going to have a ceremony, you know, family and friends."

"Like a wedding?" Matthew asked and slowly shook his head. "Ah, I don't think that would be a good idea."

"Why not?" David pulled back and looked at him.

"Someone told me recently that weddings are for straight people."

"I'm sure you know that in some states, same sex marriage is legal. If John were still alive, we would've been married."

"That's nice and all but, well, my parents aren't too thrilled with the idea of having a gay son," Matthew admitted. "I don't know what they'd do if Pete and I did that."

"I see," David said and nodded. "You know, it took me a long time to learn but you have to remember to always be true to yourself. You can't live your parents' lives any more than they can yours. If they can't handle you being gay, quite frankly, that's their problem. Just be yourself."

The words struck a chord. He smiled as he remembered his conversation with Peter. "Pete said those same words to me a year ago," he told David.

"Good advice."

Matthew nodded.

* * *

"Excuse me." The soft-spoken words interrupted Claudia's thoughts while she paced in the hallway outside the waiting room.

She stopped and looked at the woman. She was dressed in a long, dark-brown fur coat which she held closed close to her neck. Claudia was sure it was to flash the large diamond ring she wore on her finger and the diamond earrings that hung from her ears. Claudia looked at the taller gentleman at the woman's side. Dressed in a three-piece business suit, he looked equally unapproachable.

"Yes?" Claudia replied.

"We're wondering if you could tell us where we could find Claudia Wallace?" the man asked.

"Well, you've found her. I'm Claudia." She held out her hand to greet him. He politely took it and just as quickly released it. "What can I do for you?" she asked.

"We're looking for our son, Matthew. His sister told us we could find him here," the woman said in an almost arrogant tone.

Claudia glanced through the glass wall into the waiting room then turned and looked over her shoulder at the hallway behind her. She turned back at the couple. "I'm sorry. He was just here an hour ago. If you'd like you could wait here. I'm sure he'll be back soon."

"Thank you," the man said and walked into the waiting room.

His wife started to follow him but hesitated when she looked the many faces of the Wallace family. "I think I'll just wait out here," she said in a condescending tone.

"Leslie Murphy, get in here," the man ordered, standing beside two empty chairs near the door. "I've had enough of your attitude for one day!"

"Don't start with me, Raymond," Leslie challenged her husband.

"Now and not another word or so help me. . ." He did not finish his sentence, he did not need to. Leslie walked into the waiting room and obediently sat in the chair next to her husband.

Ariel quickly picked up Kevin and his toys from the floor in front of her. Leslie feigned a slight smile and looked away.

Nicholas stood up and stretched. He walked over to his parents and sat down next to his mother. "So how much longer is this going to take?" he asked, fidgeting.

"I don't know," Tamera answered. "Your Aunt Claudia said Peter's operation was only going to be an hour or two. I don't know about Aunt Patty. Your Grandpa and Uncle Roger have only been gone for a half an hour."

"Can't they hurry up?" Nicholas groaned.

"These things take time," Tamera said, patting his knee. "We just have to wait."

"Well, I'm tired of waiting."

"Here." Tamera dug in her purse, pulled out a handful of coins, and handed them to her son. "Take this and get me a soda. Get yourself something too."

"Okay." He stood up and left the room, happy to be free at last. He followed the signs that pointed toward the cafeteria but took his time. He wanted his freedom to last as long as he could.

As he rounded a corner he nearly bumped into Matthew and his Uncle David. He did not say a word to either of them. He just glared at Matthew and ran off.

Matthew ignored him and continued on his way. As he and David neared the waiting room, Matthew suddenly stopped.

"Ohmygod!" he gasped, backing against the wall

"What's the matter?" David asked, looking at Matthew curiously.

"My parents are here." He saw Raymond and Leslie approach Claudia. They said something and then Claudia turned around, looking up the hallway. She pointed at Matthew. "Oh no, here they come," Matthew said on the edge of panic.

"Remember, be true to yourself." David put his hand on Matthew's shoulder and reminded him. "You'll be fine," he tried to reassure Matthew before he continued down the hall.

"Matthew," Leslie called out and rushed to her son. She threw her arms around him.

"Mother," Matthew replied and gave her a quick

obligatory hug.

"Son," Raymond greeted stoically.

"Father," Matthew answered in the same manner. "Why didn't you tell me you were coming? How did you know I'd be here?"

"Your sister told us, first of all; and secondly, you haven't been keeping in contact with us yourself," Leslie said with a bit of annoyance in her tone.

"I've been kind of busy," Matthew replied.

"So we hear," Raymond said. "Your sister also told us you haven't been home for weeks. She said you were staying with Claudia Wallace and her son?"

"Well, yes." Matthew nodded sheepishly.

"The Wallace's," Leslie repeated and she suddenly began to remember. "Wasn't there a boy back home you used to hang around named Wallace?"

Matthew sighed out loud. "Yes, Mother. His name is Peter. He and his mother moved out here a couple of years ago. Right now he is in surgery."

"Oh my." Leslie shook her head. "That's too bad. Why don't we all go out to dinner now and catch up on what you've been doing."

"I can't right now. I need to stay here for Pete." Matthew lowered his voice and looked over his father's shoulder at the waiting room. How he longed to be inside with the Wallace family at that moment.

"Nonsense, boy," Raymond scoffed. "He's got family here. He doesn't need you."

Matthew looked at his father with rage in his eyes. "Don't ever say that again."

Raymond stiffened his back and stood straight up. "Don't you take that tone with me, boy."

"Then don't tell me what to do. I'm twenty years old. I'm not a boy anymore. I'm a man. I have my own life now," Matthew snapped back.

"You may be twenty, but you're still my son, and I will

not have you talk to me in that tone of voice." Raymond clenched his teeth and lowered his voice.

"What's so important that you need to stay here?" Leslie interrupted the argument.

Matthew looked at the floor and then at his mother. All his life he always did what they expected him to do, regardless of whether or not it was what he wanted. He always tried to please them to win their love, but any love he had for them was long gone. So was his fear. He no longer cared about them or their money. He had found something, someone, more important to him.

"I'll tell you why I have to stay here," Matthew said calmly and slowly. "Because the man I intend to spend the rest of my life with is in that operating room right now. That's why."

Leslie looked at the door behind them confused and then back at Matthew. He could tell she was lost and just shook his head.

"What?" Raymond's voice echoed down the hallway. The loudness even surprised him. He lowered his voice. "No son of mine is a stinking homo!"

"It's gay, Father," Matthew said. "If you insist on labeling me, I prefer to be called gay."

Raymond cocked his head and looked at his son. "Call it what you want. It's still obscene," he growled.

"Oh, honey, all you need is a good wife," Leslie said, putting her arm around Matthew's.

Matthew pulled back and shook his head. "No. Don't you ever listen? I don't want a woman. I am gay. I'm in love with Pete. I want to spend the rest of my life with him. If you can't accept it, then just leave me alone."

Claudia cautiously walked over to the three, hearing Raymond's loud voice down the hall. "Is there something wrong?" she said quietly.

Raymond looked at Claudia with anger in his eyes. "This is all your fault," he snapped. "You and your little queer boy."

Claudia looked confused. "Wha—"

"Just what kind of a mother are you?" Raymond interrupted her.

Claudia recoiled at the harshness of his words. She was totally caught off guard. She looked at Matthew as though asking him to tell her what was going on.

"Well, I hope you're happy," Leslie snapped at her. "You've allowed your son to turn our son against us and into some kind of a freak homo."

Matthew turned to his mother. "So, is that what you think of me?"

Leslie ignored her son, her attention and anger fixed on Claudia. "We've lost our son today because of you and I hope you lose yours."

Leslie's head suddenly jerked to the right as Claudia's hand connected with her cheek. Leslie's dark glasses hit the floor and slid down the hall. She put her hand to her cheek and looked at Claudia with wide, shocked eyes.

"How dare you say that to me!" Claudia said firmly. "As for you, Mr. Murphy, just what kind of father are you? You obviously don't know much about the goings on in your own household. If you did, you would've known about your son and mine years ago. So, don't preach to me, you self-righteous, pompous ass."

Without another word, Claudia turned around and left the three standing in the hallway. She fought hard to hold back her tears, not wanting to give them the satisfaction of knowing how much they had hurt her. She rounded the corner of the adjoining hall and burst into quiet sobs as she collapsed against the wall.

Matthew stood staring at his parents in shock and disbelief at how cruel and insensitive they were. He glanced down the hall and replayed in his mind how quickly Claudia had slapped his mother's face. He smiled to himself, remembering how she had shocked his mother speechless. *Serves her right,* he thought.

Raymond turned back to his son and breathed deeply. "So, what's it going to be? Are you coming home with us or are you staying?"

Matthew shook his head and laughed. "You just don't get it," he said calmly. "I'm staying."

Raymond set his jaw. "Stay then, but know this, you are out of our wills when we get back home."

"Go ahead." Matthew shrugged. "You've been wanting to do that for as long as I can remember. So do it! You never gave a damn about me. It's always been about money with you. Why did you even have children?"

"Oh, Matthew," Leslie gasped and covered her mouth.

"Don't *oh, Matthew* me," Matthew snapped at his mother. "After what you said, you can rot in hell for all I care."

Leslie looked at Raymond for help but he just stood stone faced, staring at his son.

"It's a boy!" a shout came from the waiting room. Matthew looked over his father's shoulder and smiled as the excited cheers spilled into the hall.

"All right, Aunt Patty," he said aloud.

"Aunt Patty?" Leslie questioned.

"Yes. You see, Pete's family accepts me for who I am, not who they think I should be; unlike you two, my own parents."

"It's because we are your parents that we can't," Raymond said, his tone much softer. "We had so much hope, so many dreams for you."

"But they were your dreams, not mine," Matthew said calmly. "You never once asked me what I wanted to do with my life. You just assumed I'd be just like you. Follow in your footsteps right into the family business. Well, I have news for you. I don't want to and never have."

"You're making a big mistake." Raymond put his hands on Leslie's shoulders.

"Well, I guess it runs in the family," Matthew retorted.

Raymond's jaw dropped. He looked at his wife. "Come

on, Leslie," he said and he steered her away. As they reached the elevator, he turned back to Matthew. "We'll be staying at the Oxford Suites, if you change your mind."

Matthew laughed and shook his head. He watched his parents step into the elevator. "You just don't listen," he shouted at them as the doors closed.

"I take it things didn't go well?" David asked, walking up behind Matthew.

"Just as I thought it would." Matthew shrugged and turned around to face him. "What can I say?"

"Well, just remember, we're all here for you. We all love you and Peter. You're part of our family now."

Matthew looked into David's brown eyes. His smile faded as the realization that he may never see his parents again struck him. "I sure could use a hug, right now," he admitted.

David took Matthew in his arms and held his firm body against his chest. David closed his eyes and a feeling of warmth filled him. A feeling he had not felt since John. It felt good to hold a man again. It felt good to hold Matthew. David opened his eyes and let go of Matthew so quickly that Matthew looked at him curiously.

"Is something wrong?" he asked.

"Ah, no," David lied and looked away, avoiding Matthew's eyes. "Let's go see the others."

The waiting room was astir when Matthew and David joined the family. Claudia walked over to Matthew and put her arms around him.

"You okay?" she asked, smiling at him with tear-dampened cheeks.

"Yes," he replied. "Thank you so much for being there for me."

"Anytime." She nodded. "You're like my own son, now, part of my family."

"Thank you," Matthew said, kissing Claudia on the cheek.

"So, how are Patty and the baby?" Tamera asked Ruth.

"Patty's fine and so is the baby. He's beautiful." Ruth smiled proudly.

"So, who got to the birth certificate first?" Ariel said loudly over the noise.

"Patty relented, but they named him Steven Colin," Carl informed the family.

"I knew it." Ariel grinned happily.

"When can we see them?" Morgan asked as everyone stood in a huddle in the center of the room.

"In a few minutes." Ruth halted the small mob. "Patty is a bit tired and wants to spend a few moments in quiet with Roger and Colin."

The family all continued to talk at once. Everyone was so caught up in the excitement of the new baby that for a split second, they had forgotten about Peter. Even Claudia and Matthew listened happily to the chatter and were swept away by the moment.

No one saw the doctor standing in the doorway, still dressed in his powder-blue scrubs. He reached up and removed his cap, looking at the joyful huddle in front of him. He bit his lip and searched for Claudia.

Ruth glanced over at the doorway and saw the doctor. Their eyes met briefly and she felt a shiver run up her spine. Her smile faded and she nudged Carl with her elbow.

Slowly the room fell silent as everyone turned their attention to the doctor.

"Excuse me, is Claudia Wallace here?" he asked and cleared his throat.

Claudia jumped when she heard his voice and stepped forward through the gathering. "Doctor Hough, how is he? Can I see him?" Claudia asked excitedly and rushed to him. She ignored the look in his eyes, refusing to see it. She grabbed his arms and held on tight.

"Ah, Mrs. Wallace." Dr. Hough tried to avoid her eyes and her grasp. "I'm sorry; please sit down for a moment."

"No," Claudia groaned as they sat down, tears filling

her eyes and streaming down her cheeks.

Matthew's heart sank at the sound of the doctor's voice. He suddenly felt as though he could not breathe. He became dizzy. The room began to close in on him.

"I need some air," he panted and bolted from the room.

Daniel looked at David. Their eyes met and David understood. Without a word, David ran after Matthew.

"Matthew, wait!" he called to him as he reached the parking lot.

Matthew stopped and fell back against the side of his car. He bent down and covered his head with his hands. His shoulders heaved as he sobbed and tried to catch his breath. *No, this can't be happening,* he thought, unable to speak. He took the ring box from his pocket and looked at it through his tear filled eyes.

"No," he groaned and cried.

"Matthew," David repeated softly as he caught up with him. Gently he placed his hand on Matthew's shoulder.

Immediately Matthew stood up and hugged David and sobbed. "He can't be," Matthew said through his tears. "He promised me he'd come back. He promised. He can't be."

"It's all right, Matthew," David consoled him. "It wasn't his fault. He would've come back to you if he could have."

"No," Matthew said while tears dampened his cheeks.

"Hush. Hush now," David whispered while he held Matthew's quivering body in his arms. He kissed Matthew's forehead.

Matthew pulled back and looked at David. His mind had not completely registering what had happened.

David's lips curled slightly. He wiped the tears from Matthew's cheeks all the while keeping his gaze fixed on Matthew's blue eyes. Gently he raised Matthew's chin and leaned closer. At first it was a quick kiss on the lips but then he felt Matthew's body lean into him and their mouths opened to each other.

* * *

The waiting room was cold and quiet. Everyone had found a chair and was seated. Ruth sat next to Carl holding onto his hand tightly.

"I'm sorry, Mrs. Wallace," Dr. Hough said, shaking his head. He crouched beside her chair. Even after twenty years in practice, he had never become used to delivering bad news. He hated this part of his job.

"No," Claudia said firmly and directly, drying her tears. "Tell me when I can see him."

"He'll be moved into the ICU shortly," the doctor said, "but Mrs. Wallace, he won't know you're there."

Tears filled Claudia's eyes again. Her heart ached and her stomach tightened. She began to pant and her eyes would not focus on anything as she searched the room for someone to hold.

Ruth rushed to her side and took her into her arms. Ruth could feel Claudia trembling and she held her tighter.

"He is going to make it," she whispered into Claudia's ear. "You have to believe that. You heard the doctor, his coma is temporary. He will wake up."

Claudia pulled away from her mother-in-law. She looked at the woman she had come to trust deeply and silently prayed she was right.

* * *

Ruth looked out the bedroom window at the darkness of the night. Finally the day was over. She sighed.

"Come to bed, dear," Carl beckoned.

Slowly she walked over to their bed and sat down. Her white cotton nightgown hung loosely on her tired shoulders. She continued staring through the window.

Carl lay watching his wife. He sat up on his knees until

his bare chest was just inches behind her head. Gently he reached over and began to rub her back. Ruth moaned as she felt herself relaxing against his touch. He smiled, pleased by her response, and continued to massage her shoulders with both hands. She responded by lying back against him and closing her eyes.

"How could I have been so blind?" Ruth reflected.

Carl raised an eyebrow. "Blind?" he repeated.

"Yes." Ruth sat forward a bit. "It's funny. You raise five children and you think you know them, what goes on in their heads. Only to find out you really don't. You were oblivious to their internal pains and torments all those years. I thought we didn't keep secrets from each other, that we were honest and open, but these past two years have really made me stop and think."

Carl listened, wrapping his arms around her.

"First Steven. Why didn't he tell us about Claudia? I think it's sad that he died and never even knew he had a son. Poor Peter, look what his secret resulted in. Then Tamera being raped and having an abortion. How could she have kept that from us? She and Daniel keeping Nicholas' adoption secret from him. I just don't understand it. I should've known." Ruth sighed and stood up. She pulled back the blankets and crawled into bed.

Carl lay back down. He wrapped his arm protectively around his wife and kissed her forehead.

"Ruth, it's not your fault. We did the best we could. You know, I guess when you think about it, we all have things about ourselves that we don't tell one another. Little secrets. They aren't meant to hurt anyone. It's just part of what makes us individuals. I guess the difficulty comes in knowing which secrets we should let go of and which secrets need to be kept."

Ruth turned her head and looked at Carl. "You don't have any secrets, do you?"

Carl smiled at her. "After forty-six years of marriage, you know all there is to know about me. I have no secrets."

A. M. Huff

"That's good," Ruth said, closing her eyes as they kissed.

* * * *

ABOUT THE AUTHOR

Author A. M. Huff's love for writing began when he was a teenager in high school. He began writing stories for his own enjoyment, for his eyes only.

Years later, he shared one of his dreams with a coworker. She urged him to "write it down. It would make a great story." He did and shared it with her. She read it and handed it back saying, "I want more." "More?" he said, "but that was the end of the dream." "I don't' care. I want more," she insisted. He returned to his computer and what followed became "*SECRETS The Wallace Family.*"

Mr. Huff is a longtime member of a writers group, Becoming Fiction, and president of the Northwest Independent Writers Association. He currently resides in Central Oregon.